THE

WALKING

DELEGATE

by

Leroy Scott

LITERATURE HOUSE / GREGG PRESS
Upper Saddle River, N. J.

Republished in 1969 by
LITERATURE HOUSE
an imprint of The Gregg Press
121 Pleasant Avenue
Upper Saddle River, N. J. 07458

Standard Book Number—8398-1853-X
Library of Congress Card—68-57549

Printed in United States of America

LEROY SCOTT

Leroy Scott was born in Fairmount, Indiana, in 1875 and died in 1929. After graduation from Indiana University in 1897 he worked on newspapers and was assistant to the Editor of the *Woman's Home Companion*. He lived for a while at Hull House in Chicago, where he became interested in settlement work. In New York he worked as assistant to the manager of the University Settlement. In 1904 he gave up settlement work in order to write. He visited Russia in 1905, and later described his experiences there, particularly the atrocities committed by terrorists.

Scott's novels and articles show that he was definitely a muckraker, but he was a moderate in his approach to social reform. He was interested in organizing the Women's Trade Union League, was an active worker for progressive child-labor laws, and was a founder and executive of the Intercollegiate Socialist Society. When muckraking declined, Scott wrote stories dealing with crime and its detection. He carefully investigated the underworld and its methods. These stories always contained the moral that the social structure was largely responsible for crime, and that methods of handling offenders against the law had to be modernized. The plots of these stories have been criticized as being romantic and improbable.

The Random House Dictionary of the English Language defines a walking delegate as "(formerly) an official appointed by a trade union to go from place to place to investigate conditions, to ascertain whether union contracts were being fulfilled, and, sometimes, to negotiate contracts between employers and unions." Buck Foley, the "walking delegate," is the head of a New York ironworkers' union. He was raised in an orphanage, ran away, and worked as a newsboy, truck driver, seaman, and assistant to a ward boss before discovering the proper outlet for his ambitions—that of labor organizer. The union which he headed had lacked effective leadership; he became president by default. His first act was to get the men on his side. He then called a strike and proved to them that he was a tougher man and a better bargainer than the contractors, by winning several pay raises. Because his salary as president and walking delegate was only thirty dollars per week, he began to accept bribes from rich contractors eager to have a tractable working force, and to avoid costly strikes. At the point where Scott begins his story, Foley is completely corrupt, but unassailable. When the workers under him complain, he silences them by a bribe or, if necessary, by intimidation. He also pleases them by maintaining a "closed shop," and "scabs" are either scared off or beaten up by his goons ("transmittin' unionism to the brain by the fist").

The better elements among the workers find a supporter in another natural leader, Tom Keating, one of the rare "proletarian" heroes who is convincing and is not a mouthpiece for the author's political views. Keating dedicates his life to making the union democratic, and this means getting rid of Foley. In order to accomplish this goal, he discovers that he must not only use the legal weapons of the ballot box, but also be as wiley, tough, and dangerous as his opponent. Keating is not a Marxist—this is not a thesis novel. He has independently reached the conclusion that "The capitalist class was now in power, and was performing its mission—the development and centralization of industries. But its decline would be even more rapid than its rise. It would be succeeded by the working class." His strongest belief is in education, which he sees as presently available only to the rich. Keating is made a sympathetic figure through his idealism, his early erroneous assumption that his battle can be won without "hitting below the belt," and by the author's portrait of his slatternly wife, who is too ill bred to recognize her husband's greatness. The complicated stratagems and counter-stratagems of the protagonists make exciting reading, and the author's unsentimental descriptions of working-class people and their daily lives provide a realistic background to the plot. A reader who might be critical of the number of riots, bombings, assaults, and miscarriages of justice which occur in this novel should refer to any scholarly study of the development of American labor unions.

Upper Saddle River, N. J.   F. C. S.
May, 1969

THE WALKING DELEGATE

The
Walking Delegate

By

Leroy Scott

With Frontispiece

New York
Doubleday, Page & Company
1905

To My Wife

CONTENTS

CONTENTS

LIST OF CHARACTERS

BUCK FOLEY, a walking delegate.

TOM KEATING, a foreman.

MAGGIE KEATING, his wife.

MR. BAXTER, President of Iron Employers' Ass'n.

MRS. BAXTER.

MR. DRISCOLL, a contractor.

RUTH ARNOLD, his secretary.

MR. BERMAN, junior partner of Mr. Driscoll.

MR. MURPHY, a contractor.

MR. BOBBS, a contractor.

MR. ISAACS, a contractor.

CONNELLY, Secretary of Iron Workers' Union.

NELS PETERSEN, a "scab."

ANNA PETERSEN, his wife.

PIG IRON PETE, a workman

JOHNSON, a workman.

BARRY, a workman.

MRS. BARRY.

JAKE HENDERSON
ARKANSAS NUMBER TWO
KAFFIR BILL   Members of
SMOKEY   "The Entertainment
HICKEY   Committee."

THE WALKING DELEGATE

Chapter I

ON THE ST. ETIENNE HOTEL

THE St. Etienne Hotel would some day be as bulky and as garishly magnificent as four million dollars could make it. Now it was only a steel framework rearing itself into the center of the overhead grayness—a black pier supporting the grimy arch of heaven.

Up on its loosely-planked twenty-first story stood Mr. Driscoll, watching his men at work. A raw February wind scraped slowly under the dirty clouds, which soiled the whole sky, and with a leisurely content thrust itself into his office-tendered flesh. He shivered, and at times, to throw off the chill, he paced across the pine boards, carefully going around the gaps his men were wont to leap. And now and then his eyes wandered from his lofty platform. On his right, below, there were roofs; beyond, a dull bar of water; beyond, more roofs: on his left there were roofs; a dull bar of water; more roofs: and all around the jagged wilderness of house-tops reached away and away till it faded into the complete envelopment of a smudgy haze. Once Mr. Driscoll caught hold of the head of a column and leaned out above the street; over its dizzy bottom erratically shifted dark specks—hats. He drew back with a shiver with which the February wind had nothing to do.

It was a principle with Mr. Driscoll, of Driscoll & Co., contractors for steel bridges and steel frames of buildings, that you should not show approval of your workmen's work. " Give 'em a smile and they'll do ten per cent. less and ask ten per cent. more." So as he now watched his men, one hand in his overcoat pocket, one on his soft felt hat, he did not smile. It was singularly easy for him not to smile. Balanced on his short, round body he had a round head with a rim of reddish-gray hair, and with a purplish face that had protruding lips which sagged at each corner, and protruding eyes whose lids blinked so sharply you seemed to hear their click. So much nature had done to help him adhere to his principle. And he, in turn, had added to his natural endowment by growing mutton-chops. Long ago someone had probably expressed to him a detestation of side-whiskers, and he of course had begun forthwith to shave only his chin.

His men were setting twenty-five foot steel columns into place,—the gang his eyes were now on, moving actively about a great crane, and the gang about the great crane at the building's other end. Their coats were buttoned to their chins to keep out the February wind; their hands were in big, shiny gloves; their blue and brown overalls, from the handling of painted iron, had the surface and polish of leather. They were all in the freshness of their manhood—lean, and keen, and full of spirit—vividly fit. Their work explained their fitness; it was a natural civil service examination that barred all but the active and the daring.

And yet, though he did not smile, Mr. Driscoll was cuddled by satisfaction as he stood on the great platform just under the sky and watched the brown men at work. He had had a deal of trouble during the past three years—accidents, poor workmen, delays due to strikes over inconsequential matters—all of which had severely taxed his profits and his profanity. So the smoothness with which this, his greatest job, progressed was his especial joy. In his heart he credited this smoothness to the brown young foreman who had just come back to his side —but he didn't tell Keating so.

"The riveters are keeping right on our heels," said Tom. "Would you like to go down and have a look at 'em?"

"No," said Mr. Driscoll shortly.

The foreman shrugged his shoulders slightly, and joined the gang Mr. Driscoll was watching. In the year he had worked for Mr. Driscoll he had learned to be philosophic over that gentleman's gruffness: he didn't like the man, so why should he mind his words?

The men had fastened a sling about a twenty-five foot column and to this had attached the hook of the pulley. The seventy-foot arm of the crane now slowly rose and drew after it the column, dangling vertically. Directed by the signals of Tom's right hand the column sank with precision to its appointed place at one corner of the building. It was quickly fastened to the head of the column beneath it with four bolts. Later the riveters, whose hammers were now maintaining a terrific rattle two floors below, would replace the four bolts by four rows of rivets.

"Get the sling, Pete," ordered Tom.

'At this a loosely-jointed man threw off his slouch hat, encircled the column with his arms, and mounted with little springs. Near its top he locked his legs around the column, and, thus supported and working with both hands, he unfastened the rope from the pulley hook and the column, and threw it below. He then stepped into the hook of the pulley, swung through the air to the flooring, picked up his hat and slapped it against his leg.

Sometimes Mr. Driscoll forgot his principle. While Pete was nonchalantly loosening the sling, leaning out over the street, nothing between him and the pavement but the grip of his legs, there was something very like a look of admiration in Mr. Driscoll's aggravating eyes. He moved over to Pete just as the latter was pulling on his slouch hat.

"I get a shiver every time I see a man do that," he said.

"That? That's nothin'," said Pete. "I'd a heap ruther do that than work down in the street. Down in the street, why, who knows when a brick's agoin' to fall on your head!"

"Um!" Mr. Driscoll remembered himself and his eyes clicked. He turned from Pete, and called to the young foreman: "I'll look at the riveters now."

"All right. Oh, Barry!"

There came toward Tom a little, stocky man, commonly known as "Rivet Head." Someone had noted the likeness of his cranium to a newly-hammered rivet, and the nickname had stuck.

"Get the other four columns up out of the street before setting any more," Tom ordered, and then walked with Mr. Driscoll to where the head of a ladder stuck up through the flooring.

Pete, with a sour look, watched Mr. Driscoll's round body awkwardly disappear down the ladder.

"Boys, if I was a preacher, I know how I'd run my business," he remarked.

"How, Pete?" queried one of the gang.

"I'd stand up Driscoll in the middle o' the road to hell, then knock off workin' forever. When they seen him standin' there every blamed sinner'd turn back with a yell an' stretch their legs for the other road."

"I wonder if Tom'll speak to him about them scabs," said another man, with a scowl at a couple of men working along the building's edge.

"That ain't Tom's business, Bill," answered Pete. "It's Rivet Head's. Tom don't like Driscoll any more'n the rest of us do, an' he ain't goin' to say any more to him 'n he has to."

"Tom ought to call him down, anyhow," Bill declared.

"You let Foley do that," put in Jake Henderson, a big fellow with a stubbly face and a scar across his nose.

"An' let him peel off a little graft!" sneered Bill.

" Close yer face! " growled Jake.

" Come on there, boys, an' get that crane around! "
shouted Barry.

Pete, Bill, and Jake sprang to the wooden lever
that extended from the base of the ninety-foot mast;
and they threw their weight against the bar, bending
it as a bow. The crane slowly turned on its bearings to the desired position. Barry, the " pusher "
(under foreman), waved his outstretched hand.
The signalman, whose eyes had been alert for this
movement, pulled a rope; a bell rang in the ears
of an engineer, twenty-one floors below. The big
boom slowly came down to a horizontal position, its
outer end twenty feet clear of the building's edge.
Another signal, and the heavy iron pulley began to
descend to the street.

After the pulley had started to slide down its
rope there was little for the men to do till it had
climbed back up the rope with its burden of steel.
Pete—who was usually addressed as " Pig Iron,"
perhaps for the reason that he claimed to be from
Pittsburg—settled back at his ease among the gang,
his back against a pile of columns, his legs stretched
out.

" I've just picked out the apartment where I'm
goin' to keep my celluloid collar when this here
shanty's finished," he remarked. " Over in the
corner there, lookin' down in both streets. I ain't
goin' to do nothin' but wear kid gloves, an' lean out
the windows an' spit on you roughnecks as you go
by. An' my boodwar is goin' to have about seventeen push-buttons in it. Whenever I want any-

thing I'll just push a button, an' up 'll hot-foot a
nigger with it in a suit o' clothes that's nothin' but
shirt front. Then I'll kick the nigger, an' push
another button. That's life, boys. An' I'll have
plush chairs, carpets a foot thick, an iv'ry bath-
tub——"

Pete's wandering gaze caught one man watching
him with serious eyes, and he broke off. " Say, Johnson, wha' d' you suppose I want a bath-tub for?"

Johnson was an anomaly among the iron-workers—
a man without a sense of humor. He never knew
when his fellows were joking and when serious; he
usually took them literally.

" To wash in," he answered.

Pete whistled. " Wash in it! Ain't you got no
respect for the traditions o' the workin' class?"

" Hey, Pig Iron; talk English!" Bill demanded.
" What's traditions?"

Pete looked puzzled, and a laugh passed about the
men. Then his sang-froid returned. " Your traditions, Bill, is the things you'd try to forget about
yourself if you had enough coin to move into a place
like this."

He turned his lean face back on Johnson. " Don't
you know what a bath-tub's for, Johnson? Don't
you never read the papers? Well, here's how it is:
The landlords come around wearin' about a sixteen-
candle-power incandescent smile. They puts in marble
bath-tubs all through all the houses. They're goin'
to elevate us. The next day they come around again
to see how we've improved. They throw up their
hands, an' let out a few yells. There's them bath-

tubs chuck full o' coal. We didn't know what they was for,—an' they was very handy for coal. That's us. It's down in the papers. An' here you, Johnson, you'd ruin our repitations by usin' the bath-tubs to bathe in."

The pulley toiled into view, dragging after it two columns. Johnson was saved the necessity of response. The men hurried to their places.

" O' course, Pig Iron, you'll be fixed all right when you've moved in here," began Bill, after the boom had reached out and the pulley had started spinning down for the other two columns. " But how about the rest of us fixers? Three seventy-five a day, when we get in only six or seven months a year, ain't makin' bankers out o' many of us."

" Only a few," admitted Pete; " an' them few ain't the whole cheese yet. Me, I can live on three seventy-five, but I don't see how you married men do."

" Especially with scabs stealin' your jobs," growled Bill, glancing again at the two men working along the building's edge.

" I told you Foley'd look after them," said Barry, who had joined the group for a moment. " It hustles most of us to keep up with the game," he went on, in answer to Pete's last remark. " Some of us don't. An' rents an' everything else goin' up. I don't know what we're goin' to do."

" That's easy," said Pete. " Get more money or live cheaper."

" How're we goin' to live cheaper? " demanded Bill.

" Yes, how? " seconded Barry.

" I'm for more money," declared Bill.

" Well, I reckon I wear the same size shoe," said Pete. " More money—that's me."

" And me," " and me," joined in the other men, except Johnson.

" It's about time we were gettin' more," Pete advanced. " The last two years the bosses have been doin' the genteel thing by their own pockets, all right."

" We've got to have more if our kids are goin' to know a couple o' facts more'n we do." Barry went over to the edge of the building and watched the tiny figures attaching the columns to the pulley hook.

" That's right," said Pete. " You don't stand no chance these days to climb up on top of a good job unless you ripped off a lot o' education when you was young an' riveted it on to your mem'ry. I heard a preacher once. He preached about education. He said if you wanted to get up anywhere you had to be educated like hell. He was right, too. If you left school when you was thirteen, why, by the time you're twenty-seven an' had a few drinks you ain't very likely to be just what I'd call a college on legs."

" Keating, he thinks we ought to go after more this spring," said Bill.

" I wonder what Foley thinks? " queried another of the men.

" If Tom's for a strike, why, Foley 'll be again' it," one of the gang answered. " You can place your money on that color."

" Tom certainly did pour the hot shot into Foley at the meetin' last night," said Bill, grinning.

"Grafter! He called Buck about thirteen diff'rent kind."

"If Keating's all right in his nut he'll not go round lookin' for a head-on collision with Buck Foley," asserted Jake, with a wise leer at Bill.

Bill answered by giving Jake his back. "Foley don't want no strike," he declared. "What's he want to strike for? He's gettin' his hand in the dough bag enough the way things is now."

"See here, the whole bunch o' you roughnecks give me a pain!" broke out Pete. "You shoot off your faces a lot when Buck's not around, but the imitation you give on meetin' nights of a collection o' mummies can't be beat. I ain't in love with Buck—not on your life! You can tell him so, Jake. But he certainly has done the union a lot o' good. Tom'd say that, too. An' you know how much Tom likes Foley. You fixers forget when you was workin' ten hours for two dollars, an' lickin' the boots o' the bosses to hold your jobs."

There was a short silence, then Johnson put forward cautiously: "I don't see the good o' strikin'."

Pete stared at him. "Why?" he demanded.

"Well, I've been in the business longer'n most o' you boys, an' I ain't found the bosses as bad as you make 'em out. When they're makin' more, they'll pay us more."

"Oh, you go tell that to a Sunday school!" snorted Pete. "D'you ever hear of a boss payin' more wages 'n he had to? Not much! Them kind 'o bosses 's all doin' business up in heaven. If we was actually earnin' twenty a day, d'you suppose we'd get a cent more'n three seventy-five till we'd licked the bosses. You do—hey? That shows the kind of a nut you've got. The boss 'ud buy a tutti-frutti yacht, or a few more automobiles, or mebbe a college or two, where they learn you how to wear your pants turned up; but all the extra money you'd get wouldn't pay for the soap used by a Dago. If ever a boss offers you an extra dollar before you've licked him, yell for a cop. He's crazy."

Pete's tirade completely flustered Johnson. " All the same, what I said 's so."

Pete snorted again. " When d'you think you're livin'? You make me tired, Johnson. Go push yourself off the roof! "

The two last columns rose swinging above the chasm's brink, and there was no more talk for that afternoon. For the next hour the men were busy setting the last of the columns which were to support the twenty-second and twenty-third stories. Then they began setting in the cross beams, walking about on these five-inch beams (perhaps on one with the pavement straight beneath it) with the matter-of-fact steps of a man on the sidewalk—a circus act, lacking a safety net below, and lacking flourishes and kisses blown to a thrilled audience.

Chapter II

THE WALKING DELEGATE

IT was toward the latter part of the after-noon that a tall, angular man, in a black overcoat and a derby hat, stepped from the ladder on to the loose planking, glanced about and walked over to the gang of men about the south crane.

"Hello, Buck," they called out on sight of him.

"Hello, boys," he answered carelessly.

He stood, with hands in the pockets of his overcoat, smoking his cigar, watching the crane accurately swing a beam to its place, and a couple of men run along it and bolt it at each end to the columns. He had a face to hold one's look—lean and long: gray, quick eyes, set close together; high cheek bones, with the dull polish of bronze; a thin nose, with a vultur-ous droop; a wide tight mouth; a great bone of a chin;—a daring, incisive, masterful face.

When the beam had been bolted to its place, Barry, with a reluctance he tried to conceal, walked over to Foley.

"How's things?" asked the new-comer, rolling his cigar into the corner of his mouth and slipping his words out between barely parted lips.

Barry was the steward on the job,—the union's representative. "Two snakes come on the job this

14

mornin'," he reported. "Them two over there,—
that Squarehead an' that Guinea. I was goin' to
write you a postal card about 'em to-night."

"Who put 'em to work?"

"They said Duffy, Driscoll's superintendent."

Foley grunted, and his eyes fastened thoughtfully
on the two non-union men.

"When the boys seen they had no cards, o' course
they said they wouldn't work with the scabs. But I
said we'd stand 'em to-day, an' let you straighten it
out to-morrow."

"We'll fix it now." The walking delegate, with
deliberate steps, moved toward the two men, who
were sitting astride an outside beam fitting in bolts.

He paused beside the Italian. "Clear out!" he
ordered quietly. He did not take his hands from his
pockets.

The Italian looked up, and without answer doggedly resumed twisting a nut.

Foley's eyes narrowed. His lips tightened upon
his cigar. Suddenly his left hand gripped the head
of a column and his right seized the shirt and coat
collar of the Italian. He jerked the man outward,
unseating him, though his legs clung about the beam,
and held him over the street. The Italian let out a
frightful yell, that the wind swept along under the
clouds; and his wrench went flying from his hand.
It struck close beside a mason on a scaffold seventeen
stories below. The mason gave a jump, looked up
and shook his fist.

"D'youse see the asphalt?" Foley demanded.

The man, whose down-hanging face was forced to

see the pavement far below, with the little hats moving about over it, shrilled out his fear again.

"In about a minute youse'll be layin' there, as flat as a picture, if youse don't clear out!"

The man answered with a mixture of Italian, English, and yells; from which Foley gathered that he was willing to go, but preferred to gain the street by way of the ladders rather than by the direct route.

Foley jerked him back to his seat, and a pair of frantic arms gripped his legs. "Now chase yourself, youse scab! Or——" Foley knew how to swear.

The Italian rose tremblingly and stepped across to the flooring. He dropped limply to a seat on a prostrate column, and moaned into his hands.

Without glancing at him or at the workmen who had eyed this measure doubtfully, Foley moved over to the Swede and gripped him as he had the Italian. "Now youse, youse sneakin' Squarehead! Get out o' here, too!"

The Swede's right hand came up and laid hold of Foley's wrist with a grip that made the walking delegate start. The scab rose to his feet and stepped across to the planking. Foley was tall, but the Swede out-topped him by an inch.

"I hold ma yob, yes," growled the Swede, a sudden flame coming into his heavy eyes.

Foley had seen that look in a thousand scabs' eyes before. He knew its meaning. He drew back a pace, pulled his derby hat tightly down on his head and bit into his cigar, every lean muscle alert.

"Get off the job! Or I'll kick youse off!"

The Swede stepped forward, his shoulders hunched up. Foley crouched back; his narrowed gray eyes gleamed. The men in both gangs looked on from their places about the cranes and up on the beams in statued expectation. Barry and Pig Iron hurried up to Foley's support.

"Keep back!" he ordered sharply. They fell away from him.

A minute passed—the two men standing on the loosely-planked edge of a sheer precipice, watching each other with tense eyes. Suddenly a change began in the Swede; the spirit went out of him as the glow from a cooling rivet. His arms sank to his side, and he turned and fairly slunk over to where lay an old brown overcoat.

The men started with relief, then burst into a jeering laugh. Foley moved toward Barry, then paused and, with hands back in his pockets, watched the two scabs make their preparation to leave, trundling his cigar about with his thin prehensile lips. As they started down the ladder, the Swede sullen, the Italian still trembling, he walked over to them with sudden decision.

"Go on back to work," he ordered.

The two looked at him in surprised doubt.

"Go on!" He jerked his head toward the places they had left.

They hesitated; then the Swede lay off his old coat and started back to his place, and the Italian followed, his fearful eyes on the walking delegate.

Foley rejoined Barry. "I'm goin' to settle this thing with Driscoll," he said to the pusher, loudly,

answering the amazed questioning he saw in the eyes
of all the men. " I'm goin' to settle the scab question for good with him. Let them two snakes work
till youse hear from me."

He paused, then asked abruptly: " Where's Keating? "

" Down with the riveters."

" So-long, boys," he called to Barry's gang; and at
the head of the ladder he gestured a farewell to the
gang about the other crane. Then his long body
sank through the flooring.

At the bottom of the thirty-foot ladder he paused
and looked around through the maze of beams and
columns. This floor was not boarded, as was the
one he had just left. Here and there were little
platforms on which stood small portable forges, a
man at each turning the fan and stirring the rivets
among the red coals; and here and there were groups
of three men, driving home the rivets. At regular
intervals each heater would take a white rivet from
his forge, toss it from his tongs sizzling through the
air to a man twenty feet away, who would deftly
catch it in a tin can. This man would seize the
glowing bit of steel with a pair of pincers, strike
it smartly against a beam, at which off would go a
spray of sparks like an exploding rocket, and then
thrust it through its hole. Immediately the terrific
throbbing of a pneumatic hammer, held hard against
the rivet by another man, would clinch it to its
destiny of clinging with all its might. And then,
flashing through the gray air like a meteor at twilight, would come another sparkling rivet.

And on all sides, beyond the workmen calmly playing at catch with white-hot steel, and beyond the
black crosswork of beams and columns, Foley could
see great stretches of housetops that in sullen rivalry
strove to overmatch the dinginess of the sky.

Foley caught sight of Tom with a riveting gang at
the southeast corner of the building, and he started
toward him, walking over the five-inch beams with a
practiced step, and now and then throwing a word at
some of the men he passed, and glancing casually
down at the workmen putting in the concrete flooring
three stories below. Tom had seen him coming, and
had turned his back upon his approach.

"H'are you, Buck!" shouted one of the gang.

Though Foley was but ten feet away, it was the
man's lips alone that gave greeting to him; the
ravenous din of the pneumatic hammer devoured
every other sound. He shouted a reply; his lip movements signaled to the man: "Hello, fellows."

Tom still kept his ignoring back upon Foley.
The walking delegate touched him on the shoulder.
"I'd like to trade some words with youse," he re-
marked.

Tom's set face regarded him steadily an instant;
then he said: "All right."

"Come on." Foley led the way across beams to
the opposite corner of the building where there was a
platform now deserted by its forge, and where the
noise was slightly less dense. For a space the two
men looked squarely into each other's face—Tom's
set, Foley's expressionless—as if taking the measure
of the other;—and meanwhile the great framework

shivered, and the air rattled, under the impact of the throbbing hammers. They were strikingly similar, and strikingly dissimilar. Aggressiveness, fearlessness, self-confidence, a sense of leadership, showed themselves in the faces and bearing of the two, though all three qualities were more pronounced in the older man. Their dissimilarity was summed up in their eyes: there was something to take and hold your confidence in Tom's; Foley's were full of deep, resourceful cunning.

" Well? " said Tom, at length.

" What's your game? " asked Foley in a tone that was neither friendly nor unfriendly. " Wha'd' youse want? "

" Nothing,—from you."

Foley went on in the same colorless tone. " I don't know. Youse 've been doin' a lot o' growlin' lately. I've had a lot o' men fightin' me. Most of 'em wanted to be bought off."

Tom recognized in these words a distant overture of peace,—a peace that if accepted would be profitable to him. He went straight to Foley's insinuated meaning.

" You ought to know that's not my size," he returned quietly. " You've tried to buy me off more than once."

The mask went from Foley's face and his mouth and forehead creased into harsh lines. His words came out like whetted steel. " See here. I would pass over the kind o' talkin' youse 've been doin'. Somebody's always growlin'. Somebody's got to growl. But what youse said at the meetin' last night,

I ain't goin' to stand for that kind o' talk. Youse understand?"

Tom's legs had spread themselves apart, his black-gloved hands had placed themselves upon his hips, and his brown eyes were looking hard defiance from beneath his cap's peak. "I don't suppose you did like it," he said calmly. "If I remember rightly I didn't say it for the purpose of pleasing you."

"Youse 're goin' to keep your mouth goin' then?"

"My mouth's my own."

"Mebbe youse knows what happened to a few other gents that started on the road youse 're travelin'?" the steely voice went on insinuatingly. "Duncan—Smith—O'Malley?"

"Threats, huh?" Tom's anger began to pass his control. He sneered. "Save 'em for somebody that's afraid of you!"

The cigar that had so far kept its place in Foley's mouth now fell out, and a few lurid words followed it. "D'youse know I can drive youse clean out o' New York? Yes, an' fix youse so youse can't get a job in the iron trade in the country? Except as a scab. Which's just about what you are!"

The defiant glow in Tom's eyes flared into a blaze of anger. He stepped up to Foley, his fists still on his hips, and fairly thrust his square face into the lean one of the walking delegate.

"If you think I'm afraid of you, Buck Foley, or your bunch of toughs, you're almighty mistaken! I'm going to say what I think about you, and say it whenever and wherever I please!"

Foley's face tightened. His hands clenched in his

pockets. But he controlled himself. He had the wisdom of a thousand fights,—which is, never to fight unless you have to, or unless there is something to gain. "I've got just one thing to say to youse, an' that's all," he said, and his low, steely voice cut distinctly through the hammer's uproar. "If I hear any more about your talk,—well, Duncan an' O'Malley 'll have some new company."

He turned about shortly, and stepped along beams to a ladder, and down that; leaving Tom struggling with a furious desire to follow and close with him. Out of the building, he made for the office of Mr. Driscoll as rapidly as street car could take him. On leaving the elevator in the Broadway building he strode to a door marked " Driscoll & Co.—Private—Enter Next Door," and without hesitation turned the knob. He found himself in a small room, very neat, whose principal furniture was a letter file and a desk bearing a typewriter. Over the desk was a brown print of William Morris. The room had two inner doors, one, as Foley knew, opening into the general offices, and the other into Mr. Driscoll's private room.

A young woman rose from the desk. "What is it?" she asked, with a coldness drawn forth by his disregard of the sign on the door.

"I want to see Mr. Driscoll. Tell him Foley wants to speak to him."

She went through Mr. Driscoll's door, and Foley heard his name announced. There was a hesitant silence, then he heard the words, "Well, let him come in, Miss Arnold."

Miss Arnold immediately reappeared. "Will you step in, please."

As he entered the door Foley put on his hat, which he had removed in the presence of the secretary, pulling it aggressively down over one eye.

"Hello, Driscoll," he greeted the contractor, who had swung about from a belittered desk; and he closed the door behind him.

Mr. Driscoll pointed to a chair, but his face deepened a shade. Foley seated himself, and leaned forward with his elbows on his knees, his bony hands clasped.

"Well, what can I do for you?" queried Mr. Driscoll shortly.

Foley knew his man. He had met Mr. Driscoll many times at conferences with the Executive Committee of the Iron Employers' Association, and had read him as though he were large print. He noted with satisfaction the color in the contractor's face.

The walking delegate spoke with extreme deliberation. "I come around, *Mister* Driscoll, to find out what the hell youse mean by workin' scabs on that St. Etienne job. Youse signed an agreement to work only union men, but if I didn't watch youse, youse 'd have your work alive with scabs. Now, damn youse, unless youse get them scabs off that job an' do it quicker 'n youse ever done anything before, youse 'll wish youse had!"

Foley made no mistake in his pre-calculation of the effect of this speech. Mr. Driscoll sprang to his feet, with a trembling that his reddish-gray whiskers exaggerated. His glasses tumbled from his nose, and his feet scrunched them unnoted into the rug. "If there's a scab on the job, I didn't know it. If those men 're scabs Duffy must have made a mistake. If—— "

"If one o' youse bosses ever breaks a contract, oh, it's always a mistake!"

"If you'd come around here and talked like a gentleman, I'd had 'em off inside of an hour," Mr. Driscoll roared. "But, by thunder, I don't let any walking delegate insult me and tell me what I've *got* to do!"

"Then youse ain't goin' to fire the scabs?"

"Not till hell freezes over!"

Mr. Driscoll's eyes clicked, and he banged his pudgy fist upon his desk.

"Then the men 'll go back to work on the day hell freezes over," returned Foley, rising to go. "But I have an idea youse 'll want to see me a day or two before then. I've come to youse this time. The next time we talk, youse 'll come to me. There's my card." And he went out with the triumphant feeling of the man who can guide events.

At ten o'clock the next morning he clambered again to the top of the St. Etienne Hotel. The Italian and Swede were still at work.

"Lay down your tools, boys!" he called out to the two gangs. "The job's struck!"

The men crowded around him, demanding information.

"Driscoll won't fire the scabs," he explained.

"Kick 'em off,—settle it that-a-way!" growled one

of the men. "We can't afford to lose wages on account o' two scabs."

"That'd only settle this one case. We've got to settle the scab question with Driscoll for good an' all. It's hard luck, boys, I know," he said sympathetically, "but we can't do nothin' but strike. We've got to lick Driscoll into shape."

Leaving the men talking hotly as they changed their clothes for the street, Foley went down the ladder to bear the same message and the same comfort to the riveters.

The next morning the general contractor for the building got Mr. Driscoll on the telephone. "Why aren't you getting that ironwork up?" he demanded.

Mr. Driscoll started into an explanation of his trouble with Foley, but the general contractor cut him short. "I don't care what the trouble is. What I care about is that you're not getting that ironwork up. Get your men right back to work."

"How?" queried Mr. Driscoll sarcastically.

"That's your business!" answered the general contractor, and rang off.

Mr. Driscoll talked it over with the "Co.," a young fellow of thirty or thereabouts, of polished manner and irreproachable tailoring. "See Foley," Mr. Berman advised.

"It's simply a game for graft!"

"That may be," said the junior partner. "But what can you do?"

"I won't pay graft!"

Mr. Berman shrugged his shapely shoulders and withdrew. Mr. Driscoll paced his office floor, tugged at his whiskers, and used some language that at least had the virture of being terse.   With the consequence, that he saw there was nothing for him but to settle as best as he could.   In furious mortification he wrote to Foley asking him to call.   The answer was a single scrawled sentence: " If you want to see me, I live at — West One Hundred and Fifteenth Street."

The instant after this note was read its fragments were in Mr. Driscoll's waste basket.   He'd suffer a sulphurous fate before he'd do it!   But the general contractor descended upon him in person, and there was a bitter half hour.   The result was that late Saturday afternoon Mr. Driscoll locked his pride in his desk, put his checkbook in his pocket, and set forth for the number on West One Hundred and Fifteenth Street.

A large woman, of dark voluptuous beauty, with a left hand like a jeweller's tray, answered his knock and led him into the parlor, on whose furnishings more money than taste had been spent.   The room was a war of colors, in which the gilt of the picture frames, enclosing oblongs of high-hued sentiment, had the best of the conflict, and in which baby blue, showing in pictures, upholstery and a fancy lamp shade, was an easy second, despite its infantility.

Foley sat in a swinging rocker, reading an evening paper, his coat off, his feet in slippers.   He did not rise.   " Hello!   Are they havin' zero weather in hell? "

Mr. Driscoll passed the remark.   " I guess you know what I'm here for."

" If youse give me three guesses, I might be able to hit it. But chair bottom's as cheap as carpet. Set down."

Mr. Driscoll sank into an upholstered chair, and a skirmish began between his purple face and the baby blue of the chair's back. " Let's get to business," he said.

" Won't youse have a drink first? " queried Foley, with baiting hospitality.

Mr. Driscoll's hands clenched the arms of the chair. " Let's get to business."

" Well,—fire away."

" You know what it is."

" I can't say's I do," Foley returned urbanely.

The contractor's hands dug again into the upholstery. " About the strike you called on the St. Etienne."

" Oh, that!—Well? "

Mr. Driscoll gulped down pride and anger and went desperately to the point. " What'll I have to do to settle it? "

" Um! Le's see. First of all, youse 'll fire the scabs? "

" Yes."

" Seems to me I give youse the chance to do that before, an' end it right there. But it can't end there now. There's the wages the men's lost. Youse 'll have to pay waitin' time."

" Extortion, you mean," Mr. Driscoll could not refrain from saying.

" Waitin' time," Foley corrected blandly.

" Well,—how much? " Mr. Driscoll remarked

to himself that he knew what part of the " waiting time " the men would get.

Foley looked at the ceiling and appeared to calculate.   " The waitin' time'll cost youse an even thousand."

" What! "

" If youse ain't learnt your lesson yet, youse might as well go back."   He made as if to resume his paper.

Mr. Driscoll swallowed hard.   " Oh, I'll pay. What else can I do?   You've got me in a corner with a gun to my head."

Foley did not deny the similitude.   " Youse 're gettin' off dirt cheap."

" When'll the men go back to work? "

" The minute youse pay, the strike's off."

Mr. Driscoll drew out his check-book, and started to fill in a check with a fountain pen.

" Hold on there! " Foley cried.   " No checks for me."

" What's the matter with a check? "

" Youse don't catch me scatterin' my name round on the back o' checks.   D'youse think I was born yesterday? "

" Where's the danger, since the money's to go to the men for waiting time? " Mr. Driscoll asked sarcastically.

" It's cash or nothin'," Foley said shortly.

" I've no money with me.   I'll bring it some time next week."

" Just as youse like.   Only every day raises the price."

Mr. Driscoll made haste to promise to deliver the

money Monday morning as soon as he could get it from his bank. And Foley thereupon promised to have the men ready to go back to work Monday afternoon. So much settled, Mr. Driscoll started to leave. He was suffocating.

"Won't youse have a drink?" Foley asked again, at the door.

Mr. Driscoll wanted only to get out of Foley's company, where he could explode without having it put in the bill. "No," he said curtly.

"Well!—now me, when I got to swallow a pill I like somethin' to wash it down."

The door slammed, and Mr. Driscoll puffed down the stairs leaving behind him a trail of language like a locomotive's plume.

Chapter III

THE RISE OF BUCK FOLEY

TOM glared at Foley till the walking delegate had covered half the distance to the ladder, then he turned back to his supervision, trying to hide the fires of his wrath. But his soul flamed within him. All that Foley had just threatened, openly and by insinuation, was within his power of accomplishment. Tom knew that. And every other man in the union was as much at his mercy,—and every man's family. And many had suffered greatly, and all, except Foley's friends, had suffered some. Tom's mind ran over the injustice Foley had wrought, and over Foley's history and the union's history during the last few years . . . and there was no sinking of the inward fire.

And yet there was a long period in the walking delegate's history on which Tom would not have passed harsh judgment. Very early in his career, in conformity with prevailing custom, Buck Foley had had a father and a mother. His mother he did not remember at all. After she had intimated a preference for another man by eloping with him, Buck's father had become afflicted with almost constant unsteadiness in his legs, an affliction that had before victimized him only at intervals. His father he remembered chiefly from having carried a tin pail to a store around the corner where a red-faced man filled it and handed it back to him over a high counter; and also from a white scar which even now his hair did not altogether conceal. One day his father disappeared. Not long after that Buck went to live in a big house with a great lot of boys, the little ones in checked pinafores, the big ones in gray suits. After six years of life here, at the age of twelve, he considered that he was fit for graduation, and so he went out into the world,—this on a very dark night when all in the big house were fast asleep.

For three years Buck was a newsboy; sleeping in a bed when he could afford one, sleeping in hallways, over warm gratings, along the docks, when he could not; winning all the newsboy's keen knowledge of human nature. At fifteen the sea fascinated him, and he lived in ships till he was twenty. Then a sailor's duties began to irk him. He came back to New York, took the first job that offered, driving a truck, and joined a political club of young men in a west side ward. Here he found himself. He rose rapidly to power in the club. Dan McGuire, the boss of the ward, had to take notice of him. He left his truck for a city job with a comfortable salary and nothing to do. At twenty-five he was one of McGuire's closest aids. Then his impatient ambition escaped his control. He plotted a revolution, which should overthrow McGuire and enthrone himself. But the Boss had thirty years of political cunning, and behind him a strong machine. For these Buck was no match. He took again to the sea.

Buck shipped as second mate on a steamer carrying steel for a great bridge in South Africa. Five years of authority had unfitted him for the subordinate position of second mate, and there were many tilts with the thick-headed captain. The result was that after the steamer had discharged her cargo Foley quitted his berth and followed the steel into the interior. The contractors were in sore need of men, and, even though Foley was not a bridgeman, they gladly gave him a job. His service as a sailor had fitted him to follow, without a twinge of fear, the most expert of the bridgemen in their daring clambering about cables and over narrow steel beams; and being naturally skillful he rapidly became an efficient workman.

Of the men sent out to this distant job perhaps one-half were union members. These formed a local branch of their society, and this Foley was induced to join. He rapidly won to influence and power in the affairs of the union, finding here the same keen enjoyment in managing men that he had first tasted in Dan McGuire's ward. After the completion of this job he worked in Scotland and Brazil, always active in the affairs of his union. At thirty-two he found himself back in New York,—a forceful leader ripe for an opportunity.

He had not been in New York a week when he discovered his chance. The union there was wofully weak—an organization only in name. The employers hardly gave it a consideration; the members themselves hardly held it in higher esteem. The men were working ten hours a day for two dollars; lacking the support of a strong union they were afraid to seek better terms. As Foley grimly expressed it, "The bosses have got youse down an' are settin' on your heads." Here in this utter disorganization Foley perceived his opportunity. He foresaw the extent to which the erection of steel-frame buildings, then in its beginning, was certain to develop. His trade was bound to become the "fundamental trade"; until his union had put up the steel frames the contractors could do nothing—the other workmen could do nothing. A strongly organized union holding this power—there was no limit to the concessions it might demand and secure.

It was a great opportunity. Foley went quietly to work on a job at twelve dollars a week, and bided his time. At the end of six months he was elected president and walking delegate of the union. He had no trouble in securing the offices. No one else wanted them. This was early in the spring. The first labor he set himself was the thorough organization of the union and the taking into its ranks of every iron-worker in the city.

The following spring there was a strike. Foley now came for the first time before the contractors' attention. They regarded him lightly, having remembrance of his predecessors. But they soon found they were facing a man who, though uneducated and of ungrammatical speech, was as keen and powerful as the best of them. The strike was won, and great was the name of Foley. In the next three years there were two more strikes for increases in wages, which were won. And the name of Foley waxed greater.

During these first four years no man could have

served the union better.   But here ended the stretch
of Foley's history on which Tom would not have
passed harsh judgment; and here began the period
whose acts of corruption and oppression were now
moving in burning procession through Tom's mind.
It is a matter of no moment whether Foley or the
employers took the initiative in starting him on the
new phase of his career as a labor leader.   It is
axiomatic that money is the ammunition of war;
among the employers there were many who were
indifferent whether this ammunition was spent in fighting or in buying.   On the other hand, Foley's training on the street and in Dan McGuire's ward was not
such as to produce an incorruptible integrity.   It is
only fair to Foley to say that the first sums he received
were in return for services which did not work any
injury or loss to the union.   It was easy to excuse to
himself these first lapses.   He knew his own worth;
he saw that men of much less capacity in the employ
of the bosses were paid big salaries.   The union paid
him thirty dollars a week.   " Who's hurt if I increase
my salary to something like it ought to be at the
expense of the bosses? " he reasoned; and took the
money with an easy conscience.

This first " easy money " made Foley hungry for
more.   He saw the many opportunities that existed
for acquiring it; he saw where he could readily create
other opportunities.   In earlier days he had envied
McGuire the chances that were his.   He had no reason to envy McGuire now.

During the first three or four years of his adminis-
tration there was no opposition to him within the

union. His work was too strenuous to be envied him by any man. But after the union had become an established power, and the position of walking delegate one of prominence, a few ambitious spirits began to aspire to his job. Also there began to be mutterings about his grafting. A party was formed which secretly busied itself with a plan to do to him what he had tried to do to Dan McGuire. He triumphed, as McGuire had triumphed. But the revolution, though unsuccessful, had a deep lesson for him. It taught him that, unless he fortified it, his position was insecure. At present he was dependent for its retention upon the favor of the members; and favor, as he knew, was not a dependable quantity.

He was determined to remain the walking delegate of the union. He had made the union, and the position. They were both his by right. He rapidly took measures to insure himself against the possibility of overthrow. He became relentless to all opposition. Those who dared talk were quick to hear from him. Some fared easily—the clever ones who were not bribe-proof. After being given jobs as foremen, and presented with neat little sums, they readily saw the justice of Foley's cause. Some, who were not worth bribing, he intimidated into silence. Those whom he had threatened and who still talked found themselves out of work and unable to get new jobs; they were forced into other trades or out of the city. A few such examples lessened the necessity for such severe action. Men with families to support perceived the value of a discreet tongue.

These methods were successful in quelling open

opposition; but they, together with the knowledge that Foley was taking money wherever it was offered, had the effect of rapidly alienating the better element in the union. This forced him into a close alliance with the rougher members, who were greatly in the minority. But this minority, never more than five hundred out of three thousand men, Foley made immensely effective. He instructed them to make the meetings as disorderly as possible. His scheme worked to perfection. The better members came less and less frequently, and soon the meetings were entirely in the hands of the roughs. As time passed Foley grew more and more jealous of his power, and more and more harsh in the methods used to guard it. He attached to himself intimately several of the worst of his followers whom grim facetiousness soon nominated " The Entertainment Committee." If any one attacked him now, the bold one did so knowing that he would probably experience the hospitality of these gentlemen the first dark night he ventured forth alone.

Such were the conditions behind the acts of tyranny that Tom furiously overhauled, as he mechanically directed the work. He had considered these conditions and acts before, but never with such fierceness as now. Hitherto he had been, as it were, merely one citizen, though a more or less prominent one, of an oppressed nation; now he, as an individual, had felt the tyrant's malevolence. He had before talked of the union's getting rid of Foley as a necessary action, and only the previous night he had gone to the length of denouncing Foley in open meeting, an adventurous act that had not been matched in the union for two years.   Perhaps, in the course of time, his patriotism alone would have pushed him to take up arms against Foley.   But now to his patriotic indignation there was added the selfish wrath of the outraged individual,—and the sum was an impulse there was no restraining.

Tom was not one who, in a hot moment, for the assuagement of his wrath, would bang down his fist and consign himself to a purpose.   Here, however, was a case where wrath made the same demand that already had been made by cool, moral judgment—the dethronement of Foley.   And Tom felt in himself the power for its accomplishment.   He was well furnished with self-confidence,—lacking which any man is an engine without fire.   During the last five years—that is, since he was twenty-five, when he began to look upon life seriously—the knowledge had grown upon him that he was abler, and of stronger purpose, than his fellows.   He had accepted this knowledge quietly, as a fact.   It had not made him presumptuous; rather it had imposed upon him a serious sense of duty.

He considered the risks of a fight against Foley. Personal danger,—plenty of that, yes,—but his hot mind did not care for that.   Financial loss,—he drew back from thinking what his wife would say; anyhow, there were his savings, which would keep them for awhile, if worst came to worst.

As the men were leaving the building at the end of the day's work, Tom drew Barry and Pete to one side.   "I know you fellows don't like Foley a lot," he began abruptly, "but I don't know how far you're willing to go. For my part, I can't stand for him any longer. Can't we get together to-night and have a talk? "

To this Barry and Pete agreed.

" Where'bouts? " asked Barry.

Tom hesitated; and he was thinking of his wife when he said, " How about your house? "

" Glad to have you," was Barry's answer.

Chapter IV

A COUNCIL OF WAR

TOM lived in the district below West Fourteenth Street, where, to the bewildered explorer venturing for the first time into that region, the jumbled streets seem to have been laid out by an egg-beater.

It was almost six o'clock when, hungry and wrathful, he thrust his latch-key into the door of his four-room flat. The door opened into blackness. He gave an irritated groan and groped about for matches, in the search striking his hip sharply against the corner of the dining table. A match found and the gas lit, he sat down in the sitting-room to await his wife's coming. From the mantel a square, gilded clock, on which stood a knight in full armor, counted off the minutes with irritating deliberation. It struck six; no Maggie. Tom's impatience rapidly mounted, for he had promised to be at Barry's at quarter to eight. He was on the point of going to a restaurant for his dinner, when, at half-past six, he heard the fumble of a latch-key in the lock, and in came his wife, followed by their son, a boy of four, crying from weariness.

She was a rather large, well-formed, and well-featured young woman, and was showily dressed in the extreme styles of the cheap department stores. She was pretty, with the prettiness of cheap jewelry.

Tom rose as she carefully placed her packages on the table. " You really decided to come home, did you? "

" Oh, I know I'm late," she said crossly, breathing heavily. " But it wasn't my fault. I started early enough. But there was such a mob in the store you couldn't get anywhere. If you'd been squeezed and pushed and punched like I was in the stores and in the street cars, well, you wouldn't say a word."

" Of course you had to go! "

" I wasn't going to miss a bargain of that kind. You don't get 'em often."

Tom gazed darkly at the two bulky packages, the cause of his delayed dinner. " Can I have something to eat,—and quick? "

By this time her hat and jacket were off. " Just as soon as I get back my breath," she said, and began to undo the packages.

The little boy came to her side.

"I'm so hungry, ma," he whined. "Gimme a piece."

" Dinner 'll be ready in a little while," she answered carelessly.

" But I can't wait! "—and he began to cry.

Maggie turned upon him sharply. " If you don't stop that bawling, Ferdie, you shan't have a bite of dinner."

The boy cried all the louder.

" Oh, you! " she ejaculated; and took a piece of coarse cake from the cupboard and handed it to him. " Now do be still! "

Ferdinand filled his mouth with the cake, and she returned to the packages. "I been wanting something to fill them empty places at the ends of the mantel this long time, and when I saw the advertisement in the papers this morning, I said it was just the thing. . . . Now there!"

Out of one pasteboard box she had taken a dancing Swiss shepherdess, of plaster, pink and green and blue, and out of the other box a dancing Swiss shepherd. One of these peasants she had put on either side of the knight, at the ends of the mantel.

"Now, don't you like that?"

Tom looked doubtfully at the latest adornment of his home. Somehow, he didn't just like it, though he didn't know why. "I guess it 'll do," he said at length.

"And they were only thirty-nine cents apiece! Now when I get a new tidy for the mantel,—a nice pink one with flowers. Just you wait!"

"Well,—but let's have dinner first."

"In just a minute." With temper restored by sight of her art treasures, Maggie went into the bedroom and quickly returned in an old dress. The dinner of round steak, fried potatoes and coffee was ready in a very short time. The steak avenged its hasty preparation by presenting one badly burnt side. But Tom ate the poor dinner without complaint. He was used to poor dinners; and his only desire was to get away and to Barry's.

Once during the meal he looked at his wife, a question in his mind. Should he tell her? But his eyes fell back to his plate and he said nothing.

She must know some time, of course—but he didn't want the scene now.

But she herself approached uncomfortably near the subject. She had glanced at him hesitatingly several times while they were eating; as he was rising from the table she began resolutely: "I met Mrs. Jones this afternoon. She told me what you said about Foley last night at the meeting. Her husband told her."

Tom paused.

"There's no sense doing a thing of that kind," she went on. "Here we are just beginning to have things a little comfortable. You know well enough what Foley can do to you if you get him down on you."

"Well?" Tom said guardedly.

"Well, don't you be that foolish again. We can't afford it."

"I'll see about it." He went into the sitting-room and returned with hat and overcoat on. "I'm going over to Barry's for awhile—on some business," he said, and went out.

Barry and Pete, who boarded with the Barrys, were waiting in the sitting-room when Tom arrived, —and with them sat Mrs. Barry and a boy of about thirteen and a girl apparently a couple of years younger, the two children with idle school books in their laps. Mrs. Barry's sitting-room, also her parlor, would not have satisfied that amiable lady, the president of the Society for Instructing Wage-Earners in House Furnishing. There was a coarse red Smyrna rug in the middle of the floor; a dingy, blue-flowered sofa, with three chairs to match (the sort seen in the windows of cheap furniture stores on bargain days, marked "Nineteen dollars for Set"); a table in one corner, bearing a stack of photographs and a glass vase holding up a bunch of pink paper roses; a half dozen colored prints in gilt-and-white plaster frames. The room, however, quite satisfied Mrs. Barry, and the amiable president of the S. I. W. E. H. F. would needs have given benign approval to the room's utter cleanliness.

Mrs. Barry, a big, red-faced woman, greeted Tom heartily. Then she turned to the boy and girl. "Come on, children. We've got to chase ourselves. The men folks want to talk." She drove the two before her wide body into the kitchen.

Tom plunged into the middle of what he had to say. "We've talked about Foley a lot—all of us. We've said other unions are managed decently, honestly—why shouldn't ours be? We've said we didn't like Foley's bulldozing ways. We didn't like the tough gang he's got into the union. We didn't like the rough-house meetings. We didn't like his grafting. We've said we ought to raise up and kick him out. And then, having said that much, we've gone back to work—me, you and all the rest of us—and he's kept on bullying us, and using the union as a lever to pry off graft. I'm dead sick of this sort of business. For one, I'm tired talking. I'm ready for doing."

"Sure, we're all sick o' Foley. But what d' you think we ought to do?" queried Barry.

"Fire him out," Tom answered shortly.

"It only takes three words to say that," said Pig Iron. "But how?"

"Fire him out!" Tom was leaning forward in his chair, his elbows on his knees, his big, red hands interlocked. There was determination in his square face, in the set of his powerful red neck, in the hunch of his big shoulders. He gazed steadily at the two men for a brief space. "Boys, my mind's made up. I'm going to fight him."

Pete and Barry looked at him in amazement.

"You're goin' to fight Buck Foley!" cried Barry.

"You're jokin'!" said Pig Iron.

"I'm in dead earnest."

"You know what'll happen to you if you lose?" queried Barry.

"Yes. And I know Foley may not even give me a chance to lose," Tom added grimly.

"You've got nerve to burn, Tom," said Pig Iron. "It's not an easy proposition. Myself, I'd as soon put on the gloves an' mix it up with the devil. An' to spit it right out on the carpet, Tom, I think Buck's done the union a lot o' good."

"You're right there, Pete. No one knows that better than I do. As you fellows know, I left town eight years ago and was bridging in the West four years. I was pretty much of a kid when I went away, but I was old enough to see the union didn't have enough energy left to die. When I came back and saw what Foley'd done, I thought he was the greatest thing that ever happened. If he'd quit right then the union'd 'a' papered the hall with his pictures. But you know how he's changed since then. The public knows it, too. Look how the newspapers have been shooting it into him. I'm not fighting Foley as he was four or five years ago, Pete, but Foley as he is now."

" There's no denyin' he's so crooked now he can't lay straight in bed," Pete admitted.

" We've got to get rid of him some time, haven't we? " Tom went on.

" Yes," the two men conceded.

" Or sooner or later he'll smash the union. That's certain. Now there's only one way to get rid of him. That's to go out after him, and go after him hard."

" But it's an awful risk for you, Tom," said Barry.

" Someone's got to take it if we ever get rid of Foley."

" One thing's straight, anyhow," declared Pete. " You're the best man in the union to go against Foley."

" Of course," said Barry.

Tom did not deny it.

There was a moment's silence. Then Pete asked: " What's your plan? "

" Election comes the first meeting in March. I'm going to run against him for walking delegate."

" If you care anything for my opinion," said Pete, " here it is: You've got about as much chance as a snowball in hell."

" You're away off, Pig Iron. You know as well as I do that five-sixths of the men in the union are against Foley. Why do they stand for him? Because they're unorganized, and he's got them bluffed out. If those men got together, Foley'd be the snow-ball. That's what I'm going to try to do,—get those men in line."

A door opened, and Mrs. Barry looked in. "I left my glasses somewhere in there. Will I bother you men much if I look for 'em?"

"Not me," said Tom. "You can stay and listen if you want to."

Mrs. Barry sat down. "I suppose you don't mind tellin' us how you're goin' to get the men in line," said Pete.

"My platform's going to be an honest adminis-tration of the affairs of the union, and every man to be treated like a man. That's simple enough, ain't it?—and strong enough? And a demand for more wages. I'm going to talk these things to every man I meet. If they can kick Foley out, and get honest management and decent treatment, just by all coming out and voting, don't you think they're going to do it? They'll all fall in line."

"That demand for more wages is a good card. Our wage contract with the bosses expires May first, you know. The men all want more money; they need it; they deserve it. If I talk for it Foley 'll be certain to oppose it, and that 'll weaken him.

"I wanted to talk this over with you fellows to get your opinion. I thought you might suggest something. But even if you don't like the scheme, and even if you don't want to join in the fight, I'm going to stick it out. My mind's made up."

Tom sank back into his chair and waited for the two men to speak.

"Well, your scheme don't sound just like an insane asylum," Pete admitted. "Count me in."

Tom looked across at Barry. Barry's face was turned down and his hands were inter-gripped. Tom understood. Barry had been out of work much during the last three years, and recent illness in the family had endowed him with debts. If he actively engaged in Tom's movement, and Foley triumphed, Foley's vengeance would see to it that Barry worked no more in New York. It was too great a risk to ask of a man situated as Barry was.

"I understand, Barry," said Tom. "That's all right. Don't you do it."

Barry made no answer.

Mrs. Barry put her hand on her husband's shoulder. "Jim, ain't we goin' to be in on this fight against Foley?"

"You know why, Mary." There was a catch in his voice.

"Yes. Because of me an' the kids. You, I know you've got as much nerve as anybody. We're goin' in, Jim. An' if we lose"—she tried to smile—"why, I ain't much of a consumptive, am I? I'll take in washin' to help out."

Tom turned his face about. Pete did the same, and their eyes met. Pete's face was set hard. He growled out something that sounded very much like an oath.

It was midnight when Tom left. The strike which Foley called on the St. Etienne Hotel the next day gave him time for much thinking about his campaign. He acquainted several of the more influ-

ential members of the union with his purpose, asking
them to keep secret what he said till he was ready to
begin an open fight. All gave him sympathy, but
most of them hesitated when it came to promising
active assistance. " Now if Foley only couldn't do
us out of our jobs, in case you lose, we'd be right
with you. But——" Fear inclined them to let bad
enough alone.

This set Tom to thinking again. On Monday
evening—that afternoon Foley had ordered the men
back to work on the St. Etienne Hotel—Tom announced a new plan to Barry and Pete. " We
want to get every argument we can to use on the
boys. It struck me we might make some use of the
bosses. It's to their interest, as well as to ours, for
us to have the right sort of delegate. If we could
say that the bosses are sick of Foley and want us to
get a decent man, and will guarantee to keep us at
work no mater what Foley says,—that might have
influence on some of the weak-kneed brothers."

" The boys'd say the bosses ain't runnin' the
union," said Pete. " If you get the bosses on your
side, the boys 'll all stand by Foley."

" I thought of that. That's what'd happen if we
got mixed up with anybody on the Executive Committee of the bosses except Baxter. The boys think
Murphy, Bobbs, and Isaacs are pretty small potatoes,
and they think Driscoll's not on the square. I guess
it's a case of the pot calling the kettle black, but you
know what Foley says about Driscoll. But with
Baxter it's different. He's friendly to the union, and
the boys know it. A word from him might help a

lot.   And he hates Foley, and Foley has no use for him.   I've heard Buck say as much."

" It's worth tryin', anyhow," Pete and Barry agreed.

" Well, I'm going to brace him to-morrow after work," said Tom.

Chapter V

TOM SEEKS HELP FROM THE ENEMY

AT the end of work the next day Tom joined the rush of men down the ladders and the narrow servants' stairways, the only ones in as yet, and on gaining the street made for the nearest saloon. Five cents invested in beer secured for him the liberty of the house. He washed himself, brushed his hair and clothing, and set forth for the office of Baxter & Co.

Baxter & Co. occupied one side of the tenth floor of a big downtown office building. Tom found himself in a large waiting-room, divided by a wooden railing, beyond which at a desk sat an imperious youth in a blue uniform.

" Is Mr. Baxter in? " Tom inquired.

The uniform noted that Tom's clothes were worn and wrinkled. " He's busy," it said stiffly.

" Is he in? "

" I s'pose he is."

" Well, you tell him I want to see him. Keating's my name. I'll wait if he's busy."

The uniform carelessly handed him a slip of paper. " Write down yer name an' business, an' I'll see if he'll see youse."

With a gleam in his eyes Tom took the printed form, wrote his name and " on business of the Iron Workers' Union."

The boy accepted the slip and calmly read it. Tom gave him a push that sent him spinning. " Get a move on you, there! I'm in a hurry."

The boy gave a startled look back, and walked quickly down an alley that ran between two rows of offices. Tom sat down in one of the leather-bottomed chairs and with a show of coolness, but with inward excitement, waited his interview with Mr. Baxter. He had never met an employer in his life, save regarding his own work or as a member of a strike committee. And now the first he was to meet in a private interview was the most prominent employer in his trade—head of the big firm of Baxter & Co., and president of the Iron Employers' Association.

Several minutes passed before the uniform reappeared and led Tom into Mr. Baxter's office, a large, airy room with red burlap walls, cherry woodwork, cherry chairs, a long cherry table, a flat-top cherry desk. The room was absolutely without attempt at decoration, and was as clean as though it had been swept and dusted the minute before. The only piece of paper in the room was an architect's drawing of a façade, which Mr. Baxter was examining.

Mr. Baxter did not look up immediately. Tom, standing with hat in hand, was impressed with his busyness. He was not yet acquainted with the devices by which men of affairs fortify their importance.

Suddenly Mr. Baxter wheeled about in his chair. " I beg your pardon. Be seated. What can I do for you? "

He was perhaps forty-five or fifty—slender, of

high, narrow brow, steely eyes, and Vandyke beard. His neatness was equal to that of his office; he looked as though he were fresh from barber, haberdasher and tailor. Tom understood the success of the man in the first glance at his face: he was as quick to act upon the opportunity as a steel trap.

Tom sat down in one of the polished chairs, and affected composure by throwing his left arm across the cherry table. "I belong to the Iron Workers' Union. To come right to the point——"

"I shall be obliged if you will. I'm really very busy."

Mr. Baxter's tone was a model of courtesy. A more analytical man than Tom might have felt the distinction that it was the courtesy a gentlemen owes himself, not the courtesy one man owes another. Tom merely felt a vague antagonism, and that put him at his ease.

"I'm busy, too," he returned quietly. "What I've come to see you about is a matter which I consider of great importance to the bosses and the union. And I've come to see you because I know you are friendly to the union."

"I believe that in most cases the interests of the employers and the interests of the union are practically the same."

"And also because you don't like Foley."

Mr. Baxter fingered his narrow watch chain a moment. "So you've come to see me about Mr. Foley?"

"Yes. There's no use going into details with you, Mr. Baxter. You know the sort Foley is as well as I do. He bullies the union. That's nothing to you. But he's not on the square with the bosses. That is. As you said awhile ago, the interests of the bosses and the union are the same. It's to the interest of both to get rid of Foley. That's so, ain't it? "

Mr. Baxter's face was inscrutable. " You're going to turn him out then? "

" We're going to try to."

" And what will be your policy then?—if you don't mind my asking it."

" To run things on the square."

" A praiseworthy purpose. Of course you'll put in a square man as delegate then."

" I'm going to run myself."

Tom thought he saw a significant look pass across Mr. Baxter's face. " Not because I'm anxious for his job," he hastened to explain. " But somebody's got to run against him."

Mr. Baxter nodded slightly. " I see. Not a very popular risk." His keen eyes never wavered from Tom's face. " How do propose to defeat Foley? But don't tell me anything you don't want to."

Tom outlined his plans for organizing the better element against Foley.

" That sounds feasible," was Mr. Baxter's comment when Tom had concluded. His eyes were still fastened on Tom's face. " And after you win, there 'll be a strike? "

This question, asked quietly but with electrical quickness, caught Tom unprepared. He floundered an instant. "We've got to bridge two or three rivers before we come to that one," he answered.

Mr. Baxter hardly moved an eyelash. "That's obvious. And now, aside from the benefit which we are to secure by the change, how does your plan concern me?"

"Since you are going to profit by the fight, if we win, I thought you might help us. And you can do it easy enough. One thing that'll keep a lot of the members from joining in the fight is that they're afraid, if Foley wins out, he'll get 'em all fired. Now if you'll simply guarantee that you'll stand by the men, why, they'll all come out against Foley and we'll beat him five to one. There'll be no chance for us to lose."

Mr. Baxter's white brow wrinkled in thought. Tom waited his words in suspense. At length he spoke.

"You will readily realize, Mr. Keating, that it is an almost unprecedented step for us to take such a part in the affairs of a union. Your suggestion is something I must think about."

Tom had been certain Mr. Baxter would fall in with his scheme enthusiastically. It required so little, merely his word, and assured so much. Mr. Baxter's judicial reception of his plan shot him through with disappointment.

"What, don't it appeal to you?" he cried.

"It certainly seems full of promise."

"It will clear us of Foley—certain! And it is to the interest of both of us that the union be run on the square."

"That's true,—very true. But the most I can say to you now, Mr. Keating, is that I'll take the matter under advisement. Come to see me again in a few days."

Mr. Baxter began to finger the drawing on his desk, whereby Tom knew the interview was at an end. Greatly dashed, but somewhat reassured by the contractor's last words, he said good-afternoon and withdrew. The uniform respectfully opened the gate in the railing. In the uniform's book of wisdow it was writ down that anyone who could be closeted with your boss was deserving of courtesy.

The instant the office door closed on Tom's back Mr. Baxter quickly rose and paced the floor for several minutes. Then he sat down at his desk, took a sheet of paper from a drawer, and dashed off a note to Foley.

Mr. Baxter did not rise to greet Foley when the walking delegate entered his office the next afternoon. "Mr. Foley," he said, with a short nod of his head.

"Youse guessed my name," said Foley, cooly helping himself to a chair. "What's doin'?"

The two men watched each other narrowly, as might two enemies who have established a truce, yet who suspect treachery on the part of the other. There was a distant superiority in the manner of Mr. Baxter,—and also the hardly concealed strain of the man who, from policy or breeding, would be polite where he loathes. Foley, tilted back in his chair, matched this manner with an air of defiant self-assertion,

Mr. Baxter rapidly sketched the outline of what Tom had said to him.

"And so Keating come to youse for help," grinned Foley. "That ain't bad!"

Mr. Baxter did not recognize Foley's equality by smiling. "I thought it to your interest to let you know this at once, for——"

"And to your interest, too."

"I knew you were not particularly desirous of having Mr. Keating elected," he continued.

"I'm just about as anxious as youse are," said Foley promptly. "Anyhow," he added carelessly, "I already knew what youse told me." Which he did not.

"Then my sending for you and telling you has served no purpose." The coldness of his voice placed a wide distance between himself and the walking delegate.

Foley perceived the distance, and took a vindictive pleasure in bridging it with easy familiarity. "Not at all, Baxter. It gives youse a chance to show how much youse like me, an' how much youse 've got the interest o' the union at heart."

The lean, sarcastic face nettled Mr. Baxter. "I think my reputation speaks for my interest in the union," he said stiffly.

"Your interest in the union!" Foley laughed.

No man had ever seen Mr. Baxter lose his self-control; but he was as near losing it now as he had ever been, else he would not have made so weak a rejoinder.

"My reputation speaks for my interest," he re-

peated. "You won't find a man in your union but
that 'll say I'm the union's friend."

Foley laughed again—a harsh, biting laugh.
"An' why do they say it, eh? Because I told 'em
so. An' youse 've got the nerve, Baxter, to sit there
an' talk that rot to me!—me, the man that made
youse!"

"Made me!"

Foley's heart leaped to see the wrathful color flame
in the white cheek of the suave and collected Mr.
Baxter—to see the white shapely hands twitch.

"Yes, made youse!" And he went on with his
grim pleasure. "Youse 're doin' twice the business
youse were three years ago. Why did youse get the
contracts for the Atwell building and the Sewanee
Hotel—the two jobs that put youse at the head o'
things in New York? Because Driscoll, Bobbs, an'
some o' the others had failed to get the jobs they
were workin' on done in contract time. An' why
didn't they get done on time? Because youse didn't
want 'em to get through on time. I saw that they
got bum men, who made mistakes,—an' I give 'em
their bellyful o' strikes."

"You didn't do these things out of love for me,"
Mr. Baxter put in meaningly. He was getting himself in hand again.

"Sure, I didn't,—not any more'n youse told me
about Keating for love o' me."

Foley went on. "The men who want buildings
put up have found youse get through on time, an'
the others don't—so youse get the business. Why
do youse get through on time? Because I see youse

get the fastest men in the union.   An' because I see youse don't have any labor trouble."

"Neither of which you do solely for love."

"Sure not.   Now don't youse say again I haven't made youse.   An' don't give me that hot air about bein' friendly to the union.   Three years ago youse seen clearer than the others that youse bosses was bound to lose the strike.   Youse 'd been fightin' the union till then, an' not makin' any more'n the rest o' the bosses.   So youse tried a new game.   Youse led the other bosses round to give in, an' got the credit o' bein' a friend o' the union.   I know how much youse like the union!"

"Pardon me if I fail to see the purpose of all this retrospection," said Mr. Baxter sarcastically.

"I just wanted to remind youse that I'm on to youse from hair to toenails—that's all," Foley answered calmly.

"I think it would be wiser to confine our conversation to the matter in hand," said Mr. Baxter coldly.   "Mr. Keating said he was certain to beat you.   What chance does he have of being elected?"

"The same as youse."

"And a strike,—how about that?"

"It follows if I'm elected, don't it, there'll not be any strike."

"That's according to our agreement," said Mr. Baxter.

"No," said Foley, as he rose, "Keating ain't goin' to trouble youse much."   A hard look came over his face.   "Nor me."

Chapter VI

IN WHICH FOLEY PLAYS WITH TWO MICE

FOLEY left Mr. Baxter's office with the purpose of making straight for the office of Mr. Driscoll; but his inborn desire to play with the mouse caused him to change the direct road to an acute angle having at its apex the St. Etienne Hotel. He paused a moment to look up at the great black skeleton,—a lofty scaffolding that might have been erected for some mural painter ambitious to fresco his fame upon the sky. He saw the crane swing a beam to its place between two of the outside columns, and saw a man step upon its either end to bolt it to its place. Suddenly the crane jerked up the beam, and the men frantically threw their arms around it. As suddenly the crane lowered it. It struck upon the head of a column. Foley saw one man fly from the beam, catch hold of the end of a board that extended over the edge of the building, hang there; saw the beam, freed in some manner from the pulley hook, start down, ridden by one man; and then saw it come whirling downward alone.

"Look out!" he shouted with all his lungs.

Pedestrians rushed wildly from beneath the shed which extended, as a protection to them, over the sidewalk. Horses were jerked rearing backwards.

The black beam crashed through the shed and through the pine sidewalk. Foley dashed inside and for the ladder.

Up on the great scaffolding hands had seized the wrists of the pendant man and lifted him to safety. All were now leaning over the platform's edge, gazing far down at the ragged hole in the shed.

"D'you see Pete?" Tom asked at large, in a strained voice.

There were several noes.

"That was certainly the last o' Pig Iron," muttered one of the gang.

He was not disputed.

"It wasn't my fault," said the signalman, as pale as paper. "I didn't give any wrong signals. Someone below must 'a' got caught in the rope."

"I'm going down," said Tom; and started rapidly for the ladder's head—to be met with an ascending current of the sort of English story books ascribe to pirates. Pete's body followed the words so closely as to suggest a possible relation between the two. Tom worked Pete's hand. The men crowded up.

"Now who the"—some pirate words—"done that?" Pete demanded.

"It was all an accident," Tom explained.

"But I might 'a' been kilt!"

"Sure you might," agreed Johnson sympathetically.

"How is it you weren't?" Tom asked.

"The beam, in whirlin' over, swung the end I

was on into the floor below. I grabbed a beam an' let it travel alone. That's all."

Foley, breathing deeply from his rapid climb, emerged this instant from the flooring, and walked quickly to the group. "Anybody kilt?" he asked.

The particulars of the accident were given him. "Well, boys, youse see what happens when youse got a foreman that ain't onto his job."

Tom contemptuously turned his back and walked away.

"I don't see why Driscoll don't fire him," growled Jake.

"Who knows what 'll happen!" Foley turned a twisted, knowing look about the group. "He's been talkin' a lot!"

He walked over to where Tom stood watching the gang about the north crane. "I'm dead onto your game," he said, in a hard, quiet voice, his eyes glittering.

Tom was startled. He had expected Foley to learn of his plan, but thought he had guarded against such an early discovery. "Well?" he said defiantly.

Foley began to play with his mouse. "I guess youse know things 'll begin to happen." He greedily watched Tom's face for signs of inward squirming. "Remember the little promise I made youse t'other day? Buck Foley usually keeps his promises, don't he—hey?"

But the mouse refused to be played with. "The other beam, boys," it called out to three men, and strode away toward them.

Foley watched Tom darkly an instant, and then turned sharply about. At the ladder's head Jake stopped him.

"Get him fired, Buck. Here's your chance to get me that foreman's job you promised me."

"We'll see," Foley returned shortly, and passed down the ladder and along the other leg of the angle to the office of Driscoll & Co. He gave his name to Miss Arnold. She brought back the message that he should call again, as Mr. Driscoll was too busy to see him.

"Sorry, miss, but I guess I'm as busy as he is. I can't come again." And Foley brushed coolly past her and entered Mr. Driscoll's office.

"Good-afternoon, Mr. Driscoll," he said, showing his yellow teeth in a smile, and helping himself to a chair. "Nice afternoon, ain't it?"

Mr. Driscoll wheeled angrily about in his chair. "I thought I sent word to you I was too busy to see you?"

"So youse did, Mr. Driscoll. So youse did."

"Well, I meant it!" He turned back to his desk.

"I s'pose so," Foley said cheerfully. He tilted back easily in his chair, and crossed his legs. "But, youse see, I could hardly come again, an' I wanted very much to see youse."

Mr. Driscoll looked as though he were going to explode. But fits of temper at a thousand dollars a fit were a relief that he could afford only now and then. He kept himself in hand, though the effort it cost him was plain to Foley.

"What d'you want to see me about? Be in a hurry. I'm busy."

The point of Foley's tongue ran gratified between his thin lips, as his eyes took in every squirm of this cornered mouse. "In the first place, I come just in a social way. I wanted to return the calls youse made on me last week. Youse see, I been studyin' up etiquette. Gettin' ready to break into the Four Hundred."

"And in the second place?" snapped Mr. Driscoll.

Foley stepped to the office door, closed it, and resumed his back-tilted seat. "In the second place, I thought I'd like to talk over one little point about the St. Etienne job."

Mr. Driscoll drew a check-book out of a pigeonhole and dipped his pen. "How much this time?"

The sarcasm did not touch Foley. He made a wide negative sweep with his right arm. "What I'm goin' to tell youse won't cost youse a cent. It's as free as religion." The point of red again slipped between his lips.

"Well?—I said I was busy."

"Well, here it is: Don't youse think youse got a pretty bum foreman on the St. Etienne job?"

"What business is that of yours?"

"Won't youse talk in a little more of a Christian spirit, Mr. Driscoll?"

It was half a minute before Mr. Driscoll could speak in any kind of a spirit. "Will you please come to the point!"

"Why, I'm there already," the walking delegate

returned sweetly. "As I was sayin', don't youse think your foreman on the St. Etienne job is a pretty bum outfit?"

"Keating?—I never had a better."

"D'youse think so? Now I was goin' to suggest, in a friendly way, that youse get another man in his place."

"Are you running my business, or am I?"

"If youse'd only talk with a little more Christian——"

The eyes clicked. The members of the church to which Mr. Driscoll belonged would have 'stuffed fingers into their horrified ears at the language in which Foley was asked to go to a place that was being prepared for him.

Foley was very apologetic. "I'm too busy now, an' I don't get my vacation till August. Then youse ain't goin' to take my advice?"

"No! I'm not!"

The walking delegate stopped purring. He leaned forward, and the claws pushed themselves from out their flesh-pads. "Let's me and youse make a little bet on that, Mr. Driscoll. Shall we say a thousand a side?"

Driscoll's eyes and Foley's battled for a moment. "And if I don't do it?" queried Mr. Driscoll, abruptly.

"I don't like to disturb youse by talkin' about unpleasant things. It would be too bad if you didn't do it. Youse really couldn't afford any more delays on the job, could youse?"

Mr. Driscoll made no reply.

Foley stood up, again purring. " It's really good advice, ain't it? I'll send youse round a good man in the mornin' to take his place. Good-by."

As Foley passed out Mr. Driscoll savagely brushed the papers before him to one side of his desk, crushing them into a crumpled heap, and sat staring into the pigeon-holes. He sent for Mr. Berman, who after delivering an opinion in favor of Foley's proposition, departed for his own office, pausing for a moment to lean over the desk of the fair secretary. Presently, with a great gulp, Mr. Driscoll touched a button on his desk and Miss Arnold appeared within the doorway. She was slender, but not too slender. Her heavy brown hair was parted in the middle and fell over either end of her low, broad forehead. The face was sensitive, sensible, intellectual. Persons chancing into Mr. Driscoll's office for the first time wondered how he had come by such a secretary.

" Miss Arnold, did you ever see a jelly fish? " he demanded.

" Yes."

" Well, here's another."

" I can't say I see much family resemblance," smiled Miss Arnold.

" It's there, all right. We ain't got any nerve."

" It seems to me you are riding the transmigration of soul theory at a pretty hard pace, Mr. Driscoll. Yesterday, when you upset the bottle of ink, you were a bull in a china shop, you know."

" When you know me a year or two longer, you'll know I'm several sorts of dumb animals. But I didn't call you to give you a natural history lecture. Get Duffy on the 'phone, will you, and tell him to send Keating around as soon as he can. Then come in and take some letters that I want you to let me have just as quick as you can get them off."

Two hours later Tom appeared in Miss Arnold's office. She had seen him two or three times when he had come in on business, and had been struck by his square, open face and his confident bearing. She now greeted him with a slight smile. " Mr. Driscoll is waiting for you," she said; and sent him straight on through the next door.

Mr. Driscoll asked Tom to be seated and continued to hold his bulging eyes on a sheet of paper which he scratched with a pencil. Tom, with a sense of impending disaster, sat waiting for his employer to speak.

At length Mr. Driscoll wheeled about abruptly. " What d'you think of Foley? "

" I've known worse men," Tom answered, on his guard.

" You must have been in hell, then! You think better of him than I do. And better than he thinks of you. He's just been in to see me. He wants me to fire you."

Tom had half-guessed this from the moment Duffy had told him Mr. Driscoll wanted him, but nevertheless he was startled by its announcement in words. He let several seconds pass, the while he got hold of himself, then asked in a hard voice: " And what are you going to do? "

Mr. Driscoll knew what he was going to do, but

his temper insisted on gratification before he told his plan. " What can I do? " he demanded testily. " It's your fault—the union's fault. And I don't have any sympathy to waste for anything that happens to any of you. Why don't you put a decent man in as your business agent? "

Tom passed all this by. " So you're going to fire me? "

" What else can I do? " Mr. Driscoll reiterated.

" Hasn't my work been satisfactory? "

" It isn't a question of work. If it's any satisfaction to you, I'll say that I never had a foreman that got as much or as good work out of the men."

" Then you're firing me because Foley orders you to? " There were both pity and indignation in Tom's voice.

Mr. Driscoll had expected to put his foreman on the defensive; instead, he found himself getting on that side. " If you want it right out, that's it. But what can I do? I'm held up."

" Do? " Tom stood up before his employer, neck and face red, eyes flashing. " Why, fight him! "

" I've tried that "—sarcastically—" thanks."

" That's what's the matter with you bosses! You think more of dollars than you do of self-respect! "

Mr. Driscoll trembled. " Young man, d'you know who you're talking to? "

" I do!" Tom cried hotly. " To the man who's firing me because he's too cowardly to stand up for what's right! "

Mr. Driscoll glared, his eyes clicked. Then he gave a great swallow. " I guess you're about right.

But if I understand the situation, I guess there's a lot of men in your union that'd rather hold their jobs than stand up for what's right."

Tom, in his turn, had his fires drawn. "And I guess you're about right, too," he had to admit.

"I may be a coward," Mr. Driscoll went on, "but if a man puts a gun to my head and says he'll pull the trigger unless I do what he says, I've got to do it, that's all. And I rather guess you would, too. But let's pass this by. I've got a plan. Foley can make me put you off one job, but he can't make me fire you. Let's see; I'm paying you thirty a week, ain't I?"

"That's it."

"Well, I'm going to give you thirty-five a week and put you to work in the shop as a superintendent. Foley can't touch you there,—or me either. Isn't that all right?" Mr. Driscoll wore a look of half-hearted triumph.

Tom had regarded Mr. Driscoll so long with dislike that even this proposal, apparently uttered in good faith, made him suspicious. He began to search for a hidden motive.

"Well?" queried Mr. Driscoll impatiently.

He could find no dishonest motive. "But if I took the job I'd have to go out of the union," he said finally.

"It oughtn't break your heart to quit Foley's company."

Tom walked to the window and looked meditatively into the street. Mr. Driscoll's offer was tempting. It was full of possibilities that appealed to his ambition. He was confident of his ability to fill this position, and was confident that he would develop capacity to fill higher positions. This chance would prove the first of a series of opportunities that would lead him higher and higher,—perhaps even to Mr. Driscoll's own desk. He knew he had it in him. And the comfort, even the little luxuries, the broader opportunities for self-development that would be his, all appealed to him. And he was aware of the joy this new career would give to Maggie. But to leave the union—to give up the fight——

He turned back to Mr. Driscoll. "I can't do it."

"What!" cried the contractor in amazement.

"I can't do it," Tom repeated.

"Do you know what you're throwing away? If you turned out well, and I know you would, why there'd be no end of chances for advancement. I've got a lot of weak men on my pay-roll."

"I understand the chance, Mr. Driscoll. But I can't take it. Do you know why Foley's got it in for me?"

"He don't like you, I suppose."

"Because he's found out, somehow, that I've begun a fight on him, and am going to try to put him out of business. If I take this job, I've got to drop the fight. And I'll never do that!" Tom was warming up again. "Do you know the sort Foley is? I suppose you know he's a grafter?"

"Yes. So does my pocket-book."

"And so does his pocket-book. His grafting alone is enough to fight him on. But there's the way he treats the union! You know what he's done to me. Well, he's done that to a lot of others. He's got some of us scared so we're afraid to breathe. And the union's just his machine. Now d'you suppose I'm going to quit the union in that shape?" He brought his big red fist thundering down on the desk before Mr. Driscoll. "No, by God! I'm going to stick by the boys. I've got a few hundred saved. They'll last me a while, if I can't get another job. And I'm going to fight that damned skate till one of us drops!"

Miss Arnold had come in the moment before with letters for Mr. Driscoll's signature, and had stood through Tom's outburst. She now handed the letters to Mr. Driscoll, and Tom for the first time noticed her presence. It struck him full of confusion. "I beg pardon, miss. I didn't know you were here. I—I hope you didn't mind what I said."

"If Miss Arnold objects to what you said, I'll fire her!" put in Mr. Driscoll.

The secretary looked with hardly-concealed admiration at Tom, still splendid in the dying glow of his defiant wrath. "If I objected, I'd deserve to be fired," she said. Then she added, smiling: "You may say it again if you like."

After Miss Arnold had gone out Mr. Driscoll looked at Tom with blinking eyes. "I suppose you think you're some sort of a hero," he growled.

Tom's sudden confusion had collapsed his indignation. "No, I'm a man looking for a job," he returned, with a faint smile.

"Well, I'm glad you didn't take the job I offered you. I can't afford to let fools help manage my business."

Tom took his hat. "I suppose this is all," he said and started for the door.

"Hold on!" Mr. Driscoll stood up. "Why don't you shake hands with a man, like a gentleman? There. That's the stuff. I want to say to you, Keating, that I think you're just about all right. If ever you want a job with me, just come around and say so and I'll give you one if I have to fire myself to make a place for you. And if your money gives out, or you need some to use in your fight, why I ain't throwing much away these days, but you can get all you want by asking for it."

Chapter VII

GETTING THE MEN IN LINE

HIS dismissal had been one of the risks Tom had accepted when he had decided upon war, and though he felt it keenly now that it had come, yet its chief effect was to intensify his resolution to overturn Buck Foley. He strode on block after block, with his long, powerful steps, his resolution gripping him fiercer and fiercer,—till the thought leaped into his mind: " I've got to tell Maggie."

He stopped as though a cold hand had been laid against his heart; then walked on more slowly, considering how he should give the news to her. His first thought was to say nothing of his dismissal for a few days. By then he might have found another job, and the telling that he had lost one would be an easy matter. But his second thought was that she would doubtless learn the news from some of her friends, and would use her tongue all the more freely because of his attempt at concealment; and, furthermore, he would be in the somewhat inglorious position of the man who has been found out. He decided to have done with it at once.

When he entered his flat Maggie looked up in surprise from the tidy on which she was working.

"What! home already!" Then she noticed his face. "Why, what's the matter?"

Tom drew off his overcoat and threw it upon the couch. "I've been fired."

She looked at him in astonishment. "Fired!"

"Yes." He sat down, determined to get through with the scene as quickly as possible.

For the better part of a minute she could not speak. "Fired? What for?" she articulated.

"It's Foley's work. He ordered Driscoll to."

"You've been talking about Foley some more, then?"

"I have."

Tom saw what he had feared, a hard, accusing look spread itself over her face. "And you've done that, Tom Keating, after what I, your wife, said to you only last week? I told you what would happen. I told you Foley would make us suffer. I told you not to talk again, and you've gone and done it!" The words came out slowly, sharply, as though it were her desire to thrust them into him one by one.

Tom began to harden, as she had hardened. But at least he would give her the chance to understand him. "You know what Foley's like. You know some of the things he's done. Well, I've made up my mind that we oughtn't to stand him any longer. I'm going to do what I can to drive him out of the union."

"And you've been talking this?" she cut in. "Oh, of course you have! No wonder he got you fired! Oh, my God! I see it all. And you, you never thought once of your wife or your child!"

"I did, and you'll see when I tell you all," Tom said harshly. "But would you have me stand for all the dirty things he does?"

"Couldn't you keep out of his way—as I asked you to? Because a wolf's a wolf, that's no reason why you should jump in his mouth."

"It is if you can do him up. And I'm going to do Foley up. I'm going to run against him as walking delegate. The situation ain't so bad as you think," he went on, with a weak effort to appease her. "You think things look dark, but they're going to be brighter than they ever were. I'll get another job soon, and after the first of March I'll be walking delegate. I'm going to beat Buck Foley, sure!"

For a moment the vision of an even greater elevation than the one from which they were falling made her forget her bitter wrath. Then it flooded back upon her, and she put it all into a laugh. "You beat Buck Foley! Oh, my!"

Her ireful words he had borne with outward calm; he had learned they were borne more easily, if borne calmly. But her sneering disbelief in him was too much. He sprang up, his wrath tugging at its leash. She, too, came to her feet, and stood facing him, hands clenched, breast heaving, sneering, sobbing. Her words tumbled out.

"Oh, you! you! Brighter days, you say. Ha! ha! You beat Buck Foley? Yes, I know how! Buck Foley 'll not let you get a job in your trade. You'll have to take up some other work—if you can get it! Begin all over! We'll grow poorer and poorer. We'll have to eat anything. I'll have to wear rags. Just when we were getting comfortable. And all because you wouldn't pay any attention to what I said. Because you were such a fo-o-ol! Oh, my God! My God!"

As she went on her voice rose to a scream, broken by gasps and sobs. At the end she passionately jerked Tom's coat and hat from the couch and threw herself upon it—and the frenzied words tumbled on, and on.

Tom looked down upon her a moment, quivering with wrath and a nameless sickness. Then he picked up hat and coat, and glancing at Ferdinand, who had shrunk terrified into a corner, walked quickly out of the flat.

He strode about the streets awhile, had dinner in a restaurant, and then, as Wednesday was the union's meeting night, he went to Potomac Hall. It fell out that he met Pete and Barry entering as he came up.

"I guess you'll have another foreman to-morrow, boys," he announced; and he briefly told them of his discharge.

"It'll be us next, Rivet Head," said Pete.

Barry nodded, his face pale.

All the men in the hall learned that evening what had happened to Tom, some from his friends, more from Foley's friends. And the manner of the latter's telling was a warning to every listener. "D'you hear Keating has been fired?" "Fired? No. What for?" A wise wink: "Well, he's been talkin' about Foley, you know."

Tom grew hot under, but ignored, the open jeering of the Foleyites. The sympathy of his friends he answered with a quiet, but ominous, " Just you wait! " There were few present of the men he had counted on seeing, and soon after the meeting ended, which was unusually early, he started home.

It was after ten when he came in. Maggie sat working at the tidy; she did not look up or speak; her passion had settled into resentful obstinacy, and that, he knew from experience, only time could overcome. He had not the least desire to assist time in its work of subjection, and passed straight into their bedroom.

Tom felt her sustained resentment, as indeed he could not help; but he did not feel that which was the first cause of the resentment—her lack of sympathetic understanding of him. At twenty-three he had come into a man's wages, and Maggie's was the first pretty face he had seen after that. The novelty of their married life had soon worn off, and with the development of his stronger qualities and of her worst ones, it had gradually come about that the only thoughts they shared were those concerning their common existence in their home. Tom had long since become accustomed to carrying his real ideas to other ears. And so he did not now consciously miss wifely sympathy with his efforts.

There was no break the next morning in Maggie's sullen resentment. After an almost wordless breakfast Tom set forth to look for another job. An opening presented itself at the first place he called. " Yes, it happens we do need a foreman," said the contractor. " What experience have you had? "

Tom gave an outline of his course in his trade, dwelling on the last two years and a half that he had been a foreman.

" Um,—yes. That sounds very good. You say you worked last for Driscoll on the St. Etienne job? "

" Yes."

" I suppose you don't mind telling why you left? Driscoll hasn't finished that job yet."

Tom briefly related the circumstances.

" So you're out with Foley." The contractor shook his head. " Sorry. We need a man, and I guess you're a good one. But if Foley did that to Driscoll, he'll do the same to me. I can't afford to be mixed up in any trouble with him."

This conversation was a more or less accurate pattern of many that followed on this and succeeding days. Tom called on every contractor of importance doing steel construction work. None of them cared to risk trouble with Foley, and so Tom continued walking the streets.

One contractor—the man for whom he had worked before he went on the St. Etienne job— offered Tom what he called some " business advice." " I'm a pretty good friend of yours, Keating, for I've found you all on the level. The trouble with you is, when you see a stone wall you think it was put there to butt your head against. Now, I'm older than you are, and had a lot more experience, and let me tell you it's a lot easier, and a lot quicker, when you see trouble across your path like a stone wall, to go round it than it is to try to butt it out of your way.

Stop butting against Foley. Make up with him, or
go to some other city. Go round him."

In the meantime Tom was busy with his campaign
against Foley. He was discharged on the fourteenth of February; the election came on the seventh
of March; only three weeks, so haste was necessary. On the days he was tramping about for a
job he met many members of the union also looking
for work, and to these he talked wherever he found
them. And every night he was out talking to the
men, in the streets, in saloons, in their own homes.

The problem of his campaign was a simple one—
to get at least five hundred of the three thousand
members of the union to come to the hall on election
night and cast their votes against Foley. His campaign, therefore, could have no spectacular methods
and no spectacular features. Hard, persistent work,
night after night—that was all.

On the evening after the meeting and on the following evening Tom had talks with several leading
men in the union. A few joined in his plan with
spirit. But most that he saw held back; they were
willing to help him in secret, but they feared the
result of an open espousal of his cause. There
were only a dozen men, including Barry and Pete,
who were willing to go the whole way with him, and
these he formed loosely into a campaign committee.
They held a caucus and nominations for all offices
were made, Tom being chosen to run for walking
delegate and president. The presidency was unsal-
aried, and during Foley's régime had become an
office of only nominal importance; all real power that

had ever belonged to the position had been gradually absorbed by the office of walking delegate. At the meeting on the twenty-first Tom's ticket was formally presented to the union, as was also Foley's.

Even before this the dozen were busy with a canvass of the union. The members agreed heartily to the plan of demanding an increase in wages, for they had long been dissatisfied with the present scale. But to come out against Foley, that was another matter. Tom found, as he had expected, that his arguments had to be directed, not at convincing the men that Foley was bad, but at convincing them it was safe to oppose him. Reformers are accustomed to explain their failure by saying they cannot arouse the respectable element to come out and vote against corruption. They would find that even fewer would come to the polls if the voters thereby endangered their jobs.

The answers of the men in almost all cases were the same.

" If I was sure I wouldn't lose my job, I'd vote against Foley in a minute. But you know well enough, Tom, that we have a hard enough time getting on now. Where'd we be if Foley blacklisted us ? "

" But there's no danger at all, if enough of us come out," Tom would reply. " We can't lose."

" But you can't count on the boys coming out. And if we lose, Foley 'll make us all smart. He'll manage to find out every man that voted against him."

Here was the place in which the guarantee he had

sought from Mr. Baxter would fit in.　Impelled by knowledge of the great value of this guarantee, Tom went to see the big contractor a few days after his first visit.　The uniform traveled down the alley between the offices and brought back word that Mr. Baxter was not in.　Tom called again and again. Mr. Baxter was always out.　Tom was sorely disappointed by his failure to get the guarantee, but there was nothing to do but to make the best of it; and so he and his friends went on tirelessly with their nightly canvassing.

The days, of course, Tom continued to spend in looking for work.　In wandering from contractor to contractor he frequently passed the building in which was located the office of Driscoll & Co.; and, a week after his discharge, as he was going by near one o'clock, it chanced Miss Arnold was coming into the street.　They saw each other in the same instant.　Tom, with his natural diffidence at meeting strange women, was for passing her by with a lift of his hat.　"Why, Mr. Keating!" she cried, with a little smile, and as they held the same direction he could but fall into step with her.

"What's the latest war news?" she asked.

"One man still out of a job," he answered, taking refuge in an attempt at lightness.　"No actual conflict yet.　I'm busy massing my forces.　So far I have one man together—myself."

"You ought to find that a loyal army."　She was silent for a dozen paces, then asked impulsively: "Have you had lunch yet?"

Tom threw a surprised look down upon her.　"Yes.

Twelve o'clock's our noon hour. We men are used to having our lunch then."

"I thought if you hadn't we might have lunched in the same place," she hastened to explain, with a slight flush of embarrassment. "I wanted to ask you some questions. You see, since I've been in New York I've been in a way thrown in contact with labor unions. I've read a great deal on both sides. But the only persons I've had a chance to talk to have all been on the employers' side,—persons like Mr. Driscoll and my uncle, Mr. Baxter."

"Baxter, the contractor—Baxter & Co.?"

"Yes."

Tom wondered what necessity had forced the niece of so rich a man as Mr. Baxter to earn her living as a stenographer.

"I've often wanted to talk with some trade union man, but I've never had the chance. I thought you might tell me some of the things I want to know."

The note of sincere disappointment in Miss Arnold's voice brought a suggestion to Tom's mind that both embarrassed and attracted. He was not accustomed to the society of women of Miss Arnold's sort, whose order of life had been altogether different from his own, and the idea of an hour alone with her filled him with a certain confusion. But her freshness and her desire to know more of the subject that was his whole life allured him; and his interest was stronger than his embarrassment. "For that matter, I'm not busy, as you know. If you would like it, I can talk to you while you eat."

For the next hour they sat face to face in the quiet

little restaurant to which Miss Arnold had led the
way. The other patrons found themselves looking
over at the table in the corner, and wondering what
common subject could so engross the refined young
woman in the tailored gown and the man in ill-fitting
clothes, with big red hands, red neck and crude,
square face. For their part these two were unconscious of the wondering eyes upon them. With a
query now and then from Miss Arnold, Tom spirit-
edly presented the union side of mooted questions
of the day,—the open shop, the strike, the sympathetic strike, the boycott. The things Miss Arnold
had read had dealt coldly with the moral and economic principles involved in these questions. Tom
spoke in human terms; he showed how every point
affected living men, and women, and children. The
difference was the difference between a treatise and
life.

Miss Arnold was impressed,—not alone by what
Tom said, but by the man himself. The first two or
three times she had seen him, on his brief visits to
the office, she had been struck only by a vague bigness—a bigness that was not so much of figure as
of bearing. On his last visit she had been struck
by his bold spirit. She now discovered the crude,
rugged strength of the man: he had thought much;
he felt deeply; he believed in the justice of his cause;
he was willing, if the need might be, to suffer for
his beliefs. And he spoke well, for his sentences,
though not always grammatical, were always vital.
He seemed to present the very heart of a thing, and
let it throb before the eyes.

When they were in the street again and about to go their separate ways, Miss Arnold asked, with impulsive interest: " Won't you talk to me again about these things—some time? "

Tom, glowing with the excitement of his own words and of her sympathetic listening, promised. It was finally settled that he should call the following Sunday afternoon.

Back at her desk, Miss Arnold fell to wondering what sort of man Tom would be had he had four years at a university, and had his life been thrown among people of cultivation. His power, plus these advantages, would have made him—something big, to say the least. But had he gone to college he would not now be in a trade union. And in a trade union, Miss Arnold admitted to herself, was where he was needed, and where he belonged.

Tom went on his way in the elation that comes of a new and gratifying experience. He had never before had so keen and sympathetic a listener. And never before had he had speech with a woman of Miss Arnold's type—educated, thoughtful, of broad interests. Most of the women he had known necessity had made into household drudges—tired and uninteresting, whose few thoughts rarely ranged far from home. Miss Arnold was a discovery to him. Deep down in his consciousness was a distinct surprise that a woman should be interested in the big things of the outside world.

He was fairly jerked out of his elation, when, on turning a corner, he met Foley face to face in front of a skyscraper that was going up in lower Broadway. It was their first meeting since Foley had tried to have grim sport out of him on the St. Etienne Hotel.

Foley planted himself squarely across Tom's path. "Hello, Keating! How're youse? Where youse workin' now?"

The sneering good-fellowship in Foley's voice set Tom's blood a-tingling. But he tried to step to one side and pass on. Again Foley blocked his way.

"I understand youse 're goin' to be the next walkin' delegate o' the union. That's nice. I s'pose these days youse 're trainin' your legs for the job?"

"See here, Buck Foley, are you looking for a fight? If you are, come around to some quiet place and I'll mix it up with you all you want."

"I don't fight a man till he gets in my class."

"If you don't want to fight, then get out of my way!"

With that Tom stepped forward quickly and butted his hunched-out right shoulder against Foley's left. Foley, unprepared, swung round as though on a pivot. Tom brushed by and continued on his way with unturned head.

Again the walking delegate proved that he could swear.

Chapter VIII

THE COWARD

TWO days before his meeting with Miss Arnold Tom had been convinced that any more time was wasted that was spent in looking for a job as foreman. He had before him the choice of being idle or working in the gang. He disliked to do the latter, regarding it as a professional relapse. But he was unwilling to draw upon his savings, if that could be avoided, so he decided to go back into the ranks. The previous evening he had heard of three new jobs that were being started. The contractors on two of them he had seen during the morning; and after his encounter with Foley he set out to interview the third. The contractor was an employer of the smallest consequence—a florid man with little cunning eyes. "Yes, I do need some men," he replied to Tom's inquiry. "How much d'you want?"

"Three seventy-five a day, the regular rate."

The contractor shook his head. "Too much. I can only pay three."

"But you signed an agreement to pay the full rate!" Tom cried.

"Oh, a man signs a lot o' things."

Tom was about to turn away, when his curiosity got the better of his disgust. For a union man to work under the scale was an offense against the union. For an employer to pay under the scale was an offense against the employers' association. Tom decided to draw the contractor out. "Well, suppose I go to work at three dollars, how do we keep from being discovered?" he asked.

The little eyes gleamed with appreciation of their small cunning. "I make this agreement with all my men: You get the full amount in your envelope Saturday. Anybody that sees you open your envel- · ope sees that you're gettin' full scale. Then you hand me back four-fifty later. That's for money I advanced you durin' the week. D'you understand?"

"I do," said Tom. "But I'm no three dollar man!"

"Hold on!" the contractor cried to Tom's back. His cunning told him in an instant that he had made a mistake; that this man, if let go, might make trouble. "I was just foolin' you. Of course, I'll pay you full rate."

Tom knew the man was lying, but he had no real proof that the contractor was breaking faith both with the union and his fellow employers; so, as he needed the money, he took the offered position and went to work the next morning. The job was a fire-engine house just being started on the upper west side of the island. The isolation of the job and the insignificance of the contractor made Tom feel there was a chance Foley might overlook him for the next two weeks.

On the following Saturday morning three new men began work on the job. One of them Tom was certain he knew—a tall, lank fellow, chiefly knobs

and angles, with wide, drooping shoulders and a big
yellow mustache. Tom left his place at the crane
of the jimmy derrick and ran down a plank into the
basement to where this man and four others were
rolling a round column to its place.

He touched the man on the shoulder. " Your
name's Petersen, ain't it? "

" Yah," said the big fellow.

" And you worked for a couple of days on the St.
Etienne Hotel? "

" Yah."

Tom did his duty as prescribed by the union rules.
He pointed out Petersen as a scab to the steward.
Straightway the men crowded up and there was a
rapid exchange of opinions. Tom and the steward
wanted that a demand for Petersen's discharge be
made of the contractor. But the others favored
summary action, and made for where the big Swede
was standing.

" Get out! " they ordered.

Petersen glowered at the crowd. " I lick de whole
bunch! " he said with slow defiance.

The men were brought to a pause by his threatening attitude. His resentful eyes turned for an
instant on Tom. The men began to move forward
cautiously. Then the transformation that had taken
place on the St. Etienne Hotel took place again.
The courage faded from him, and he turned and
started up the inclined plank for the street.

Jeers broke from the men. Caps and greasy
gloves pelted Petersen's retreating figure. One man,
the smallest of the gang, ran up the plank after him.

"Do him up, Kid!" the men shouted scrambling up to the sidewalk.

Kid, with showy valiance, aimed an upward blow at the Swede's head. Petersen warded off the fist with automatic ease, but made no attempt to strike back. He started away, walking sidewise, one eye on his path, one on his little assailant who kept delivering fierce blows that somehow failed to reach their mark.

"If he ain't runnin' from Kid!" ejaculated the men. "Good boy, Kid!"

The blows became faster and fiercer. At the corner Petersen turned back, held his foe at bay an instant, and a second time Tom felt the resentment of his eyes. Then he was driven around the corner. A minute later the little man came back, puffed out and swaggering.

"What an infernal coward!" the men marveled, as they went back to work.

That was a hard evening for Tom. He not only had to work for votes, but he met two or three lieutenants who were disheartened by the men's slowness to promise support, and to these friends he had to give new courage. Twice, as he was talking to men on the street, he glimpsed the tall, lean figure of Petersen, standing in a doorway as though waiting for someone.

The end of his exhausting evening's work found him near the Barrys', and he dropped in for an exchange of experiences. Barry and Pig Iron Pete had themselves come in but a few minutes before.

" Got work on your job for a couple more men? "
asked Pete after the first words had been spoken.

" Hello! You haven't been fired? "

" That's it," answered Pete; and Barry nodded.

" Foley's work, I suppose? "

" Sure. Foley put Jake Henderson up to it. Oh,
Jake makes a hot foreman! Driscoll ought to pay
him ten a day to keep off the job. Jake complained
against us an' got us fired. Said we didn't know our
business."

" Well, it's only for another week, boys," Tom
cheered them.

" If you think that then you've had better luck
with the men than me 'n' Barry has," Pete declared
in disgust. " They're a bunch o' old maids!
Foley's too good for 'em. I don't see why we
should try to force 'em to take somethin' better."
The whole blankety-blanked outfit had Pete's per-
mission to go where they didn't need a forge to heat
their rivets.

" You don't understand 'em, Pete," returned Tom.
" They've got to think first of all of how to earn a
living for their families. Of course they're going
to hesitate to do anything that will endanger their
chance to earn a living. And you seem to forget
that we've only got to get one man in five to win
out."

" An' we've got to get him! " said Barry, almost
fiercely.

" D'you think there's much danger of your losin',
Tom? " Mrs. Barry queried anxiously.

" Not if we work. But we've got to work."

Mrs. Barry was silent for several moments, during which the talk of the men ran on. Suddenly, she broke in: " Don't you think the women'd have some influence with their husbands? "

Tom was silent for a thoughtful minute. " Some of them, mebbe."

" More'n you think, I bet! " Mrs. Barry declared. " It's worth tryin', anyhow. Here's what I'm goin' to do: I'm goin' to start out to-morrow an' begin visitin' all the union women I know. I can get the addresses of others from them. An' I'll keep at it every afternoon I can get away till the election. I'll talk to 'em good an' straight an' get 'em to talk to other women. An' we'll get a lot o' the men in line, see if we don't! "

Tom looked admiringly at Mrs. Barry's homely face, flushed with determination. " The surest thing we can do to win is to put you up for walking delegate. I'll hustle for you."

" Oh, g'wan with you, Tom! " She smiled with pleasure, however. " I've got a picture o' myself climbin' up ladders an' buyin' drinks for the men."

" If you was the walkin' delegate," said Pete, " we'd always work on the first floor, an' never drink nothin' but tea."

" You shut up, Pete! " Mrs. Barry looked at Tom. " I suppose you're wife'll help in this, too? "

Tom looked steadily at the scroll in Mrs. Barry's red rug. " I'm afraid not," he said at length. " She —she couldn't stand climbing the stairs."

It was after eleven o'clock when Tom left the Barrys' and started through the quiet cross street toward a car line. A man stepped from an adjoining doorway, and fell in a score of paces behind him. Tom heard rapid steps drawing nearer and nearer, but it was not till the man had gained to within a pace that it occurred to him perhaps he was being followed. Then it was too late. His arm was seized in a grip of steel.

The street was dark and empty. Thoughts of Foley's entertainment committee flashed through his head. He whirled about and struck out fiercely with his free arm. His wrist was caught and held by a grip like the first. He was as helpless as if handcuffed.

" I vant a yob," a savage voice demanded.

Tom recognized the tall, angular figure. " Hello, Petersen! What d'you want? "

" I vant a yob."

" A job. How can I give you a job? "

" You take to-day ma yob avay. You give me a yob! "

In a flash Tom understood. The Swede held him accountable for the incident of the morning, and was determined to force another job from him. Was the man crazy? At any rate 'twould be wiser to parley than to bring on a conflict with one possessed of such strength as those hands betokened. So he made no attempt to break loose.

" I can't give you a job, I say."

" You take it avay! " the Swede said, with fierce persistence. " You make me leave! "

" It's your own fault. If you want to work, why don't you get into the union? "

Tom felt a convulsive shiver run through the man's big frame. " De union? Ah, de union! Ev'ryvare I ask for yob. Ev'ryvare! ' You b'long to union?' de boss say. ' No,' I say. De boss give me no yob. De union let me not vork! De union——! " His hands gripped tighter in his impotent bitterness.

" Of course the union won't let you work."

" Vy? I am strong!—yes. I know de vork."

Tom felt that no explanation of unionism, however lucid, would quiet this simple-minded excitement. So he said nothing.

" Vy should I not vork? Dare be yobs. I know how to vork. But no! De union! I mak dis mont' two days. I mak seven dollar. Seven dollar! " He fairly shook Tom, and a half sob broke from his lips. " How de union tank I live? My family?—me? Seven dollar? "

Tom recognized with a thrill that which he was hearing. It was the man's soul crying out in resentment and despair.

" But you can't blame the union," he said weakly, feeling that his answer did not answer.

" You tank not? " Petersen cried fiercely. " You tank not? " He was silent a brief space, and his breath surged in and out as though he had just paused from running. Suddenly he freed Tom's wrists and set his right hand into Tom's left arm. " Come! I show you vot de union done."

He started away. Those iron fingers locked about the prisoner's arm were a needless fetter. The Swede's despairing soul, glimpsed for a moment, had thrown a spell upon Tom, and he would have followed willingly.

Their long strides matched, and their heel-clicks coincided. Both were silent. At the end of ten minutes they were in a narrow street, clifted on its either side with tenements that reached up darkly. Presently the Swede turned down a stairway, sentineled by garbage cans. Tom thought they were entering a basement. But Petersen walked on, and in the solid blackness Tom was glad of the hand locked on his arm. They mounted a flight of stone steps, and came into a little stone-paved court. Far above there was a roof-framed square of stars. Petersen led the way across the court and into the doorway of a rear tenement. The air was rotting. They went up two flights of stairs, so old that the wood shivered under foot. Petersen opened a door. A coal oil lamp burned on an otherwise barren table, and beside the table sat a slight woman with a quilt drawn closely about her.

She rose, the quilt fell from her shoulders, and she stood forth in a faded calico wrapper. " Oh, Nels! You've come at last! " she said. Then she saw Tom, and drew back a step.

" Yah," said Petersen. He dragged Tom after him into the room and swept his left arm about. " See!—De union! "

The room was almost bare. The table, three wooden chairs, a few dishes, a cooking-stove without fire,—this was the furniture. Half the plastering was gone from the ceiling, the blue kalsomine was scaling leprously from the walls, in places the floor was worn almost through. In another room he saw a child asleep on a bed.

There was just one picture on the walls, a brown-framed photograph of a man in the dress and pose of a prize fighter—a big, tall, angular man, with a drooping mustache. Tom gave a quick glance at Petersen.

" See!—De union! " Petersen repeated fiercely.

The little woman came quickly forward and laid her hand on Petersen's arm. " Nels, Nels," she said gently.

" Yah, Anna. But he is de man vot drove me from ma yob."

" We must forgive them that despitefully use us, the Lord says."

Petersen quieted under her touch and, dropped Tom's arm.

She turned her blue eyes upon Tom in gentle accusation. " How could you? Oh, how could you? "

Tom could only answer helplessly: " But why don't he join the union? "

" How can he? "

The words echoed within Tom. How could he? Everything Tom saw had not the value of half the union's initiation fee.

There was an awkward silence. " Won't you sit down, brother." Mrs. Petersen offered Tom one of the wooden chairs, and all three sat down. He noted that the resentment was passing from Petersen's eyes, and that, fastened on his wife, they were filling with submissive adoration.

"Nels has tried very hard," the little woman said. They had been in the West for three years, she went on; Nels had worked with a non-union crew on a bridge over the Missouri. When that job was finished they had spent their savings coming to New York, hearing there was plenty of work there. "We had but twenty dollars when we got here. How could Nels join the union? We had to live. An' since he couldn't join the union, the union wouldn't let him work. Brother, is that just? Is that the sort o' treatment you'd like to get?"

Tom was helpless against her charges. The union was right in principle, but what was mere correctness of principle in the presence of such a situation?

"Would you be willing to join the union?" he asked abruptly of Petersen.

It was Petersen's wife who answered. "O' course he would."

"Well, don't you worry any more then. He won't have any trouble getting a job."

"How?" asked the little woman.

"I'm going to get him in the union."

"But that costs twenty-five dollars."

"Yes."

"But, brother, we haven't got *one!*"

"I'll advance it. He can pay it back easy enough afterwards."

The little woman rose and stood before Tom. Her thin white face was touched up faintly with color, and tears glistened in her eyes. She took Tom's big red hand in her two frail ones.

" Brother, if you ain't a Christian, you've got a Christian heart! " she cried out, and the thin hands tightened fervently. She turned to her husband. " Nels, what did I say! The Lord would not forget them that remembered him."

Tom saw Petersen stand up, nothing in his eyes now but adoration, and open his arms. He turned his head.

For the second time Tom took note of the brown-framed photograph, with " The Swedish Terror " in black letters at its bottom, and rose and stood staring at it. Presently, Mrs. Petersen drew to his side.

" We keep it before us to remind us what wonders the Lord can work, bless His holy name! " she explained. " Nels was a terrible fightin' man before we was married an' I left the Salvation Army. A terrible fightin' man! " Even in her awe of Petersen's one-time wickedness Tom could detect a lurking admiration of his prowess. " The Lord has saved him from all that. But he has a terrible temper. It flares up at times, an' the old carnal desire to fight gets hold o' him again. That's his great weakness. But we pray that God will keep him from fightin', an' God does! "

Tom looked at the little woman, a bundle of religious ardor, looked at Petersen with his big shoulders, thought of the incident of the morning. He blinked his eyes.

Tom stepped to the table and laid down a five-dollar bill. " You can pay that back later." He moved quickly to the door. " Good-night," he said, and tried to escape.

But Mrs. Petersen was upon him instantly.
" Brother! Brother! " She seized his hands again
in both hers, and looked at him with glowing eyes.
" Brother, may God bless you! "

Tom blinked his eyes again. " Good-night," he
said.

Petersen stepped forward and without a word took
Tom's arm. The grasp was lighter than when they
had come up. Again Tom was glad of the guidance
of that hand as they felt their way down the shivering stairs, and out through the tunnel.

" Good-night," he said once more, when they had
gained the street.

Petersen gripped his hand in awkward silence.

Chapter IX

RUTH ARNOLD

RUTH ARNOLD was known among her friends as a queer girl. Neither the new ones in New York nor the old ones of her birth town understood her " strange impulses." They were constantly being shocked by ideas and actions which they considered, to phrase it mildly, very unusual. The friends in her old home were horrified when she decided to become a stenographer. Friends in both places were horrified when, a little less than a year before, it became known she was going to leave the home of her aunt to become Mr. Driscoll's secretary. " What a fool! " they cried. " If she had stayed she might have married ever so well! " Mrs. Baxter had entreated, and with considerable elaboration had delivered practically these same opinions. But Ruth was obstinate in her queerness, and had left.

However, only a few weeks before, Mrs. Baxter had had a partial recompense for Ruth's disappointing conduct. She had noted the growing intimacy between Mr. Berman, who was frequently at her house, and Ruth, and by delicate questioning had drawn the calm statement from her niece that Mr. Berman had asked her in marriage.

" Of course you said ' yes,' " said Mrs. Baxter.

Ruth had not.

" My child! Why not? "

" I don't love him."

" What of that? " demanded her aunt, who loved her husband. " Love will come. He is educated, a thorough gentleman, and has money. What more do you want in a husband? And your uncle says he is very clever in business."

Thus brought to bay, Ruth had taken her aunt into the secret that her refusal had not been final and that Mr. Berman had given her six months in which to make up her mind. This statement was Mrs. Baxter's partial recompense. " Then you'll marry him, Ruth! " she declared, and kissed her lightly.

Ruth understood herself no better than did her friends. She was not conscious that she had in a measure that rare endowment—the clear vision which perceives the things of life in their true relation and at their true value, plus the instinct to act upon that vision. It was the manifestations of this instinct that made her friends call her queer. Her instinct, however, did not hold her in sole sway. Her training had fastened many governing conventions upon her, and she was not always as brave as her inward promptings. Her actions made upon impulse were usually in accord with this instinct. Her actions that were the result of thought were frequently in accord with convention.

It was her instinct that had impelled her to ask Tom to call. It was convention that, on Sunday afternoon, made her await his coming with trepidation. She was genuinely interested in the things for which Tom stood, and her recent-born admiration of him was sincere. Nevertheless his approaching visit was in the nature of an adventure to her. This workingman, transferred from the business world to the social world, might prove himself an embarrassing impossibility. Especially, she wondered, with more than a little apprehension, how he would be dressed. She feared a flaming necktie crawling up his collar, and perhaps in it a showy pin; or a pair of fancy shoes; or a vest of assertive pattern; or, perhaps, hair oil!

When word was brought her by a maid that Tom was below, she gave an order that he was to wait, and put on her hat and jacket. She did not know him well enough to ask him to her room. She could not receive him in the parlor common to all the boarding-house. Her instinctive self told her it would be an embarrassment to him to be set amid the gossiping crowd that gathered there on Sunday afternoon. Her conventional self told her that, if he were but a tenth as bad as was possible, it would be more than an embarrassment for her to sit beside him amid those curious eyes. The street was the best road out of the dilemma.

He was sitting in the high-backed hall chair when she came down. "Shall we not take a walk?" she asked. "The day is beautiful for February."

Tom acceded gratefully. He had glanced through the parted portières into the parlor, and his minutes of waiting had been minutes of consternation.

The first thing Ruth noted when they came out into the light of the street was that his clothes were all in modest taste, and she thrilled with relief. Mixed with this there was another feeling, a glow of pleasure that he was vindicating himself to her conventional part.

Ruth lived but a few doors from Central Park. As they started across Central Park West a big red automobile, speeding above the legal rate, came sweeping down upon them, tooting its arrogant warning. Tom jerked Ruth back upon the sidewalk. She glared at the bundled-up occupants of the scurrying car.

" Don't it make you feel like an anarchist when people do that? " she gasped.

" Not the bomb-throwing sort."

" Why not? When people do that, I've got just one desire, and that's to throw a bomb! "

" What good would a bomb here or there do? Or what harm? " Tom asked humorously. "What's the use trying to destroy people that're already doomed?"

Ruth was silent till they gained the other side of the street. "Doomed? What do you mean? " she then asked.

" Every dog has his day, you know. Them rich people are having theirs. It's a summer day, and I guess it's just about noon now. But it's passing."

Ruth had learned during her conversation with him on the previous Tuesday that a large figurative statement such as this was likely to have a great many ideas behind it, so she now proceeded to lead him to the ideas' expression. The sun, drawing good-humoredly from his summer's store, had brought thousands to the Park walks, and with genial presumption had unbuttoned their overcoats. The bare gray branches of bush and tree glinted dully in the warm light, as if dreamfully smiling over the budding days not far ahead. But Tom had attention for the joy of neither the sun nor his dependents. He thought only of what he was saying, for he had been led to speech upon one of his dearest subjects.

Though he had left school at thirteen to begin work, he had attended night school for a number of years, had belonged to a club whose chief aim was debating, had read a number of solid books and had done a great deal of thinking for himself. As a result of his reading, thinking and observation he had come into some large ideas concerning the future of the working class. In the past, he now said to Ruth, classes had risen to power, served their purpose, and been displaced by new classes stimulated by new ideas. The capitalist class was now in power, and was performing its mission—the development and centralization of industries. But its decline would be even more rapid than its rise. It would be succeeded by the working class. The working class was vast in numbers, and was filled with surging energy. Its future domination was certain.

"And you believe this?" Ruth queried when he came to a pause.

"I know it."

"Admitting that all these things are coming about—which I don't—don't you honestly think it would be disastrous to the general interest for the workingman to come into power?"

" You mean we would legislate solely in our own interests? What if we did? Hasn't every class that ever came into power done that? Anyhow, since we make up nine-tenths of the people we'd certainly be legislating in the interests of the majority— which can't always be said now. And as for our ability to run things, I'd rather have an honest fool than a grafter that knows it all. But if you mean we're a pretty rough lot, and haven't much education, I guess you're about right. How can we help it? We've never had a chance to be anything else. But think what the working class was a hundred years ago! Haven't we come up? Thousands of miles! That's because we've been getting more and more chances, like chances for an education, that used to belong only to the rich. And our chances are increasing. Another hundred years and we won't know ourselves. We'll be fit for anything! "

" I see you're very much of a dreamer."

" Dreamer? Not at all! If you were to look ahead and say in a hundred years from now it'll be 2000, would you call that a dream? "

" Hardly! " Ruth admitted with a smile.

" Well, what I'm telling you is just as certain as the passage of time. I'm anything but a dreamer. I believe in a present for the working class as well as a future. I believe that we, if we work hard, have the right, now, to-day, to a comfortable living, and with enough over to give our children as good an education as the children of the bosses; and with enough to buy a few books, see a little of the world, and to save a little so we'll not have ahead of us the terrible fear that we and our families may starve when we get too old to work. That's the least we ought to have. But we lack an almighty lot of having it, Miss Arnold.

"Take my own trade—and we're a lot better off than most workingmen—we get three seventy-five a day. That wouldn't be so bad if we made it three hundred days a year, but you know we don't average more than six months' work. Less than seven hundred dollars a year. What can a man with a family do in New York on seven hundred dollars a year? Two hundred for rent, three hundred for food, one hundred for clothes. There's six hundred gone in three lumps. Twenty-five cents a day left for heat, light, education, books, amusement, travel, street-car fare,—and to save for your old age!

"And then our trade's dangerous. I think half of our men are killed. If you saw the obituary list that's published monthly of all the branches of our union in the country, you'd think so, too! Every other name—crushed, or something broke and he fell. Only the other day on a steel bridge near Pittsburg a piece of rigging snapped and ten men dropped two hundred feet. They landed on steel beams in a barge anchored below—and were pulp. And after the other names, it's pneumonia or consumption. D'you know what that means? It means exposure at work. Killed by their work! . . . Well, that's our work,—and we get seven hundred a year!

"And then our work takes the best part of our lives, and throws us away. So long as we're strong

and active, we can be used. But the day we begin
to get a little stiff—if we last that long!—we're out
of it. It may be at forty. We've got to learn how
to do something else, or just wait for the end.
There's our families. And you know how much
we've got in the bank!

"Well, that's how it is in our union. Is seven
hundred a year enough?—when we risk our lives
every day we work?—when we're fit for work only
so long as we're young men? We're human beings,
Miss Arnold. We're men. We want comfortable
homes, we want to keep our children in school, we'd
like to save something up for the time when we can't
work. Seven hundred a year! How 're we going
to do it, Miss Arnold? How 're we going to
do it?"

Ruth looked up at his glowing set face, and
for the moment forgot she was allied to the other
side. "Demand higher wages!" her instinct answered promptly.

"That's the only thing! And that's what we're
going to do! More money for the time we do
work!"

He said no more. Now that the stimulant of his
excited words was gone, Ruth felt her fatigue. En-
grossed by his emotions he had swung along at a
pace that had taxed her lesser stride.

"Shall we not sit down," she suggested; and they
found a bench on a pinnacle of rock from whence
they looked down through a criss-cross of bare
branches upon a sun-polished lagoon, and upon the
files of people curving along the paths. Tom

removed his hat, and Ruth turning to face him took in anew the details of his head—the strong, square, smooth-shaven face, the broad forehead, moist and banded with pink where his hat had pressed, the hair that clung to his head in tight brown curls. Looked,—and felt herself growing small, and the men of her acquaintance growing small. And thought. . . . Yes, that was it; it was his purpose that made him big.

"You have kept me so interested that I've not yet asked you about your fight against Mr. Foley," she said, after a moment.

Tom told her all that had been done.

"But is there no other way of getting at the men except by seeing them one by one?" she asked. "That seems such a laborious way of carrying on a campaign. Can't you have mass-meetings?"

Tom shook his head. "In the first place it would be hard to get the men out; they're tired when they come home from work, and then a lot of them don't want to openly identify themselves with us. And in the second place Foley'd be likely to fill the hall with his roughs and break the meeting up."

"But to see the men individually! And you say there are twenty-five hundred of them. Why, that's impossible!"

"Yes. A lot of the men we can't find. They're out when we call."

"Why not send a letter to every member?" asked Ruth, suggesting the plan to her most obvious.

"A letter?"

"A letter that would reach them a day or two

before election! A short letter, that drove every point home!" She leaned toward him excitedly.

"Good!" Tom brought his fist down on his knee.

Ruth knew the money would have to come from his pocket. "Let's see. It would cost, for stamps, twenty-five dollars; for the letters—they could be printed—about fifteen dollars; for the envelopes six or seven dollars. Say forty-five or fifty dollars."

Fifty dollars was a great deal to Tom—saved little by little. But he hesitated only a moment. "All right. If we can influence a hundred men, one in twenty-five, it 'll be worth the money."

A thoughtful look came over his face.

"What is it?" Ruth asked quickly.

"I was thinking about the printing and other things. Wondering how I could get away from work to see to it."

"Won't you let me look after that for you?" Ruth asked eagerly. "I look after all our printing. I can leave the office whenever I'm not busy, you know. It would take only a few minutes of my time."

"It really wouldn't?" Tom asked hesitantly.

"It wouldn't be any trouble at all. And I'd be glad to do it."

Tom thanked her. "I wouldn't know how to go about a thing of that sort, anyhow, even if I could get away from work," he admitted.

"And I could see to the addressing, too," Ruth pursued.

He sat up straight. "There's the trouble! The addresses!"

" The addresses? Why? "

" There's only one list of the men and where they live. That's the book of the secretary and treasurer."

" Won't he lend it to you? "

Tom had to laugh. " Connelly lend it to me! Connelly's one of the best friends Foley's got."

" Then there's no way of getting it? "

" He keeps it in his office, and when he's not there the office is locked. But we'll get it somehow."

" Well, then if you'll write out the letter and send it to me in a day or two, I'll see to having it printed right away."

It flashed upon Tom what a strong concluding statement to the letter the guarantee from Mr. Baxter would make. He told Ruth of his idea, of his attempts to get the guarantee, and of the influence it would have on the men.

" He's probably forgotten all about it," she said. " I think I may be able to help you to get it. I can speak to Aunt Elizabeth and have her speak to him."

But her quick second thought was that she could not do this without revealing to her aunt a relation Mrs. Baxter could not understand. " No, after all I can't be of any use there. You might try to see him again, and if you fail then you might write him."

Tom gave her a quick puzzled glance, as he had done a few days before when she had mentioned her relation to Mr. Baxter. She caught the look.

" You are wondering how it is Mr. Baxter is my uncle," she guessed.

" Yes," he admitted.

" It's very simple. All rich people have their

poor relatives, I suppose? Mrs. Baxter and my mother were sisters. Mr. Baxter made money. My father died before he had a chance. After mamma died, I decided to go to work. There was only enough money to live a shabby-genteel, pottering life—and I was sick of that. I have no talents, and I wanted to be out in the world, in contact with people who are doing real things. So I learned stenography. A little over a year ago I came to New York. I lived for awhile with my uncle and aunt; they were kind, but the part of a poor relation didn't suit me, and I made up my mind to go to work again. They were not pleased very well; they wanted me to stay with them. But my mind was made up. I offered to go to work for my uncle, but he had no place for me, and got me the position with Mr. Driscoll. And that's all."

A little later she asked him for the time. His watch showed a quarter of five. On starting out she had told him that she must be home by five, so she now remarked: " Perhaps we'd better be going. It 'll take us about fifteen minutes to walk back."

They started homeward across the level sunbeams that were stretching themselves out beneath barren trees and over brown lawns for their night's sleep. As they drew near to Ruth's boarding-house they saw a perfectly-tailored man in a high hat go up the steps. He was on the point of ringing the bell when he sighted them, and he stood waiting their coming. A surprised look passed over his face when he recognized Ruth's companion.

As they came up the steps he raised his hat to

Ruth. "Good-afternoon, Miss Arnold." And to Tom he said carelessly: "Hello, Keating."

Tom looked him squarely in the eyes. "Hello, Berman," he returned.

Mr. Berman started at the omission of the "Mr." Tom lifted his hat to Ruth, bade her good-afternoon, and turned away, not understanding a sudden pang that shot into his heart.

Mr. Berman's eyes followed Tom for a dozen paces. "A very decent sort—for a workingman," he remarked.

"For any sort of a man," said Ruth, with an emphasis that surprised her. She took out her latch-key, and they entered.

Chapter X

LAST DAYS OF THE CAMPAIGN

AFTER supper, which was eaten in the customary silence, Tom started for the Barrys' to talk over the scheme of circularizing the members of the union. He met Pete coming out of the Barrys' tenement. He joined him and, as they walked away, outlined the new plan.

"That's what I call a mighty foxy scheme," Pete approved. "It's a knock-out blow. It 'll come right at the last minute, an' Foley won't have time to hit back."

Tom pointed out the difficulty of getting the membership list. "You leave that to me, Tom. It's as easy as fallin' off the twenty-third story an' hittin' the asphalt. You can't miss it."

"But what kind of a deal will you make with Connelly? He's crooked, you know."

"Yes, he has got pretty much of a bend to him," Pete admitted. "But he ain't so worse, Tom. I've traveled a lot with him. When d'you want the book?"

"We've got to get it and put it back without Connelly knowing it's been gone. We'd have to use it at night. Could you get it late, and take it back the next morning?"

"That'd be runnin' mighty close. What's the matter with gettin' it Saturday night an' usin' it Sunday?"

"Sunday's pretty late, with the election coming Wednesday. But it 'll do, I guess."

Tom spent the evening at one corner of the dining-table from which he had turned back the red cloth, laboriously scratching on a sheet of ruled letter paper. He had never written when he could avoid it. His ideas were now clear enough, but they struggled against the unaccustomed confinement of written language. The words came slowly, with physical effort, and only after crossing out, and interlining, and crossing out again, were they joined into sentences.

At ten o'clock Maggie, who had been calling on a friend, came in with Ferdinand. The boy made straight for the couch and was instantly asleep. Maggie was struck at once by the unwonted sight of her husband writing, but her sulkiness fought her curiosity for more than a minute, during which she removed her hat and jacket, before the latter could gain a grudged victory. "What are you doing?" she asked shortly.

"Writing a letter," he answered, keeping his eyes on the paper.

She leaned over his shoulder and read a few lines. Her features stiffened. "What're you going to do with that?"

"Print it."

"But you'll have to pay for it."

"Yes."

" How much? "

" About fifty dollars."

She gasped, and her sullen composure fled. " Fifty dollars! For that—that——" Breath failed her.

Tom looked around. Her black eyes were blazing. Her hands were clenched. Her full breast was rising and falling rapidly.

" Tom Keating, this is about the limit! " she broke out. " Hain't your foolishness learnt you anything yet? It's cost you seven dollars a week already. And here you are, throwing fifty dollars away all in one lump! Fifty dollars! " Her breath failed her again. " That's like you! You'll throw money away, and let me go without a decent rag to my back! "

Tom arose. " Maggie," he said, in a voice that was cold and hard, " I don't expect any sympathy from you. I don't expect you to understand what I'm about. I don't think you want to understand. But I do expect you to keep still, if you've got nothing better to say than you've just said! "

Maggie had lost herself. " Is that a threat? " she cried furiously. " Do you mean to threaten me? Why, you brute! D'you think you can make me keep still? You throw away money that's as much mine as yours!—you make me suffer for it!—and yet you expect me never to say a word, do you? "

Tom glared at her. His hands tingled to lay hold of her and shake her. But, as he glared, he thought of the woman he had so recently left, and a sense of shame for his desire crept upon him. And, too, he began vaguely to feel, what it was inevitable he should some time feel, the contrast between his wife . . . and this other.

His silence added to her frenzy. " You threaten me? What do I care for your threats! You can't do anything worse than you already have done,—and are doing. You're ruining us! Well, what are you standing there for? Why——"

There was but one thing for Tom to do, that which he had often had to do before,—go into the street. He put the scribbled sheets into his coat, and left her standing there in the middle of the floor pouring out her fury.

He walked about till he thought she would be asleep, then returned. A glance into their bedroom showed her in bed, and Ferdinand in his cot at the bed's foot. He sat down again at the table and resumed his clumsy pencil.

It was midnight before the two-hundred-word production was completed and copied. He put it into an envelope, enclosed a note saying he expected to have the list of names over the following Sunday, and took the letter down and dropped it into a mail-box. Then removing shoes, coat, and collar, he lay down on the sofa with his overcoat for covering, and presently fell asleep.

Ruth's heart sank when she received the letter the next afternoon. Her yesterday's talk with him had left her with a profound impression of his power, and that impression had been fresh all the morning. This painfully written letter, with its stiff, hard sentences, headed " Save the Union! " and beginning " Brothers," recalled to her with a shock another element of his personality. It was as though his crudity had dissociated itself from his other qualities and laid itself, bare and unrelieved, before her eyes.

As she read the letter a second time she felt a desire to improve upon his sentences; but she thought this might give him offense; and she thought also, and rightly, that his stilted sentences, rich with such epithets, as " tyrant," " bully," " grafter," would have a stronger effect on his readers than would more polished and controlled language. So she carried the letter to the printer as it had left Tom's hand.

She wrote Tom that Mr. Driscoll was willing her office should be used for the work of Sunday. Tom's answer was on a postal card and written in pencil. She sighed.

The week passed rapidly with Tom, the nights in canvassing, the days in work. Every time he went to work, he did so half expecting it would be his last day on the job. But all went well till Friday morning. Then the expected happened. As he came up to the fire-house a hansom cab, which had turned into the street behind him, stopped and Foley stepped out.

" Hold on there, Keating! " the walking delegate called.

Tom paused, three or four paces from the cab. Foley stepped to his side. " So this's where youse 've sneaked off to work! "

Tom kept his square jaw closed.

" I heard youse were at work. I thought I'd look youse up to-day. So I followed youse. Now, are youse goin' to quit this job quiet, or do I have to get youse fired? "

Tom answered with dangerous restraint. " I haven't got anything against the contractor. And I know what you'd do to him to get me off. I'll go."

" Move then, an' quick! "

" There's one thing I want to say to you first," said Tom; and instantly his right fist caught the walking delegate squarely on the chin. Foley staggered back against the wheel of the hansom. Without giving him a second look Tom turned about and walked toward the car line.

When Foley recovered himself Tom was a score of paces away. Half a dozen of the workmen were looking at him in waiting silence. He glared at Tom's broad back, but made no attempt to follow. " To-day ain't the only day! " he said to the men, closing his eyes to ominous slits; and he stepped back into the cab and drove away.

That evening Tom had an answer to the letter he had written Mr. Baxter, after having failed once more to find that gentleman in. It was of but a single sentence.

After giving thorough consideration to your suggestion, I have decided that it would be neither wise nor in good taste for me to interfere in the affairs of your union.

Tom stared at the letter in amazement. Mr. Baxter had little to risk, and much to gain. He could not understand. But, however obscure Mr. Baxter's motive, the action necessitated by his decision was as clear as a noon sun; a vital change had to be made in the letter to the members of the union. Certain of Mr. Baxter's consent, Tom had set down the guarantee to the men as the last paragraph in the letter and had held the proof awaiting Mr. Baxter's formal authorization of its use. He now cut out the paragraph that might have meant a thousand votes, and mailed the sheet to Ruth.

He talked wherever he could all the next day, and the next evening. After going home he sat up till almost one o'clock expecting Pete to come in with the roster of the members. But Pete did not appear. Early Sunday morning Tom was over at the Barrys'. Pete was not yet up, Mrs. Barry told him. Tom softly opened the door of Pete's narrow room and stepped in. Pete announced himself asleep by a mighty trumpeting. Tom shook his shoulders. He stirred, but did not open his eyes. "Doan wan' no breakfas'," he said, and slipped back into unconsciousness. Tom shook him again, without response. Then he threw the covers back from Pig Iron's feet and poured a little water on them. Pete sat suddenly upright; there was a meteoric shower of language; then he recognized Tom.

"Hello, Tom! What sort of a damned society call d'you call this?"

"If you only worked as hard as you sleep, Pete, you could put up a building alone," said Tom, exasperated. "D'you get the book?"

"Over there." Pete pointed to a package lying on the floor.

Tom picked it up eagerly, sat down on the edge of

the bed—Pete's clothes were sprawling over the only chair—and hastily opened it. Within the wrapping paper was the secretary's book.

"How'd you get it, Pete?"

"The amount o' licker I turned into spittoons last night, Tom, was certainly an immoral waste. If I'd put it where it belonged, I'd be drunk for life. Connelly, he'll never come to. Now, s'pose you chase along, Tom, an' let me finish things up with my bed."

"What time d'you want the book again?"

"By nine to-night."

"Will you have any trouble putting it back in the office?"

"Sure not. While I had Connelly's keys I made myself one to his office. I took a blank and a file with me last night."

At ten o'clock, the hour agreed upon, Tom was in Ruth's office. Ruth and a business-looking woman of middle age, who was introduced as a Mrs. Somebody, were already there when he came. Five boxes of envelopes were stacked on a table, which had been drawn to the center of the room, the letters were on a smaller table against one wall, and sheets of stamps were on the top of Ruth's desk.

Tom was appalled when he saw what a quantity twenty-five hundred envelopes were. "What! We can't write names on all those to-day!"

"It 'll take the two of us about seven hours with you reading the names to us," Ruth reassured him. "I had the letters come folded from the printers. We'll put them in the envelopes and put on the stamps to-morrow. They'll all be ready for the mail Monday night."

Until five o'clock, with half an hour off for lunch, the two women wrote rapidly, Tom, on the opposite side of the table, reading the names to them alternately and omitting the names of the adherents of Foley.

Now that she was with him again Ruth soon forgot all about Tom's crudity. His purposeful power, which projected itself through even so commonplace an occupation as reading off addresses, rapidly remade its first impression. It dwarfed his crudity to insignificance.

When he left her at her door she gave him her hand with frank cordiality. "You'll come Thursday evening then to tell me all about it as you promised. When I see you then I'm sure it will be to congratulate you."

Chapter XI

IN FOLEY'S "OFFICE"

BUCK FOLEY'S greatest weakness was the consciousness of his strength. Two years before he would have been a much more formidable opponent, for then he was alert for every possible danger and would have put forth his full of strength and wits to overwhelm an aspiring usurper. Now he was like the ring champion of several years' standing who has become too self-confident to train.

Foley felt such security that he made light of the first reports of Tom's campaigning brought him by his intimates. "He can't touch me," he said confidently. "After he rubs sole leather on asphalt a few more weeks, he'll be so tame he'll eat out o' my hand."

It was not till the meeting at which Tom's ticket was presented that Foley awoke to the possibility of danger. He saw that Tom was tremendously in earnest, that he was working hard, that he was gaining strength among the men. If Tom were to succeed in getting out the goody-goody element, or even a quarter of it—— Foley saw the menacing possibility.

Connelly hurried up to him at the close of the

meeting. "Say, Buck, this here looks serious!" he whispered. "A lot o' the fellows are gettin' scared."

"What's serious?"

"Keating's game."

"I'd forgotten that. I keep forgettin' little things. Well, s'pose youse get the bunch to drop in at Mulligan's."

Half an hour later Foley, who knew the value of coming late, sauntered into the back room of Mulligan's saloon, which drinking-place was distant two blocks from Potomac Hall. This back room was commonly known as "Buck's Office," for here he met and issued orders to his lieutenants. It was a square room with a dozen chairs, three tables, several pictures of prize fighters and several nudes of the brewers' school of art. Connelly, Jake Henderson, and six other men sat at the tables, beer glasses before them, talking with deep seriousness.

Foley paused in the doorway. "Hello, youse coffin-faces! None o' this for mine!" He started out.

"Hold on, Buck!" Connelly cried, starting up.

Foley turned back. "Take that crape off your mugs, then!"

"We were talkin' about Keating," Connelly explained. "It strikes us he means business."

It was a principle in Foley's theory of government not to ask help of his lieutenants in important affairs except when it was necessary; it fed his love of power to feel them dependent upon his action. But it was also a principle that they should feel an absolute confidence in him. He now saw dubiety on every face;

an hour's work was marked out. He sat down, threw open his overcoat, put one foot on a table and tipped back in his chair. "Yes, I s'pose Keating thinks he does mean business."

With his eyes fixed carelessly on the men he drew from a vest pocket a tight roll of bills, with 100 showing at either end, and struck a match; and moved the roll, held cigar-wise between the first and second fingers of his left hand, and the match toward his mouth. With a cry Connelly sprang forward and seized his wrist.

"Now what the hell——" Foley began, exasperatedly. His eyes fell to his hand, and he grinned. "Well! Now I wonder where that cigar is." He went one by one through the pockets of his vest. "Well, I reckon I'll have to buy another. Jake, ask one o' the salesladies to fetch in some cabbage."

Jake Henderson stepped to the door and called for cigars. Mulligan himself responded, bearing three boxes which he set down before Foley. "Five, ten and fifteen," he said, pointing in turn at the boxes.

Foley picked up the cheapest box and snuffed at its contents. "These the worst youse got?"

"Got some two-fers."

"Um! Make youse think youse was mendin' the asphalt, I s'pose. I guess these's bad enough. Help youselves, boys." But it was the fifteen-cent box he started around.

The men took one each, and the box came back to Foley. "Hain't youse fellows got no vest pockets?" he demanded, and started the box around again.

When the box had completed its second circuit

Mulligan took it and the two others and started out. " Hold on, Barney," said Foley. " What's the matter with your beer? "

" My beer? "

" Been beggin' the boys to have some more, but they don't want it."

" My beer's—— "

" Hi, Barney! Don't youse see he's shootin' hot air into youse? " cried Jake delightedly. " Chase in the beer! "

" No, youse don't have to drink nothin' youse don't like. Bring in some champagne, Barney. I'm doin' a scientific stunt. I want to see what champagne does to a roughneck."

" How much? " asked Mulligan.

" Oh, about a barrel." He drew from his trousers pocket a mixture of crumpled bills, loose silver, and keys. From this he untangled a twenty-dollar bill and handed it to Mulligan.

" Fetch back what youse don't want. An' don't move like your feet was roots, neither."

Two minutes later Mulligan returned with four quart bottles. Immediately behind him came a girl in the dress of the Salvation Army. " Won't you help us in our work? " she said, holding her tin box out to Foley.

" Take what youse want." He pointed with his cigar to the change Mulligan had just laid upon the table.

With hesitation she picked up a quarter. " This much? " she asked, smiling doubtfully.

" No wonder youse 're poor! " He swept all the

change into his palm. "Here!" and he thrust it into her astonished hands.

After she had stammered out her thanks and departed, Foley began to fill the glasses from a bottle Mulligan had opened. Jake, moistening his lips, put out his hand in mock refusal.

"Only a drop for me, Buck."

Foley filled Jake's glass to the brim. "Well, there's several. Pick your choice."

He filled the other glasses, then lifted his own with a "Here's how!" They all raised the fragile goblets clumsily and emptied them at a gulp. "Now put about twenty dollars' worth o' grin on your faces," Foley requested.

"But what about Keating?" asked Connelly anxiously, harking back to the first subject. "He's startin' a mighty hot fight. An' really, Buck, he's a strong man."

"Yes, I reckon he is." Foley put one hand to his mouth and yawned mightily behind it. "But he's sorter like a big friend o' mine who went out to cut ice in July. His judgment ain't good."

"Of course, he ain't got no chance."

"The same my friend had o' fillin' his ice-house."

"But it strikes me we ought to be gettin' busy," Connelly persisted.

"See here, Connelly. Just because I ain't got a couple o' niggers humpin' to keep the sweat wiped off me, youse needn't think I'm loafin'," Foley returned calmly.

The others, who had shared Connelly's anxiety, were plainly affected by Foley's large manner.

"Youse can just bet Buck 'll be there with the goods when the time comes," Jake declared confidently.

"That's no lie," agreed the others.

"Oh, I ain't doubtin' Buck. Never a once!" said Connelly. "But what's your plans, Buck?"

Foley gazed mysteriously over their heads, and slowly blew out a cloud of smoke. "Youse just keep your two eyes lookin' my way."

Foley knew the value of coming late. He also knew the value of leaving as soon as your point is made. His quick eyes now saw that he had restored the company's confidence; they knew he was prepared for every event.

"I guess I'll pull out," he said, standing up. "Champagne ain't never been the same to me since me an' Morgan went off in his yacht, an' the water give out, an' we had to wash our shirts in it." He looked through the door into the bar-room. "Say, Barney, if these roughnecks want anything more, just put it down to me." He turned back to the men. "So-long, boys," he said, with a wave of his hand, and went out through the bar-room.

"The man that beats Buck Foley's got to beat five aces," declared Jake admiringly.

"Yes," agreed Connelly. "An' he don't keep a strangle holt on his money, neither."

Which two sentiments were variously expressed again and again before the bottoms of the bottles were reached.

If Foley was slow in getting started, he was not slow to act now that he was started. During the following two weeks any contractor that so wished could have worked non-union men on his jobs for all the trouble Foley would have given him. Buck had more important affairs than the union's affairs.

Foley's method of electioneering was even more simple than Tom's. He saw the foreman on every important job in the city. To such as were his friends he said:

"Any o' that Keating nonsense bein' talked on this job?" If there was not: "Well, it's up to youse to see that things stay that way." If there was: "Shut it up. If any o' the men talk too loud, fire 'em. If youse ain't got that authority, find somethin' wrong with their work an' get 'em fired. It's your business to see that not a man on your job votes again' me!"

To such few as he did not count among his friends he said:

"Youse know enough to know I'm goin' to win. Youse know what's the wise thing for youse to do, all right. I like my friends, an' I don't like the men that fight me. I ain't likely to go much out o' my way to help Keating an' his push. I think that's enough, ain't it?"

It was—especially since it was said with a cold look straight into the other's eyes. An hour's speech could not have been more effective.

Foley made it his practice to see as many of the doubtful workmen as possible during their lunch hour. He had neither hope nor desire that they should come out and vote for him. His wish was merely that they should not come out and vote for Tom. To them his speech was mainly obvious threats. And he called upon the rank and file of his followers to help him in this detail of his campaign. "Just tell 'em youse think they won't enjoy the meetin' very much," was his instruction, given with a grim smile; and this opinion, with effective elaboration, his followers faithfully delivered.

When Foley dropped into his office on the Tuesday night before election he found Jake, Connelly and the other members of his cabinet anxiously awaiting him. Connelly thrust a copy of Tom's letter into his hands. "Now wha'd'you think o' that?" he demanded. "Blamed nigh every man in the union got one to-night."

As Foley read the blood crept into his face. "'Bully,' 'blood-suckin' grafter', 'trade union pirate', 'come out and make him walk the plank'," Jake quoted appreciatively, watching Foley's face.

By the time he reached the end Foley had regained his self-control. "Well, that's a purty nice piece o' writin', ain't it, now?" he said, looking at the sheet admiringly. "Didn't know Keating was buttin' into literchure. Encouragin', ain't it, to see authors springin' up in every walk o' life. This here'll get Keating the votes o' all the lit'ry members, sure."

"It 'll get him too many!" growled Connelly anxiously.

"A-a-h, go count yourself, Connelly!" Foley looked at the secretary with a pity that was akin to disgust. "Youse give me an unpleasant feelin' in my abdomen!"

He pushed the letter carelessly across to Connelly. "O' course it 'll bring the boys out," he said, in his previous pleasant voice. " But the trouble with Keating is, he believes in the restriction o' output. He believes a man oughtn't to cast more'n one vote a day."

But Foley, for all his careless jocularity, was aware of the seriousness of Tom's last move, and till long after midnight the cabinet was in session—to the great profit of Barney Mulligan's cash register.

Chapter XII

THE ELECTION

TOM set out for Potomac Hall Wednesday evening with the emotions of a gambler who had placed his fortune on a single color; his all was risked on the event of that night. However, he had a bracing confidence running through his agitation; he felt that he controlled the arrow of fortune. The man to man canvass; the feminine influence made operative by Mrs. Barry; the letters with which Ruth had helped him, —these, he was certain, had drawn the arrow's head to the spot where rested his stake and the union's.

Tom reached the hall at six-thirty. The polls did not open till seven, but already thirty or forty of Foley's men stood in knots in front of the building.

"Hello, boys! Now don't he think he's It!" said one admiringly.

"Poor Buck! This's the last o' him!" groaned another.

There was a burst of derisive laughter, and each of the party tossed a bit of language in his way; but Tom made no answer and passed them unflinchingly. At the doorway he was stopped by the policeman who was regularly stationed at Potomac Hall on meeting nights.

"Goin' to have a fist sociable to-night?" the

policeman asked, anxiously watching the men in the street.

"Can't say, Murphy. Ask Foley. He'll be floor manager, if there is one."

As he went through the hallway toward the stairs, Tom paused to glance through a side door into the big bar-room, which, with a café, occupied the whole of the first floor. A couple of score of Foley men stood at the bar and sat about the tables. It certainly did look as if there might be festivities.

Tom mounted the broad stairway and knocked at the door of the union's hall. Hogan, the sergeant-at-arms, a Foley man, gingerly admitted him. The hall in which he found himself was a big rectangular room, perhaps fifty by one hundred feet. The walls had once been maroon in color, and had a broad moulding of plaster that had been white and gilt; the ceiling had likewise once been maroon, and was decorated with plaster scroll-work and crudely painted clusters of fruits and flowers—scroll-work and paintings lacking their one-time freshness. From the center of the ceiling hung a great ball of paper roses; at the front of the room was a grand piano in a faded green cover. The sign advertising the hall, nailed on the building's front, had as its last clause: "Also available for weddings, receptions, and balls."

Tom's glance swept the room. All was in readiness for the election. The floor was cleared of its folding chairs, they being now stacked at the rear of the room; down the hall's middle ran a row of tables, set end to end, with chairs on either side; Bill Jackson, one of his supporters, was at Hogan's elbow, ready to hand out the ballots as the men were admitted; the five tellers—Barry, Pete, Jake and two other Foley men—were smoking at the front of the room, Jake lolling on the piano, and the other four on the platform where the officers sat at the regular meetings.

Tom joined Pete and Barry, and the three drew to one side to await the opening of the door. "Anything new?" Tom asked.

"Nothin'," answered Pete. "But say, Tom, that letter was certainly hot stuff! I've heard some o' the boys talkin' about it. They think it's great. It's bringin' a lot o' them out."

"That's good."

"An' we're goin' to win, sure."

Tom nodded. "If Foley don't work some of his tricks."

"Oh, we'll look out for that," said Pete confidently.

Promptly at seven o'clock Hogan unlocked the door. The men began to mount the stairway. As each man came to the door Hogan examined his membership card, and, if it showed the holder to be in good standing, admitted him. Jackson then handed him a ballot, on which the names of all the candidates were printed in a vertical row, and he walked to one of the tables and made crosses before the names of the men for whom he desired to vote.

Five minutes after the door had been opened there were thirty or forty men in the room, an equal number of each party, Foley among them. Jake, who was chief teller, rose at the center table on the platform to discharge the formality of offering the ballot-box for inspection. He unlocked the box, which was about twelve inches square, and performing a slow arc presented the open side to the eyes of the tellers and the waiting members. The box was empty.

" All right? " he asked.

" Sure," said the men carelessly. The tellers nodded.

Foley began the telling of a yarn, and was straightway the center of the group of voters. In the meantime Jake locked the box and started to carry it to its appointed place on a table at one end of the platform, to reach which he had to pass through the narrow space between the wall and the chair-backs of the other tellers. As he brushed through this alley, Tom, whose eyes had not left him, saw the ballot-box turn so that its slot was toward the wall, and glimpsed a quick motion of Jake's hand from a pocket toward the slot—a motion wholly of the wrist. He sprang after the chief teller and seized his hand.

" You don't work that game! " he cried.

Foley's story snapped off. His hearers pivoted to face the disturbance.

Jake turned about. " What game? "

" Open your hand! " Tom demanded.

Jake elevated his big fist, then opened it. It held nothing. He laughed derisively, and set the box down in its place. A jeering shout rose from Foley's crowd.

For an instant Tom was taken aback. Then he

stepped quickly to the table and gave the box a light shake. He triumphantly raised it on high and shook it violently. From it there came an unmistakable rattle.

"This's how Foley'd win!" he cried to the crowd.

Jake, his derision suddenly changed to fury, would have struck Tom in another instant, for all his wits were in his fists; but the incisive voice of Foley sounded out: "A clever trick, Keating."

"How's that?" asked several men.

"A trick to cast suspicion on us," Foley answered quietly. "Keating put 'em in there himself."

Tom stared at him, then turned sharply upon Jake. "Give me the key. I'll show who those ballots are for."

Jake, not understanding, but taking his cue from Foley, handed over the key. Tom unlocked the box, and took out a handful of tightly-folded ballots. He opened several of them and held them up to the crowd. The crosses were before the Foley candidates.

"Of course I put 'em in!" Tom said sarcastically, looking squarely at Foley.

"O' course youse did," Foley returned calmly. "To cast suspicion on us. It's a clever trick, but it's what I call dirty politics."

Tom made no reply. His eyes had caught a slight bulge in the pocket of Jake's coat from which he had before seen Jake's hand emerge ballot-laden. He lunged suddenly toward the chief teller, and thrust a hand into the pocket. There was a struggle of an instant; the crowd saw Tom's hand come out of the pocket filled with packets of paper; then Tom broke loose. It all happened so quickly that the crowd had no time to move. The tellers rose just in time to lay hands upon Jake, who was hurling himself upon Tom in animal fury.

Tom held the ballots out toward Foley. They were bound in packets half an inch thick by narrow bands of papers which were obviously to be snapped as the packet was thrust into the slot of the box. " I suppose you'll say now, Buck Foley, that I put these in Henderson's pocket! "

For once Foley was at a loss. Part of the crowd cursed and hissed him. His own men looked at him expectantly, but the trickery was too apparent for his wits to be of avail. He glared straight ahead, rolling his cigar from side to side of his mouth.

Tom tossed the ballots into the open box. " Enough votes there already to elect Foley. Now I demand another teller instead of that man." He jerked his head contemptuously toward Jake.

Foley's composure was with him again. " Anything to please youse, Tom. I guess nobody's got a kick again' Connelly. Connelly, youse take Jake's place."

As the exchange was being made the Foleyites regarded their leader dubiously; not out of disapproval of his trickery, but because his attempted jugglery had failed. Foley had recourse again to his confidence-compelling glance—eyes narrowed and full of mystery. " It's only seven-thirty, boys! " he said in an impressive whisper, and turned and went out. Jake glowered at Tom and followed him.

Tom transferred the ballots from the box to his pockets, locked the box, turned over the key to the tellers, and was resuming his seat when he saw a man of disordered dress at the edge of the platform, who had been anxiously awaiting the end of this episode, beckoning him. Tom quickly stepped to his side. " What's the matter? "

" Hell's broke loose downstairs, Tom," said the man. " Come down."

" Look out for any more tricks," Tom called to Pete, and hurried out. The stairway was held from top to botttom by a line of Foley men. Foley supporters were marching up, trading rough jests with these guardsmen; but not a single man of his was on the stairs. He saw one of his men start up, and receive a shove in the chest that sent him upon his back. A laugh rose from the line. Tom's fists knotted and his eyes filled with fire. The head guardsman tried to seize him, and got one of the fists in the face.

" Look out, you——! " He swore mightily at the line, and plunged downward past the guards, who were held back by a momentary awe. The man below rose to his feet, hotly charged, and was sent staggering again. Tom, descending, caught the assailant by the collar, and with a powerful jerk sent him sprawling upon the floor. He turned fiercely upon the line. But before he could even speak, half of it charged down upon him, overbore him and swept him through the open door into the street. Then they melted away from him and returned to their posts.

Tom, bruised and dazed, would have followed the

men back through the doorway, but his eyes came upon a new scene. On his either hand in the street, which was weakly illumined by windows and corner lights, several scuffles were going on, six or seven in each; groups of Foley men were blocking the way of his supporters, and blows and high words were passing; farther away he could dimly see his men standing about in hesitant knots—having not the reckless courage to attempt passage through such a rowdy sea.

The policeman was trying to quell one of the scuffles with his club. Tom saw it twisted from his hand. Murphy drew his revolver. The club sent it spinning. He turned and walked quickly out of the street.

All this Tom saw in two glances. The man beside him swore. "Send for the police, Tom. Nothing else 'll save us." His voice barely rose above the cries and oaths.

"It won't do, Smith. We'd never hear the last of it."

And yet Tom realized, with instant quickness, the hopelessness of the situation. Against Foley's organized ruffianism, holding hall and street, his unorganized supporters, standing on the outskirts, could do nothing. There was but one thing to be done—to get to his men, organize them in some way, wait till their number had grown, and then march in a body to the ballot-box.

Ten seconds after his discharge into the street Tom was springing away on this errand, when out of the tail of his eye he saw Foley come to the door and glance about. He wheeled and strode up to the walking delegate.

"Is this your only way of winning an election?" he cried hotly.

"Well! well! They're mixin' it up a bit, ain't they," Foley drawled, looking over Tom's head. "That's too bad!"

"Don't try any of your stage business on me! Stop this fighting!"

"What could I do?" Foley asked deprecatingly. "If I tried, I'd only get my nut cracked." And he turned back into the hall.

"Come on!" Tom cried to Smith; and together they plunged eastward, in which direction were the largest number of Tom's friends. Before they had gone a dozen paces they were engulfed in the fray. Several of his men swept in from the outskirts to his support; more Foley men rushed into the conflict; the fight that had before been waged in skirmishes was now a general engagement. For a space that seemed an hour to Tom, but that in reality was no more than its quarter, it was struggle at the top of his strength. He warded off blows. He stung under fists. He struck out at dim faces. He swayed fiercely in grappling arms. He sent men down. He went down again and again himself. And oaths were gasped and shouted, and deep-lunged cries battered riotously against the street's high walls . . . And so it was all around him—a writhing, striking, kicking, swearing whirlpool of men, over whose fierce turbulence fell the dusky light of bar-room and tenement windows.

After a time, when his breath was coming in gasps, and his strength was well-nigh gone, he saw the vindictive face of Jake Henderson, with the bar-room's light across it, draw nearer and nearer through the struggling mob. If Jake should reach him, spent as he was—— He saw his limp, out-stretched body as in a vision.

But Jake's vengeance did not then fall. Tom heard a cry go up and run through the crowd: "Police! Police!" In an instant the whirlpool half calmed. The cry brought to their feet the two men who had last borne him down. Tom scrambled up, saw the mob untangle itself into individuals, and saw, turning the corner, a squad of policemen, clubs drawn, Murphy marching at the captain's side.

The captain drew his squad up beside the doorway of the hall, and himself mounted the two steps. "If there's any more o' this rough house, I'll run in every one o' you!" he shouted, shaking his club at the men.

The Foleyites laughed, and defiance buzzed among them, but they knew the better part of valor. It was a Foley principle to observe the law when the law is observing you.

Five minutes later the captain's threat was made even more potent for order by the appearance of the reserves from another precinct; and in a little while still another squad leaped from clanging patrol wagons, making in all fifty policemen that had answered Murphy's call. Twenty of these were posted in the stairway, and the rest were placed on guard in the street.

A new order came from the bar-room, and Foley's men withdrew to beyond the limits of police influence and intercepted the men coming to vote, using blandishment and threats, and leading some into the bar-room to be further convinced.

Tom, who stood outside watching the restoration of order, now started back to the hall. On the way he glanced through the side door into the bar-room. It was heavy with smoke, and at the bar was a crowd, with Foley as its center. "I don't know what youse think about Keating callin' in the police," he was saying, "but youse can bet I know what Buck Foley thinks! A man that 'll turn the police on his own union!" And then as a fresh group of men were led into the room: "Step right up to the counter, boys, an' have your measure taken for a drink. I've bought out the place, an' am givin' it away. Me an' Carnegie's tryin' to die poor."

Tom mounted to the hall with a secret satisfaction in the protection of the broad-chested bluecoats that now held the stairway. A fusillade of remarks from the men marking their ballots greeted his entrance, but he passed up to the platform without making answers.

Pete's mouth fell agape at sight of him. "Hello! You look like you been ticklin' a grizzly under the chin!"

Tom noted the relishing grins of the Foley tellers. "The trouble downstairs is all over. I'll tell you all about it after awhile," he said shortly; and sat down just behind Pete to watch the voting.

Up to this time the balloting had been light. But

now the hall began to fill, and the voting proceeded rapidly—and orderly, too, thanks to the policemen on stairway and in street. Tom, his clothes " lookin' like he tried to take 'em off without unbuttonin'," as a Foley teller whispered, his battered hat down over his eyes, sat tilted against the wall scanning every man that filed past the box. As man after man had his membership card stamped " voted," and dropped in his ballot, Tom's excitement rose, for he recognized the majority of the men that marched by as of his following.

At nine o'clock Pete leaned far back in his chair. " Lookin' great, ain't it? " he whispered.

" If it only keeps up like this." That it might not was Tom's great fear now.

" Oh, it will, don't you worry."

The line of voters that marched by, and by, bore out Pete's prediction, as Tom's counting .eyes saw. He had the wild exultation and throbbing weakness of the man who is on the verge of success. But the possibility of failure, the cause of his weakness, became less and less as time ticked on and the votes dropped into the ballot box. His enthusiasm grew. Dozens of plans flashed through his head. But his eyes never left that string of men who were deciding his fate and that of the union.

At half past ten Tom was certain of his election. Pete leaned back and gripped his hand. " It's a cinch, Tom. It's a shame to take the money," he whispered.

Tom acquiesced in Pete's conviction with a jerk of his head, and watched the passing line, now grown thin and slow, drop in their ballots, his certainty growing doubly sure.

Fifteen minutes later Foley entered the hall, whispered a moment with Hogan at the door, a moment with Connelly, and then went out again. Tom thought he saw anxiety showing through Foley's ease of manner, and to him it was an advance taste of triumph.

Tom wished eleven o'clock had come and the door was locked. The minutes passed with such exhausting slowness. A straggling voter dropped in his ballot—and another straggler—and another. Tom looked at his watch. Two minutes had passed since Foley's visit. Another straggling voter. And then four men appeared in a body at the hall door, all apparently the worse for Foley's hospitality. Tom saw the foremost present his card. Hogan glanced at it, and handed it back. " You can't vote that card; it's expired," Tom heard him say.

" What's that? " demanded the man, threateningly.

" The card's expired, I said! You can't vote it! Get out! "

" I can't vote it, hey! " There was an oath, a blow—a surprisingly light blow to produce such an effect, so it seemed to Tom—and Hogan staggered back and went to the floor. There was a scuffle; the tables on which lay the ballots toppled over, and the ballots went fluttering. By this time Tom reached the door, policemen had rushed in and settled the scuffle, and the four men were being led from the room.

Hogan was unhurt, but Jackson was so dazed from a blow that Tom had to put another man in his place.

The minutes moved toward eleven with slow, ticking steps. Two stragglers . . . at long intervals. At a few minutes before eleven the exhausting monotony was enlivened by the entrance of eight men, singing boisterously and jostling each other in alcoholic jollity. They marked their ballots and staggered in a group to the ballot-box. Two tried to deposit their ballots at once.

"Leave me alone, will youse!" cried one, with an oath, and struck at the other.

The ballot-box slipped across to the edge of the table. Connelly, who sat just behind the box, made no move for its safety. "Hey, stop that!" cried Pete and sprang across to seize it. But he was too late. The one blow struck, the eight were all instantly delivering blows, and pushing and swearing. The box was knocked forward upon the floor, and the eight sprawled pell-mell upon it.

Tom and the tellers sprang from behind the tables upon the scuffling heap, and several policemen rushed in from the hallway. The men, once dragged apart, subsided and gave no trouble. They were allowed to drop their ballots in the box, now back in its place on the table, and were then led out in quietness by the officers.

Pete turned about, struck with a sudden fear. "I wonder if that was a trick?" he whispered.

Tom's face was pale. The same fear had come to him. "I wonder!"

In another five minutes the door was locked and the tellers were counting the ballots. Among the first hundred there were perhaps a score that bore no mark except a cross before Foley's name. Pete looked again at Tom. With both fear had been replaced by certainty.

"The box's been stuffed!" Pete whispered.

Tom nodded.

His only hope now was that not enough false ballots had been got into the box to carry the election. But as the count proceeded, this hope left him. And the end was equal to his worst fears. The count stood: for walking delegate, Foley 976, Keating 763; for president, Keating 763, Foley's man 595; all the other Foley candidates won by a slight margin. The apparent inconsistencies of this count Tom readily understood even in the first wild minutes. Foley's running ahead of his ticket was to be explained on the ground that the brief time permitted of a cross being put before his name alone on the false ballots; his own election to the unimportant presidency, and the failure of his other candidates, was evidently caused by several of his followers splitting their tickets and voting for the minor Foley candidates.

As the count had proceeded Tom had exploded more than once, and Pete had made lurid use of his gift. When Connelly read off the final results Tom exploded again.

"It's an infernal steal!" he shouted.

"Even if it is, what can we do?" returned Connelly.

Words ran high. But Tom quickly saw the use-lessness of protests and accusations at this time. His great desire now was to take his heat and disap-pointment out into the street; and so he gave evasive answers to Pete and Barry, who wanted to talk it over, and made his way out of the hall alone.

Cheers and laughter were ascending from the bar-room. As he was half-way down the stairs the door of the saloon opened, and Foley came out and started up, followed by a number of men. Among them Tom saw several of the drunken group that had upset the ballot-box; and he also saw that they prob-ably had not been more sober in years.

"Why, hello, Tom!" Foley cried out on sight of him. "D'youse hear the election returns?"

Tom looked hard at Foley's face with its leering geniality, and he was almost overmastered by a de-sire to hurl himself upon Foley and annihilate him. "You infernal thief!" he burst out.

Foley sidled toward him across the broad step. "I'll pass that by. I can afford to, for youse 're about wiped out. I guess youse 've had enough."

"Enough?" cried Tom. "I've just begun!"

With that he brushed by Foley and passed through the door out into the street.

Chapter XIII

THE DAY AFTER

THE distance to Tom's home was half a hundred blocks, but he chose to walk. Anger, disappointment, and underlying these the hopeless sense of being barred from his trade, all demanded the sympathy of physical exertion—and, too, there was the inevitable meeting with his wife. Walking would give him an hour before that.

It was after one when he opened the hall door and stepped into his flat. Through the dining-room he could see the gas in the sitting-room was turned down to a point, and could see Maggie lying on the couch, a flowered comforter drawn over her. He guessed she had stayed up to wait for his report. He listened. In the night's dead stillness he could faintly hear her breath come deep and regular. Seizing at the chance of postponing the scene, he cautiously closed the hall door, and, sitting down on a chair beside it, removed his shoes. He crossed on tip-toe toward their bedroom, but its door betrayed him by a creak. He turned quickly about. There was Maggie, propped up on one arm, the comforter thrown back.

She looked at him for a space without speaking.

145

Through all his other feelings Tom had a sense that he made anything but a brave figure, standing in his stocking feet, his shoes in one hand, hat and over-coat on.

"Well?" she demanded at length.

Tom returned her fixed gaze, and made no reply to her all-inclusive query.

Her hands gripped her covering. She gave a gasp. Then she threw back the comforter and slipped to her feet.

"I understand!" she said. "Everything! I knew it! O-o-h!" There were more resentment and re-crimination packed into that prolonged "oh" than she could have put into an hour's upbraiding.

Tom kept himself in hand. He knew the futility of explanation, but he explained. "I won, fairly. But Foley robbed me. He stuffed the ballot-box."

"It makes no difference how you lost! You lost! That's what I've got to face. You know I didn't want you to go into this. I knew you couldn't win. I knew Foley was full of tricks. But you went in. You lost wages. You threw away money—*our* money! And what have you got to show for it all?"

Tom let her words pass in silence. On his long walk he had made up his mind to bear her fury quietly.

"Oh, you!" she cried through clenched teeth, stamping a bare foot on the floor. "You do what you please, and I suffer for it. You wouldn't take my advice. And now you're out of a job and can't get one in your trade. How are we to live? Tell me that, Tom Keating? How are we to live?"

Only the word he had passed with himself enabled Tom to hold himself in after this outburst. " I'll find work."

" Find work! A hod-carrier! Oh, my God! "

She turned and flung herself at full length upon the couch, and lay there sobbing, her hands passionately gripping the comforter.

Tom silently watched the workings of her passion for a moment. He realized the measure of right on her side, and his sense of justice made his spirit unbend. " If we have to live close, it 'll only be for a time," he said.

" Oh, my God! " she moaned.

He grimly turned and went into the bedroom. After a while he came out again. She had drawn the comforter over her, but her irregular breathing told him she was still awake.

" Aren't you coming to bed? " he asked.

She made no answer, and he went back. For half an hour he tossed about. Then he came into the sitting-room again. Her breath was coming quietly and regularly. He sat down and gazed at her handsome face for a long, long time, with misty, wondering thoughts. Then he rose with a deep-drawn sigh, took part of the covering from the bed, and spread it over her sleeping figure.

He tossed about long before he fell into a restless sleep. It was early when he awoke. He looked into the sitting-room. Maggie was still sleeping. He quickly dressed himself in his best suit (the one he had had on the night before was beyond further wearing), noting with surprise that his face bore few marks of conflict, and stole quietly out.

Tom's disappointment and anger were too fresh to allow him to put his mind upon plans for the future. All day he wandered aimlessly about, talking over the events of the previous night with such of his friends as chance put in his path. Late in the afternoon he met Pete and Barry, who had been looking for work since morning. They sat down in a saloon and talked about the election till dinner time. It was decided that Tom should protest the election and appeal to the union—a move they all agreed had little promise. Tom found a soothing gratification in Pete's verbal handling of the affair; there was an ease, a broadness, a completeness, to Pete's profanity that left nothing to be desired; so that Tom was prompted to remark, with a half smile: " If there was a professorship of your kind of English over at Columbia University, Pete, you'd never have to put on overalls again."

Tom had breakfasted in a restaurant, and lunched in a restaurant, and after Pete and Barry left he had dinner in one. It was a cheap and meager meal; with his uncertain future he felt it wise to begin to count every cent. Afterwards he walked about the streets till eight, bringing up at Ruth's boarding-house. The colored maid who answered his ring brought back the message: " Miss Arnold says will you please come up."

He mounted the stairway behind the maid. Ruth was standing at the head of the stairs awaiting him.

She wore a loose white gown, held in at the waist
by a red girdle, and there was a knot of red in her
heavy dark hair. Tom felt himself go warm at
sight of her, and there began a throbbing that beat
even in his ears.

"You don't mind my receiving you in my room,
do you?" she said, opening her door, after she had
greeted him.

"Why, no," said Tom, slightly puzzled. His
acquaintance with the proprieties was so slight that
he did not know she was then breaking one.

She closed the door. "I'm glad to see you. I
know what happened last night; we heard at the
office." She held out her hand again. The grip
was warm and full of sympathy.

The hand sent a thrill through Tom. In his
fresh disappointment it was just this intelligent sympathy that he was hungry for. For a moment he
was unable to speak or move.

She gently withdrew her hand. "But we heard
only the bare fact. I want you to tell me the whole
story."

Tom laid his hat and overcoat upon the couch,
which had a dull green cover, glancing, as he did
so, about the room. There were a few prints of
good pictures on the walls; a small case of books; a
writing desk; and in one corner a large screen whose
dominant color was a dull green. The thing that
struck him most was the absence of the knick-knack-
ery with which his home was decorated. Tom was
not accustomed to give attention to his surroundings,
but the room pleased him; and yet it was only an

ordinary boarding-house room, plus the good taste of a tasteful woman.

Tom took one of the two easy chairs in the room, and once again went over the happenings of the previous night. She interrupted again and again with indignant exclamations.

"Why, you didn't lose at all!" she cried, when he had finished the episode of the eight drunken men. "You won, and it was stolen from you! Your Mr. Foley is a—a——" Whichever way she turned for an adequate word she ran against a restriction barring its use by femininity. "A robber!" she ended.

"But aren't you going to protest the election?"

"I shall—certainly. But there's mighty little chance of the result being changed. Foley 'll see to that."

He tried to look brave, but Ruth guessed the bitterness within. She yearned to have him talk over things with her; her sympathy for him now that she beheld him dispirited after a daring fight was even warmer than when she had seen him pulsing with defiant vigor. "Won't you tell me what you are going to do? If you don't mind."

"I'd tell if I knew. But I hardly have my bearings yet."

"Are you sure you can't work at your trade?"

"Not unless I kiss Foley's shoes."

She did not like to ask him if he were going to give in, but the question was in her face, and he saw it.

"I'm not that bad licked yet."

"There's Mr. Driscoll's offer," she suggested,

" Yes. I've thought of that. I don't know what move I'll make next. I don't just see now how I'm going to keep at the fight, but I'm not ready to give it up. If I took Mr. Driscoll's job, I'd have to drop the fight, for I'd practically have to drop out of the union. If the protest fails—well, we'll see."

Ruth looked at him thoughtfully, and she thrilled with a personal pride in him. He had been beaten; the days just ahead looked black for him; but his spirit, though exhausted, was unbroken. As a result of her experience she was beginning to regard business as being largely a compromise between self-respect and profit. In Tom's place she guessed what Mr. Baxter would do, and she knew what Mr. Driscoll would do; and the thing they would do was not the thing that Tom was doing. And she wondered what would be the course of Mr. Berman.

At the moment of parting she said to him, in her frank, impulsive way: " I think you are the bravest man I have ever known." He could only stumble away from her awkwardly, for to this his startled brain had no proper answer. His courage began to bubble back into him; and the warmth aroused by her words grew and grew—till he drew near his home, and then a chill began to settle about him.

Maggie was reading the installment of a serial story in an evening paper when he came in. She glanced up, then quickly looked back at her paper without speaking.

He started into the bedroom in silence, but paused hesitant in the doorway and looked at her. " What are you reading, Maggie? "

" The Scarlet Stain."

He held his eyes upon her a moment longer, and then with a sigh went into the bedroom and lit the gas. The instant he was gone from the doorway Maggie took her eyes from the story and listened irresolutely. All day her brain had burnt with angry thoughts, and all day she had been waiting the chance to speak. But her obstinate pride now strove to keep her tongue silent.

" Tom! " she called out, at length.

He appeared in the doorway. " Yes."

" What are you going to do? "

He was silent for a space. " I don't just know yet."

" I know," she said in a voice she tried to keep cold and steady. " There's only one thing for you to do. That's to get on the square with Foley."

Their eyes met. Hers were cold, hard, rebellious.

" I'll think it over," he said quietly; and went back into the bedroom.

Chapter XIV

NEW COURAGE AND NEW PLANS

THE next morning after breakfast Tom sat down to take account of his situation. But his wife's sullen presence, as she cleared away the dishes, suffocated his thoughts. He went out and walked south a few blocks to a little park that had formerly served the neighborhood as a burying-ground. A raw wind was chattering among the bare twigs of the sycamore trees; the earth was a rigid shell from the night's frost, and its little squares and oblongs of grass were a brownish-gray; the sky was overcast with gray clouds. The little park, this dull March day, was hardly more cheerful than the death it had erewhile housed, but Tom sat down in its midst with a sense of grateful relief.

His mind had already passed upon Maggie's demand of the previous evening. But would it avail to continue the fight against Foley? He had slept well, and the sleep had strengthened his spirit and cleared his brain; and Ruth's recurring words, " I think you are the bravest man I have ever known," were to him a determining inspiration. He went over the situation detail by detail, and slowly a new plan took shape.

Foley had beaten him by a trick. In six months there would be another election. He would run again, and this next time, profiting by his dear experience of Wednesday night, he would see that guard was set against every chance for unfair play. During the six months he would hammer at Foley's every weak spot, and emphasize to the union the discredit of Foley's discreditable acts.

He would follow up his strike agitation. He had already put Foley into opposition to a demand for more money. If he could induce the union to make the demand in the face of Foley's opposition it would be a telling victory over the walking delegate. Perhaps, even, he might head the management of the strike—if it came to a strike. And if the strike were won, it would be the complete undoing of Foley. As for Maggie, she would oppose the plan, of course, but once he had succeeded she would approve what he had done. In the meantime he would have to work at some poorly paid labor, and appease her as best he could.

At dinner that night little was said, till Maggie asked with a choking effort: " Did you see Foley to-day? "

" No," said Tom. He ate a mouthful, then laid down knife and fork, and looked firmly into her face. " I didn't try to see him. And I might as well tell you, Maggie, that I'm not going to see him."

" You'll not see him? " she asked in a dry voice. " You'll not see him? "

" Most likely it would not do any good if I did see him. You mark what I say, Maggie," he went on, hopefully. " Foley thinks I'm down, and you do, too, but in a few months things 'll be better than they ever were. We may see some hard times—but in the end ! "

" You were just that certain last week. But how'll we live ? "

" I'll find some sort of a temporary job."

She looked at him tensely; then she rose abruptly and carried her indignant grief into the kitchen. She had decided that he must be borne with. But would he never, never come to his senses !

After he had finished his dinner, which had been ready earlier than usual, Tom hurried to the Barrys', and found the family just leaving the table. He rapidly sketched his new plan.

" You're runnin' again' Foley again in six months is all right, but where's the use our tryin' to get more money ? " grumbled Pete. " Suppose we fight hard an' win the strike. What then ? We get nothin' out of it. Foley won't let us work."

" Oh, talk like a man, Pete ! " requested Mrs. Barry. " You know you don't think that way."

" If we win the strike, with Foley against it, it 'll be the end of him," said Tom, in answer to Pete.

" But suppose things turn out with Foley in control o' the strike ? " questioned Barry.

" That won't happen. But if it would, he'd run it all on the square. And he'd manage it well, too. You know what he has done. Well, he'd do the same again if he was forced into a fight.

" It won't be hard to work the men up to make the demand for an increase," Tom went on. " All the men who voted for me are in favor of it, and a lot more, too. All we've got to do is to stir them up a bit, and get word to them to come out on a certain night. Foley 'll hardly dare put up a fight against us in the open."

"Whoever runs the strike, we certainly ought to have more money," said Mrs. Barry decidedly.

"And the bosses can afford to give us more," declared Tom. "They've never made more than they have the last two years."

"Sure, they could divide a lot o' the money we've made with us, an' still not have to button up their own clothes," averred Mrs. Barry.

"Oh, I dunno," said Pete. "They're hard up, just the same as us. What's a hundred thousand when you've got to spend money on yachts, champagne an' Newport, an' other necessities o' life? The last time I was at the Baxters', Mrs. Baxter was settin' at the kitchen table figgerin' how she could make over the new dress she had last summer an' wonderin' how she'd ever pay the gas bill."

Mrs. Barry grunted.

"I got a picture o' her!"

Tom brought the talk back to bear directly upon his scheme, and soon after left, accompanied by Pete, to begin immediately his new campaign.

As soon as they had gone Mrs. Barry turned eagerly to her husband. "If we get that ten per cent. raise, Henry won't have to go to work when he's fourteen like we expected."

"Yes. I was thinkin' o' that."

"An' we could keep him in school mebbe till he's

eighteen. Then he could get a place in some office or business. By that time Annie 'll be old enough to go to normal college. She can go through there and learn to be a teacher."

" An' mebbe I can get you some good clothes, like I've always wanted to."

" Oh, you! D'you think you can buy everything with seventy dollars! " She leaned over with glowing eyes and kissed him.

Rapid work was required by the new campaign, for Tom had settled upon the first meeting in April as the time when he would have the demand for more wages put to a vote. The new campaign, however, would be much easier than the one that had just come to so disastrous an ending. As he had said, the men were already eager to make the demand for more money; his work was to unite this sentiment into a movement, and to urge upon the men that they be out to vote on the first Wednesday in April.

Tom's first step was to enlist the assistance of the nine other men who had helped him in his fight against Foley. He found that the vengeance of the walking delegate had been swift; seven had abruptly lost their jobs. When he had explained his new plan, eight of the nine were with him. The spirit of the ninth was gone.

" I've had enough," he said bitterly. " If I hadn't mixed in with you, I'd be all right now." Upon this man Tom promptly turned his back. He was an excellent ally to be without.

Tom, with Pete, Barry, and his eight other helpers, began regularly to put in each evening in calling upon the members of the union. Every man they saw was asked to talk to others. And so the word spread and spread.

And to Foley it came among the first. Jake Henderson heard it whispered about the St. Etienne Hotel Saturday, and when the day's work was done he hurried straight to Foley's home in order to be certain of catching Buck when he came in to dinner. He had to wait half an hour, but that time was not unpleasantly spent, inasmuch as Mrs. Foley set forth a bottle of beer.

When Foley caught the tenor of Jake's story his face darkened and he let out an oath. But immediately thereafter he caught hold of his excitement. While Jake talked Foley's mind worked rapidly. He did not want a strike for three sufficient reasons. First of all, that the move was being fathered by Tom was enough to make him its opponent. Secondly, he had absolutely nothing to gain from a strike; his power was great, and even a successful strike could not add to it. And last, he would lose financially by it; his arrangement with Baxter and one or two other contractors would come to an end, and in the management of a general strike so many persons were involved that he would have no chance to levy tribute.

Before Jake had finished his rather long-winded account Foley cut him short. " Yes. I'm glad youse come in. I was goin' to send for youse to-night about this very thing."

"What! Youse knew all about it already?"

Foley looked surprise at him. " D'youse think I do nothin' but sleep?"

"Nobody can't tell youse anything," said Jake admiringly. "Youse 're right up to the minute."

"Some folks find me a little ahead." He pulled at his cigar. "I got a little work for youse an' your bunch."

Jake sprang up excitedly. "Not Keating?"

"If youse could guess that well at the races youse 'd always pick the winner. This business's got to stop, an' I guess that's the easiest way to stop it." And, Foley might have added, the only way.

"He ought to've had it long ago," said Jake, with conviction.

"He'll enjoy it all the more for havin' to wait for it." He stood up, and Jake, accepting his dismissal, took his hat. "Youse have a few o' the boys around to-night, an' I'll show up about ten. Four or five ought to be enough—say Arkansas, Smoky, Kaffir Bill, and Hickey."

Foley saw Connelly and two or three other members of his cabinet during the evening, and gave orders that the word was to go forth among his followers that he was against Keating's agitation; he knew the inside facts of present conditions, and knew there was no chance of winning a strike. At ten o'clock he sauntered into the rear room of Mulligan's saloon. Five men were playing poker. With the exception of one they were a group to make an honest man fall to his knees and quickly confess his sins. Such a guileless face had the one that the honest man would have been content with him as confessor. In past days the five had worked a little, each in his own part of the world, and not liking work had procured their living in more congenial ways; and on landing in New York, in the course of their wanderings, they had been gathered in by Foley as suited to his purpose.

"Hello, Buck!" they called out at sight of Foley.

"Hello, gents," he answered. He locked the door with a private key, and kicked a chair up to the table.

"Say, Buck, I got a thirst like a barrel o' lime," remarked he of the guileless face, commonly known as Arkansas Number Two. "D'you know anything good for it?"

"The amount o' money I spend in a year on other men's drinks 'd support a church," Foley answered. But he ordered a quart of whisky and glasses. "Now let's get to business," he said, when they had been placed on the table. "I guess youse 've got an idea in your nuts as to what's doin'?"

"Jake put us next," grinned Kaffir Bill. "Keating."

"Yes. He's over-exertin' his throat. He's likely to spoil his voice, if we don't sorter step in an' stop him."

"But Jake didn't tell us how much youse wanted him to have," said Kaffir Bill. "Stiff?"

"Not much. Don't youse remember when youse made an undertaker's job out o' Fleischmann? An' how near youse come to takin' the trip to Sing Sing? We don't want any more risks o' that sort. Leave your guns at home." Foley gulped down the raw whisky. "A couple months' vacation 'd be about right for Keating. It 'd give him a chance to get acquainted with his wife."

He drew out a cigar and fitted it to one corner of his mouth. " He's left handed, youse know. An' anyhow he works mostly with his mouth."

" An' he's purty chesty," said Jake, following up Foley's cue with a grin.

" That's the idea," said Foley. " A wing, an' say two or three slats. Or a leg."

The five understood and pledged the faithful discharge of their trust in a round of drinks.

" But what's in it for us? " asked Arkansas Number Two.

" It's an easy job. Youse get him in a fight, he goes down; youse do the business with your feet. Say ten apiece. That's plenty."

" Is that all it's worth to you? " Arkansas asked cunningly.

" Make it twenty-five, Buck," petitioned Kaffir Bill. " We need the coin. What's seventy-five more to youse? "

The other four joined in the request.

" Well, if I don't I s'pose every son-of-a-gun o' youse 'll strike," said Foley, assuming the air of a defeated employer. " All right—for this once. But this ain't to be the regular union rate."

" You're all to the good, Buck! " the five shouted.

Foley rose and started out. At the door he paused. " Youse can't ask me for the coin any too soon," he said meaningly.

The five held divergent opinions upon many subjects, but upon one point they were as one mind— esteem for the bottle. So when Buck's quart of whisky was exhausted they unanimously decided to remove themselves to Potomac Hall, in whose bar-room there usually could be found someone that, after a dark glance or two, was delighted to set out the drinks.

They quickly found a benefactor in the person of Johnson, also a devotee of the bottle. They were disposing of the third round of drinks when Pete, who had been attending a meeting of the Membership Committee of the union, passed through the bar-room on his way out. Jake saw him, and, three parts drunk, could not resist the opportunity for advance satisfaction. "Hold on, Pig Iron," he called after him.

Pete stopped, and Jake walked leeringly up to him. "This here ———" the best Jake could do in the way of profanity, " Keating is goin' to get what's comin' to him! " Jake ended with a few more selections from his repertoire of swear-words.

Pete retorted in kind, imperatively informing Jake that he knew where he could go, and walked away. Pete recognized the full meaning of Jake's words; and a half hour later he was knocking on Tom's door. He found a tall, raw-boned man sitting in one of Tom's chairs. Maggie had gone to bed.

" Shake hands with Mr. Petersen, Pete," said Tom sleepily. " He's just come into the union."

" Glad to know you," said Pete, and offered a hand to the Swede, who took it without a word. He turned immediately about on Tom. " I guess you're in for your thumps, Tom." And he told about his meeting with the five members of the entertainment committee.

" I expected 'em before the election. Well, I'll be ready for 'em," Tom said grimly.

A light had begun to glow in Petersen's heavy eyes as Pete talked. He now spoke for the first time since Pete had come in. " Vot day do? " he asked.

Pete explained in pantomine, thrusting rapid fists close to various parts of Petersen's face. " About five men on you at once."

Petersen grunted.

When Pete left, the Swede remained in his chair with anxiety showing through his natural stolidity. Tom gave a helpless glance at him, and followed Pete out into the hall.

" For God's sake, Pete, help me out! " Tom said in a whisper. " He's the fellow I helped get into the union. I told you about him, you know. He came around to-night to tell me he's got a job. When I came in at half past ten he'd been here half an hour already. It's eleven-thirty now. And he ain't said ten words. I want to go to bed, but confound him, he don't know how to leave! "

Pete opened the door. " Say, Petersen, ain't you goin' my way? Come on, we'll go together."

Petersen rose with obvious relief. He shook hands with Tom in awkward silence, and together he and Pete went down the stairs.

Monday morning Tom bought the first revolver he had ever possessed. If he had had any doubt as to the correctness of Pete's news, that doubt would not have been long with him. During the morning, as he went about looking for a job, he twice caught a glimpse of three members of the entertainment committee watching him from the distance; and he knew they were waiting a safe chance to close in upon him. The revolver in his inner vest pocket pressed a welcome assurance against his ribs.

That night when he came down from dinner to carry his new plan from ear to ear, he found Petersen, hands in his overcoat pockets, standing patiently without the doorway of the tenement.

" Hello, Petersen," he said in surprise.

" Hello," said Petersen.

Tom wanted no repetition of his experience of Saturday night. " Got a lot of work to do to-night," he said hurriedly. " So-long."

He started away. The Swede, with no further words, fell into step beside him. For several blocks they walked in silence, then Tom came to a pause before a tenement in which lived a member of the union.

" Good-by, Petersen," he said.

" Goo'-by," said Petersen.

They shook hands.

When Tom came into the street ten minutes later there was Petersen standing just where he had left him. Again the Swede fell into step. Tom, though embarrassed and irritated by the man's silent, persistent company, held back his words.

At the second stop Tom said shortly: " I'll be here a long while. You needn't wait."

But when he came down from the call, which he had purposely extended, Petersen was waiting beside the steps. This was too much for Tom. " Where are you going? " he demanded.

" 'Long you," the Swede answered slowly.

" I don't know's I need you," Tom returned shortly, and started away.

For half a dozen paces there was no sound but his own heel-clicks. Then he heard the heel-clicks of the Swede. He turned about in exasperation. " See here! What's your idea in following me around like this? "

Petersen shifted his feet uncomfortably. " De man, last night, he say——" He finished by placing his bony fists successively on either side of his jaw. " I tank maybe I be 'long, I be some good."

A light broke in on Tom. And he thought of the photograph on Petersen's leprous wall. He shoved out his hand. " Put it there, Petersen! " he said.

And all that evening Tom's silent companion marched through the streets beside him.

Chapter XV

MR. BAXTER HAS A FEW CONFERENCES

CAPTAINS of war have it as a common practice to secure information, in such secret ways as they can, about their opponents' plans and movements, and to develop their own plans to match these; and this practice has come into usage among captains of industry. The same afternoon that Jake brought news of Tom's scheme to Foley, a man of furtive glance whom a member of the union would have recognized as Johnson requested the youth in the outer office of Baxter & Co. to carry his name to the head of the firm.

"Wha' d'youse want to see him 'bout?" demanded the uniform.

"A job."

"No good. He don't hire nobody but the foremen."

"It's a foreman's job I'm after," returned Johnson, glancing about.

The debate continued, but in the end Johnson's name went in to Mr. Baxter, and Johnson himself soon followed it. When he came out Mr. Baxter's information was as complete as Buck Foley's.

That evening Johnson's news came into the conversation of Mr. Baxter and his wife. After dinner she drew him into the library—a real library, booked to the ceiling on three sides, an open wood fire on the other—to tell him of a talk she had had that day with chance-met Ruth. With an aunt's privilege she had asked about the state of affairs between her and Mr. Berman.

"There's no telling what she's going to do," Mrs. Baxter went on, with a gentle sigh. "I do hope she'll marry him! People are still talking about her strange behavior in leaving us to go to work. How I did try to persuade her not to do it! I knew it would involve us in a scandal. And the idea of her offering to go to work in your office!"

Mr. Baxter continued to look abstractedly into the grate, as he had looked ever since she had begun her half-reminiscent strain. Now that she was ended, she could but note that his mind was elsewhere.

"James!"

"Yes." He turned to her with a start.

"Why, you have not spoken a word to me. Is there something on your mind?"

He studied the flames for a moment. "I learned this afternoon that the Iron Workers' Union will probably demand a ten per cent. increase in wages."

"What! And that means a strike?"

"It doubtless does, unless we grant their demand."

"But can you afford to?"

"We could without actually running at a loss."

Mrs. Baxter was on the board of patronesses of one or two workingwomen's clubs and was a contributor to several fashionable charities, so considered herself genuinely thoughtful of the interests of wage-earners. "If you won't lose anything, I suppose you might as well increase their salaries. Most of them can use a little more money. They're respectable people who appreciate everything we do for them. And you can make it up by charging higher prices."

Mr. Baxter sat silent for a space looking at his wife, quizzically, admiringly. He was inclined to scoff in his heart at his wife's philanthropic hobbies, but he indulged her in them as he did in all her efforts to attain fashionable standing. He had said, lover fashion, in their courtship days, that she should never have an ungratified wish, and after a score of years he still held warmly to this promise. He still admired her; and little wonder, for sitting with her feet stretched toward the open fire, her blonde head gracefully in one hand, her brown eyes fixed waitingly on him, looking at least eight less than her forty-three years, she was absolutely beautiful.

"Elizabeth," he said at length, "do you know how much we spent last year?"

"No."

"About ninety-three thousand dollars."

"So much as that? But really, it isn't such a big sum. A mere nothing to what some of our friends spend."

"This year, with our Newport house, it 'll be a good thirty thousand more; one hundred and twenty-five thousand, anyway. Now I can't make the owners pay the raise, as you seem to think." He smiled slightly at her business naïveté. "The estimates on the work I'll do this year were all made on the present scale, and I can't raise the estimates. If the ten per cent. increase is granted, it 'll have to come out of our income. Our income will be cut down for this year to at least seventy-five thousand. If things go bad, to fifty thousand."

Mrs. Baxter rose excitedly to her feet. "Why, that's absurd!"

"We'd have to give up the Newport house," he went on, "put the yacht out of commission and lessen expenses here."

She looked at her husband in consternation. After several years of effort Mrs. Baxter was just getting into the outer edge of the upper crust of New York society. At her husband's words she saw all that she had striven for, and which of late had seemed near of attainment, withdraw into the shadowy recesses of an uncertain future.

"But we can't cut down!" she cried desperately. "We simply can't! We couldn't entertain here in the manner we have planned. And we'd have to go to Atlantic City this summer, or some other such place!—and who goes to Atlantic City? Why, we'd lose everything we've gained! We can never give the raise, James. It's simply out of the question!"

"And we won't," said Mr. Baxter, gently tapping a forefinger upon the beautifully carved arm of his chair.

"Anyhow, suppose we do spend a hundred and twenty-five thousand, why the working people get everything back in wages," she added ingeniously.

Mr. Baxter realized the economic fallacy of this last statement; but he refrained from exposing her sophistry since her conscience found satisfaction in it.

Monday morning, in discharge of his duty as president of the Iron Employers' Association, Mr. Baxter got Murphy, Bobbs, Isaacs, and Driscoll, the other four members of the Executive Committee, on the telephone. At eleven o'clock the five men were sitting around Mr. Baxter's cherry table. Bobbs, Murphy, and Isaacs already had knowledge of Tom's plans; Mr. Baxter was not the only one having unionists on his payroll who performed services other than handling beams and hammering rivets. Mr. Driscoll alone was surprised when Mr. Baxter stated the object of calling the committee thus hastily together.

" Why, I thought we'd been assured the old schedule would be continued! " he said.

" So Mr. Foley gave us to understand," answered Mr. Baxter. " But it's another man, a man named Keating, that's stirring this up."

" Keating! " Mr. Driscoll's lips pouted hugely, and his round eyes snapped. For a man to whom he had taken a genuine liking to be stirring up a fight against his interest was in the nature of a personal affront to him.

" I think I know him," said Mr. Murphy. " He ain't such a much! "

" That shows you don't know him! " said Mr. Driscoll sharply. " Well, if there is a strike, we'll at least have the satisfaction of fighting with an honest man."

" That satisfaction, of course," admitted Mr. Baxter, in his soft, rounded voice. " But what shall be our plan? It is certainly the part of wisdom for us to decide upon our attitude, and our course, in advance."

"Fight 'em!" said Mr. Driscoll.

"What is the opinion of you other gentlemen?"

"They don't deserve an increase, so I'm against it," said Mr. Bobbs. Had he spoken his thought his answer would have been: "It 'll half ruin me if we give the increase. Fact is, I've gone in pretty heavy in some real estate lately. If my profits are cut down, I can't meet my payments."

"Same as Driscoll," said Mr. Murphy, a blowzed, hairy man, a Tammany member of the Board of Aldermen. He swore at the union. "Why, they're already gettin' twice what they're worth!"

Mr. Baxter raised his eyebrows the least trifle at Mr. Murphy's profanity. "Mr. Isaacs."

"I don't see how we can pay more. And yet if we're tied up by a strike for two or three months we'll lose more than the increase of wages would come to."

Mr. Baxter answered the doubtful Mr. Isaacs in his smooth, even tones. "You seem to forget, Mr. Isaacs, that if we grant this without a fight, there'll be another demand next spring, and another the year after. We're compelled to make a stand now if we would keep wages within reasonable bounds."

"Yes, I suppose so," agreed Mr. Isaacs.

"Besides, if there is a strike it is not at all likely that it will last any time," Mr. Baxter continued. "We should break the strike easily, with a division in the union, as of course you see there is,—this Mr. Keating on one side, Mr. Foley on the other. I've met Mr. Keating. I dare say he's honest enough, as Mr. Driscoll says. But he is inexperienced, and I am sure we can easily outgeneral him."

" Beat 'em easy, an' needn't spit on our hands to do it neither," said Mr. Murphy. He started to swing one foot upon the cherry table, but catching Mr. Baxter's eye he checked the leg in mid-career.

Straightway the five plunged into an excited discussion of the chance of beating the strike, of plans for fighting it, and of preparation that should be made in anticipation of it.

When they had gone Mr. Baxter sat down to his desk and began writing a note. He had listened to the talk of the four, to him mere chatter, with outward courtesy and inward chafing, not caring to mention to them the plan upon which he had already decided. His first impulse had been to fight the union, and fight it hard. He hated trade unionism for its arrogation of powers that he regarded as the natural right of the employer; it was his right, as the owner of a great business, and as the possessor of a superior intelligence, to run his affairs as he saw fit—to employ men on his own terms, work them such hours and under such conditions as he should decide—terms, hours, and conditions, of course, to be as good as he could afford. But his business training, his wholly natural instinct for gain, and later his large family expenses, had fixed upon him the profitable habit of seeking the line of least resistance. And so, succeeding this first hot impulse, was a desire that the strike be avoided—if that were possible.

His first thought had been of Foley. But the fewer his meetings with the walking delegate of the iron workers, the more pleased was he. Then came the second thought that it was better to deal directly with the threatening cause—and so the letter he now wrote was to Tom Keating.

The letter was delivered Tuesday morning before Tom left home. He read it in wonderment, for to him any letter was an event:

"Will you please call at my office as soon as you can find it convenient. I have something to say that I think will interest you."

Guessing wildly as to what this something might be, Tom presented himself at ten o'clock in the outer office of Baxter & Co. The uniform respectfully told him that Mr. Baxter would not be in before twelve. At twelve Tom was back. Yes, Mr. Baxter was in, said the uniform, and hurried away with Tom's name. Again there was a wait before the boy came back, and again a wait in a sheeny chair before Mr. Baxter looked up.

"Oh, Mr. Keating," he said. "I see you got my letter."

"Yes. This morning."

Mr. Baxter did not lose a second. "What I wanted to see you about is this: I understand that some time ago you were inquiring here for a position. It happens that I have a place just now that I'm desirous of filling with an absolutely trustworthy man. Mr. Driscoll spoke very highly to me of you, so I've sent for you."

This offer came to Tom as a surprise. His uppermost guess as to the reason for his being summoned had been that Mr. Baxter, repenting of his late non-participation, now wished to join in the fight against Foley. Under other circumstances Tom would have accepted the position, said nothing, and held the job as long as he could. But the fact that the offer was coming to him freely and in good faith prompted him to say: "You must know, Mr. Baxter, that if you give me a job Foley 'll make trouble for you."

"I have no fear of Mr. Foley's interference," Mr. Baxter answered him quietly.

"You haven't!" Tom leaned forward in sudden admiration. "You're the first boss I've struck yet that's not afraid of Foley! He's got 'em all scared stiff. If you'd come out against him——"

Tom would have said more but Mr. Baxter's cold reserve, not a change of feature, chilled his enthusiasm. He drew up in his chair. "What's the job?"

"Foreman. The salary is forty a week."

Tom's heart beat exultantly—and he had a momentary triumph over Maggie. "I'll take it," he said.

"Can you begin at once?"

"Yes."

"Very well. Then I'll want you to leave to-morrow."

Tom started. "Leave?"

"Yes. Didn't I mention that the job is in Chicago?"

Mr. Baxter watched Tom closely out of his steely gray eyes. He saw the flush die out of Tom's face, saw Tom's clasped hands suddenly tighten—and knew his answer before he spoke.

" I can't do it," he said with an effort. " I can't leave New York."

Mr. Baxter studied Tom's face an instant longer . . . But it was too honest.

He turned toward his desk with a gentle abruptness. " I am very sorry, Mr. Keating. Good-day."

With Mr. Baxter there was small space between actions. He had already decided upon his course in case this plan should fail. Tom was scarcely out of his office before he was writing a note to Buck Foley.

Foley sauntered in the next morning, hands in overcoat pockets, a cigar in one corner of his mouth. " What's this I hear about a strike? " Mr. Baxter asked, as soon as the walking delegate was seated.

" Don't youse waste none o' the thinks in your brain-box on no strike," returned Foley. He had early discovered Mr. Baxter's dislike of uncouth expressions.

" But there's a great deal of serious talk."

" There's always wind comin' out o' men's mouths."

Mr. Baxter showed not a trace of the irritation he felt.

" Is there going to be a strike? "

" Not if I know myself. And I think I do." He blew out a great cloud of smoke.

" But one of your men—a Mr. Keating—is stirring one up."

"He thinks he is," Foley corrected. "But he's got another think comin'. He's a fellow youse ought to know, Baxter. Nice an' cultivated; God-fearin' an' otherwise harmless."

Mr. Baxter's face tightened. "I know, Mr. Foley, that this situation is much more serious than you pretend," he said sharply.

Foley tilted back in his chair. "If youse seen a lion comin' at youse with a yard or so of open mouth youse'd think things was gettin' a little serious. But if youse knew the lion 'd never make its last jump, youse wouldn't go into the occupation o' throwin' fits, now would youse?"

"What do you mean?"

"Nothin'. Only there'll be no last jump for Keating."

"How's that?"

"How? That's my business." He stood up, relit his cigar, striking the match on the sole of his shoe. "Results is what youse's after. The how belongs to me."

At the door he paused, half closed one eye, and slowly blew forth the smoke of his cigar. "Now don't get brain-fag," he said.

Chapter XVI

BLOWS

IT was about half past twelve when Tom left Mr. Baxter's office. As he came purposeless into the street it occurred to him that he was but a few blocks from the office of Mr. Driscoll, and in the same instant his chance meeting with Ruth three weeks before as she came out to lunch flashed across his memory. He turned his steps in the direction of Mr. Driscoll's office, and on gaining the block it was in walked slowly back and forth on the opposite side of the street, eagerly watching the revolving door of the great building. At length she appeared. Tom started quickly toward her. Another quarter revolution of the door and a man was discharged at her side. The man was Mr. Berman; and they walked off together, he turning upon her glances whose meaning Tom's quickened instinct divined at once.

The sight of these two together, Mr. Berman's eyes upon her with an unmistakable look, struck him through with jagged pain. He was as a man whose sealed vision an oculist's knife has just released. Amid startled anguish his eyes suddenly opened to things he, in his blindness, had never guessed. He saw what she had come to mean to him. This was so great that, at first, it well-nigh obscured all else. She filled him,—her sympathy, her intelligence, her high womanliness. And she, she that filled him, was . . . only a great pain.

And then (he had mechanically followed them, and now stood watching the door within which they had disppeared—the door through which he had gone with her three weeks before) he saw, his pain writhing within him the while, the double hopelessness of his love: she was educated, cultured—she could care nothing for a mere workman; and even if she could care, he was bound.

And then (he was now moving slowly through the Broadway crowd, scarcely conscious of it) he saw how poor he was in his loveless married life. Since his first liking for Maggie had run its so brief course, he had lapsed by such slow degrees to his present relations with her that he had been hardly more conscious of his life's lacking than if he had been living with an unsympathetic sister. But now that a real love had discovered itself to him, with the suddenness of lightning that rips open the night, he saw, almost gaspingly, how glorious life with love could be; and, by contrast, he saw how sordid and commonplace his own life was; and he saw this life without love stretching away its flat monotony, year after year.

And there were things he did not see, for he had not been made aware by the unwritten laws prevailing in a more self-conscious social stratum. And one of these things was, he did not see that perhaps in his social ignorance he had done Ruth some great injury.

That night Maggie kept his dinner warm on the

back of the kitchen range, to no purpose; and that
night Petersen waited vainly on the tenement steps.
It was after twelve when Tom came into the flat,
his face drawn, his heart chilled. He had seen his
course vaguely almost from the first moment of his
vision's release; he had seen it clearer and more
clear as hour after hour of walking had passed; and
he felt himself strong enough to hold to that course.

The next morning at breakfast he was gentler
with Maggie than he had been in many a day; so that
once, when she had gone into the kitchen to refill her
coffee cup, she looked in at him for a moment in a
kind of resentful surprise. Not being accustomed to
peering inward upon the workings of his soul, Tom
himself understood this slight change in his attitude
no better than did his wife. He did not realize that
the coming of the knowledge of love, and the coming
of sorrow, were together beginning to soften and
refine his nature.

The work Tom had marked out for himself permitted him little time to brood over his new unhap-
piness. After breakfast he set out once more upon
his twofold purpose: to find a job, if one could be
found; to talk strike to as many members of the
union as he could see. In seeking work he was
limited to such occupations as had not yet been union-
ized. He walked along the docks, thinking to find
something to do as a longshoreman, but the work
was heavy and irregular, the hours long, the pay
small; and he left the river front without asking for
employment. He looked at the men in the tunnel of
the underground railway; but he could not bring him-

self to ask employment among the low-waged Italians he saw there. He did go into three big stores and make blind requests for anything, but at none was there work for him.

As he went about Tom visited the jobs near which he passed, on which members of his union were at work. One of these was a small residence hotel just west of Fifth Avenue, whose walls were up, but which was as yet unfinished on the inside. He climbed to the top in search of members employed on the iron stairways and the elevator shafts, but did not find a man. He reached the bottom of the stairway just in time to see three men enter the doorway. One of the three he recognized as Jake Henderson, and he knew the entertainment committee had him cornered. He grimly changed his revolver from his vest pocket to his left coat pocket, and filling his right coat pocket from a heap of sand beside him, quietly awaited their coming.

The three paused a moment inside the door, evidently to accustom their eyes to the half darkness, for all the windows were boarded up. At length they sighted him, standing before the servants' staircase in the further corner. They came cautiously across the great room, as yet unpartitioned, Jake slightly in the lead. At ten paces away they came to a halt.

" I guess we got youse good an' proper at last," said Jake gloatingly. " It won't do youse no good to yell. We'll give youse all the more if youse do. An' we can give it to youse, anyhow, before the men can get down."

Tom did not answer. He had no mind to cry for help. He stood alertly watching them, his hands in his coat pockets.

Jake laid off his hat and coat—there was leisure, and it enlarged his pleasure to take his time—and moved forward in advance of his two companions.

"Good-by," he said leering. He was on the point of lunging at his victim, when Tom's right hand came out and a fistful of sand went stinging full into his face. He gave a cry, but before he could so much as make a move to brush away the sand Tom's fist caught him on the ear. He dropped limply.

The two men sprang forward, to be met in the face by Tom's revolver.

"If you fellows want button-holes put into you, just move another step!" he said.

They took another step, several of them—but backward steps. Tom kept them covered for a minute, then moved toward the light, walking backward, his eyes never leaving them. On gaining the door he slipped the revolver into his vest pocket and stepped quickly into the blinding street.

When Tom, entering the union hall that evening, passed Jake at his place at the door, the latter scowled fiercely, but the presence of several of Tom's friends, who had been acquainted with the afternoon's encounter, pacified his fists.

"Why, what's the matter with your eyes, Jake?" asked Pig Iron Pete sympathetically.

Jake consigned Pete to the usual place, and whispered in Tom's ear: "Youse just wait! I'll git youse yet!"

That night Tom sat his first time in the president's chair. His situation was painfully grotesque,—instead of being the result of the chances of election, it might well have been an ironic jest of Foley: there was Connelly, two tables away, at his right; Brown, the vice-president, at the table next him; Snyder, the corresponding secretary, at his left; Jake Henderson, sergeant-at-arms, at the door;—every man of them an intimate friend of Foley. And it was not long before Tom felt the farce-tragedy of his position. Shortly after he rapped the meeting to order a man in the rear of the hall became persistently obstreperous. After two censured outbreaks he rose unsteadily amid the discussion upon a motion. "I objec'," he said.

"What's your objection?" Tom asked, repressing his wrath.

The man swore. "Ain't it 'nough I objec'!"

"If the member is out of order again he'll have to leave the hall." Tom guessed this to be a scheme of Foley to annoy him.

"Put me out, you——" And the man offered some remarks upon Tom's character.

Tom pounded the table with his gavel. "Sergeant-at-arms, put that man out!"

Jake, who stood at the door whispering to a man, did not even turn about.

"Sergeant-at-arms!"

Jake went on with his conversation.

"Sergeant-at-arms!" thundered Tom, springing to his feet.

Jake looked slowly around.

" Put that man out! " Tom ordered.

" Can't youse see I'm busy? " said Jake; and turned his broad back.

Several of Tom's friends sprang up, but all in the room waited to see what he would do. For a moment he stood motionless, a statue of controlled fury, and for that moment there was stillness in the hall. Then he tossed the gavel upon the table and strode down the center aisle. He seized the offending member, who was in an end seat, one hand on his collar and one on his wrist. The man struck out, but a fierce turn of his wrist brought from him a submissive cry of pain. Tom pushed him, swearing, toward the door. No one offered interference, and his ejection was easy, for he was small and half drunken.

Tom strode back to his table, brought the gavel down with a blow that broke its handle and looked about with blazing eyes. Again the union waited his action in suspense. His chest heaved; he swallowed mightily. Then he asked steadily: " Are you ready for the question? "

This is but one sample of the many annoyances Tom suffered during the meeting, and of the annoyances he was to suffer for many meetings to come. A man less obstinately strong would have yielded his resignation within an hour—to force which was half the purpose of the harassment; and a man more violent would have broken into a fury of words, which, answering the other half of the purpose, would have been to Foley's crew what the tirade of a beggar is to teasing schoolboys.

When "new business" was reached Tom yielded the chair to Brown, the vice-president, and rose to make the protest on which he had determined. He had no great hope of winning the union to the action he desired; but it had become a part of his nature never to give up and to try every chance.

The union knew what was coming. There were cheers and hisses, but Tom stood waiting minute after minute till both had died away. "Mr. Chairman, I move we set aside last week's election of walking delegate," he began, and went on to make his charges against Foley. Cries of "Good boy, Tom!" "Right there!" came from his friends, and various and variously decorated synonyms for liar came from Foley's crowd; but Tom, raising his voice to a shout, spoke without pause through the cries of friends and foes.

When he ended half the crowd was on foot demanding the right to the floor. Brown dutifully recognized Foley.

Foley did not speak from where he stood in the front row, but sauntered angularly, hands in trousers pockets, to the platform and mounted it. With a couple of kicks he sent a chair from its place against the wall to the platform's edge, leisurely swung his right foot upon the chair's seat, rested his right elbow upon his knee, and with cigar in the left corner of his mouth, and his side to his audience, he began to speak.

"When I was a kid about as big as a rivet I used to play marbles for keeps," he drawled, looking at the side wall. "When I won, I didn't make no kick.

When I lost, a deaf man could 'a' heard me a mile. I said the other kid didn't play fair, an' I went cryin' around to make him give 'em up."

He paused to puff at his cigar. " Our honorable president, it seems he's still a kid. Me an' him played a little game o' marbles last week. He lost. An' now he's been givin' youse the earache. It's the same old holler. He says I didn't play fair. He says I tried to stuff the box at the start. But that was just a game on his part, as I said then, to throw suspicion on me; an,' anyhow, no ballots got in. He says I stuffed it by a trick at the last. What's his proof? He says so. Convincin'—hey? Gents, if youse want to stop his bawlin', give him back his marbles. Turn me down, an' youse 'll have about what's comin' to youse—a cry baby sport."

He kicked his chair back against the wall and sat down; and amidst all the talk that followed he did not once rise or turn his face direct to the crowd. But when, finally, Brown said, " Everybody in favor of the motion stand up," Foley rose to his full height with his back against the wall, and his withheld gaze now struck upon the crowd with startling effect. It was a phenomenon of his close-set eyes that each man in a crowd thought them fixed upon himself. Upon every face that gaze seemed bent—lean, sarcastic, menacing.

" Everybody that likes a cry baby sport, stand up! " he shouted.

Men sprang up all over the hall, and stood so till the count was made.

" Those opposed," Brown called out.

A number equally great rose noisily. A glance showed Tom the motion was lost, since a two-thirds' vote was necessary to rescind an action. But as his hope had been small, his disappointment was now not great.

Foley's supporters broke into cheers when they saw their leader was safe, but Foley himself walked with up-tilted cigar back to his first seat in an indifferent silence.

Chapter XVII

THE ENTERTAINMENT COMMITTEE

DURING the three weeks that followed Tom kept busy day and night,—by day looking for work and talking to chance-met members, by night stirring the members to appear on the first Wednesday of April to vote for the demand for higher wages. He was much of the time dogged by part of the entertainment committee, but he had become watchful, and the knowledge that he was armed made them wary, so day after day passed without another conflict. At first his committee's delay in the discharge of their duty stirred Foley's wrath. " Youse 're as slow as fat angels! " he informed them in disgust. Later the delay stirred his anxiety, and he raised his offer from twenty-five dollars a man to one hundred.

Every night Tom was met at his street door by Petersen and left there by him a few hours later. His frequent appearance with Tom brought Petersen into some prominence; and he was promptly nick-named " Babe " by a facetious member who had been struck by his size, and " Rosie " by a man who saw only his awkwardness. Both names stuck. His relation to Tom had a more unpleasant result: it made the story of his discomfiture by a man of half his size, while on the fire-house job, decidedly worth the telling; and so it rapidly came into general circulation, and the sight of Petersen was the signal for jeers, even among Tom's own friends. Petersen flushed at the taunts, but bore them dumbly and kept his arms at his side.

All this while Ruth was much in Tom's mind. Had it not been that he kept himself busy he could have done little else but think of her. As it was, he lay awake long hours at night, very quietly that he might not rouse his wife, in wide-eyed dreams of her; and several times by day he caught himself out of thoughts of her to find himself in a street far out of his way. And once, in the evening, he had puzzled the faithful Petersen by walking back and forth through an uptown block and gazing at a house in which no member of the Iron Workers' Union could possibly be living. But he held firmly to the course he had recognized as his only course.

For three weeks he maintained his determination, against desire scarcely less strong than his strength, till the evening of the first Tuesday of April, the night before the vote upon the strike. Then, either he was weaker, or desire was stronger. He was overwhelmed. His resolve to keep away from her, his intention to spend this last evening in work, were nothing before his wish to see her again. He was fairly swept up to her door, not heeding Petersen, and not giving a thought to Jake, whom he glimpsed once in the street car behind when a brief blockade let it gain the tail of his own.

"You needn't wait for me," he said mechanically to Petersen as he rang the bell. Again the maid

brought back word for him to come up. This time
Ruth was not waiting him at the head of the stairs.
He stood before her door a moment, with burning
brain, striving for mastery over himself, before he
could knock. She called to him to enter, and he
found her leaning against her little case of books,
unusually pale, but with eyes brighter than he had
ever seen them.

She took a step toward him, and held out her
hand. " I'm so glad you called, Mr. Keating."

Tom, for his part, could make no answer; his
throat had suddenly gone cracking dry. He took her
hand; his grip was as loose as an unconscious man's.

As was the first minute, so were the two hours that
followed. In answer to her questions he told her
of his new plans, without a vestige of enthusiasm;
and presently, to save the situation, she began to
talk volubly about nothing at all. They were hours
of mutual constraint. Tom hardly had knowledge
of what he said, and he hardly heard her words.
His very nearness to her made more ruthlessly clear
the wideness that lay between them. He felt with
its first keenness the utter hopelessness of his love.
Every moment that he sat with his hot eyes upon her
he realized that he should forthwith go. But still
he sat on in a silence of blissful agony.

At length there came an interruption—a knock at
the door. Ruth answered it, and when she turned
about she held out an envelope to Tom. " A letter
for you," she said, with a faint show of surprise.
" A messenger brought it."

Tom tore it open, looking first to the signature.

It was from Pete. " I have got a bunch of the fellows in the hall over the saloon at — Third Avenue," read the awkward scramble of words. " On the third floor. Can't you come in and help me with the spieling? "

At another time Tom might have wondered at this note: how Pete had come to be in a hall with a crowd of men, how Pete had learned where he was. But now the note did not raise a doubt in his fevered brain.

He folded the note, and put it into a pocket. " I've got some work to do yet to-night," he explained, and he took up his hat. It was an unusually warm evening for the first of April and he had worn no overcoat.

" You must come again soon," she said a few moments later, as he was leaving. Tom had nothing to say; he could not tell her the truth—that he expected never to see her again. And so he left her, awkwardly, without parting word of any kind. At the foot of the stairs he paused and looked up at her door, at the head of the first flight, and he looked for a long, long space before he stepped forth into the night.

A little round man stood bareheaded on the stoop; Petersen was pacing slowly to and fro on the sidewalk. The little man seized Tom by the arm. " Won't you send a policeman, please," he asked excitedly, in an inconsequential voice, such as belongs properly to the husband of a boarding-house mistress.

" What for? "

"That man there has been walking just so, back and forth, for the last two hours. From the way he keeps looking up at the house it is certain he is contemplating some nefarious act of burglary."

"I'll do better than send a cop," said Tom. "I'll take him away myself."

He went down the steps, took Petersen's arm and started off with him. "Thank you exceedingly, sir!" called out the little man.

They took an Eighty-sixth Street cross-town car to Third Avenue, and after five minutes' riding southward Tom, keeping watch from the end of the car, spied a number near to the one for which he was searching. They got out and easily found the place designated in Pete's note. It was that great rarity, a saloon in the middle of a New York block. The windows of the second floor were dark; a soft glow came through those of the floor above.

With the rattle of the elevated trains in their ears Tom and Petersen entered the hallway which ran alongside the saloon, and mounted two flights of stairs so dark that, at the top of the second, Tom had to grope for the door. This discovered, he opened it and found himself at the rear of the hall. This was a barren, dingy room, perhaps forty feet long, with double curtains of some figured cloth at the three front windows. Four men sat at the front end of the room playing cards; there were glasses and beer bottles on the table, and the men were smoking.

All this Tom saw within the time of the snapping of an instantaneous shutter; and he recognized, with the same swiftness, that he had been trapped. But before he could shift a foot to retreat, a terrific shove from behind the door sent him staggering against the side wall. The door was slammed shut by the same force, grazing Petersen as he sprang in. The bolt of the lock clicked into place.

"We've got youse this time!" Tom heard a harsh voice cry out, and on the other side of Petersen, who stood on guard with clenched fists, he saw Jake Henderson, a heavy stick in his right hand.

In the same instant the men at the table had sprung to their feet. "Why, if it ain't Rosie!" cried Kaffir Bill, advancing at the head of the quartette.

"Say, fellows, tie my two hands behind me, so's me an' Rosie can have an even fight," requested Arkansas Number Two.

"If youse want Rosie to fight, youse 've got to tie his feet together," said Smoky; and this happy reference to the time Petersen ran away brought a laugh from the three others.

Tom, recovering from his momentary dizziness, drew his revolver and levelled it at the four. "The first man that moves gets the first bullet."

The men suddenly checked their steps.

For an instant the seven made a tableau. Then Petersen sprang in at Jake. A blow from the club on his left shoulder stopped him. Again he sprang in, this time breaking through Jake's guard, but only to grasp Jake's left arm with his half-numbed left hand. This gave Jake his chance. His right hand swung backward with the club, his eyes on Tom.

"Look out!" cried Petersen.

Tom, guessing danger in the warning, pulled the trigger. With a cry Hickey dropped to the floor, a bullet in his leg. In the very flash of the revolver the whizzing club sent the weapon flying from Tom's hand. Tom made a rush after the pistol, and Jake, breaking from Petersen's grip, made a plunge on the same errand. Both outstretched hands closed upon it, and the two men went sprawling to the floor in a struggle for its possession.

Petersen faced quickly about upon the men whom Tom's revolver had made hesitant. Hickey lay groaning and swearing, a little pool of blood beginning to form on the bare floor. The other three, in their lust for their reward now so nearly won, gave Hickey hardly a glance, but advanced upon Petersen with the confidence that comes of being three to one and of knowing that one to be a coward. Petersen slipped off his coat, threw it together with his derby hat upon the floor near the wall, and with swelling nostrils quietly awaited their onslaught.

Arkansas stepped forth from his fellows. "Where'll I hit you first, Rosie? Glad to give you your pref'rence." And he spat into the V of Petersen's vest.

That was the last conscious moment of Arkansas for an hour. Petersen took a step forward, his long arm shot out, and Arkansas went to the floor all a-huddle.

Tom's eyes, glancing an instant from his own adversary, saw the " Swedish Terror " of the photograph: left foot advanced, fists on guard, body low-crouched. " Come on! " Petersen said, with a joyous snarl, to the two men who had fallen back a step. "Come on. I vant you bod!"

Kaffir Bill looked hesitantly upon his companion. "It was only a lucky lick, Smoky; Arkansas wasn't lookin'," he explained doubtfully.

"Yes," said the other.

"Sure. It couldn't 'a' been nothin' else. Why, Kid Morgan done him up."

"Come on then!" cried Smoky.

Together they made a rush, Bill a step in advance. Petersen's right landed over Bill's heart. Bill went tottering backward and to the floor. Smoky shot in and clinched; but after Petersen's fists, like alternating hammers, had played a terrific tattoo against his two cheeks, he loosed his hold and staggered away with his arms about his ears. Bill rose dizzily to his feet, and the pair leaned against the further wall, whispering and watching Petersen with glowering irresolution.

"Come on, bod! Come on vid you!" Petersen shouted, his fists moving back and forth in invitation, his indrawn breath snoring exultantly.

Jake let out an oath. "Get into him!" he said.

"Yah! Come on vid you!"

They conferred a moment longer, and then crept forward warily. Hickey stopped his groaning and rose to his elbows to watch the second round. At five feet away the two paused. Then suddenly Smoky made a feint, keeping out of reach of the Swede's swinging return, and under cover of this Kaffir Bill ducked and lunged at Petersen's legs.

Petersen went floundering to the floor, and

Smoky hurled himself upon his chest. The three became a whirling, tumbling tangle,—arms striking out, legs kicking,—Petersen now in under, now half free, striking and hugging with long-untasted joy, breathing fierce grunts and strange ejaculations. The two had thought, once off his feet, the Swede would be an easy conquest. But Petersen had been a mighty rough-and-tumble scrapper before he had gone into the prize ring, and for a few tumultuous moments the astounded twain had all they could do to hold their own.

"Slug him, can't youse!" gasped Bill, who was looking after Petersen's lower half, to Smoky, who was looking after the upper.

Smoky likewise saw that only a blow in the right place could give them victory over this heaving force. So far it had taken his best to hold these long arms. But he now loosed his hug to get in the victorious blow. Before he could strike, Petersen's fist jammed him in the face.

"Ya-a-h!" grunted the Swede.

Smoky fell instantly to his old position. "Hit him yourself!" he growled from Petersen's shirt front.

Bill, not having seen what had happened to Smoky, released a leg so that he might put his fist into Petersen's stomach. The leg kicked his knee. Bill, with a shriek, frantically re-embraced the leg.

The two now saw they could do no more than merely hold Petersen, and so the struggle settled to a stubborn equilibrium.

In the meantime the strife between Tom and Jake

had been like that of two bulls which stand braced, with locked horns. Jake's right hand had gained possession of the revolver, having at first had the better hold on it; Tom had a fierce grip on his forearm. The whole effort of one was to put the weapon into use; the whole effort of the other was to prevent its use, and perhaps to seize it for himself. Neither dared strike lest the act give the other his chance.

When he saw nothing was coming of the struggle between Bill and Smoky and Petersen, a glimpse of the wounded man, raised on his elbows, gave Jake an idea. With a jerk of his wrist he managed to toss the revolver a couple of feet away, beyond his own and Tom's reach.

"Hickey!" he called out. "Get it!"

The wounded man moved toward them, half crawling, half dragging himself. A vengeful look came into his eyes. Tom needed no one to tell him what would happen when the man he had shot laid hand upon his weapon. Hickey drew nearer and nearer, his bloody trouser leg leaving a moist trail on the bare floor. His head reached their feet—passed them—his right hand stretched out for the revolver. Tom saw his only chance. With a supreme effort he turned Jake, who in watching Hickey was momentarily off his guard, upon his back; and with all the strength of his leg he drove his foot into the crawling man's stomach. The man collapsed with a groaning outrush of breath.

Tom saw that the deadlock was likely to be ended, and the victory won, by the side gaining possession of the revolver; and he saw the danger to Petersen and himself that lay in the possibility of either of the unconscious men regaining his senses. Petersen's slow mind worked rapidly enough in a fight; he, too, saw the danger Tom had seen. Anything to be done must be done at once.

But a nearer danger presented itself. Jake strained his neck till his eyes were on the trio. " Can't one o' youse hold him? " he gasped. " T'other git the gun."

Smoky was on his back crosswise beneath Petersen's chest, his arms tight about Petersen's neck, clamping Petersen's hot cheek against his own. Kaffir Bill lay upon the Swede's legs, arms locked about them just below the hips. Bill was the freer to obey the order of the chief, and he began to slip his arms, still embracing the legs, slowly downward.

Certainly anything to be done must be done at once, for Petersen, lost to passion though he was, knew that in another moment Bill's arms would have slipped to his feet, and there would be a spring to be clear of his kick and a rush for the revolver. With a fierce grunt, he quickly placed his broad hands on either side of Smoky's chest and slowly strained upward. Bill, not knowing what this new move meant, immediately regripped Petersen's thighs. Slowly Petersen rose, lifting Smoky's stiffened body after him, cheek still tight against cheek, till his elbows locked. Then his hips gradually raised till part of his weight was on his knees. His back arched upward, and his whole body stiffened till it was like a bar of iron.

Suddenly his arms relaxed, and he drove downward, his weight and strength concentrated against Smoky's cheek. Smoky's head battered the floor. His arms loosened; a quick blow on the jaw made them fall limp. Petersen whirled madly over to dispose of Bill, but in the same tick of the watch Bill sprang away, and to his feet, and made a dash for the revolver. Instantly Petersen was up and but two paces behind him. Bill's lunging hand fell upon the weapon, Petersen's fist fell upon Bill, and the revolver was Petersen's.

When Jake saw Petersen come up with the pistol he took his arms from about Tom. " Youse 've got me done. I give in," he growled.

The two were rising when a wild voice sounded out hoarsely: " Come on! Come on now vid you! "

Tom, on his feet, turned toward Petersen. The Swede, left hand gripping the revolver about its barrel, stood in challenging attitude, his eyes blazing, saliva trickling from one corner of his mouth. " Yah! Come on! "

Tom recognized what he was seeing,—that wild Swedish rage that knows neither when it has beat nor when it is beaten; in this case all the less controllable from its long restraint.

Pete, Smoky, and Bill were now all on their feet and leaning against the wall. Petersen strode glaring before them, shaking his great fists madly. " Come on now! "

" Petersen! " Tom called.

" Come on vid you! I vant all dree! " The harsh voice rose into a shriek.

The three did not move. " For God's sake, Petersen! The fight's over! " Tom cried.

" Afraid! Yah! Afraid! I lick you all dree! "

With an animal-like roar he rushed at the three men. Smoky and Bill ducked and dashed away, but Jake stood his ground and put up his fists. A blow and he went to the floor. Petersen flung about to make for Smoky and Bill. Tom seized his arm.

" God, man! Stop! They've give in! "

" Look out! " A shove sent Tom staggering, and Petersen was away. " I lick 'em all, by God! " he roared.

With annihilating intent he bore down upon Bill and Smoky, who stood back to wall on fearful defense. An inspiration flashed upon Tom. " Your wife, Petersen! Your wife! " he cried.

Petersen's raging strides checked. He looked slowly about. " Vot? "

" Your wife! "

" Anna! . . . Anna! " Dazed, breathing heavily, he stared at Tom. Something like a convulsion went through him. His face faded to dullness, then to contrition.

" Better let me have the gun, " Tom said quietly, after a minute had passed.

Petersen handed it over.

" Now get your hat and coat, and we'll go. "

Without glancing at the three, who were staring at him in utter bewilderment, Petersen dully put on his hat and coat. A moment later he and Tom were backing toward the door. But before they reached it Tom's steady gaze became conscious of the curtains at the further end of the room. His square face tightened grimly with sudden purpose.

"Take down those curtains, Petersen," he said.

Petersen removed the six curtains, dusty and stained with tobacco juice, from their places and brought them to Tom.

"Tear five of 'em into two strips."

The three men, and Hickey from the floor, looked on curiously while Petersen obeyed.

"Tie Jake up first; hands behind his back," was Tom's next order.

"I'll see youse in hell first!" Jake backed away from Petersen and raised his fists.

"If you make any trouble, I'll give you a quick chance to look around there a bit!"

Jake gazed a moment at the revolver and the gleaming eye behind it, and his fists dropped. Petersen stepped behind him and went to work, twisting the strip of muslin into a rope as he wound it about Jake's wrists. The job was securely done in a minute, for Petersen had once followed the sea.

"Now his feet," said Tom; and to Jake: "It 'll be easier for you if you lay down."

Jake hesitated, then with an oath dropped to his knees and tumbled awkwardly on his side. In another minute Jake's feet were fastened; and at the end of ten minutes the other four men had been bound, even the wounded Hickey.

Tom put his revolver in his outside coat pocket, and unlocked the door. "Good-night," he said; and he and Petersen stepped out. He locked the door and put the key in his pocket.

" Police? " asked Petersen, when they had gained the street.

" No. That's what they ought to have. But when you've been a union man longer you'll know we boys don't ask the police to mix in our affairs. When there's a strike, they're always turned against us by the bosses. So we leave 'em alone."

They were but half a dozen squares from Mulligan's saloon. Tom set out in its direction, and five minutes later, with Petersen behind him, he walked into the doorway of the room beyond the bar. As he had expected, there sat Foley, and with him were three of his men. Foley started, and half rose from his chair, but settled back again. His discomposure confirmed what Tom had already guessed—that Foley's was the brain behind the evening's stratagem, and that he was awaiting his deputies' report.

" I guess you were expecting somebody else," Tom said grimly from the doorway, one hand on the revolver in his coat pocket. " I just dropped in to tell you Jake Henderson and his bunch are waiting for you up over Murphy's saloon."

Foley was dazed, as he could not help but be, thus learning his last plan had failed. " Youse saw 'em? "

" I did."

He looked Tom over. And then his eyes took in the figure of Petersen just within the doorway. He grasped instinctively at the chance to raise a laugh. " Was Rosie there? " he queried.

The three dutifully guffawed.

" Yes," said Tom. " Rosie was there."

Foley took a bracing hold of himself, and toyed with the stem of his beer glass. " Much obliged for comin' in to tell me," he said, with a show of carelessness. " But I guess the boys ain't in no hurry."

" No, I guess not," Tom agreed. " They said they'd wait till you came."

With that he tossed the key upon the table, turned and strode forth from the saloon. Outside he thrust a gripping arm through Petersen's, which straightway took on an embarrassed limpness, and walked away.

Chapter XVIII

THE STOLEN STRIKE

TOM mounted the stairs of Potomac Hall early the next evening. During the day he had told a few friends the story of the encounter of the night before. The story had spread in versions more or less vague and distorted, and now on his entry of the hall he was beset by a crowd who demanded a true and detailed account of the affair. This he gave.

"Oh, come now, Tom! This's hot air you're handin' us out about Babe!" expostulated one of the men.

"It's the truth."

"Get out! I saw Kid Morgan chase him a block. He can't fight."

"You think not? Well, there's one way you can convince yourself."

"How's that?"

"Try it with him for about a minute," answered Tom.

There was a laugh, in which the man joined. "I tell you what, boys," he said, after it had subsided. "I hit Babe on the back o' the neck with a glove the day Kid chased him. If what Tom says is straight, I'm goin' to beg Babe's pardon in open meetin'."

" Me, too," chimed in another.

" It's so," said Tom, thinking with a smile of what was in store for Petersen.

For some reason, perhaps one having to do with their personal pride, Jake and his fellows did not appear that night, though several hundred men waited their coming with impatient greetings. But just before Tom opened the session Petersen entered the hall and slipped into an obscure seat near the door.

He was immediately recognized. " Petersen! " someone announced. Straightway men arose all over the hall and turned about to face him. " Petersen! " " Petersen! " " What's the matter with Petersen! " the cries went up, and there was a great clapping of hands.

Petersen sprang to his feet in wild consternation. Yes, they were looking at him. Yes, that was his name. He didn't know what it meant——

But the next instant he had bolted out of the hall.

When the shouting had died away Tom called the union to order. He was filled with an exultant sense of certain triumph; he had kept an estimating eye on the members as they had filed in; an easy majority of the men were with him, and as their decision would be by open vote there would be no chance for Foley to stuff a ballot-box.

Pete, the instructed spokesman for Tom's party, was the first man on his feet. " Mr. President," he said, " I move we drop the reg'lar order o' business an' proceed at once to new business."

Tom put the motion to rising vote. His confidence grew as he looked about the hall, for the rising vote on the motion showed how strong his majority really was.

"Motion carried!" he shouted, and brought down his gavel.

The next instant a dozen men were on their feet waving their right hands and crying, "Mr. Chairman." One was Pete, ten were good-intentioned but uninformed friends, and one was Foley. Tom's eyes fastened upon Foley, and his mind worked quickly.

"Mr. Foley," he said.

A murmur of surprise ran among Tom's friends. But he had his reason for this slight deviation from his set plan. He knew that Foley was opposed to a strike; if he let Foley go on record against it in a public speech, then his coming victory over the walking delegate would be all the more decisive.

Foley looked slowly about upon the men, and for a moment did not speak. Then he said suddenly, in a conversational tone: "Boys, how much youse gettin'?"

"Three seventy-five," several voices answered.

"How long youse been gettin' it?"

"Two years."

"Yes," he said, his voice rising and ringing with intensity. "Two years youse 've been workin' for three seventy-five. The bosses' profits have been growin' bigger an' bigger. But not a cent's raise have youse had. Not a cent, boys! Now here's what I say."

He paused, and thrust out his right arm impressively. Tom regarded him in sickened, half-comprehending amazement.

"Here's what I say, boys! I say it's time we had more money. I say we ought to make the bloodsuckin' bosses give up a part o' what's comin' to us. That's what I say!" And he swung his doubled fist before his face in a great semi-circle.

He turned to Tom, with a leer in his eyes that was for Tom alone. "Mr. President, I move we demand a ten per cent. increase o' wages, an' if the bosses won't give it, strike for it!"

Tom sank stupefied back in his chair. Foley's own men were bewildered utterly. A dead silence of a minute or more reigned in the hall, while all but the walking delegate strove to recover their bearing.

It was Connelly who broke the general trance. Connelly did not understand, but there was Foley's standing order, "Watch me, an' do the same." "I second the motion," he said.

A little later Foley's strike measure was carried without a single dissenting vote. Foley, Connelly, Brown, Pete, and Tom, with Foley as chairman, were elected the committee to negotiate with the employers for higher wages, and, if there should be a strike, to manage it.

The adoption of the strike measure meant to Foley that the income derived from Mr. Baxter, and two or three others with whom he maintained somewhat similar relations, was to be cut off. But before he reached home that night he had discovered a compensation for this loss, and he smiled with grim satisfaction. The next morning he presented himself in the office of Mr. Baxter, and this same grim smile was on his face.

"Hello, Baxter! How youse stackin' up this mornin'?" And he clapped a hand on Mr. Baxter's artistically padded shoulder.

The contractor started at this familiarity, and a slight frown showed itself on his brow. "Very well," he said shortly.

"Really, now. Why, youse look like youse slept alongside a bad dream." Foley drew forth his cigar-case and held it out. He knew Mr. Baxter did not smoke cigars and hated their smell.

"No, thank you."

The walking delegate put one in his mouth and scratched a match under the edge of the cherry table. "I don't s'pose youse know there was doin's at the union last night?"

"I understand the union decided to strike."

"Wonderful, ain't it, how quick news travels?"

Mr. Baxter disregarded Foley's look of mock surprise. "You seem to have failed utterly to keep your promise that there would be no strike," he said coldly.

"It was Keating stirred it up," Foley returned, calmly biting a bit off his cigar and blowing it out upon the deep red rug.

"You also failed to stop Mr. Keating," Mr. Baxter pursued.

"Mr. Baxter, even the best of us makes our mistakes. I bet even youse ain't cheated every man youse 've counted on cheatin'."

Mr. Baxter gave another little start, as when Foley

had slapped his shoulder. " Furthermore, I understand you, yourself, made the motion to strike."

" The way youse talk sometimes, Baxter, makes
me think youse must 'a' been born about minute before last," Foley returned blandly. "As an amachure
diplomat, youse 've got Mayor Low skinned to death.
Sure I made the motion. An' why did I make the
motion? If I hadn't 'a' made it, but had opposed
it, where'd I 'a' been? About a thousand miles outside the outskirts o' nowhere,—nobody in the union,
an' consequently worth about as much to youse as a
hair in a bowl o' soup. I stood to lose both. I still
got the union."

" What do you propose that we do? " Mr. Baxter held himself in, for the reason that he supposed
the old relation would merely give place to a new.

" Well, there's goin' to be strike. The union 'll
make a demand, an' I rather guess youse 'll not give
up without a fight."

" We shall certainly fight," Mr. Baxter assured
him.

" Well," he drawled, " since I've got to lead the
union in a strike an' youse 're goin' to fight the strike,
it seems like everything 'd have to be off between us,
don't it? "

Mr. Baxter did not reply at once, and then did not
answer the question. " What are you going to do? "

" To tell youse, that is just what I came here for."
In a flash Foley's manner changed from the playful
to the vindictive, and he leaned slowly forward in
his chair. " I'm goin' to fight youse, Baxter, an' fight
youse like hell! " he said, between barely parted teeth.

And his gray eyes, suddenly hard, gazed maliciously
into Mr. Baxter's face.

" I'm goin' to fight like hell! " he went on. " For
two years I've been standin' your damned manicured
manners. Youse 've acted like I wasn't fit to touch.
Why d'youse s'pose I've stood it? Because it was
money to me. Now that there's no money in it,
d'youse s'pose I'm goin' to stand it any longer? Not
much, by God! And d'youse think I've forgotten
the past—your high-nosed, aristocratic ways? Well,
youse 'll remember 'em too! My chance's come, an'
I'm goin' to fight youse like hell! "

At the last Foley's clenched fist was under Mr.
Baxter's nose. The contractor did not stir the
breadth of a hair. " Mr. Foley," he said in his cold,
even voice, " I think you know the shortest way out
of this office."

" I do," said Foley. " An' it's a damned sight too
long! "

He gave Mr. Baxter a long look, full of defiant
hate, contemptuously filliped his half-smoked cigar
on Mr. Baxter's spotless desk, and strode out.

Chapter XIX

FOLEY TASTES REVENGE

FOLEY'S threat that, under cover of the strike, he was going to make Mr. Baxter suffer, was anything save empty bluster. But twenty years of fighting had made him something of a connoisseur of vengeance. He knew, for instance, that a moment usually presented itself when revenge was most effective and when it tasted sweetest. So he now waited for time to bring him that moment; and he waited all the more patiently because a month must elapse ere the beginning of the strike would afford him his chance.

The month passed dully. Buck had spoken from certain knowledge when he had remarked to Mr. Baxter that the contractors would not yield without a fight. During April there were no less than half a dozen meetings between the union's committee and the Executive Committee of the employers' association in a formal attempt at peaceful settlement. The public attitude of Foley and Baxter toward each other for the past two years had been openly hostile. That attitude was not changed, but it was now sincere. In these meetings the unionists presented their case; the employers gave their side; every point, pro and con, was gone over again and again. On the thirtieth of

April the situation was just as it had been on the first:
" We're goin' to get all we're askin' for," said Foley;
" We can concede nothing," said Mr. Baxter. On
the first of May not a man was at work on an iron
job in New York City.

During these four weeks Foley regained popularity
with an astounding rapidity. He was again the
Foley of four or five years ago, the Foley that had
won the enthusiastic admiration of the union, fierce-
tongued in his denunciation of the employers at
union meetings, grimly impudent to members of the
employers' Executive Committee and matching their
every argument,—at all times witty, resourceful,
terribly determined, fairly hurling into others a confidence in himself. He was feeling with almost its
first freshness the joy of being in, and master of, a
great fight. Men that for years had spoken of him
only in hate, now cheered him. And even Tom himself had to yield to this new Foley a reluctant admiration, he was so tireless, so aggressive, so equal to
the occasion.

Tom had become, by the first of May, a figure of
no importance. True, he was a member of the strike
committee, but Foley gave him no chance to speak;
and, anyhow, the walking delegate said what there
was to be said so pointedly, albeit with a virulence
that antagonized the employers all the more, that
there was no reason for his saying aught. And as
for his position as president, that had become pathet-
ically ludicrous. As though in opposite pans of a
balance, the higher Foley went in the union's estima-
tion, the lower went he. Even his own friends, while

not abandoning him, fell in behind Foley. He was that pitiable anomaly, a leader without a following and without a cause. Foley had stolen both. He tried to console himself with the knowledge that the walking delegate was managing the strike for the union's good; but only the millionth man has so little personal ambition that he is content to see the work he would do being well done by another . . . And yet, though fallen, he hung obstinately on and waited—blindly.

Tom was now in little danger from the entertainment committee, for Foley's disquiet over his influence had been dissipated by his rapid decline. And after the first of May Tom gave Foley even less concern, for he had finally secured work in the shipping department of a wholesale grocer, so could no longer show himself by day among the union men.

During April the contractors had prepared for the coming fight by locating non-union ironworkers, and during the first part of May they rushed these into the city and set them to work, guarded by Pinkerton detectives, upon the most pressing jobs. The union, in its turn, picketed every building on which there was an attempt to continue work, and against the scabs the pickets waged a more or less pacific warfare. Foley was of himself as much as all the pickets. He talked to the non-union men as they came up to their work, as they left their work, as they rode away on street cars, as they sat in saloons. Some he reached by his preachment of the principles of trade unionism. And some he reached by such brief speech as this: "This strike 'll be settled soon. Our men 'll all go

back to work. What 'll happen to youse about then?
The bosses 'll kick youse out. If youse 're wise
youse 'll join the union and help us in the strike."
This argument was made more effective by the temporary lifting of the initiation fee of twenty-five
dollars, by which act scabs were made union men
without price. There was also a third method, which
Foley called " transmittin' unionism to the brain by
the fist," and he reached many this way, for his fist
was heavy and had a strong arm behind it.

The contractors, in order to retain the non-union
men, raised their wages to fifty cents a day more than
the union demanded, but even then they were able
to hold only enough workers to keep a few jobs going
in half-hearted fashion. There were many accidents
and delays on these buildings, for the workers were
boilermakers, and men who but half knew the trade,
and men who did not know the trade at all. As
Pete remarked, after watching, from a neighboring
roof, the gang finishing up the work on the St. Etienne
Hotel, " The shadder of an ironworker would do
more'n three o' them snakes." The contractors
themselves realized perfectly what poor work they
were getting for so extravagant a price, and would
have discharged their non-union gangs had this not
been a tacit admission of partial defeat.

From the first of May there of course had been
several hot-heads who favored violent handling of
the scabs. Tom opposed these with the remnant
of his influence, for he knew the sympathy of the
public has its part in the settlement of strikes, and
public sympathy goes not to the side guilty of outrage.

The most rabid of all these advocates of violence was Johnson, who, after being summoned to Mr. Baxter's office, began diligently to preach this substance: " If we put a dozen or two o' them snakes out o' business, an' fix a job or two, the bosses 'll come right to time."

" It strikes me, Johnson, that you change your ideas about as often as you ought to change your shirt," Pete remarked one day, after listening to Johnson's inflammatory words. " Not long ago you were all against a strike."

For a moment Johnson was disconcerted. Then he said: " But since there is a strike I'm for measures that 'll settle it quick. What you got against smashin' a few scabs?"

" Oh, it's always right to smash a scab," Pete agreed. " But you ought to know that just now there's nothin' the bosses'd rather have us do. They'd pay good money to get us to give the hospitals a chance to practice up on a few snakes."

Johnson looked at Pete searchingly, fearing that Pete suspected. But Pete guessed nothing, and Johnson went about his duty.

There were a number of encounters between the strikers and the strike-breakers, and several of these set-tos had an oral repetition in the police courts; but nothing occurred so serious as to estrange public sympathy till the explosion in the Avon, a small apartment house Mr. Baxter was erecting as a private investment. And with this neither Johnson nor the rank and file, on whose excitable feelings he tried to play, had anything to do.

Foley's patience mastered his desire for vengeance

easily enough during April, but when May had
reached its middle without offering the chance he
wanted, his patience weakened and desire demanded
its rights. At an utterly futile meeting between the
committees of the union and the employers, toward the
end of the month, arranged for by the Civic Federation, the desire for vengeance suddenly became the
master. This was the first meeting since the strike
began, and was the first time Foley had seen Mr.
Baxter since then. The contractor did not once look
at Foley, and did not once address speech to him; he
sat with his back to the walking delegate, and put all
his remarks to Brown, the least important member of
the strikers' committee. Foley gave as good as he
received, for he selected Isaacs, who was nothing
more than a fifth man, and addressed him as head of
the employers' committee; and rather better, for he
made Mr. Baxter the object of a condescending affa-
bility that must have been as grateful as salt to raw
and living flesh.

But Foley was not appeased. When he and Connelly were clear of the meeting he swore fiercely.
" He won't be so cool to-morrow! " he said, and
swore again. " An' the same trick 'll help bring 'em
all to time," he added.

Foley had already had vengeful eyes upon the
Avon, which stood on a corner with a vacant lot on
one side and an open space between its rear and the
next building. Jake had carefully reconnoitered its
premises, with the discovery that one of the two
Pinkerton guards was an acquaintance belonging to
the days when he himself had been in the service of

the Pinkerton agency. That night Jake sauntered by the Avon, chatted awhile with the two guards, and suggested a visit to a nearby saloon. As soon as the three were safely around the corner Kaffir Bill and Arkansas Number Two slipped into the doorway of the Avon, leaving Smoky on watch without. Bill and Arkansas had their trouble: to find their way about in the darkness, to light the fuse—and then they had to cut off an unignitable portion of the fuse; and then in their nervous eagerness to get away their legs met a barrel of cement and they went sprawling behind a partition. Several moments passed ere they found the doorway, the while they could hear the sputtering of the shortened fuse, and during which they heard Smoky cry out, " Come on! " When they did come into the street it was to see the two Pinkertons not twenty paces away. Before their haste could take them to the opposite sidewalk the pavement jumped under their feet, and the building at their backs roared heavily. The guards, guessing the whole trick, began shooting at the two. A policeman appeared from around the corner with drawn pistol—and that night Jake, Bill, and Arkansas slept in a cell.

The next morning, after getting on the car that carried him to his work, Tom took up his paper with a leisure that straightway left him, for his eyes were instantly caught by the big headlines sketching the explosion in the Avon. He raced through the three columns. He could see Foley behind the whole outrage, and he thrilled with satisfaction as he foresaw the beginning of Foley's undoing in the police court.

There was no work for him that morning. He leaped off the car and took another that brought him near the court where the three men were to have their preliminary hearing.

It was half-past eight when he reached the court. As he entered the almost empty court-room he saw Foley and a black-maned man of lego-theatric appearance standing before a police sergeant, and he heard Foley say: " This is their lawyer; we want to see 'em straight off." Tom preferred to avoid meeting Foley, so he turned quickly back and walked about for half an hour. When he returned the small court-room was crowded, the clerks were in place, the policemen and their prisoners stood in a long queue having its head at the judge's desk and its tail without the iron railing that fenced off the spectators.

Tom had been in the court-room but a few minutes when an officer motioned him within the railing. The court attorney stepped to his side. " You were pointed out to me as the president of the Iron Workers' Union," said the attorney.

" Yes."

" And I was told you didn't care particularly for the prisoners in this explosion case."

" Well? "

" Would you be willing to testify against them— not upon the explosion, which you didn't see, but upon their character? "

Tom looked at Jake, Arkansas, and Bill, standing at the head of the queue in charge of the two Pinkertons and a couple of policemen, and struggled a moment with his thoughts. Ordinarily it was a point

of honor with a union man not to aid the law against
a fellow member; but this was not an ordinary case.
The papers had thrown the whole blame for the outrage upon the union. The union's innocence could
be proved only by fastening the blame upon Foley
and the three prisoners.

" I will," he consented.

There was a tiresome wait for the judge. About
ten o'clock he emerged from his chambers and took
his place upon his platform. He was a cold-looking
man, with an aristocratic face, deeply marked with
lines of hard justice, and with a time-tonsured pate.
His enemies, and they were many, declared his judg-
ments ignored the law; his answer was that he ad-
ministered the law according to common sense, and
not according to its sometimes stupid letter.

The bailiff opened the court, and the case of Jake,
Arkansas, and Bill was called. The two Pinkertons recited the details of the explosion and the two
policemen added details of the arrest. Then Mr.
Baxter, looking pale, but as much the self-controlled
gentleman as ever, testified to the damage done by
the dynamite. The Avon still stood, but its steel
frame was so wrenched at the base that it was liable
to fall at any moment. The building would have
to be reconstructed entirely. Though much of the
material could be used again, the loss, at a conserva-
tive estimate, would be seventy-five thousand dollars.

Tom came next before the judge's desk. Exclamations of surprise ran among the union men in the room
when it was seen Tom was to be a witness, and the
bailiff had to pound with his gavel and shout for

order. Tom testified that the three were known in
the union as men ready for any villainy; and he managed to introduce in his answers to the questions
enough to make it plain that the union was in no
degree responsible for the outrage, that it abhorred
such acts, that responsibility rested upon the
three—"And someone else," he added meaningly.

"Who's that?" quickly demanded the court
attorney.

"Buck Foley."

"I object!" shouted the prisoners' attorney.
Foley, who sat back in the crowd with crossed legs,
did not alter his half-interested expression by a
wrinkle.

"Objection over-ruled," said the judge.

"Will you please tell what you know about Mr.
Foley's connection with the case," continued the
court attorney.

"I object, your Honor! Mr. Foley is not on
trial."

"It's the duty of this court to get at all the facts,"
returned the judge. "Does the witness speak from
his own knowledge, or what he surmises?"

"I'm absolutely certain he's at the bottom of this."

"But is your evidence first-hand information?"

"It is not," Tom had to confess. "But I couldn't
be more certain if I had seen him——"

"Guess-work isn't evidence," cut in the judge.

Tom, however, had attached Foley to the case—he
had seen the reporters start at his words as at a fresh
sensation—and he gave a look of satisfaction at Foley
as he stepped away from the judge's desk. Foley

gave back a half-covered sneer, as if to say, " Just youse wait! "

Arkansas was the first of the prisoners to be called —the reason for which priority, as Tom afterwards guessed, being his anomalous face that would not have ill-suited a vest that buttoned to the chin and a collar that buttoned at the back. Arkansas, replying to the questions of his long-haired attorney, corroborated the testimony of the policemen and the Pinkertons in every detail. When Arkansas had answered the last query the lawyer allowed several seconds to pass, his figure drawn up impressively, his right hand in the breast of his frock coat.

The judge bent over his docket and began to write. " This seems a perfectly plain case. I hold the three prisoners for the grand jury, each in ten thou-sand——"

The attorney's right hand raised itself theatrically. " Hold! " he cried.

The judge looked up with a start. Tom's eyes, wandering to Foley's face, met there a malign grin.

" The case is not ended, your Honor. The case is just begun." The attorney brushed back his mane with a stagy movement of his hand, and turned upon Arkansas. " You and the other prisoners did this. You do not deny it. But now tell his Honor why you did it."

Arkansas, with honesty fairly obtruding from his every feature, looked nervously at Tom, and then said hesitantly: " Because we had to."

" And why did you have to? "

Again Arkansas showed hesitation.

"Speak out," encouraged the attorney. "You're in no danger. The court will protect you."

"We was ordered to. If we hadn't done it we'd been thrown out o' the union, an' been done up."

"Explain to the court what you mean by 'done up'."

"Slugged an' kicked—half killed."

"In other words, what you did was done in fear of your life. Now who ordered you to blow up the Avon, and threatened to have you 'done up' if you didn't?"

"Mr. Keating, the president o' the union."

The judge, who had been leaning forward with kindling eyes, breathed a prolonged "A-a-ah!"

For a moment Tom was astounded. Then he sprang to Arkansas's side. "You infernal liar!" he shouted, his eyes blazing.

The judge's hammer thundered down. "Silence!" he roared.

"But, your Honor, he's lying!"

"Five dollars for contempt of court! Another word and I'll give you the full penalty."

Two officers jerked Tom back, and surging with indignant wrath he had to listen in silence to the romance that had been spun for Arkansas's lips and which he was now respinning for the court's ears; and he quickly became aware that newspaper artists had set their pencils busy over his face. Once, glancing at Jake, he was treated with a leer of triumph.

Arkansas plausibly related what had passed between Tom and himself and his two companions; and then Bill took the stand, and then Jake. Each repeated the story Arkansas, with the help of his face, had made so convincing.

"And now, your Honor," the prisoners' attorney began when his evidence was all in, "I think I have made plain my clients' part in this most nefarious outrage. They are guilty—yes. But they were but the all too weak instruments of another's will, who galvanized them by mortal fear to do his dastardly bidding. He, he alone——"

"Save your eloquence, councilor," the judge broke in. "The case speaks best for itself. You here." He crooked his forefinger at Tom.

Tom was pushed by policemen up before the judge. "Now what have you to say for yourself?" the judge demanded.

"It's one string of infernal lies!" Tom exploded. And he launched into a hot denial, strong in phrasing but weak in comparison with the inter-corroborative stories of the three, which had the further verisimilitude gained by tallying in every detail with the officers' account of the explosion.

"What you say is merely denial, the denial we hear from every criminal," his Honor began when Tom had finished. "I do not say I believe every word of the testimony of the three prisoners. But it is more credible than your statements.

"What has been brought out here to-day—the supreme officer of a union compelling members to commit an act of violence by threat of economic disablement and of physical injury, perhaps death—is in perfect accord with the many diabolical practices that have recently been revealed as existing among trade unions. It is such things as this that force all right-minded men to regard trade unionism as the most menacing danger which our nation now confronts." And for five minutes he continued in his arraignment of trade unions.

"In the present circumstances," he ended, "it is my duty to order the arrest of this man who appears to be the chief conspirator—this president of a union who has had the supreme hardihood to appear as a witness against his own tools, doubtless hoping thereby to gain the end of the thief who cried 'stop thief.' I hold him in fifteen thousand dollars bond to await the action of the grand jury. The three prisoners are held in five thousand dollars bail each."

Jake, Bill, and Arkansas were led away by their captors, and Tom, utterly dazed by this new disaster that had overtaken him when he had thought there was nothing more that could befall, was shoved over to the warrant clerk. And again he caught Foley's eyes; they were full of malicious satisfaction.

As he waited before the warrant clerk's desk he saw Mr. Baxter, on his way to the door, brush by Foley, and in the moment of passing he saw Foley's lips move. He did not hear Foley's words. They were two, and were: "First round!"

A few minutes later Tom was led down a stairway, through a corridor and locked in a cell.

Chapter XX

TOM HAS A CALLER

LATE in the afternoon, as Tom lay stretched in glowering melancholy on the greasy, dirt-browned board that did service as chair and bed to the transitory tenants of the cell, steps paused in the corridor without and a key rattled in his door. He rose dully out of his dejection. A scowling officer admitted a man, round and short and with side whiskers, and locked the door upon his back.

"This is a pretty how-to-do!" growled the man, coming forward.

Tom stared at his visitor. "Why, Mr. Driscoll!" he cried.

"That's who the most of my friends say I am," the contractor admitted gruffly.

He deposited himself upon the bench that had seated and bedded so much unwashed misfortune, and, his back against the cement wall, turned his sour face about the bare room. "This is what I call a pretty poor sort of hospitality to offer a visitor," he commented, in his surly voice. "Not even a chair to sit on."

"There is also the floor; you may take your choice," Tom returned, nettled by the other's manner. He himself took the bench.

Mr. Driscoll stared at him with blinking eyes, and he stared back defiantly. In Tom's present mood of wrath and depression his temper was tinder waiting another man's spark.

"Huh!" Mr. Driscoll ran his pudgy forefinger easefully about between his collar and his neck, and removing his spectacles mopped his purple face. "What's this funny business you've been up to now?" he asked.

"What do you mean?" Tom demanded, his irritation mounting.

"You ought to read the papers and keep posted on what you do. I just saw a *Star*. There's half a page of your face, and about a pint of red ink."

Tom groaned, and his jaws clamped ragefully.

"What I read gave me the impression you'd been having a sort of private Fourth of July celebration," Mr. Driscoll pursued.

Tom turned on the contractor half savagely. "See here! I don't know what you came here for, but if it was for this kind of talk—well, you can guess how welcome you are!"

Mr. Driscoll emitted a little chuckling sound, or Tom thought for an instant he did. But a glance at that sour face, with its straight pouting mouth, corrected Tom's ears.

"Now, what was your fool idea in blowing up the Avon?"

Tom uprose wrathfully. "Do you mean to say you believe the lies those blackguards told this morning?"

"I only know what I read in the papers."

" If you swallow everything you see in the papers, you must have an awful maw ! "

" Yes, I suppose you have got some sort of a story you put up."

Tom glared at his pudgy visitor who questioned with such an exasperating presumption. " Did I ask you here? " he demanded.

The contractor's eyes snapped, and Tom expected hot words. But none came. " Don't get hot under the collar," Mr. Driscoll advised, running his comforting finger under his own. " Come, what's your side of the story? "

Tom was of half a mind to give a curt refusal. But his wrong was too great, too burning, for him to keep silent upon it. He would have talked of it to any one—to his very walls. He took a turn in the cell, then paused before his old employer and hotly explained his innocence and Foley's guilt.

While Tom spoke Mr. Driscoll's head nodded excitedly.

" Just what I said! " he cried when Tom ended, and brought his fist down on his knee. " Well, we'll show him ! "

" Show him what? " Tom asked.

Mr. Driscoll stopped his fist midway in another excited descent. He stood up, for he saw the officer's scowling face at the grated front of the cell. " Oh, a lot of things before he dies. As for you, keep your courage up. What else's it for? "

He held out his hand. Tom took it with bewildered perfunctoriness.

Mr. Driscoll passed through the door, held open

by the officer. Outside he turned about and growled through the bars: " Now don't be blowing up any more buildings! "

Tom, stung anew, would have retorted in kind, but Mr. Driscoll's footsteps had died away down the corridor before adequate words came to him.

It was about an hour later that the officer appeared before his cell again and unlocked his door. " Come on," he said shortly.

Tom, supposing he was at length to be removed to the county jail, put on his hat and stepped outside the cell. He had expected to find policemen in the corridor, and to be handcuffed. But the officer was alone.

Two cells away he saw Jake's malignant face peering at him through the bars. " I guess this puts us about even! " Jake called out.

Tom shook his fist. " Wait till the trial! We'll see! " he cried vengefully.

" Shut up, youse! " shouted the surly watchman. He pushed Tom through the corridor and up a stairway. At its head Tom was guided through a door, and found himself in the general hall of the police station.

" Here youse are," said the officer, starting for the sergeant's desk. " Come on and sign the bail bond."

Tom caught his arm. " What's this mean? " he cried.

" Don't youse know? Youse 're bailed out."

" Bailed out! Who by? "

" Didn't he tell youse? " Surprise showed in the

crabbed face of the officer. "Why, before he done anything he went down to talk it over with youse."

"Not Mr. Driscoll?"

"I don't know his name. That red-faced old geezer in the glasses. Huh!—his coin comes easier'n mine."

Tom put his name to the bond, already signed by Mr. Driscoll, and stumbled out into the street, half blinded by the rush of sunlight into his cell-darkened eyes, and struck through with bewilderment at his unexpected liberation. He threw off a number of quizzing reporters, who had got quick news of his release, and walked several aimless blocks before he came back to his senses. Then he set out for Mr. Driscoll's office, almost choking with emotion at the prospect of meeting Ruth again. But he reached it too late to spend his thanks or to test his self-control. It was past six and the office was locked.

He started home, and during the car ride posted himself upon his recent doings by reading the accounts of the trial and his part in the Avon outrage. On reaching the block in which he lived he hesitated long before he found the courage to go up to the ordeal of telling Maggie his last misfortune. When he entered his flat it was to find it empty. He sat down at the window, with its backyard view of clothes-lines and of fire-escape landings that were each an open-air pantry, and rehearsed the sentences with which he should break the news to her, his suspense mounting as the minutes passed. At length her key sounded in the lock, he heard her footsteps, then saw her dim shape come into the sitting-room.

In the same instant she saw him at the window. " What—Tom ! " she cried, with the tremulous relief of one who ends a great suspense.

He had been nerving himself to face another mood than this. He was taken aback by the unexpected note in her voice—a sympathetic note he had not heard for such a time it seemed he had never heard it at all.

He rose, embarrassed. " Yes," he said.

She had come quickly to his side, and now caught his arm. " You are here, Tom? "

" Why, yes," he answered, still dazed and at a loss. " Where have you been, Maggie? "

Had the invading twilight not half blindfolded him, Tom could have seen the rapid change that took place in Maggie's face—the relief at finding him safe yielding to the stronger emotion beneath it. When she answered her voice was as of old. " Been? Where haven't I been? To the jail the last place."

" To the jail? " He was again surprised. " Then . . . you know all? "

" Know all? " She laughed harshly, a tremolo beneath the harshness. " How could I help knowing all? The newsboys yelling down in the street! The neighbors coming in with their sympathy ! " She did not tell him how to these visitors she had hotly defended his innocence.

" I didn't know you were at the police station," he said weakly, still at a loss.

" Of course not. When I got there they told me you'd been let out." Her breath was coming rapidly, deeply. " What a time I had ! I didn't know how to get to the jail! Dragging myself all over town! Those awful papers everywhere! Everybody looking at me and guessing who I was! Oh, the disgrace! The disgrace!"

"But, Maggie, I didn't do this!"

"The world don't know that!" The rage and despair that had been held in check all afternoon by her concern for him now completely mastered her. "We're disgraced! You've been in jail! You're now only out on bail! Fifteen thousand dollars bail! Why that boss, Mr. Driscoll, went on it, heaven only knows! You're going to be tried. Even if you get off we'll never hear the last of it. Hadn't we had trouble enough? Now it's disgrace! And why's this come on us? You tell me that!"

She was shaking all over, and for her to speak was a struggle with her sobs. She supported herself with arms on the table, and looked at him fiercely, wildly, through the dim light.

Tom took her arm. "Sit down, Maggie," he said, and tried to push her into a chair.

She repulsed him. "Answer me. Why has this trouble come on us?"

He was silent.

"Oh, you know! Because you wouldn't take a little advice from your wife! Other men got along with Foley and held their jobs. But you wanted to be different; you wanted to fight Foley. Well, you've had your way; you've fought him. And what of it? We're ruined! Disgraced! You're working for less than half what you used to get. We're ashamed to show our faces in the street. All because you wouldn't pay any attention to me. And me—how I've got to suffer for it! Oh, my God! My God!"

Tom recognized the justice, from her point of view, in her wild phrases and did not try to dispute her. He again tried to push her into a chair.

She threw off his hand, and went hysterically on, now beating her knuckles upon the table. "Leave me alone! I've made up my mind about one thing. You won't listen to reason. I've given you good advice. I've been right every time. You've paid no attention to me and we're ruined! Well, I've made up my mind. If you do this sort of thing again, I'll lock you out of the house! D'you hear? I'll lock you out of the house!"

She fell of her own accord into a chair, and with her head in her hands abandoned herself to sobbing. Tom looked at her silently. In a narrow way, she was right. In a broad way, he knew he was right. But he could not make her understand, so there was nothing he could say. Presently he noticed that her hair had loosened and her hat had fallen over one cheek. With unaccustomed hands he took out the pins and laid the hat upon the table. She gave no sign that she had noted the act . . . Her sobs became fewer and less violent.

Tom quietly lit the gas. "Where's Ferdinand?" he asked, in his ordinary voice.

"I left him with Mrs. Jones," she answered through her hands.

When Tom came back with the boy she was in the kitchen, a big apron over her street dress, beginning the dinner. Tom looked in upon her, then obeying

an impulse long unstirred he began to set the table.
She glanced furtively at this unusual service, but said
nothing. She sat through the meal with hard face,
but did not again refer to the day's happenings; and,
since the day was Wednesday, as soon as he had
eaten Tom hurried away to Potomac Hall.

Tom was surrounded by friends the minute he
entered the hall. The ten o'clock edition of the
evening papers, out before seven, had acquainted
them with his release. The accounts in this edition
played up the anomaly of this labor ruffian, shown by
his act to be the arch-enemy of the employers, being
bailed out by one of the very contractors with whom
the union was at war. Two of the papers printed
interviews with Mr. Driscoll upon the question, why
had he done it? One interview was, "I don't
know"; the other, "None of your business."

Tom's friends had the curiosity of the papers, and
put to him the question the news sheets had put to Mr.
Driscoll. "If Mr. Driscoll don't know, how can I?"
was all the answer he could give them. Their curiosity, however, was weak measured by their indignation over the turn events had taken in the court-
room. They would stand by him at his trial, they
declared, and show what his relations had been with
Jake, Bill and Arkansas.

Before the meeting was opened there was talk
among the Foleyites against Tom being allowed to
preside, but he ended their muttering by marching to
his table and pounding the union to order. He
immediately took the floor and in a speech filled with
charges against Foley gave to the union his side of

the facts that had already been presented them from a different viewpoint in the papers. When he ended Foley's followers looked to their chief to make reply, but Foley kept his seat. Connelly, seeing it his duty to defend his leader, was rising to his feet when a glance from Foley made him sink back into his chair. The talk from Tom's side went hotly on for a time, but, meeting with no resistance, and having no immediate purpose, it dwindled away.

The union then turned to matters pertaining to the management of the strike. As the discussion went on followers of Foley slipped quietly about the hall whispering in the ears of their brethren. The talk became tedious. Tom's friends, wearied and uninterested, sat in silence. Foleyites spoke at great length upon unimportant details. Foley himself made a long speech, the like of which had never before come from him, it was that dull and purposeless. At half-past ten, by which time the men usually were restless to be out of the hall and bound toward their beds, adjournment seemed as far off as at eight. Sleepy and bored by the stupid discussion, members began to go out, and most of those that left were followers of Tom. The pointless talk went on; men kept slipping out. At twelve o'clock not above two hundred were in the hall, and of these not two dozen were Tom's friends.

Tom saw Foley cast his eyes over the thinned crowd, and then give a short nod at Connelly. The secretary stood up and claimed Tom's recognition.

" Mr. President, I move we suspend the constitution."

The motion was instantly seconded. Tom promptly ruled it out of order, on the ground that it was unconstitutional to suspend the constitution. But he was over-ruled, only a score siding with him. The motion was put and was carried by the same big majority that had voted against his decision.

Connelly rose a second time. " I make a motion that we remove the president from office on the charge that he is the instigator of an outrage that has blackened the fair name of our union before all the world."

A hundred voices cried a second to the motion. Tom rose and looked with impotent wrath into the faces of the crowd from which Foley's cunning had removed his followers. Then he tossed the gavel upon the table.

" I refuse to put the motion! " he shouted; and picking up his hat he strode down the middle aisle. Half-way to the door he heard Connelly, in the absence of the vice-president, put the motion; and turning as he passed out he glimpsed the whole crowd on its feet.

The next morning Tom saw by his newspaper that Connelly was the union's new president; also that he had been dropped from the strike committee, Hogan now being in his place. The reports in the papers intimated that the union had partially exonerated itself by its prompt discardure of the principal in the Avon explosion. The editorial pages expressed surprise that the notorious Foley bore no relation to an outrage that seemed a legitimate offspring of his character.

Tom had not been at work more than an hour when

a boy brought him word that the superintendent of the shipping department desired to see him. He hurried to his superior's office.

" You were not at work yesterday? " the superintendent said.

" No," Tom admitted.

The head of the department drew a morning paper from a pigeon-hole and pointed at a face on its first page. " Your likeness, I believe."

" It was intended for me."

He touched a button, and a clerk appeared. " Phillips, make out Keating's time check." He turned sharply back upon Tom. " That's all. We've got no use for anarchists in our business."

Chapter XXI

WHAT MIGHT HAVE BEEN

WHEN Ruth carried a handful of letters she had just finished into Mr. Driscoll's office —this while he sat talking to Tom in the latter's cell—she saw staring luridly at her from the desk the newspaper that had sent her employer to the jail on his errand of gruff mercy. There was a great drawing of Tom's face, brutalized, yet easily recognizable, and over it the heavy crimson heading:

TOOLS OF UNION PRESIDENT
FORCED BY DEATH THREATS BLEW UP THE AVON

The stare of that brutal face and of those red words sent her sinking into Mr. Driscoll's chair, and the letters fluttered to the floor. After a moment she reached in eager revulsion for the paper, and her eyes reeled through the high-colored account of the court scene. What was printed there was the newest of news to her; she had lunched early, and the paper she had bought to learn the latest developments in the Avon case had carried her only to the beginning of the trial. As she read, a dizzy sickness ran through all her body. The case against Tom, as the papers made it out, was certainly strong; and the fact that he, the instigator of the outrage, had attempted to escape blame by seeking to help convict his own tools was emphasized as the most blackening phase of the whole black affair. But strong as the case appeared, within her sickened, bewildered self there was something that protested the story could not possibly be true.

During the weeks that had passed since she had last seen Tom she had wondered much that he had not come again, guessing every reason but the right one. When ten days had passed without a visit from him she had concluded that he must be too busy in the management of the strike to spare an evening; she did not know how completely Tom had been crowded off the stage by Foley. When more days had passed, and still no call from him, her subtle woman's nature had supplied another reason, and one that was a sufficient explanation to her even to the present. She knew what Tom's feelings were toward her; a woman needs precious little insight to discover when a man loves her. For all her instinctive democracy, she was perfectly conscious of the social difference between herself and him, and with not unnatural egotism she endowed Tom with the same consciousness. He loved her, but felt their social inequality, and felt it with such keenness that he deemed it hopeless to try to win her, and so had decided to see her no more.

Such was her explanation of his absence. She pitied him with a warm romantic pity for his renunciation. Held away by such a reason, she knew that if ever he came it must be at her bidding. At times she had been impelled to send for him to come. To her this was not an impulse of prohibitive unmaidenliness; she could bend to a man who thought himself beneath her as she never could to a man on her own level. But she had not sent. To do so without being prepared to give him what he desired would be to do him a great wrong, and to give him this she was neither able nor ready. She admired all that was good in him; but she could not blind her eyes to his shortcomings, and to go into his world, with its easily imagined coarseness, with its ignorance of books and music and painting, and all the little refinements that were dear to her, she could not. And yet her heart had ached that he had not come.

But now as she read the story of his disgrace, and as the reflux of wits and strength began, all her heart was one protest of his innocence, and she forgot all the little differences that had before halted her desire to see him; and this desire, freed of its checks, suddenly expanded till it filled the uttermost recesses of her soul.

Her first impulse, when she had reached the story's end, was to go straight to him, and she went so far as to put on her hat. But reason stopped her at the door. She could do him no good, and her call would be but an embarrassment to them both. She removed her hat, and sat down to surging thoughts.

She was sitting at her desk, white and weak, reading anew the lurid story in the paper, when Mr. Driscoll passed through her room into his office with hat drawn over his eyes. She looked through his open door for several minutes—and then, obeying the desire for the relief of speech, she went in.

" Did you see this article about Mr. Keating? "
she asked, trying to keep her personal interest in Tom
from showing in her voice.

Mr. Driscoll's hat brim was still over his eyes.
He did not look up. " Yes," he said gruffly.

" You remember him, don't you?—one of the foremen? "

The hat brim moved affirmatively.

She had to summon all her strength to put her next
question with calmness. " What will be done with
him? "

" I don't know. Blowing up buildings isn't a very
innocent amusement."

" But he didn't do it! "

" He didn't? Hum! "

Ruth burned to make a hot defense. But instead
she asked: " Do you think he's the sort of a man to
do a thing of that sort? He says he didn't."

" What d'you suppose he'd say? "

She checked her rising wrath. " But what do you
think will be done with him? "

" Hung," growled Mr. Driscoll.

She glared at him, but his hat brim shielded off
her resentment; and without another word she swept
indignantly out of the room.

Ruth went home in that weakening anxiety which
is most felt by the helpless. On the way she bought
an evening paper, but there was nothing new in it.
After a dinner hardly touched she went into the
street and got a ten o'clock edition. It had the story
of Tom's release on bail.

" Why, the dear old bear! " she gasped, as she dis-

covered that Mr. Driscoll had gone Tom's bond. She
hurried to her room and in utter abandonment to her
emotion wrote Tom a note asking him to call the following evening.

The next morning Tom, discharged but half an
hour before, walked into Ruth's office. He had stood
several minutes in front of the building before he had
gained sufficient control to carry him through the
certain meeting with her. She went red at sight of
him, and rose in a throbbing confusion, but subdued
herself to greet him with a friendly cordiality.

" It's been a long time since I've seen you," she
said, giving him her hand. It was barely touched,
then dropped.

" Yes. I've been—very—busy," Tom mumbled,
his big chest heaving. It seemed that his mind, his
will, were slipping away from him. He seized his
only safety. " Is Mr. Driscoll in? "

" Yes." Suddenly chilled, she went into Mr. Driscoll's room. " He says he's too busy to see you," she
said on her return; and then a little of her greeting
smile came back: " But I think you'd better go in,
anyhow."

As Tom entered Mr. Driscoll looked up with something that was meant to be a scowl. He had had one
uncomfortable scene already that morning. " Didn't
I say I was busy? " he asked sharply.

" I was told you were. But you didn't think I'd
go away without thanking you? "

" It's a pity a man can't make a fool of himself
without being slobbered over. Well, if you've got to,
out with it! But cut it short."

Tom expressed his thanks warmly, and obediently made them brief. " But I don't know what you did it for? " he ended.

" About fifty reporters have been asking that same thing."

The telephone in Ruth's office began to ring. He waited expectantly.

" Mr. Bobbs wants to speak to you," said Ruth, appearing at the door.

" Tell him I'm out—or dead," he ordered, and went on to Tom: " And he's about the seventeenth contractor that's asked the same question, and tried to walk on my face. Maybe because I don't love Foley. I don't know myself. A man goes out of his head now and then, I suppose." His eyes snapped crossly.

" If you're sorry this morning, withdraw the bail and I'll——"

" Don't you try to be a fool, too! All I ask of you is, don't skip town, and don't blow up any more buildings."

Tom gave his word, smiling into the cross face; and was withdrawing, when Mr. Driscoll stood up. " When this strike you started is over come around to see me." He held out his hand; his grasp was warm and tight. " Good-by."

Tom, having none of that control and power of simulation which are given by social training, knew of but one way to pass safely by the danger beyond Mr. Driscoll's door. He hurried across Ruth's office straight for the door opening into the hallway. He had his hand on the knob, when he felt how brutal was his discourtesy. He turned his head. Ruth sat before the typewriter, her white face on him.

" Good-by," he said.

She did not answer, and he went dazedly out.

Ruth sat in frozen stillness for long after he had gone. This new bearing of Tom toward her fitted her explanation for his long absence—and did not fit it. If he had renounced her, though loving her, he probably would have borne himself in the abrupt way he had just done. And he might have acted in just this same way had he come to be indifferent to her. This last was the chilling thought. If he had received her letter then his abrupt manner could mean only that this last thought struck the truth. When she had written him she had been certain of his feeling for her; that certainty now changed to uncertainty, she would have given half her life to have called the letter back with unbroken seal.

She told herself that he would not come,—told herself this as she automatically did her work, as she rode home in the car, as she made weak pretense of eating dinner. And yet, after dinner, she put on the white dress that his eyes had told her he liked so well. And later, when Mr. Berman's card was brought her, she sent down word that she was ill.

Presently . . . he came. He did not speak when she opened the door to him, nor did she. There was an unmastering fever burning in his throat and through all his body; and all her inner self was the prisoner of a climacteric paralysis. They held hands for a time, laxly, till one loosed, and then both swung limply back to their places.

" I just got your letter to-night—when I got home,"
he said, driving out the words. But he said nothing
of his struggle: how he had fought back his longing
and determined not to come; and how, the victory
won, he had madly thrown wisdom aside and rushed
to her.

They found seats, somehow, she in a chair, he on
the green couch, and sat in a silence their heart-beats
seemed to make sonant. She was the first to recover
somewhat, and being society bred and so knowing the
necessity of speech, she questioned him about his
arrest.

He started out on the story haltingly. But little
by little his fever lost its invalidating control, and
little by little the madness in his blood, the madness that had forced him hither, possessed his brain
and tongue, and the words came rapidly, with spirit.
Finishing the story of his yesterday he harked back
to the time he had last seen her, and told her what
had happened in the second part of that evening in
the hall over the Third Avenue saloon; told her how
Foley had stolen the strike; how he had declined to
his present insignificance. And as he talked he eagerly
drank in her sympathy, and loosed himself more and
more to the enjoyment of the mad pleasure of being
with her. To her his words were not the account of
the more or less sordid experiences of a workingman; they were the story of the reverses of the hero
who, undaunted, has given battle to one whom all
others have dared not, or cared not, fight.

" What will you do now? " she asked when he had
ended.

" I don't know. Foley says he has me down and
out—if you know what that means."

She nodded.

" I guess he's about right. Not many people want
to hire men who blow up buildings. I had thought
I'd work at whatever I could till October—our next
election's then—and run against Foley again. But if
he wins the strike he may be too strong to beat."

" But do you think he'll win the strike? "

" He'll be certain to win, though this explosion will
injure us a lot. He's in for the strike for all he's
worth, and when he fights his best he's hard to beat.
The bosses can't get enough iron-men to keep their
jobs going. That's already been proved. And in a
little while all the other trades will catch up to where
we left off; they'll have to stop then, for they can't
do anything till our work's been done. That 'll be
equivalent to a general strike in all the building trades.
We'll be losing money, of course, but so 'll the bosses.
The side 'll win that can hold out longest, and we're
fixed to hold out."

" According to all the talk I hear the victory is
bound to go the opposite way."

" Well, you know some people then who'll be
mighty disappointed! " Tom returned.

She did not take him up, and silence fell between
them. Thus far their talk had been of the facts of
their daily lives, and though it had been unnatural
in that it was far from the matter in both their hearts,
yet by help of its moderate distraction they had managed to keep their feelings under control. But now,
that distraction ended, Tom's fever began to burn

back upon him. He sat rigidly upright, his eyes avoiding her face, and the fever flamed higher and higher. Ruth gazed whitely at him, hands gripped in her lap, her faculties slipping from her, waiting she hardly knew what. Minutes passed, and the silence between them grew intenser and more intense.

Amid her throbbing dizziness Ruth's mind held steadily to just two thoughts: she was again certain of Tom's love, and certain that his pride would never allow him to speak. These two thoughts pointed her the one thing there was for her to do; the one thing that must be done for both their sakes—and finally she forced herself to say: " It has been a long time since you have been to see me. I had thought you had quite forgotten me."

" I have thought of you often? " he managed to return, eyes still fixed above her, his self-control tottering.

" But in a friendly way?—No.—Or you would not have been silent through two months."

His eyes came down and fastened upon that noble face, and the words escaped by the guard he tried to keep at his lips: " I have never had a friend like you."

She waited.

" You are my best friend," the words continued. She waited again, but he said nothing more.

She drove herself on. " And yet you could—stay away two months?—till I sent for you? "

He stood up, and walked to the window and stood as if looking through it—though the shade was drawn. She saw the fingers at his back writhing and knotting themselves. She waited, unwinking, hardly breathing, all her life in the tumultuous beating of her heart.

He turned about. His face was almost wild. " I stayed away—because I love you——" His last word was a gasp, and he did not have the strength to say the rest.

It had come! Her great strain over, she fairly collapsed in a swooning happiness. Her head drooped, and she swayed forward till her elbows were on her knees. For a moment she existed only in her great, vague, reeling joy. Then she heard a spasmodic gasp, and heard his hoarse words add:

" And because—I am married."

Her head uprose slowly, and she looked at him, looked at him, with a deadly stupefaction in her eyes. A sickening minute passed. " Married? " she whispered.

" Yes—married."

A terrified pallor overspread her face, but the face held fixedly to his own. He stood rigid, looking at her. Her strange silence began to alarm him.

" What is it? " he cried.

Her face did not change, and seconds passed. Suddenly a gasp, then a little groan, broke from her. " Married! " she cried.

For a moment he was astounded; then he began dimly to understand. " What, you don't mean——" he commenced, with dry lips. He moved, with uncertain steps, up before her. " You don't—care for me? "

The head bowed a trifle.

"Oh, my God!" He half staggered backward into a chair, and his face fell into his hands. He saw, in an agonizing vision, what might have been his, and what never could be his; and he saw the wide desert of his future.

"You!" He heard her voice, and he looked up. She was on her feet, and was standing directly in front of him. Her hands were clenched upon folds of her skirt. Her breath was coming rapidly. Her eyes were flashing.

"You! How could you come to see me as you have, and you married?" She spoke tremulously, fiercely, and at the last her voice broke into a sob. Tears ran down her cheeks, but she did not heed them.

Tom's face dropped back into his hands; he could not stand the awful accusation of that gaze. She was another victim of his tragedy, an innocent victim— and *his* victim. He saw in a flash the whole ghastly part he, in ignorance, had played. A groan burst from his lips, and he writhed in his self-abasement.

"How could you do it?" he heard her fiercely demand again. "Oh, you! you!" He heard her sweep across the little room, and then sweep back; and he knew she was standing before him, gazing down at him in anguish, anger, contempt.

He groaned again. "What can I say to you— what?"

There was silence. He could feel her eyes, unchanging, still on him. Presently he began to speak into his hands, in a low, broken voice. "I can make no excuse. I don't know that I can explain. But I never intended to do this. Never! Never!

"You know how we met, how we came to be together the first two or three times. Afterwards . . . I said awhile ago that you were my best friend. I have had few real friends—none but you who sympathized with me, who seemed to understand me. Well, afterwards I came because—I never stopped to think why I came. I guess because you understood, and I liked you. And so I came. As a man might come to see a good man friend. And I never once thought I was doing wrong. And I never thought of my wife—that is, you understand, that she made it wrong for me to see you. I never thought—— If you believe in me at all, you must believe this. You must! And then—one day—I saw you with another man, and I knew I loved you. I awoke. I saw what I ought to do. I tried to do it—but it was very hard —and I came to see you again—the last time. I said once more I would not see you again. It was still hard, very hard—but I did not. And then—your letter—came——"

His words dwindled away. Then, after a moment, he said very humbly: "Perhaps I don't just understand how to be a gentleman."

Again silence. Presently he felt a light touch on his shoulder. He raised his eyes. She was still gazing at him, her face very white, but no anger in it.

"I understand," she said.

He rose—weak. "I can't ask that you forgive me."

"No. Not now."

"Of course. I have meant to you only grief—pain. And can mean only that to you, always."

She did not deny his words.

"Of course," he agreed. Then he stood, without words, unmoving.

"You had better go," she said at length.

He took his hat mechanically. "The future?"

"You were right."

"You mean—we should not meet again?"

"This is the last time."

Again he stood silent, unmoving.

"You had better go," she said. "Good-night."

"Good-night."

He moved sideways to the door, his eyes never leaving her. He paused. She stood just as she had since she had touched his shoulder. He moved back to her, as in a trance.

"No." She held up a hand, as if to ward him off.

He took the hand—and the other hand. They were all a-tremble. And he bent down, slowly, toward her face that he saw as in a mist. The face did not recede. Their cold lips met. At the touch she collapsed, and the next instant she was sobbing convulsively in his arms.

And all that night she lay dressed on her couch . . . And all that night he walked the streets.

Chapter XXII

THE PROGRESS OF THE STRIKE

WHEN morning began to creep into the streets, and while it was yet only a dingy mist, Tom slipped quietly into his flat and stretched his wearied length upon the couch, his anguish subdued to an aching numbness by his lone walk. He lay for a time, his eyes turned dully into the back yard, watching the dirty light grow cleaner; and presently he sank into a light sleep. After a little his eyes opened and he saw Maggie looking intently at him from their bedroom door.

For a moment the two of them maintained a silent gaze. Then she asked: " You were out all night? "

" Yes," he answered passively.

" Why? "

He hesitated. " I was walking about—thinking."

" I should think you would be thinking! After what happened to you Wednesday, and after losing your job yesterday!"

He did not correct her misinterpretation of his answer, and as he said nothing more she turned back into the bedroom, and soon emerged dressed. As she moved about preparing breakfast his eyes rested on her now and then, and in a not unnatural selfishness he dully wondered why they two were married. Her feeling for him, he knew, was of no higher sort than that attachment which dependence upon a man and the sense of being linked to him for life may engender in an unspiritual woman. There was no love between them; they had no ideas in common; she was not this, and not this, and not this. And all the things that she was not, the other was. And it was always to be Maggie that he was to see thus intimately.

He had bowed to the situation as the ancients bowed to fate—accepted it as a fact as unchangeable as death that has fallen. And yet, as he lay watching her, thinking it was to be always so,—always!—his soul was filled with agonizing rebellion; and so it was to be through many a day to come. But later, as his first pain began to settle into an aching sense of irreparable loss, his less selfish vision showed him that Maggie was no more to blame for their terrible mistake than he, and not so much; and that she, in a less painful degree, was also a pitiable victim of their error. He became consciously considerate of her. For her part, she at first marveled at this gentler manner, then slowly yielded to it.

But this is running ahead. The first days were all the harder to Tom because he had no work to share his time with his pain. He did not seek another position; as he had told Ruth, he knew it would be useless to ask for work so long as the charge of being a dynamiter rested upon him. He walked about the streets, trying to forget his pain in mixing among his old friends, with no better financial hope than to wait till the court had cleared his name. Several times he met Pig Iron Pete, who, knowing only the public

cause for Tom's dejection, prescribed a few drinks
as the best cure for such sorrow, and showed his faith
in his remedy by offering to take the same medicine.
And one evening he brought his cheerless presence to
the Barrys'. "Poor fellow!" sighed Mrs. Barry
after he had gone. "He takes his thumps hard."

One day as he walked about the streets he met
Petersen, and with the Swede was a stocky, red-faced,
red-necked man wearing a red necktie whose brilliance
came to a focus in a great diamond pin. Petersen
had continued to call frequently after nightly atten-
dance had become unnecessary. Two weeks before
Tom had gleaned from him by hard questioning that
the monthly rent of twelve dollars was overdue, the
landlord was raging, there was nothing with which
to pay, and also nothing in the house to eat. The
next day Tom had drawn fifteen dollars from his little
bank account, and held it by him to give to Petersen
when he next called. But he had not come again.
Now on seeing him Tom's first feeling was of guilt
that he had not carried the needed money to Petersen's home.

The stocky man, when he saw the two were
friends, withdrew himself to the curb and began to
clean his nails with his pocket knife. "How are
you, Petersen?" Tom asked.

"I'm purty good," Petersen returned, glancing
restlessly at the stocky man.

"You don't need a little money, do you?" Tom
queried anxiously.

"No. I'm vorkin'." He again looked restlessly
at his manicuring friend.

" You don't say! That's good. What at? "

Petersen's restlessness became painful. " At de docks."

Tom saw plainly that Petersen was anxious to get away, so he said good-by and walked on, puzzled by the Swede's strange manner, by his rather unusual companion, and puzzled also as to how his work as longshoreman permitted him to roam the streets in the middle of the afternoon.

When Tom met friends in his restless wanderings and stopped to talk to them, the subject was usually the injustice he had suffered or the situation regarding the strike. Up to the day of the Avon explosion the union as a whole had been satisfied with the strike's progress. That event, of course, had weakened the strikers' cause before the public. But the promptness with which the union was credited to have renounced the instigator of the outrage partially restored the ironworkers to their position. They were completely restored three days after the explosion, when Mr. Baxter, smarting under his recent loss and not being able to retaliate directly upon Foley, permitted himself to be induced by a newspaper to express his sentiments upon labor unions. The interview was an elaboration of the views which are already partly known to the reader. By reason of the rights which naturally belong to property, he said, by reason of capital's greatly superior intelligence, it was the privilege of capital, nay even its duty, to arrange the uttermost detail of its affairs without any consultation whatever with labor, whose views were always selfish and necessarily always unintelligent. The high assumption of superiority in Mr. Baxter's interview, its paternalistic, even monarchical, character, did not appeal to his more democratic and less capitalized readers, and they drew nearer in sympathy to the men he was fighting.

As the last days of May passed one by one, Tom's predictions to Ruth began to have their fulfillment. By the first of June a great part of the building in the city was practically at a standstill; the other building trades had caught up with the ironworkers on many of the jobs, and so had to lay down their tools. The contractors in these trades were all checked more or less in their work. Their daily loss quickly overcame their natural sympathy with the iron contractors and Mr. Baxter was beset by them. "We haven't any trouble with our men," ran the gist of their complaint. "Why should we be losing money just because you and your men can't agree? For God's sake, settle it up so we can get to work!"

Owners of buildings in process of construction, with big sums tied up in them, began to grow frantic. Their agreements with the contractors placed upon the latter a heavy fine for every day the completion of the buildings was delayed beyond the specified time; but the contracts contained a "strike clause" which exempted the bosses from penalties for delays caused by strikes. And so the loss incurred by the present delay fell solely upon the owners. "Settle this up somehow," they were constantly demanding of Mr. Baxter. "You've delayed my building a month. There's a month's interest on my money, and my natural profits for a month, both gone to blazes!"

To all of these Mr. Baxter's answer was in substance the same: " The day the union gives up, on that day the strike is settled." And this he said with unchangeable resolution showing through his voice. The bosses and owners went away cursing and looking hopelessly upon an immediate future whose only view to them was a desert of loss.

But Mr. Baxter did not have in his heart the same steely decision he had in his manner. Events had not taken just the course he had foreseen. The division in the union, on which he had counted for its fall, had been mended by the subsidence of Tom. The union's resources were almost exhausted, true, but it was receiving some financial assistance from its national organization, and its fighting spirit was as strong as ever. If the aid of the national organization continued to be given, and if the spirit of the men remained high, Mr. Baxter realized that the union could hold out indefinitely. The attempt to replace the strikers by non-union men had been a failure; Mr. Driscoll and himself were the only contractors who still maintained the expensive farce of keeping a few scabs at work. And despite his surface indifference to it, the pressure of the owners of buildings and of the bosses in other trades had a little effect upon Mr. Baxter, and more than a little upon some other members of the Executive Committee. A few of the employers were already eager to yield to the strikers' demand, preferring decreased profits to a long period of none at all; but when Mr. Isaacs attempted to voice the sentiments of these gentlemen in a meeting of the Executive Committee, a look from Mr. Baxter's steady gray eyes was enough to close him up disconcerted.

So Buck Foley was not without a foundation in fact for his hopeful words when he said in his report to the union at the first meeting in June: "The only way we can lose this strike, boys, is to give it away."

Which remark might be said, by one speaking from the vantage of later events, to have been a bit of unconscious prophecy.

Chapter XXIII

THE TRIUMPH OF BUSINESS SENSE

MR. BAXTER had to withstand pressure from still another source—from himself. His business sense, as had owners and contractors, demanded of him an immediate settlement of the strike. In its frequent debates with him it was its habit to argue by repeating the list of evils begotten by the strike, placing its emphasis on his losses that promised to continue for months to come. Unlike most reformers and other critics of the *status quo,* Mr. Baxter's business sense was not merely destructive; it offered a practicable plan for betterment—a plan that guaranteed victory over the strikers and required only the sacrifice of his pride.

But Mr. Baxter's pride refused to be sacrificed. His business sense had suggested the plan shortly after the union had voted to strike. He would have adopted the plan immediately, as the obvious procedure in the situation, had it not been for the break with Foley. But the break had come, and his pride could not forget that last visit of Foley to his private office; it had demanded that the walking delegate be humiliated—utterly crushed. His business sense, from the other side, had argued the folly of allowing mere emotion to stand in the way of victory and the profitable resumption of work. Outraged pride had been the stronger during April and May, but as the possibility of its satisfaction had grown less and less as May had dragged by, the pressure of his business sense had become greater and greater. And the Avon explosion had given business sense a further chance to greaten. "Try the plan at once," it had exhorted; "'if you don't, Foley may do it again." However, for all the pressure of owners and contractors and of his business sense—owners and contractors urging any sort of settlement, so that it be a settlement, business sense urging its own private plan—in the early days of June Mr. Baxter continued to present the same appearance of wall-like firmness. But his firmness was that of a dam that can sustain a pressure of one hundred, and is bearing a pressure of ninety-nine with its habitual show of eternal fixedness.

Mr. Baxter had to withstand pressure from yet another source—from his wife. When he had told her in early May that the strike was not going to be settled as quickly as he had first thought, and had asked her to practice such temporary economy as she could, she had acquiesced graciously but with an aching heart; and instead of going to Europe as she had intended, she and her daughter had run up to Tuxedo, where with two maids, carriage, and coachman, they were managing to make both ends meet on three hundred dollars a week. But when the first days of June had come, and no prospect of settlement, she began to think with swelling anxiety of the Newport season.

"Why can't this thing be settled right off?" she said to her husband who had run up Friday evening— the Friday after the Wednesday Foley had assured the union of certain victory—to stay with her over Saturday and Sunday. And she acquainted him with her besetting fears.

Only another unit of pressure was needed to overturn the wall of Mr. Baxter's resistance, and the stress of his wife's words was many times the force required. During his two days at Tuxedo Mr. Baxter sat much of the time apart in quiet thought. Mrs. Baxter was too considerate a wife to repeat to him her anxieties, or to harass him with pleas and questions, but just before he left early Monday morning for the city she could not refrain from saying: "You will try, won't you, dear, to end the strike soon?"

"Yes, dear."

She beamed upon him. "How soon?"

"It will last about three more weeks."

She fell on his neck with a happy cry, and kissed him. She asked him to explain, but his business sense had told him it would be better if she did not know the plan, and his love had given him the same counsel; so he merely answered, "I am certain the union will give up," and plead his haste to catch his train as excuse for saying nothing more.

That afternoon a regular meeting of the Executive Committee took place in Mr. Baxter's office. It was not a very cheerful quintet that sat about the cherry table: Isaacs, in his heart ready to abandon the fight; Bobbs, Murphy, and Driscoll, determined

to win, but with no more speedy plan than to continue the siege; and Baxter, cold and polite as usual,
and about as inspiring as a frozen thought.

There was nothing in the early part of the meeting
to put enthusiasm into the committee. First of all,
Mr. Baxter read a letter from the Civic Federation,
asking the committee if it would be willing to meet
again, in the interest of a settlement, with the
strikers' committee.

" Why not? " said Isaacs, trying to subdue his
eagerness to a business-like calm. " We've got
nothing to lose by it."

" And nothing to gain! " snorted Driscoll.

" Tell the Civic Federation, not on its life," advised Murphy. " And tell 'em to cut their letters
out. We're gettin' tired o' their eternal buttin' in."

Baxter gave Murphy a chilly glance. " We'll
consider that settled then," he said quietly. In his
own mind, however, he had assigned the offer of the
Civic Federation to a definite use.

There were several routine reports on the condi-
tion of the strike; and the members of the committee
had a chance to propose new plans. Baxter was not
ready to offer his—he hung back from broaching
it; and the others had none. " Nothin' to do but
set still and starve 'em out," said Murphy, and no
one contradicted him.

At the previous meeting, when pride was still
regnant within him, Mr. Baxter had announced that
he had put detectives on the Avon case with the hope
of gaining evidence that would convict Foley of
complicity in the explosion. Since then the detec-

tives had reported that though morally certain of Foley's direct responsibility they could find not one bit of legal evidence against him. Furthermore, business sense had whispered Mr. Baxter that it would be better to let the matter drop, for if brought to trial Foley might, in a fit of recklessness, make some undesirable disclosures. So, for his own reasons, Mr. Baxter had thus far guarded the Avon explosion from the committee's talk. But at length Mr. Driscoll, restless at the dead subjects they were discussing, avoided his guard and asked: " Anything new in the Avon business? "

" Nothing. My detectives have failed to find any proof at all of Mr. Foley's guilt."

" Arrest him anyhow," said Driscoll. " If we can convict him, why the back of the strike's broken."

" There's no use arresting a man unless you can convict him."

" Take the risk! You're losing your nerve, Baxter."

Baxter flushed the least trifle at Driscoll's words, but he did not retort. His eyes ran over the faces of the four with barely perceptible hesitancy. He felt this to be his opening, but the plan of his business sense was a subject difficult and delicate to handle.

" I have a better use for Mr. Foley," he said steadily.

" Yes? " cried the others, and leaned toward him. When Baxter said this much, they knew he had a vast deal more to say.

" If we could convict him I'd be in favor of his

arrest. But if we try, we'll fail; and that will be a triumph for the union. So to arrest him is bad policy."

" Go on," said Murphy.

" Whatever we may say to the public, we know among ourselves this strike is nowhere near its end. It may last all summer—the entire building season."

The four men nodded.

Baxter now spoke with apparent effort. " Why not make use of Foley and win it in three weeks? "

" How? " asked Driscoll suspiciously.

" How? " asked the others eagerly.

" I suppose most of you have been held up by Foley? "

There were four affirmative answers.

" You know he's for sale? "

" I've been forced to buy him! " said Driscoll.

Baxter went on more easily, and with the smoothness of a book. " We have all found ourselves, I suppose, compelled to take measures in the interests of peace or the uninterrupted continuance of business that were repugnant to us. What I am going to suggest is a thing I would rather not have to do; but we are face to face with two evils, and this is the lesser.

" You will bear me out, of course, when I say the demands of the union are without the bounds of reason. We can't afford to grant the demands; and yet the fight against the union may use up the whole building season. We'll lose a year's profits, and the men will lose a year's wages, and in the end we'll win. Since we are certain to win, anyhow, it seems to me that any plan that will enable us to win at once, and save our profits and the men's wages, is justifiable."

" Of course," said three of the men.

" What do you mean? " Driscoll asked guardedly.

" Many a rebellion has been quelled by satisfying the leader."

" Oh, come right out with what you mean," demanded Driscoll.

" The quickest way of settling the strike, and the cheapest, for both us and the union, is to—well, see that Foley is satisfied."

Driscoll sprang to his feet, his chair tumbling on its back, and his fist came down upon the table. " I thought you were driving at that! By God, I'm getting sick of this whole dirty underhand way of doing business. I'd get out if I had a half-way decent offer. The union is in the wrong. Of course it is! But I want to fight 'em on the square —in the open. I don't want to win by bribing a traitor! "

" It's a case where it would be wrong not to bribe —if you want to use so harsh a word," said Baxter, his face tinged the least bit with red. " It is either to satisfy Mr. Foley or to lose a summer's work and have the men and their families suffer from the loss of a summer's wages. It's a choice between evils. I'll leave to the gentlemen here, which is the greater."

" Oh, give your conscience a snooze, Driscoll! " growled Murphy.

" I think Baxter's reasoning is good," said Bobbs. Isaacs corroborated him with a nod,

" It's smooth reasoning, but it's rotten!—as rotten as hell! " He glared about on the four men. " Are you all in for Baxter's plan? "

" We haven't heard it all yet," said Bobbs.

" You've heard enough to guess the rest," snorted Driscoll.

" I think it's worth tryin'," said Murphy.

" Why, yes," said Bobbs.

" We can do no less than that," said Isaacs.

" Then you'll try it without me! " Driscoll shouted. " I resign from this committee, and resign quick! "

He grabbed his hat from Baxter's desk and stamped toward the door. Mr. Baxter's smooth voice stopped him as his hand was on the knob.

" Even if you do withdraw, of course you'll keep secret what we have proposed."

Driscoll gulped for a moment before he could speak; his face deepened its purplish red, and his eyes snapped and snapped. " Damn you, Baxter, what sort d'you think I am! " he exploded. " Of course! "

He opened the door, there was a furious slam, and he was gone.

The four men looked at each other questioningly. Baxter broke the silence. " A good fellow," he said with a touch of pity. " But his ideas are too inelastic for the business world."

" He ought to be runnin' a girls' boardin' school," commented Murphy.

" Perhaps it's just as well he withdrew," said Baxter. " I take it we're pretty much of one mind."

" Anything to settle the strike—that's me," said
Murphy.   " Come on now, Baxter; give us the
whole plan.   Just handin' a roll over to Foley ain't
goin' to settle it.   That'd do if it was his strike.
But it ain't.   It's the union's—about three thousand
men.   How are you goin' to bring the union
around ? "

" The money brings Foley around; Foley brings
the union around.   It's very simple."

" As simple as two and two makes seven," growled
Murphy.   " Give us the whole thing."

Baxter outlined his entire plan, as he expected it
to work out.

" That sounds good," said Bobbs.   " But are you
certain we can buy Foley off ? "

" Sure thing," replied Murphy, answering for
Baxter.   " If we offer him enough."

"How much do you think it 'll take ? " asked
Isaacs.

Baxter named a figure.

" So much as that ! " cried Isaacs.

" That isn't very much, coming from the Association," said Baxter.   " You're losing as much in a
week as your assessment would come to."

" I suppose you want the whole Association to
know all about this," remarked Murphy.

" Only we four are to know anything."

" How'll you get the Association to give you the
money then ? " Murphy followed up.

" I can get the emergency fund increased.   We
have to give no account of that, you know."

" You seem to have thought o' everything, Baxter," Murphy admitted. " I say we can't see Foley any too soon."

Bobbs and Isaacs approved this judgment heartily.

" I'll write him, then, to meet us here to-morrow afternoon. There's one more point now." He paused to hunt for a phrase. " Don't you think the suggestion should—ah—come from him? "

The three men looked puzzled. " My mind don't make the jump," said Murphy.

Baxter coughed. It was not very agreeable, this having to say things right out. " Don't you see? If we make the offer, it's—well, it's bribery. But if we can open the way a little bit, and lead him on to make the demand, why we're——"

" Held up, o' course! " supplied Murphy admiringly.

" Yes. In that case, if the negotiations with Foley come to nothing, or there is a break later, Foley can't make capital out of it, as he might in the first case. We're safe."

" We couldn't help ourselves! We were held up! " Alderman Murphy could not restrain a joyous laugh, and he held out a red hairy hand. " Put 'er there, Baxter! There was a time when I classed you with the rest o' the reform bunch you stand with in politics —fit for nothin' but to wear white kid gloves and to tell people how good you are. But say, you're the smoothest article I've met yet! "

Baxter, with hardly concealed reluctance, placed his soft slender hand in Murphy's oily paw.

Chapter XXIV

BUSINESS IS BUSINESS

IT had been hard for Baxter to broach his plan to the Executive Committee. The next step in the plan was far harder—to write the letter to Foley. His revolted pride upreared itself against this act, but his business sense forced him to go on with what he had begun. So he wrote the letter—not an easy task of itself, since the letter had to be so vague as to tell Foley nothing, and yet so luring as to secure his presence—and sent it to Foley's house by messenger.

The next afternoon at a quarter past two the committee was again in Baxter's office. Foley had been asked to come at half-past. The fifteen minutes before his expected arrival they spent in rehearsing the plan, so soon to be put to its severest test.

" I suppose you'll do all the talking, Baxter," said Bobbs.

" Sure," answered Murphy. " It's his game. I don't like to give in that any man's better than me, but when it comes to fine work o' this kind we ain't one, two, three with Baxter."

Baxter took the compliment with unchanged face.

Foley was not on time. At two-forty he had not come, and that he would come at all began to be doubted. At two-fifty he had not arrived. At three none of the four really expected him.

"Let's go," said Murphy. "He'd 'a' been here on time if he was comin' at all. I ain't goin' to waste my time waitin' on any walkin' delegate."

"Perhaps there has been some mistake—perhaps he didn't get the letter," suggested Baxter. But his explanation did not satisfy himself; he had a growing fear that he had humiliated himself in vain, that Foley had got the letter and was laughing at him— a new humiliation greater even than the first. " But let's wait a few minutes longer; he may come yet," he went on; and after a little persuasion the three consented to remain half an hour longer.

At quarter past three the office boy brought word that Foley was without. Baxter ordered that he be sent in, but before the boy could turn Foley walked through the open door, derby hat down over his eyes, hands in his trousers pockets. Baxter stood up, and the other three rose slowly after him.

"Good-afternoon, gents," Foley said carelessly, his eyes running rapidly from face to face. " D'I keep youse waitin'?"

"Only about an hour," growled Murphy.

"Is that so, now? Sorry. I always take a nap after lunch, an' I overslep' myself."

Foley's eyes had fixed upon Baxter's, and Baxter's returned their gaze. For several seconds the two stood looking at each other with expressionless faces, till the other three began to wonder. Then Baxter seemed to swallow something. " Won't you please be seated, Mr. Foley," he said.

" Sure," said Foley in his first careless tone.

The five sat down.   Foley again coolly scanned the committee.   " Well? " he said.

The three looked at Baxter to open the conversation.   He did not at once begin, and Foley took out his watch.   " I can only give youse a few minutes, gents.   I've got an engagement up town at four.   So if there's anything doin', s'pose we don't waste no time in silent prayer."

" We want to talk over the strike with you," began Baxter.

" Really.   If I'd known that now I'd 'a' brought the committee along."

Murphy scowled at this naïveté.   " We don't want to talk to your committee."

" I'm nobody without the committee.   The committee's runnin' the strike."

" We merely desire to talk things over in a general way with you in your capacity as an individual," said Baxter quickly, to head off other remarks from Murphy.

" A general talk?   Huh!   Youse talk two hours; result—youse 've talked two hours."   He slowly rose and took his hat, covering a yawn with a bony hand. " Interestin'.   I'd like it if I had the time to spare. But I ain't.   Well—so-long."

" Hold on! " cried Baxter hastily.   Foley turned. " We thought that possibly, as the result of our talk, we might be able to reach some compromise for the settlement of the strike."

" If youse 've got any plans, that's different." Foley resumed his chair, resting an elbow on the table.

"But remember I've got another engagement, an' cut 'em short."

There were five chairs in the room. Baxter had placed his own with its back to the window, and Foley's so that the full light fell straight in the walking delegate's face. His own face, in the shadow, was as though masked.

Baxter had now immediately before him the task of opening the way for Foley to make the desired demand. "This strike has been going on over five weeks now," he began, watching the walking delegate's face for any expression significant that his words were having their effect. "You have been fixed in your position; we have been fixed in ours. Your union has lost about three hundred and fifty thousand dollars. I won't say how much we've lost. We both seem to be as firmly fixed in our determination as ever. The strike may last all summer. The question is, do we both want to keep on losing money —indefinitely?"

Foley did not take the opening. "That's the question," he said blandly.

It was a few seconds before Baxter went on. "I judge that we do not. You have——"

"Excuse me," said Foley, rising, "but I got weak eyes, an' this light hurts 'em. Suppose me an' youse changes chairs." He calmly stepped over to Baxter's side and waited.

There was nothing for Baxter but to yield the seat, which he did. Foley sat down, tilted back against the window sill, and hooked his heels over a chair rung.

"Your union has perhaps a million dollars at stake," Baxter continued at the same even pitch. "We have—a great deal, and the owners stand to lose heavily. If by talking an hour we can devise a plan by which this can be saved, it's worth while, is it not?"

"Sure. Speakin' as an individual, I'm willin' to talk twice as long for half as much," Foley drawled.

There was a silence. The three men, their elbows on the polished table, looked on as though spectators at a play.

"I wonder if you have anything to propose?" asked Baxter guardedly.

"Me? I come to use my ears, not my tongue."

The two men watched each other narrowly. The advantage, if there could be advantage in the case of two faces under perfect control, was all with Foley. The contractor had caught no sign revealing whether his insinuative words were having effect.

"But you perhaps have thought of some plan that is worth considering," he went on.

Foley hesitated, for the first time. "Well—yes."

"What is it?"

"I——" He broke off, and seemed to listen with suspicion.

Baxter's face quickened—the least trifle. The three men leaned further across the table, excitement tugging in their faces.

"You are perfectly safe," Baxter assured him. "No one can hear."

"The plan's dead simple. But mebbe it's occurred to youse."

" Go on! " said Baxter. The men hardly breathed.

"The quickest way o' settlin' the strike is for "—
he paused—" youse bosses to give in."

Baxter's face went a little pale. Something very
like a snarl came from the spectators.

Foley gave a prolonged chuckle. " If youse 'll pay
me for my time, I'm willin' to play tag in the dark so
long's the coin lasts. But if youse ain't, come to business, or I'll go."

" I don't understand," returned Baxter blankly.

" Oh, tell the truth now an' then, Baxter. It sorter
gives contrast to the other things youse say. Youse
understand all right enough."

Baxter continued his blank look.

Foley laughed dryly. "Now why do youse keep
up that little game with me, Baxter? But keep it up,
if youse like it? It don't fool no one, so where's the
harm. I see through youse all right, even if youse
don't understand me."

" Yes? "

"Mebbe youse 'd like to have me tell youse why
youse sent for me? "

There was no answer.

" I'll tell then, since youse don't seem to want to.
I only expect to live till I'm seventy-five, so I ain't got
no time to waste on your way o' doin' business."
Tilted at his ease against the window sill, he gave
each of the four a slow glance from his sharp eyes.
"Well, youse gents sent for me to see if I wouldn't
offer to sell out the strike."

This was hardly the manner in which the four had
expected he would be led on to hold them up. There

was a moment of suppressed disconcertment. Then Baxter remarked: " It seems to me that you are doing some very unwarranted guessing."

" I may be wrong, sure." A sardonic grin showed through the shadow-mask on his face. " Well, what did youse want to talk to me about then? "

Again there was a pause. The three twisted in uncomfortable suspense. Baxter had the control of a bronze. " Suppose that was our purpose? " he asked quietly. " What would you say? "

" That's pretty fair; youse 're gettin' out where there's daylight," Foley approved. " I'd say youse was wastin' time. It can't be done—even if anybody wanted it done."

" Why? "

" There's three thousand men in the union, an' every one o' them has a say in settlin' the strike. An' there's five men on the strike committee. I s'pose it's necessary to tell four such honest gents that a trick o' this sort's got to be turned on the quiet. Where's the chance for quiet? A committee might fool a union—yes. But there's the committee."

Foley looked at his watch. " I've got to move if I keep that engagement." He stood up, and a malignant look came over his face. " I've give youse gents about the only sort of a reason youse 're capable of appreciatin'—I couldn't if I wanted to. But there's another—I don't want to. The only way o' settlin' this strike is the one I said first, for youse bosses to give in. I've swore to beat youse out, an', by God, I'm goin' to do it! "

Bobbs and Isaac blinked dazedly. Murphy rose

with a savage look, but was sent to his chair by a glance from Baxter. Save for that glance, Foley's words would have made no more change on Baxter's face than had it indeed been of bronze.

"When youse 're ready to give in, gents, send for me, an' I'll come again. Till then, damn youse, good-by!"

As his hand was on the knob Baxter's even voice reached him: "But suppose a man could fool the committee?"

Foley turned slowly around. "What?"

"Suppose a man could fool the committee?"

"What youse drivin' at?"

"Suppose a man could fool the committee?"

Foley's eyes were of blazing intentness. "It can't be done."

"I know of only one man who could do it."

"Who?"

"I think you can guess his name."

Foley came slowly back to his chair, with a gaze that fairly clutched Baxter's face. "Don't youse fool with me!" he snarled.

Baxter showed nothing of the angler's excitement who feels the fish on his hook. "Suppose a man could fool the committee? What would you say?"

Foley held his eyes in piercing study on Baxter's face. "See here, are youse talkin' business?" he demanded.

"Suppose I say I am."

The shadow could not hide a wolf-like gleam of Foley's yellow teeth. "Then I might say, 'I'll listen.'"

" Suppose a man could fool the committee," Baxter
reiterated. " What would you say? "

" S'pose I was to say, ' how'? "

Baxter felt sure of his catch. Throwing cautious
speech aside, he outlined the plan of his business
sense, Foley watching him the while with unshifting
gaze, elbows on knees, hands gripped. " Negotiations between your committee and ours might be
resumed. You might be defiant for one or two meetings of the two committees. You might still be defiant
in the meetings, but you might begin to drop a few
words of doubt on the outside. They will spread, and
have their effect. You can gradually grow a little
weaker in your declarations at the meetings and a little
stronger in your doubts expressed outside. Some
things might happen, harmless in themselves, which
would weaken the union's cause. Then you might
begin to say that perhaps after all it would be better
to go back to work on the old scale now, than to hold
out with the possibility of having to go back at the
old scale anyhow after having lost a summer's work.
And so on. In three weeks, or even less, you would
have the union in a mood to declare the strike off."

Foley's gaze dropped to the rug, and the four
waited his decision in straining suspense. The walking delegate's mind quickly ran over all the phases of
this opportunity for a fortune. None of the four
men present would tell of the transaction, since, if
they did, they would be blackened by their own words.
To the union and all outside persons it would seem
nothing more than a lost strike. The prestige he
would lose in the union would be only temporary; he

could regain it in the course of time. Other walking delegates had lost strikes and kept their places as leaders.

Even Baxter had begun to show signs of nervous strain when Foley raised his eyes and looked hesitatingly at the three men. Every man was one more mouth, so one more danger.

"What is it?" asked Baxter.

"I ain't used to doin' business with more'n one man."

"Oh, we're all on the level," growled Murphy. "Come out with it."

"Well, then, I say yes—with an ' if '."

"And the 'if '?" queried Baxter.

"If the price is right."

"What do you think it should be?"

Foley studied the men's faces from beneath lowered eyebrows. "Fifty thousand."

This was the sum Baxter had mentioned the afternoon before. But Isaacs cried out, "What!"

"That—or nothing!"

"Half that's enough," declared Murphy.

Foley sneered in Murphy's face. "As I happen to know, twenty-five thousand is just what youse got for workin' in the Board o' Aldermen for the Lincoln Avenue Traction Franchise. Good goods always comes higher."

The alderman's red face paled to a pink. But Baxter cut in before he could retort. "We won't haggle over the amount, Mr. Foley. I think we can consider the sum you mention as agreed upon."

Foley's yellow teeth gleamed again. He summed

up his terms concisely: " Fifty thousand, then. Paid in advance. No checks. Cash only."

" Pay you in advance! " snorted Murphy. " Well I rather guess not! "

" Why? "

" Well—we want somethin' for our money! "

Foley's face grew dark. " See here, gents. We've done a little quiet business together, all of us. Now can any one o' youse say Buck Foley ever failed to keep his part o' the agreement? "

The four had to vindicate his honor. But nevertheless, for their own reason, they seemed unwilling to pay now and trust that he would do the work; and Foley, for his reason, seemed unwilling to do the work and trust that they would pay. After much discussion a compromise was reached: the money was to be paid by Baxter in the morning of the day on which the union would vote upon the strike; the committee could then feel certain that Foley would press his measure through, for he would have gone too far to draw back; and Foley, if payment should not be made, could still balk the fulfillment of the plan.

When this agreement had been reached Baxter was ready with another point. " I believe it would be wise if all our future dealings with Mr. Foley should be in the open, especially my dealings with him. If we were seen coming from an apparently secret meeting, and recognized—as we might be, for we are both known to many people—suspicions might be aroused and our plan defeated."

The four gave approval to the suggestion.

At five o'clock all was settled, and Foley rose to go. He looked irresolutely at Baxter for a moment, then said in a kind of grudging admiration: " I've never give youse credit, Baxter. I knew youse was the smoothest thing in the contractin' business, but I never guessed youse was this deep."

For an instant Baxter had a fear that he would again have to shake a great hairy hand. But Foley's tribute did not pass beyond words.

Chapter XXV

IN WHICH FOLEY BOWS TO DEFEAT

THE minute after Foley had gone Mr. Baxter was talking over the telephone to the secretary of the Conciliation Committee of the Civic Federation. "We have considered your offer to try to bring our committee and the committee of the ironworkers together," he said. "We are willing to reopen negotiations with them." A letter would have been the proper and more dignified method of communication. But this was the quicker, and to Mr. Baxter a day was worth while.

The secretary believed in the high mission of his committee, and was enthusiastic to make a record for it in the avoidance of strikes and assistance in their settlement. So he laid down the telephone receiver and called for a stenographer. Within twenty minutes a messenger left his office bearing a letter to Foley.

When Foley got home, an hour after leaving Mr. Baxter's office, his wife handed him the letter. It read:

My Dear Mr. Foley:

Mr. Baxter, speaking for the Executive Committee of the Iron Employers' Association, has signified their willingness to meet your committee and again discuss possible measures for the ending of the strike. Notwithstanding the barrenness of previous meetings I sincerely hope your committee will show the same willingness to resume negotiations. Permit me to urge upon your attention the extreme seriousness of the present situation: the union, the contractors, the owners, all losing money, the public discommoded by the delay in the completion of buildings; all these demand that your two committees get together and in a spirit of fairness reach some agreement whereby the present situation will be brought to an end.

Our rooms are at the service of your two committees. As time is precious I have secured Mr. Baxter's consent, for his committee, to meet you here at palf-past two to-morrow afternoon. I hope this will suit you. If not, a later date can be arranged.

Though his appetite and dinner were both ready, Foley put on his hat and went to the home of Connelly. The secretary was just sitting down to his own dinner.

"I just happened to be goin' by," said Foley, "an' I thought I'd run in an' show youse a letter I got to-day." He drew out the letter and handed it to Connelly.

Foley chatted with Mrs. Connelly while the letter was being read, but all the time his eyes were watching its effect upon Connelly. When he saw the end had been reached, he remarked: "It don't amount to nothin'. I guess we might as well write 'em to go to hell."

Connelly hesitated. It usually took more than a little courage to express a view contrary to Foley's. "I don't know," he said doubtfully. "Baxter knows how we stand. It strikes me if he offers to talk things over with us, that means he realizes he's licked an' is willin' to make concessions."

"Um! Maybe youse 're right."

Encouraged by this admission Connelly went on:

" It might be worth our while to meet 'em, anyhow. Suppose nothin' does come of it, what have we lost? "

Foley looked half-convinced. " Well, mebbe our committee might as well talk the letter over."

" Sure thing."

" I suppose then we ought to get together to-night. If we get word to the other three boys, we've got to catch 'em at dinner. Can youse see to that? "

Connelly looked regretfully at his untasted meal. " I guess I can."

" All right. In your office then, say at eight."

The five men were in the office on time, though Connelly, to make it, had to content himself with what he could swallow in a few minutes at a quick lunch counter. The office was a large, square room, a desk in one corner, a few chairs along the sides, a great cuspidor in the center; at the windows were lace curtains, and on one wall was a full-length mirror in a gilt frame—for on nights when Potomac Hall was let for weddings, receptions, and balls, Connelly's office had over its door, " Ladies' Dressing Room."

The five men lit cigars, Foley's cigars, and drew chairs around the cuspidor, which forthwith began to bear the relation of hub to their frequent salivary spokes. " Connelly told youse about the letter from the Civic Federation, that's gettin' so stuck on runnin' God's business they'll soon have him chased off his job," Foley began. " But I guess I might as well read the letter to youse."

" Take the offer, o' course! " declared Pete, when Foley had ended.

"That's what I said," Connelly joined.

Hogan and Brown, knowing how opposed Foley was to the proposition, said nothing.

"We've wasted enough time on the bosses' committee," Foley objected. "No use talkin' to 'em again till we've put 'em down an' out."

"The trouble with you, Foley, is, you like a fight so well you can't tell when you've licked your man," said Pete in an exasperated tone. "What's the use punchin' a man after he's give in?"

"We've got 'em licked, or they'd never ask to talk things over," urged Connelly.

Foley looked in scowling meditation at his cigar ash. Then he raised his eyes to Brown and Hogan. "What do youse think?"

Thus directly questioned; they had to admit they stood with Pete and Connelly.

"Oh, well, since we ain't workin', I suppose we won't be wastin' much if we do chin a bit with 'em," he conceded. But the four easily perceived that he merely yielded to their majority, did not agree.

The next afternoon Foley and his committee were led by the secretary of the Conciliation Committee into one of the rooms of the Civic Federation's suite, where Mr. Baxter and his committee were already in waiting. The secretary expressed a hope that they arrive at an understanding, and withdrew in exultation over this example of the successful work his committee was doing.

There was a new member on the employers' committee—Mr. Berman. Mr. Baxter, exercising the power vested in him to fill vacancies temporarily, had chosen Mr. Berman as Mr. Driscoll's successor for two reasons: his observations of Mr. Berman had made him certain the latter had elastic ideas; and, more important, for Mr. Driscoll's own partner to take the vacant place would quiet all suspicions as to the cause of Mr. Driscoll's unexpected resignation. Of the five, Bobbs and Isaacs were rather self-conscious; Murphy, who had had previous experience in similar situations, wore a large, blustering manner; Berman, for all his comparative inexperience, was most promisingly at his ease; and Baxter was the Baxter he was three hundred and sixty-five days in the year.

The strikers' committee presented the confident front of expected victory. Foley, slipped far down in his chair, eyed the contractors with a sideling, insolent glance.

"If this here's to be another o' them hot air festivals, like we attended in April an' May, say so now," he growled. "We ain't got no time for talkin' unless youse mean business."

Connelly, whose chair was beside Foley's, leaned over anxiously. "Don't you think you're goin' at 'em pretty rough, Buck?" he whispered. "If you get 'em mad, they'll go right back to where they stood."

"Oh, youse leave 'em to me," Foley returned knowingly.

It would serve no purpose to give the details of this meeting. Mr. Baxter, ignoring Foley's insolence of manner, outlined in well-balanced sentences the reasons that made it imperative to both sides for the strike to be settled, and then went on to give anew the contractors' side of the questions at issue. Now and then Foley broke in with comments which were splenetic outbursts rather than effective rejoinders. When the meeting was over and his committee was out in the street, Foley shed his roughly defiant manner. " Boys," he said with quiet confidence, " we've got 'em beat to death."

The next afternoon was occupied with a debate between Mr. Baxter and Foley upon their respective claims. Foley's tongue was as sharp as ever, but his fellow committeemen had to acknowledge to their secret hearts there was more of convincing substance in what Mr. Baxter said. They wondered somewhat at the sudden declension in the effectiveness of their leader's speech, which perhaps they would not have done had they been parties to a conference that morning at which Foley had pointed out to Mr. Baxter the vulnerable spots in the union's claims, and schooled him in the most telling replies to the statements he, Foley, intended making.

After the meeting Foley again declared his certainty of winning, but there was a notable decrease of confidence in his voice.

" Yes," said Connelly, without much spirit. " But Baxter, he puts up a good talk."

" He seems to have facts to talk from," explained Brown.

" So have we," said Foley.

" Yes, but somehow at the meetin's his facts seem stronger," said Connelly.

" Oh, what o' that," Foley returned encouragingly.

" More'n once in poker I've seen a strong bluff win over a strong hand."

The next meeting was a repetition of the second. Foley was keen in his wit, and insolently defiant; but Mr. Baxter got the better of every argument. The union's committee began to admit, each man to himself, that their position was weaker, and the contractors' much stronger, than they had thought.

And so, day by day, Foley continued to undermine their confidence. So skillfully did he play his part, they never guessed that he was the insinuating cause of their failing courage; more, his constant encouragement made them ashamed to speak of their sinking spirit.

But on the fifth day, at a consultation in Connelly's office, it came out. There had been an hour of talk, absolutely without a touch of enthusiasm, when Connelly, who had been looking around at the men's faces for some time, said with an effort: " On the level now, boys, d'you think we've got any chance o' winnin'? "

Foley swore. " What's that? " he demanded. " Why o' course we're goin' to win! "

But Connelly's words had their effect; the silence broken, the men spoke hesitatingly of the growing doubts they had been trying to hide. Foley stood up. " Boys, if youse 're goin' to talk this kind o' rot, youse 've got to talk it without me," he said, and went out.

Foley gone, they spoke freely of their doubts; and they also talked of him. " D'you notice how the ring's all gone out o' his voice? " asked Brown.

" I bet he ain't got no more confidence than any o' the rest of us," said Pete.

" I bet so, too," agreed Connelly. " He talks big just to cheer us up. Then it's mighty hard for Buck to give up. He'll always fight to his last drop o' blood."

The decline of the committee's enthusiasm had already begun to have a disquieting effect in the union. It now rapidly spread that the committee had little confidence of winning the strike, and that Foley, for all his encouraging words, believed at heart as did the rest of the committee.

The first meeting of the union after the resumption of negotiations was a bitter one. The committee made a vague report, in which Foley did not join, that made apparent their fallen courage. Immediately questioning men were on their feet all over the hall, Tom among them. The committee, cornered by queries, had to admit publicly that it had no such confidence as it had had a week before. The reasons for this were demanded. No more definite reason could be given than that the bosses were stronger in their position than the union had believed.

There were sneers and hot words for the four members who participated in the report. Cries went up for Foley, who had thus far kept out of the discussion; and one voice, answering the cries, shouted: "Oh, he's lost his nerve, too, the same as the others!"

Foley was on his feet in an instant, looking over the excited crowd. " If any man here has heard me say I'm for givin' in, let him get up on his two feet!"

No one stood up. " I guess youse all know I'm

for fightin' as long's there's anything worth fightin' for," he declared, and sank back into his seat.

But there had been no wrath in his eyes as he had looked over the crowd, and no ferocity in his words of vindication. The whisper ran about that it was true, he was losing his nerve. And if Foley, Foley the fighter, were losing confidence, then the situation must indeed be desperate.

The courage of a large body of men, especially of one loosely organized, is the courage of its leaders. Now that it was known the committee's confidence was well-nigh gone, and guessed that Foley's was going, the courage of the men ebbed rapidly. It began to be said: " If there's no chance of winning the strike, why don't we settle it at once, and get back to work? " And the one who spoke loudest and most often in this strain was Johnson.

Two days after the meeting Foley had a conference with Mr. Baxter, at which the other members of the union's committee were not present. And that same night there was another explosion in one of Mr. Baxter's buildings that chanced to be unguarded. The explosion was slight, and small damage was done, but a search discovered two charges of dynamite in the foundation, with fuses burned almost to the fulminating caps.

If the dynamite did not explode, the newspapers did. The perpetrators of this second outrage, which only fate had prevented, should be hunted down and made such an example of as would be an eternal warning against like atrocities. The chief of police should apprehend the miscreants at whatever cost, and the district attorney should see that they had full justice—and perhaps a little more.

The chief of police, for his part, declared he'd have the guilty parties if it took his every man to run them down. But his men searched, days passed, and the waiting cells remained empty.

Mr. Baxter, interviewed, said it was obvious that the union was now determined to stop at nothing in its efforts to drive the contractors into submission. The union, at a special meeting, disclaimed any responsibility for the attempted outrage, and intimated that this was a scheme of the contractors themselves to blacken the union's character. When a reporter " conveyed this intelligence to Mr. Baxter, that gentleman only smiled."

The chief result of this second explosion was that so much as remained to the union of public sympathy was lost in what time it took the public to read its morning paper. Had a feeling of confidence prevailed in the union, instead of one of growing doubt, this charge might have incited the union to resistance all the stouter. But the union, dispirited over the weakness of its cause, saw its cause had been yet further weakened, and its courage fled precipitately.

Three days after the explosion there was another joint meeting of the two committees. At this Mr. Baxter, who had before been soft courtesy, was all ultimatum. The explosion had decided them. They would not be intimidated; they would not make a single concession. The union could return to work on the old terms, if it liked; if not, they would fight till there was nothing more to fight with, or for.

Foley, with much bravado, gave ultimatum for ultimatum; but when his committee met, immediately after leaving the employers', to consider Mr. Baxter's proposition, he sat in gloomy silence, hardly heeding what was being said. As they talked they turned constantly to Foley's somber face, and looking at that face their words became more and more discouraged.

Finally Pete asked of him: "Where d'you stand, Buck?"

He came out of his reverie with a start. "I'm against givin' up," he said. "Somethin' may turn up yet."

"What's the use holdin' on?" demanded Connelly. "We're bound to be licked in the end. Every day we hold out the men lose a day's pay."

Foley glanced sadly about. "Is that what youse all think?"

There were four affirmative answers.

"Well, I ain't goin' to stand out——"

He broke off, and his face fell forward into his palm, and he was silent for a long space. The four watched him in wordless sympathy.

"Boys," he said, huskily, into his hand, "this's the first time Buck Foley's ever been licked."

Chapter XXVI

PETERSEN'S SIN

THE first news of the committee's failing confidence that reached Tom's ears he discredited as being one of the rumors that are always flying about when large powers are vested in a small body of men. That the strike could fail was too preposterous for his belief. But when the committee was forced to admit in open meeting that its courage was waning, Tom, astounded, had to accept what but yesterday he had discredited. He thought immediately of treachery on Foley's part, but in his hot remarks to the union he made no mention of his suspicions; he knew the boomerang quality of an accusation he could not prove. Later, when he went over the situation with cool brain, he saw that treachery was impossible. Granting even that Foley could be bought, there was the rest of the committee, —and Pete, on whose integrity he would have staked his own, was one of its members.

And yet, for all that reason told him, a vague and large suspicion persisted in his mind. A few days after the meeting he had a talk with Pete, during which his suspicion got into words. "Has it occurred to you, Pete, that maybe Foley is up to some deep trick?" he asked.

"You're away off, Tom!" was the answer, given with some heat. "I ain't missed a single committee

meetin', an' I know just where Foley stands. It's the
rest of us that're sorter peterin' out. Buck's the
only one that's standin' out for not givin' in. Mebbe
he's not above dumpin' us all if he had the chance.
But he couldn't be crooked here even if he wanted to.
We're too many watchin' him."

All this Tom had said to himself before, but his
saying it had not dispelled his suspicion, and no
more did the saying of it now by Pete. The negotiations seemed all open and above board; he could not
lay his finger on a single flaw in them. But yet the
strike seemed to him to have been on too solid a
basis to have thus collapsed without apparent cause.

At the union meeting following the committee conference where Foley had yielded, a broken man, the
advisability of abandoning the strike came up for
discussion. Foley sat back in his chair, with overcast
face, and refused to speak. But his words to the
committee had gone round, and now his gloomy
silence was more convincing in its discouragement
than any speech could have been. Tom, whose mind
could not give up the suspicion that there was trickery, even though he could not see it, had a despairing
thought that if action could be staved off time
might make the flaw apparent. He frantically opposed the desire of a portion of the members that the
strike be given up that very evening. Their defeat
was not difficult; the union was not yet ready for the
step. It was decided that the matter should come up
for a vote at the following meeting.

While Tom was at breakfast the next morning
there was a knock at the door. Maggie answered it,

and he heard a thin yet resonant voice that he seemed to have heard before, inquire: "Is Mr. Keating in?"

He stepped to the door. In the dim hallway he saw indistinctly a small, thin woman with a child in her arms. "Yes," he answered for himself.

"Don't you remember me, Brother Keating?" she asked, with a glad note in her voice, shifting the child higher on her breast and holding out a hand.

"Mrs. Petersen!" he cried. "Come right in."

She entered, and Tom introduced her to Maggie, who drew a chair for her up beside the breakfast table.

"Thank you, sister." She sank exhausted into the chair, and turned immediately on Tom. "Have you seen Nels lately?" she asked eagerly.

"Not for more than two weeks."

The excitement died out of her face; Tom now saw, by the light of the gas that had to be burned in the dining-room even at midday, that the face was drawn and that there were dark rings under the eyes. "Is anything wrong?" he asked.

"He ain't been home for two nights," she returned tremulously. "I said to myself last night, if he don't come to-night I'll come over to see you early this morning. Mebbe you'd know something about him."

"Not a thing." He wanted to lighten that wan face, so he gave the best cheer that he could. "But I guess nothing's wrong with him."

"Yes, there is, or he'd never stay away like this," she returned quickly. Her voice sank with resignation. "I suppose all I can do is to pray."

"And look," Tom added. "I'll look."

She rose to go. Maggie pressed her to have breakfast, but she refused, a faint returning hope in her
eyes. " Mebbe the Lord's brung him home while
I've been here."

A half minute after the door had closed upon her
Tom opened it and hurried down the three flights of
stairs. He caught her just going into the street.

He fumbled awkwardly in his pocket. " Do you
need anything? "

" No. Bless you, Brother Keating. Nels left me
plenty o' money. You know he works reg'lar on the
docks."

Two causes for Petersen's absence occurred as possible to Tom—arrest and death. He looked through
the record of arrests for the last two days at police
headquarters. Petersen's name was not there, and
to give a false name would never have occurred to
Petersen's slow mind. So Tom knew he was not in
a cell. He visited the public morgues and followed
attendants who turned back sheets from cold faces.
But Petersen's face he did not see.

The end of the day brought also the end of
Tom's search. He now had three explanations for
Petersen's absence: The Swede was dead, and his
body unrecovered; he had wandered off in a fit of
mental aberration; he had deserted his wife. The
first he did not want to believe. The third, remembering the looks that had passed between the two the
night he had visited their home, he could not believe.
He clung to the second; and that was the only one he
mentioned to Mrs. Petersen when he called in the
evening to report.

" He'll come to suddenly, and come back," he encouraged her. " That's the way with such cases."

" You think so? " She brightened visibly.

A fourth explanation flashed upon him. " Perhaps he got caught by accident on some boat he had been helping load, and got carried away."

She brightened a little more at this. " Just so he's alive! " she cried.

" He'll be certain to be back in a few days," Tom said positively. He left her greatly comforted by his words, though he himself did not half believe them.

There was nothing more he could do toward discovering the missing man. It must be admitted that, during the next few days, he thought of Petersen much less frequently than was the due of such a friend as the Swede had proved. The affairs of the union held his mind exclusively. Opinion was turning overwhelmingly toward giving up the strike, and giving it up immediately. Wherever there was a man who still held out, there were three or four men pouring words upon him. " Foley may not be so honest as to hurt him, but he's a fighter from 'way back, an' if he thinks we ought to stop fightin' now, then we ought to 'a' stopped weeks ago "—such was the substance of the reasoning in bar-room and street that converted many a man to yielding.

And also, Tom learned, a quick settlement was being urged at home. As long as the men had stood firm for the strike, the women had skimped at every point and supported that policy. But when they discovered that the men's courage was going, the women, who feel most the fierce economy of a strike, were for the straight resumption of work and income. Maggie, Tom knew, was beginning to look forward in silent eagerness to a settlement; he guessed that she hoped, the strike ended, he might go back to work untroubled by Foley.

Tom undertook to stand out against the proposal of submission, but he might as well have tried to shoulder back a Fundy tide. Men remembered it was he who had so hotly urged them into a strike that thus far had cost them seven weeks' wages. " I suppose you'd have us lose seven more weeks' money," they sneered at him. They said other things, and stronger, for your ironworker has studied English in many places.

Monday evening found Tom in a chair at one of the open windows of his sitting-room, staring out at nothing at all, hardly conscious of Maggie, who was reading, or of Ferdinand, who lay dozing on the couch. He was completely discouraged—at the uttermost end of things. He had searched his mind frantically for flaws in the negotiations and in Foley's conduct, flaws which, if followed up, clue by clue, would reveal Foley's suspected treachery. But he found none. There seemed nothing more he could do. The vote would come on Wednesday evening, and its result was as certain as if the count had already been made.

And so he sat staring into the line of back yards with their rows and rows of lighted windows. His mind moved over the past five months. They had held nothing for him but failure and pain. He had fought for honor in the management of the union's affairs, staking his place in his trade on the result—and honor in the contest with dishonesty had gone down in defeat. He had urged the union to strike for better wages, and now the strike was on the eve of being lost. He would have to begin life over anew, and he did not know where he could begin. Moreover, he had lost all but a few friends; and he had lost all influence. This was what his fight for right had brought him, and in five months.

And this was not the sum of the bitterness the five months had brought him—no, nor its greater part. He had learned how mighty real love can be—and how hopeless!

He had been sitting so, dreaming darkly, for an hour or more when Maggie asked him if he had heard whether Petersen had come back. The question brought to his mind that he had neglected Mrs. Petersen for four days. He rose, conscience-smitten, told Maggie he would be back presently, and set forth for the tenement in which the Petersens had their home. He found Mrs. Petersen, her child asleep in her lap, reading the Bible. She appeared to be even slighter and paler than when he had last seen her, but her spirit seemed to burn even higher through the lessened obscuration of her thinning flesh.

No, Petersen had not yet come back. " But I fetched my trouble to God in prayer," she said. " An' He helped me, glory to His name! He told me Nels is comin' back."

Tom had nothing to give to one so fired by hope,

and he slipped away as soon as he could and returned home. On entering his flat, his eyes going straight through the dining-room into the sitting-room, he saw Maggie gazing in uncomfortable silence at a man— a lean, brown man, with knobby face, and wing-like mustache, who sat with bony hands in his lap and eyes fastened on his knees.

Tom crossed the dining-room with long strides. Maggie, glad of the chance to escape, passed into the bedroom.

" Petersen ! " he cried. " Where on earth 've you been ? "

Petersen rose with a glad light in his face and grasped the hand Tom offered. Immediately he disengaged his hand to slip it into a trousers pocket. Tom now noted that Petersen's face was slightly discolored,—dim yellows, and greens, and blues— and that his left thumb was brown, as though stained with arnica.

" I come to pay vot I loan," Petersen mumbled. His hand came forth from the pocket grasping a roll of bills as big as his wrist. He unwrapped three tens and silently held them out.

Tom, who had watched this action through with dumb amazement, now broke out: " Where d'you get all that money ? Where've you been ? "

The three tens were still in Petersen's outstretched hand. " For vot you give de union, and vot you give me."

" But where've you been ? " Tom demanded, taking the money.

Fear, shame, and contrition struggled for control

of Petersen's face.   But he answered doggedly: " I
vorked at de docks."

" You know that's not so, Petersen.   You haven't
been home for a week.   And your wife's scared half
to death."

" Anna scared?   Vy? "   He started, and his
brown face paled.

" Why shouldn't she be? "   Tom returned wrathfully.   " You went off without a word to her, and
not a word from you for a week!   Now see here,
Petersen, where've you been? "

" Vorkin' at de docks," he repeated, but weakly.

" And got that wad of money for it!   Hardly."
He pushed Petersen firmly back into his chair.
" Now you've got to tell me all about it."

All the dogged resistance faded from Petersen's
manner, and he sat trembling, with face down.   For
a moment Tom was in consternation lest he break
into tears.   But he controlled himself and in shame
told his story, aided by questions from Tom.   Tom
heard him without comment, breathing rapidly and
gulping at parts of the brokenly-told story.

When the account was ended Tom gripped Petersen's hand.   " You're all right, Petersen! " he said
huskily.

Tears trickled down from Petersen's eyes, and his
simple face twitched with remorse.

Tom fell into thought.   He understood Petersen's
fear to face his wife.   He, too, was uncertain how
Mrs. Petersen, in her religious fervor, would regard
what Petersen had done.   He had to tell her, of
course, since Petersen had shown he could not.   But

how should he tell her—how, so that the woman, and not the religious enthusiast, would be reached?

Presently Tom handed Petersen his hat, and picked up his own. " Come on," he said; and to Maggie he called through the bedroom door: " I'll be back in an hour."

As they passed through the tunnel Tom, who had slipped his hand through Petersen's arm for guidance, felt the Swede begin to tremble; and it was so across the little stone-paved court, with the square of stars above, and up the nervous stairway, whose February odors had been multiplied by the June warmth. Before his own door Petersen held back.

Tom understood. " Wait here for me, then," he said, and knocked upon the door.

" Who's there? " an eager voice questioned.

" Keating."

When she answered, the eagerness in the voice had turned to disappointment. " All right, Brother Keating. In just a minute."

Tom heard the sounds of rapid dressing, and then a hand upon the knob. Petersen shrank back into the darkness of a corner.

The door opened. " Come in, Brother Keating," she said, not quite able to hide her surprise at this second visit in one evening.

A coal oil lamp on the kitchen table revealed the utter barrenness and the utter cleanness—so far as unmonied effort could make clean those scaling walls and that foot-hollowed floor—which he had seen on his first visit five months before. He was hardly within the door when her quick eyes caught the strain in his manner. One thin hand seized his arm excitedly. " What is it, brother? Have you heard from Nels?"

" Ye-es," Tom admitted hesitatingly. He had not planned to begin the story so.

" And he's alive? Quick! He's alive?"

" Yes."

She sank into a chair, clasped both hands over her heart, and turned her eyes upward. " Praise the Lord! I thank Thee, Lord! I knew Thou wouldst keep him."

Immediately her wide, burning eyes were back on Tom. " Where is he?"

" He's been very wicked," said Tom, shaking his head sadly, and lowering himself into the only other chair. " So wicked he's afraid you can never forgive him. And I don't see how you can. He's afraid to come home."

"God forgives everything to the penitent, an' I try to follow after God," she said, trembling. A sickening fear was on her face. " Tell me, brother! What's he done? Don't try to spare me! God will help me to bear it. Not—not—murder?"

" No. He's fallen in another way," Tom returned, with the sad shake of his head again. " Shall I tell you all?"

" All, brother! An' quickly!" She leaned toward him, hands gripped in the lap of her calico wrapper, with such a staring, fearing attention as seemed to stand out from her gray face and be of itself a separate presence.

" I'll have to tell you some things you know already, and know better than I do," Tom said, watching to see how his words worked upon her. " After Petersen got in the union he held a job for two weeks. Then Foley knocked him out, and then came the strike. It's been eleven weeks since he earned a cent at his trade. The money he'd made in the two weeks he worked soon gave out. He tried to find work and couldn't. Days passed, and weeks. They had little to eat at home. I guess they had a pretty hard time of it. He——"

" We did, brother! "

" He saw his wife and kid falling off—getting weaker and weaker," Tom went on, not heeding the interruption. " He got desperate; he couldn't see 'em starve. Now the devil always has temptation ready for a desperate man. About four weeks ago when his wife was so weak she could hardly move, and there wasn't a bite in the house, the devil tempted Petersen. He happened to meet a man who had been his partner in his old wicked days, his manager when he was a prize fighter. The manager said it was too bad Petersen had left the ring; he was arranging a heavy-weight bout to come off before a swell athletic club in Philadelphia, a nice purse for the loser and a big fat one for the winner. They walked along the street together for awhile, and all the time the devil was tempting Petersen, saying to him: ' Go in and fight—this once. It's right for a man to do anything rather than let his wife and kid starve.' But Petersen held out, getting weaker all the time, though. Then the devil said to him: ' He's a pretty poor sort of a man that loves his promise not to fight more than he loves his wife and kid.' Petersen fell. He decided to commit the sin."

Tom paused an instant, then added in a hard voice: "But because a man loves his wife so much he's willing to do anything for her, that don't excuse the sin, does it?"

"Go on!" she entreated, leaning yet further toward him.

"Well, he said to the manager he'd fight. They settled it, and the man advanced some money. Petersen went into training. But he was afraid to tell us what an awful thing he was doing,—doing because he didn't want his wife to starve,—and so he told us he was working at the docks. So it was for three weeks, and his wife and kid had things to eat. The fight came off last Wednesday night——"

"And who won? Who?"

"Well,—Petersen."

"Yes! Of course!" she cried, exultation for the moment possessing her face. "He is a terrible fighter! He——"

She broke off and bowed her head with sudden shame; when it came up the next instant she wore again the tense look that seemed the focus of her being.

Tom had gone right on. "It was a hard fight. He was up against a fast hard hitter. But he fought better than he ever did before. I suppose he was thinking of his wife and kid. He won, and got the big purse. But after the fight was over, he didn't dare come home. His face was so bruised his wife would have known he'd been fighting,—and he knew it would break her heart for her to know he'd been at it again. And so he thought he'd stay away till his face got well. She needn't ever have the pain then of knowing how he'd sinned. He never even thought how worried she'd be at not hearing from him. So he stayed away till his face got well, almost—till to-night. Then he came back, and slipped up to his door. He wanted to come in, but he was still afraid. He listened at the door. His wife was praying for him, and one thing he heard was, she asked God to keep him wherever he was from wrong-doing. He knew then he'd have to tell her all about it, and he knew how terrible his sin would seem to her. He knew she could never forgive him. So he slipped down the stairs, and went away. Of course he was right about what his wife would think," Tom drove himself on with implacable voice. "I didn't come here to plead for him. I don't blame you. It was a terrible sin, a sin——"

She rose tremblingly from her chair, and raised a thin authoritative hand. "Stop right there, brother!" she cried, her voice sob-broken. "It wasn't a sin. It—it was glorious!"

Tom sprang toward the door. "Petersen!" he shouted. He flung it open, and the next instant dragged Petersen, shrinking and eager, fearful, shamefaced, and yet glowing, into the room.

"Oh, Nels!" She rushed into his arms, and their mighty length tightened about the frail body. "It—was—glorious—Nels! It——"

But Tom heard no more. He closed the door and groped down the shivering stairway.

Chapter XXVII

THE THOUSANDTH CHANCE

MR. DRISCOLL was the chairman of the building committee of a little independent church whose membership was inclined to regard him somewhat dubiously, notwithstanding the open liking of the pastor. The church was planning a new home, and of late the committee had been holding frequent meetings. In the afternoon of this same Monday there had been a session of the committee; and on leaving the pastor's study Mr. Driscoll had hurried to his office, but Ruth, whom he had pressed into service as the committee's secretary, had stopped to perform a number of errands. When she reached the office she walked through the open hall door—the weather was warm, so it had been wide all day—over the noiseless rug to her desk, and began to remove her hat. Voices came to her from Mr. Driscoll's room, Mr. Driscoll's voice and Mr. Berman's; but their first few sentences, on business matters, passed her ears unheeded, like the thousand noises of the street. But presently, after a little pause, Mr. Berman remarked upon a new topic: "Well, it's the same as settled that the strike will be over in two days."

Almost unconsciously Ruth's ears began to take

in the words, though she continued tearing the sheets of stamps, one of her purchases, into strips, preparatory to putting them away.

"Another case in which right prevails," said Mr. Driscoll, a touch of sarcasm in his voice.

"Why, yes. We are altogether in the right."

"And so we win." Silence. Then, abruptly, and with more sarcasm: "But how much are we paying Foley?"

Ruth started, as when amid the street's thousand noises one's own name is called out. She gazed intently at the door, which was slightly ajar.

Silence. "What? You know that?"

"Why do you suppose I left the committee?"

"I believed what you said, that you were tired of it."

"Um! So they never told you. Since you're a member of the committee I'm breaking no pledge in telling you where I stand. I left when they proposed buying Foley——"

Mr. Berman made a hushing sound.

"Nobody 'll hear. Miss Arnold's out. Besides, I wouldn't mind much if somebody did hear, and give the whole scheme away. How you men can stand for it is more than I know."

"Oh, it's all right," Mr. Berman returned easily.

The talk went on, but Ruth listened for no more. She hastily pinned on her hat, passed quietly into the hall, and caught a descending elevator. After a walk about the block she came back to the office and moved around with all the legitimate noise she could make. Mr. Driscoll's door softly closed.

In a few minutes Mr. Berman came out and, door knob in hand, regarded her a moment as she sat at her desk making a pretense of being at work. Then he crossed the room with a rare masculine grace and bent above her.

" Miss Arnold," he said.

Ruth rarely took dictation from Mr. Berman, but she now reached for her note-book in instinctive defense against conversation. " Some work for me? " She did not look up.

" Something for you to make a note of, but no work," he returned in his low, well-modulated voice that had seemed to her the very vocalization of gentlemanliness. " I remember the promise you made me give—during business hours, only business. But I have been looking for a chance all day to break it. I want to remind you again that the six months are up to-morrow night."

" Yes. My answer will be ready."

He waited for her to say something more, but she did not; and he passed on to his own room.

Ruth had two revelations to ponder; but it was to the sudden insight she had been given into the real cause of the contractors' approaching victory that she gave her first thought, and not to the sudden insight into the character of Mr. Berman. From the first minute there was no doubt as to what she should do, and yet there was a long debate in her mind. If she were to give Tom the bare fact that had been revealed to her, and, using it as a clue, he were to uncover the whole plan, there would come a disgraceful exposure involving her uncle, her em-

ployers, and, to a degree, all the steel contractors.
And another sentiment threw its influence against
disclosing her information: her natural shrinking
from opening communication with Tom; and mixed
with this was a remnant of her resentment that he
had treated her so. She had instinctively placed
him beside Mr. Berman, and had been compelled to
admit with pain: " Mr. Berman would never have
done it."

But her sense of right was of itself enough to
have forced her to make the one proper use of the
information chance had given her; and besides this
sense of right there was her love, ready for any
sacrifice. So she covertly scribbled the following
note to Tom:

MY DEAR MR. KEATING:
    Are you sure Mr. Foley is not playing the union false?
                                            RUTH ARNOLD.
He is.

With curious femininity she had, at the last
moment, tried to compromise, suggesting enough by
her question to furnish a clue to Tom, and yet
saying so little that she could tell herself she had
really not betrayed her friends; and then, in two
words, she had impulsively flung him all her
knowledge.

The note written, she thought of the second revelation; of the Mr. Berman she had really liked so well
for his æsthetic taste, for his irreproachable gentlemanliness, for all the things Tom was not. " Oh, it's
all right," he had said easily. And she placed him

beside Tom, and admitted with pain-adulterated happiness: "Mr. Keating would never have done that."

When her work for the day was over she hurried to the postoffice in Park Row and dropped the letter into the slot marked "Special Delivery." And when Tom came back from his second call at the Petersen home Maggie was awaiting him with it. At sight of the handwriting on the envelope the color left his face. He tore open the envelope with an eagerness he tried to conceal in an assumed care-lessness, and read the score of words.

When he looked up from the note, Maggie's eyes were fastened on his face. A special delivery letter had never come to their home before. "What is it?" she asked.

"Just a note about the strike," he answered, and put the letter into his pocket.

The explanation did not satisfy Maggie, but, as it was far past their bedtime, she turned slowly and went into the bedroom.

"I'm not coming to bed for a little while," he called to her.

The next minute he was lost in the excitement begotten by the letter. It was true, then, what he had suspected. Ruth, he knew, would never have written the note unless she had been certain. His head filled with a turmoil of thoughts—every third one about Ruth; but these he tried to force aside, for he was face to face with a crisis and needed all his brain. And some of his thoughts were appalling ones that the union was so perilously near its betrayal;

and some were exultant, that he was right after all. But amid this mental turmoil one thought, larger than any of the others, with wild steadfastness held the central place of his brain: there was a chance that, even yet, he could circumvent Foley and save the union—that, fallen as low as he was, he might yet triumph.

But by what plan? He was more certain than ever of Foley's guilt, but he could not base a denunciation of Foley upon mere certitude, unsupported by a single fact. He had to have facts. And how to get them? One wild plan after another acted itself out as a play in his excited brain, in which he had such theatric parts as descending accusingly upon Mr. Baxter and demanding a confession, or cunningly trapping Foley into an admission of the truth, or gaining it at point of pistol. As the hours passed his brain quieted somewhat, and he more quickly saw the absurdity of schemes of this sort. But he could find no practicable plan, and a frantic fear began to possess him: the meeting was less than two days off, and as yet he saw no effective way of balking the sale of the strike.

He sat with head on the table, he lay on the couch, he softly paced the floor; and when the coming day sent its first dingy light into the back yards and into the little sitting-room he was still without a feasible scheme. A little later he turned down the gas and went into the street. He came back after two hours, still lacking a plan, but quieter and with better control of his mind.

"I suppose you settled the strike last night?" said Maggie, who was preparing breakfast.

" I can hardly say I did," he returned abstractedly. She did not immediately follow up her query, but in a few minutes she came into the sitting-room where Tom sat. Determination had marked her face with hard lines. " You're planning something," she began. " And it's about the strike. It was that letter that kept you up all night. Now you're scheming to put off settling the strike, ain't you? "

" Well,—suppose I am? " he asked quietly. He avoided her eyes, and looked across at the opposite windows that framed instant-long pictures of hurrying women.

" I know you are. I've been doing some thinking, too, while you were out this morning, and it was an easy guess for me to know that when you thought all night you weren't thinking about anything else except how you could put off ending up the strike."

One thing that his love for Ruth had shown Tom was that mental companionship could, and should, exist between man and wife; and one phase of his gentleness with Maggie was that latterly he had striven to talk to her of such matters as formerly he had spoken of only out of his own home.

" Yes, you're right; I am thinking what you say," he began, knowing he could trust her with his precious information. " But you don't understand, Maggie. I am thinking how I can defeat settling the strike because I know Foley is selling the union out."

Incredulity smoothed out a few of Maggie's hard lines. " You can prove it? "

" I am going to try to get the facts."

" How? "

" I don't know," he had to admit, after a pause.

She gave a little laugh, and the hard lines came back. " Another crazy plan. You lose the best job you ever had. You try to beat Foley out as walking delegate, and get beat. You start a strike; it's the same as lost. You push yourself into that Avon business—and you're only out on bail, and we'll never live down the disgrace. You've ruined us, and disgraced us, and yet you ain't satisfied. Here you are with another scheme. And what are you going on? Just a guess, nothing else, that Foley's selling out! "

Tom took it all in silence.

" Now you listen to me! " Her voice was fiercely mandatory, yet it lacked something of its old-time harshness; Tom's gentleness had begun to rouse its like in her. " Everything you've tried lately has been a failure. You know that. Now don't make us any worse off than we are—and you will if you try another fool scheme. For God's sake, let the strike be settled and get back to work! "

" I suppose you think you're right, Maggie. But —you don't understand," he returned helplessly.

" Yes, I do understand," she said grimly. " And I not only think I'm right, but I know I'm right. Who's been right every time? "

Tom did not answer her question, and after looking down on him a minute longer, she said, " You remember what I've just told you," and returned to the preparation of breakfast.

As soon as he had eaten Tom escaped into the street and made for the little park that had once been a burying-ground. Here his mind set to work again.

It was more orderly now, and soon he was proceeding systematically in his search for a plan by the method of elimination. Plan after plan was discarded as the morning hurried by, till he at length had this left as the only possibility, to follow Baxter and Foley every minute during this day and the next. But straightway he saw the impossibility of this only possible plan: he and any of his friends were too well known by Foley to be able to shadow him, even had they the experience to fit them for such work. A few minutes later, however, this impossibility was gone. He could hire detectives.

He turned the plan over in his mind. There was, perhaps, but one chance in a thousand the detectives would discover anything—perhaps hardly that. But this fight was his fight for life, and this one chance was his last chance.

At noon a private detective agency had in its safe Petersen's thirty dollars and a check for the greater part of Tom's balance at the bank.

Chapter XXVIII

THE EXPOSURE

TOM'S arrangement with the detective agency was that Baxter and Foley were to be watched day and night, and that he was to have as frequent reports as it was possible to give. Just before six o'clock that same afternoon he called at the office for his first report. It was ready—a minute account of the movements of the two men between one and five. There was absolutely nothing in it of value to him, except that its apparent completeness was a guarantee that if anything was to be found the men on the case would find it.

Never before in Tom's life had there been as many hours between an evening and a morning. He dared not lessen his suspense and the hours by discussing his present move with friends; they could not help him, and, if he told them, there was the possibility that some word might slip to Foley which would rouse suspicion and destroy the thousandth chance. But at length morning came, and at ten o'clock Tom was at the detective agency. Again there was a minute report, the sum of whose worth to him was—nothing.

He went into the street and walked, fear and suspense mounting higher and higher. In ten hours the union would meet to decide, and as yet he had no bit of evidence. At twelve o'clock he was at the office again. There was nothing for him. Eight more hours. At two o'clock, dizzy and shaking from suspense, he came into the office for the third time that day. A report was waiting.

He glanced it through, then trying to speak calmly, said to the manager: " Send anything else to my house."

Tom had said to himself that he had one chance in a thousand. But this was a miscalculation. His chance had been better than that, and had been made so by Mr. Baxter's shrewd arrangement for his dealings with Foley, based upon his theory that one of the surest ways of avoiding suspicion is to do naturally and openly the thing you would conceal. Mr. Baxter's theory overlooked the possibility that suspicion might already be roused and on watch.

Tom did not look at the sheet of paper in the hallway or in the street; with three thousand union men in the street, all of whom knew him, one was likely to pounce upon him at any minute and gain his secret prematurely. With elation hammering against his ribs, he hurried through a cross street toward the little park, which in the last five months had come to be his study. The sheet of paper was buttoned tightly in his coat, but all the time his brain was reading a few jerky phrases in the detail-packed report.

In the park, and on a bench having the seclusion of a corner, he drew the report from his pocket and read it eagerly, several times. Here was as much as he had hoped for—evidence that what he had suspected was true. With the few relevant facts of the report as a basis he began to reconstruct the secret proceedings of the last three weeks. At each step he tested conjectures till he found the only one that perfectly fitted all the known circumstances. Progress from the known backward to the unknown was not difficult, and by five o'clock the reconstruction was complete. He then began to lay his plans for the evening.

Tom preferred not to face Maggie, with her demands certain to be repeated, so he had his dinner in a restaurant whose only virtue was its cheapness. At half past seven he arrived at Potomac Hall, looking as much his usual self as he could. He passed with short nods the groups of men who stood before the building—some of whom had once been his supporters, but who now nodded negligently—and entered the big bar-room. There were perhaps a hundred men here, all talking loudly; but comparatively few were drinking or smoking—money was too scarce. He paused an instant just within the door and glanced about. The men he looked for were not there, and he started rapidly across the room.

"Hello, Keating! How's your strike?" called one of the crowd, a man whom, two months before, he himself had convinced a strike should be made.

"Eat-'Em-Up Keating, who don't know when he's had enough!" shouted another, with a jeer.

"Three cheers for Keating!" cried a third, and led off with a groan. The three groans were given heartily, and at their end the men broke into laughter.

Tom burned at these crude insults, but kept straight on his way.

There were also friends in the crowd,—a few.

When the laughter died down one cried out: " What's
the matter with Keating? " The set answer came,
" He's all right! "—but very weak. It was followed
by an outburst of groans and hisses.

As Tom was almost at the door the stub of a cigar
struck smartly beneath his ear, and the warm ashes
slipped down inside his collar. There was another
explosion of laughter. Tom whirled about, and with
one blow sent to the floor the man who had thrown
the cigar. The laugh broke off, and in the sudden
quiet Tom passed out of the bar-room and joined the
stream of members going up the broad stairway and
entering the hall.

The hall was more than half filled with men—
some sitting patiently in their chairs, some standing
with one foot on chair seats, some standing in the
aisles and leaning against the walls, all discussing the
same subject, the abandonment of the strike. The
general mood of the men was one of bitter eagerness,
as it was also the mood of the men below, for all
their coarse jesting,—the bitterness of admitted defeat, the eagerness to be back at their work without
more delay.

Tom glanced around, and immediately he saw Petersen coming toward him, his lean brown face glowing.

" Hello, Petersen. I was looking for you," he said
in a whisper when the Swede had gained his side.
" I want you by me to-night."

" Yah."

Petersen's manner announced that he wanted to
speak, and Tom now remembered, what he had for-

gotten in his two days' absorption, the circumstances under which he had last seen the Swede. "How are things at home?" he asked.

"Ve be goin' to move. A better house." After this bit of loquacity Petersen smiled blissfully—and said no more.

Tom told Petersen to join him later, and then hurried over to Barry and Jackson, whom he saw talking with a couple other of his friends in the front of the hall. "Boys, I want to tell you something in a minute," he whispered. "Where's Pete?"

"The committee's havin' a meetin' in Connelly's office," answered Barry.

Tom hurried to Connelly's office and knocked. "Come in," a voice called, and he opened the door. The five men were just leaving their chairs.

"Hello, Pete. Can I see you as soon's you're through?" Tom asked.

"Sure. Right now."

Connelly improved the opportunity by offering Tom some advice, emphasized in the customary manner, and ended with the request: "Now for God's sake, keep your wind-hole plugged up to-night!"

Tom did not reply, but as he was starting away with Pete he heard Foley say to the secretary: "Youse can't blame him, Connelly. Some o' the rest of us know it ain't so easy to give up a fight."

Tom found Barry, Petersen and the three others waiting, and with them was Johnson, who having noticed Tom whispering to them had carelessly joined the group during his absence. "If you fellows 'll step back here I'll finish that little thing I was telling," he said, and led the way to a rear corner, a dozen yards away from the nearest group.

When he turned to face the six, he found there were seven. Johnson had followed. Tom hesitated. He did not care to speak before Johnson; he had always held that person in light esteem because of his variable opinions. And he did not care to ask Johnson to leave; that course might beget a scene which in turn would beget suspicion. It would be better to speak before him, and then see that he remained with the group.

" Don't show the least surprise while I'm talking; act like it was nothing at all," he began in a whisper. And then he told them in a few sentences what he had discovered, and what he planned to do.

They stared at him in astonishment. " Don't look like that or you'll give away that we've got a scheme up our sleeves," he warned them. " Now I want you fellows to stand by me. There may be trouble. Come on, let's get our seats. The meeting will open pretty soon."

He had already picked out a spot, at the front end on the right side, the corner formed by the wall and the grand piano. He now led the way toward this. Half-way up the aisle he chanced to look behind him. There were only six men. Johnson was gone.

" Take the seats up there," he whispered, and hurried out of the hall, with a fear that Johnson at that minute might be revealing what he had heard to Foley. But when he reached the head of the stairway he saw at its foot Foley, Hogan, and Brown starting slowly up. With sudden relief he turned

back and joined his party. A little later Connelly
mounted the platform and gave a few preliminary
raps on his table, and Johnson was forgotten.

The men standing about the hall found seats.
Word was sent to the members loitering below that
the meeting was beginning, and they came up in a
straggling body, two hundred strong. Every chair
was filled; men had to stand in the aisles, and along
the walls, and in the rear where there were no seats.
It was the largest gathering of the union there had
been in three years. Tom noted this, and was glad.

All the windows were open, but yet the hall was
suffocatingly close. Hundreds of cigars were mo-
mently making it closer, and giving the upper stratum
of the room's atmosphere more and more the appearance of a solid. Few coats were on; they hung over
the arms of those standing, and lay in the laps of
those who sat. Connelly, putting down his gavel,
took off his collar and tie and laid them on his table,
an example that was given the approval of general
imitation. Everywhere faces were being mopped.

Connelly rapped again, and stood waiting till quiet
had spread among the fifteen hundred men. " I
guess you all know what we're here for," he began.
" If there's no objection I guess we can drop the regular order o' business and get right to the strike."

There was a general cry of " consent."

" Very well. Then first we'll hear from the strike
committee."

Foley, as chairman of the strike committee, should
have spoken for it; but the committee, being aware
of the severe humiliation he was suffering, and to

save him what public pain it could, had sympathetically decided that some other member should deliver
its report. And Foley, with his cunning that extended
even to the smallest details, had suggested Pete, and
Pete had been selected.

Pete now rose, and with hands on Tom's shoulders,
calmly spoke what the committee had ordered. The
committee's report was that it had nothing new to
report. After carefully considering every circum-
stance it saw no possible way of winning the strike.
It strongly advised the union to yield at once, as
further fighting meant only further loss of wages.

Pete was hardly back in his seat when it was moved
and seconded that the union give up the strike. A
great stamping and cries of " That's right! " " Give
it up! " " Let's get back to work! " joined to give
the motion a tremenduous uproar of approval.

" You have heard the motion," said Connelly.
" Any remarks? "

Men sprang up in all parts of the crowd, and for
over an hour there were brief speeches, every one in
favor of yielding. In substance they were the same:
" Since the strike's lost, let's get back to work and not
lose any more wages." Every speaker was applauded
with hand-clapping, stamps, and shouts; an enthusiasm for retreat had seized the crowd. Foley was
called for, but did not respond. Other speakers did,
however, and the enthusiasm developed to the spirit
of a panic. Through speeches, shouts, and stamping
Tom sat quietly, biding his time.

Several of the speakers made bitter flings at the
leadership that had involved them in this disastrous

strike. Finally one man, spurred to abandon by applause, ended his hoarse invective by moving the expulsion of the members who had led the union into the present predicament. So far Foley had sat with face down, without a word, in obvious dejection. But when this last speaker was through he rose slowly to his feet. At sight of him an eager quiet possessed the meeting.

" I can't say's I blame youse very much for what youse 've said," he began, in a voice that was almost humble, looking toward the man who had just sat down. " I helped get the union into the strike, yes, an' I want youse boys "—his eyes moved over the crowd—" to give me all the blame that's comin' to me."

A pause. " But I ain't the only one. I didn't do as much to bring on the strike as some others." His glance rested on Tom. " The fact is, I really didn't go in for the strike till I saw all o' youse seemed to be in for it. Then o' course I did, for I'm always with youse. An' I fought hard, so long's there was a chance. Mebbe there's a few "—another glance at Tom—" that'd like to have us keep on fightin'—an' starve. Blame me all youse want to, boys—but Buck Foley don't want none o' youse to starve."

He sank slowly back into his chair. " You did your best, Buck! " a voice shouted, and a roar of cheers went up. To those near him he seemed to brighten somewhat at this encouragement.

" Three cheers for Keating! " cried the man who had raised this shout in the bar-room, springing to his feet. And again he led off with three groans, which the crowd swelled to a volume matching the cheers for Foley. Connelly, in deference to his office, pounded with his gavel and called for silence—but weakly.

Tom flushed and his jaw tightened, but he kept his seat.

The crowd began once more to demand Foley's views on the question before the house. He shook his head at Connelly, as he had repeatedly done before. But the meeting would not accept his negative. They added the clapping of hands and the stamping of feet to their cries. Foley came up a second time, with most obvious reluctance.

" I feel sorter like the man that was run over by a train an' had his tongue cut out," he began, making what the union saw was a hard effort to smile. " I don't feel like sayin' much.

" It seems to me that everything worth sayin' has been said already," he went on in his previous humble, almost apologetic, tone. " What I've got to say I'll say in the shadow of a minute. I size up the whole thing like this : We went into this strike thinkin' we'd win, an' because we needed more money. An' boys, we ought to have it ! But we made a mistake somewhere. I guess youse 've found out that in a fight it ain't always the man that's right that wins. It's the strongest man. The same in a strike. We're right, and we've fought our best, but the other fellows are settin' on our chests. I guess our mistake was, we wasn't as strong when we went into the fight as we thought we was.

" Now. the question, as I see it, is : Do we want

to keep the other fellow on our chests, we all fagged out, with him mebbe punchin' our faces whenever he feels like it?—keep us there till we're done up forever? Or do we want to give in an' say we've had enough? He'll let us up, we'll take a rest, we'll get back our wind an' strength, an' when we're good an' ready, why, another fight, an' better luck! I know which is my style, an' from what youse boys 've said here to-night, I can make a pretty good guess as to what's your style."

He paused for a moment, and when he began again his voice was lower and there was a deep sadness in it that he could not hide. " Boys, this is the hardest hour o' my life. I ain't very used to losin' fights. I think youse can count in a couple o' days all the fights I lost for youse. [A cry, " Never a one, Buck! "] An' it comes mighty hard for me to begin to lose now. If I was to do what I want to do, I'd say, ' Let's never give in.' But I know what's best for the union, boys . . . an' so I lose my first strike."

He sank back into his seat, and his head fell forward upon his breast. There was a moment of sympathetic silence, then an outburst of shouts: " It ain't your fault! " " You've done your best! " " You take your lickin' like a man! " But these individual shouts were straightway lost in cries of " Foley! " " Foley! " and in a mighty cheer that thundered through the hall. Next to a game fighter men admire a game loser.

This was Tom's moment. He had been waiting till Foley should place himself on record before the entire union. He now stood up and raised his right hand to gain Connelly's attention. "Mr. Chairman!" he called.

"Question!" "Question!" shouted the crowd, few even noticing that Tom was claiming right of speech.

"Mr. Chairman!" Tom cried again.

Connelly's attention was caught, and for an instant he looked irresolutely at Tom. The crowd, following their president's eyes, saw Tom and broke into a great hiss.

"D'you want any more speeches?" Connelly put to the union.

"No!" "No!" "Question!" "Question!"

"All in favor of the motion——"

The desperate strait demanded an eminence to speak from, but the way to the platform was blocked. Tom vaulted to the top of the grand piano, and his eyes blazed down upon the crowd.

"You shall listen to me!" he shouted, breaking in on Connelly. His right arm pointed across the hall to where Foley was bowed in humiliation. "Buck Foley has sold you out!"

In the great din his voice did not carry more than a dozen rows, but upon those rows silence fell suddenly. "What was that?" men just behind asked excitedly, their eyes on Tom standing on the piano, his arm stretched toward Foley. A tide of explanation moved backward, and the din sank before it.

Tom shouted again: "Buck Foley has sold you out!"

This time his words reached the farthest man in

the hall. There was an instant of stupefied quiet. Then Foley himself stood up. He seemed to have paled a shade, but there was not a quaver in his voice when he spoke.

" This's a nice little stage play our friend's made up for the last minute. He's been fightin' a settlement right along, an' this is his last trick to get youse to put it off. He's sorter like a blind friend o' mine who went fishin' one day. He got turned with his back to the river, an' he fished all day in the grass. I think Keating's got turned in the wrong direction, too."

A few in the crowd laughed waveringly; some began to talk excitedly; but most looked silently at Tom, still stunned by his blow-like declaration.

Tom paid no attention to Foley's words. " Fifty thousand dollars was what he got!" he said in his loudest voice.

For the moment it was as if those fifteen hundred men had been struck dumb and helpless. Again it was Foley who broke the silence. He reared his long body above the bewildered crowd and spoke easily. " If youse boys don't see through that lie youse' re blind. If I was runnin' the strike alone an' wanted to sell it out, what Keating's said might be possible. But I ain't runnin' it. A committee is— five men. Now how d'youse suppose I could sell out with four men watchin' me—an' one o' them a friend o' Keating? "

He did not wait for a response from his audience. He turned to Connelly and went on with a provoked air: " Mr. Chairman, youse know, an' the rest o' the committee knows, that it was youse who suggested we give up the strike. An' youse know I held out again' givin' in. Now ain't we had enough o' Keating's wind? S'pose youse put the question."

What Foley had said was convincing; and, even at this instant, Tom himself could but admire the self-control, the air of provoked forbearance, with which he said it. The quiet, easy speech had given the crowd time to recover. As Foley sat down there was a sudden tumult of voices, and then loud cries of "Question!" "Question!"

"Order, Mr. Chairman! I demand the right to speak!" Tom cried.

"No one wants to hear you, and the question's called for."

Tom turned to the crowd. "It's for you to say whether you'll hear me or——"

"Out of order!" shouted Connelly.

"I've got facts, men! Facts! Will it hurt you to hear me? You can vote as you please, then!"

"Question!" went up a roar, and immediately after it a greater and increasing roar of "Keating!" "Keating!"

Connelly could but yield. He pounded for order, then nodded at Tom. "Well, go on."

Tom realized the theatricality of his position on the piano, but he also realized its advantage, and did not get down. He waited a moment to gain control of his mind, and his eyes moved over the rows and rows of faces that gleamed dully from sweat and excitement through the haze of smoke.

What he had to say first was pure conjecture, but

he spoke with the convincing decision of the man who has guessed at nothing. "You've heard the other men speak. All I ask of you is to hear me out the same way. And I have something far more important to say than anything that's been said here to-night. I am going to tell you the story of the most scoundrelly trick that was ever played on a trade union. For the union has been sold out, and Buck Foley lies when he says it has not, and he knows he lies!"

Every man was listening intently. Tom went on: "About three weeks ago, just when negotiations were opened again, Foley arranged with the bosses to sell out the strike. Fifty thousand dollars was the price. The bosses were to make a million or more out of the deal, Foley was to make fifty thousand, and we boys were to pay for it all! Foley's work was to fool the committee, make them lose confidence in the strike, and they of course would make the union lose confidence and we'd give up. That was his job, and for it he was to have fifty thousand dollars.

"Well, he was the man for the job. He worked the committee, and worked it so slick it never knew it was being worked. He even made the committee think it was urging him to give up the strike. How he did it, it's beyond me or any other honest man even to guess. No one could have done it but Foley. He's the smoothest crook that ever happened. I give you that credit, Buck Foley. You're the smoothest crook that ever happened!"

Foley had come to his feet with a look that was more of a glaring scowl than anything else: eyebrows drawn down shaggily, a gully between them—nose drawn up and nostrils flaring—jaws clenched—the whole face clenched. " Mr. President, are youse goin' to let that man go on with his lies?" he broke in fiercely.

The crowd roused from its tension. " Go on, Keating! Go on!"

" If he goes on with them lies, I for one ain't goin' to stay to listen to 'em!" Foley grabbed his coat from the back of his chair and started to edge through to the aisle.

" If you leave, Buck Foley, it's the same as a confession of guilt!" shouted Tom. " Stay here and defend yourself like a man, if you can!"

" Against youse?" He laughed a dry cackling laugh, and his returning self-mastery smoothed out his face. And then his inherent bravado showed itself. On reaching the aisle, instead of turning toward the door, he turned toward the platform and seated himself on its edge, directing a look of insouciant calm upon the men.

" Whatever lies there are, are all yours, Buck Foley," Tom went on. He looked again at the crowd, bending toward him in attention. " The trick worked. How well is shown by our being on the point of voting to give up the strike. Little by little our confidence was destroyed by doubt, and little by little Foley got nearer to his money—till to-day came. I'm speaking facts now, boys. I've got evidence for everything I'm going to tell you. I know every move Foley's made in the last thirty-six hours.

"Well, this morning,—I'll only give the big facts, facts that count,—this morning he went to get the price of us—fifty thousand dollars. Where do you suppose he met Baxter? In some hotel, or some secret place? Not much. Cunning! That word don't do justice to Foley. He met Baxter in Baxter's own office!—and with the door open! Could anything be more in harmony with the smooth scheme by which he fooled the committee? He left the door wide open, so everyone outside could hear that nothing crooked was going on. He swore at Baxter. He called him every sort of name because he would not make us any concession. After a minute or two he came out, still swearing mad. His coat was buttoned up—tight. It was unbuttoned when he went in. And the people that heard thought what an awful calling-down Baxter had got.

"Foley went first to the Independence Bank. He left seventeen thousand there. At the Jackson Bank he left fifteen thousand, and at the Third National eighteen thousand. Fifty thousand dollars, boys— his price for selling us out! And he comes here to-night and pretends to be broken-hearted. ' This is the hardest hour of my life,' he says; ' and so I lose my first strike.' Broken-hearted!—with fifty thousand put in the bank in one day! "

There was a tense immobility through all the crowd, and a profound stillness, quickly broken by Foley before anyone else could forestall him. There was a chance that Tom's words had not caught hold— his thousandth chance.

" If that fool is through ravin', better put the

motion, Connelly," he remarked the instant Tom ended, in an even tone that reached the farthest edge of the hall. No one looking at him at this instant, still sitting on the edge of the platform, would have guessed his show of calmness was calling from him the supreme effort of his life.

Voices buzzed, then there rose a dull roar of anger.

It had been Foley's last chance, and he had lost. He threw off his control, and leaped to his feet, his face twisted with vengeful rage. He tossed his hat and coat on the platform, and without a word made a rush through the men toward Tom.

"Let him through, boys!" Tom shouted, and sprang from the piano. Petersen stepped quickly to his side, but Tom pushed him away and waited in burning eagerness in the little open space. And the crowd, still dazed by the revelations of the last scene, looked fascinated upon this new one.

But at this moment an interruption came from the rear of the hall. "Letter for Foley!" shouted a voice. "Letter for Foley!"

Foley paused in his rush, and turned his livid face toward the cry. The sergeant-at-arms was pushing his way through the center aisle, repeating his shout, his right hand holding an envelope aloft. He gained Foley's side and laid the letter in the walking delegate's hand. "Messenger just brought it! Very important!" he cried.

Foley glared at Tom, looked at the letter, hesitated, then ripped open the envelope with a bony forefinger. The crowd looked on, hardly breathing, while he read.

Chapter XXIX

IN WHICH MR. BAXTER SHOWS HIMSELF
A MAN OF RESOURCES

IT was just eight o'clock when Johnson gave three excited raps with the heavy iron knocker on the door of Mr. Baxter's house in Madison Avenue. A personage in purple evening clothes drew the door wide open, but on seeing the sartorial character of the caller he filled the doorway with his own immaculate figure.

"Is Mr. Baxter at home?" asked Johnson eagerly.

"He is just going out," the other condescended to reply.

That should have been enough to dispose of this common fellow. But Johnson kept his place. "I want to see him, for just a minute. Tell him my name. He'll see me. It's Johnson."

The personage considered a space, then disappeared to search for Mr. Baxter; first showing his discretion by closing the door—with Johnson outside of it. He quickly reappeared and led Johnson across a hall that was as large as Johnson's flat, up a broad stairway, and through a wide doorway into the library, where he left him, standing, to gain what he could from sight of the rows and rows of leather-backed volumes.

Almost at once Mr. Baxter entered, dressed in a dinner coat.

"You have something to tell me?" he asked quickly.

"Yes."

"This way." Mr. Baxter led Johnson into a smaller room, opening upon the library, furnished with little else besides a flat-top walnut desk, a telephone, and a typewriter on a low table. Here Mr. Baxter sometimes attended to his correspondence, with the assistance of a stenographer sent from the office, when he did not feel like going downtown; and in here, when the mood was on him, he sometimes slipped to write bits of verse, a few of which he had published in magazines under a pseudonym.

Mr. Baxter closed the door, took the chair at the desk and waved Johnson to the stenographer's. "I have only a minute. What is it?"

For all his previous calls on Mr. Baxter, this refined presence made Johnson dumb with embarrassment. He would have been more at his ease had he had the comfort of fumbling his hat, but the purple personage had gingerly taken his battered derby from him at the door.

"Well?" said Mr. Baxter, a bit impatiently.

Johnson found his voice and rapidly told of Tom's discovery, as he had heard it from Tom twenty minutes before, and of the exposure that was going to be made that evening. At first Mr. Baxter seemed to start; the hand on the desk did certainly tighten. But that was all.

"Did Mr. Keating say, in this story he proposes

to tell, whether we offered Mr. Foley money to sell out, or whether Mr. Foley demanded it?" he asked, when Johnson had ended.

"He didn't say. He didn't seem to know."

Mr. Baxter did not speak for a little while; then he said, with a quiet carelessness: "What you have told me is of no great importance, though it probably seems so to you. It might, however, have been of great value. So I want to say to you that I thoroughly appreciate the promptness with which you have brought me this intelligence. If I can still depend upon your faithfulness, and your secrecy——" Mr. Baxter paused.

"Always," said Johnson eagerly.

"And your secrecy—" this with a slight emphasis, the gray eyes looking right through Johnson; "you can count upon an early token of appreciation, in excess of what regularly comes to you."

"You've always found you could count on me, ain't you?"

"Yes."

"And you always can!"

Mr. Baxter touched a button beneath his desk. "Have Mitchell show Mr. Johnson out," he said to the maid who answered the ring. "Do you know where Mrs. Baxter is?"

"In her room, sir."

Johnson bowed awkwardly, and backed away after the maid.

"Good-night," Mr. Baxter said shortly, and followed the two out. He crossed the library with the intention of going to the room of his wife, who had come to town to be with him during the crisis of the expected victory, but he met her in the hall ready to go out.

" My dear, some important business has just come up," he said. " I'm afraid there's nothing for me to do but to attend to it to-night."

" That's too bad! I don't care for myself, for it's only one of those stupid musical comedies. I only cared to go because I thought it would help you through the suspense of the evening."

After the exchange of a few more words he kissed her and she went quietly back to her room. He watched her a moment, wondering if she would bear herself with such calm grace if she knew what awaited him in to-morrow's papers.

He passed quickly back into the little office, and locked the door behind him. Then the composure he had worn before Johnson and his wife swiftly vanished; and he sat at the desk with interlocked hands, facing the most critical situation of his life. There was no doubting what Johnson had told him.

When to-morrow's papers appeared with their certain stories—first page, big headlines—of how he and other members of the Executive Committee, all gentlemen of reputation, had bribed a walking delegate, and a notoriously corrupt walking delegate, to sell out the Iron Workers' strike—the members of the committee would be dishonored forever, and he dishonored more than all. And his wife, how could she bear this? How could he explain to her, who believed him nothing but honor, once this story was out?

He forced these sickening thoughts from his brain. He had no time for them. Disgrace must be avoided, if possible, and every minute was of honor's consequence. He strained his mind upon the crisis. The strike was now nothing; of first importance, of only importance, was how to escape disgrace.

It was the peculiar quality of Mr. Baxter's trained mind that he saw, with almost instant directness, the best chance in a business situation. Two days before it had taken Tom from eleven to eleven, twelve hours, to see his only chance. Mr. Baxter now saw his only chance in less than twelve minutes.

His only chance was to forestall exposure, by being the first to tell the story publicly. He saw his course clearly—to rush straight to the District Attorney, to tell a story almost identical with Tom's, and that varied from the facts on only two points. First of these two points, the District Attorney was to be told that Foley had come to them demanding fifty thousand dollars as the price of settlement. Second, that they had seen in this demand a chance to get the hands of the law upon this notorious walking delegate; that they had gone into the plan with the sole purpose of gaining evidence against him and bringing him to justice; that they had been able to secure a strong case of extortion against him, and now demanded his arrest. This same story was to go to the newspapers before they could possibly get Tom's. The committee would then appear to the world in no

worse light than having stooped to the use of somewhat doubtful means to rid themselves and the union
of a piratical blackmailer.

Mr. Baxter glanced at his watch. It was half-
past eight. He stepped to the telephone, found the
number of the home telephone of the District Attorney, and rang him up. He was in, luckily, and
soon had the receiver at his ear. Could Mr. Baxter
see him in half an hour on a matter of importance—
of great public importance? Mr. Baxter could.

He next rang up Mr. Murphy, who had been with
him in his office that morning when the money had
been handed to Foley. Mr. Murphy was also at
home, and answered the telephone himself. Could
Mr. Baxter meet him in fifteen minutes in the lobby
of the Waldorf-Astoria? Very important. Mr.
Murphy could.

As he left the telephone it struck him that while
the committee must seemingly make every effort to
secure Foley's arrest, it would be far better for them
if Foley escaped. If arrested, he would naturally
turn upon them and tell his side of the affair. Nobody would believe him, for he was one against five,
but all the same he could start a most unpleasant
story.

One instant the danger flashed upon Mr. Baxter.
The next instant his plan for its avoidance was ready.
He seated himself at the typewriter, drew off its
black sole-leather case, ran in a sheet of plain white
paper, and, picking at the keys, slowly wrote a message to Foley. That finished, he ran in a plain
envelope, which he addressed to Foley at Potomac

Hall. This letter he would leave at the nearest messenger office.

Five minutes later Mr. Baxter, in a business suit, passed calmly through his front door, opened for him by the purple personage, and out into the street.

Chapter XXX

THE LAST OF BUCK FOLEY

THE letter which Foley read, while the union looked on, hardly breathing, was as follows:

All is over. The District Attorney will be told to-night you held them up, forcing them to give you the amount you received. They have all the evidence; you have none. Their hands are clean. Against you it is a perfect case of extortion.

Though the note was unsigned, Foley knew instantly from whom it came. The contractors, then, were going to try to clear themselves, and he was to be made the scapegoat. He was to be arrested; perhaps at once. Foley had thought over his situation before, its possibilities and its dangers. His mind worked quickly now. If he came to trial, they had the witnesses as the note said—and he had none. As they would be able to make it out, it would be a plain case of extortion against him. He could not escape conviction, and conviction meant years in Sing Sing. Truly, all was over. He saw his only chance in an instant—to escape.

The reading of the note, and this train of thought, used less than a minute. Foley crushed the sheet of paper and envelope into a ball and thrust them into a trousers pocket, and looked up with the determination to try his only chance. His eyes fell upon what in the tense absorption of the minute he had almost forgotten—fifteen hundred men staring at him with fixed waiting faces, and one man staring at him with clenched fists in vengeful readiness.

At sight of Tom his decision to escape was swept out of him by an overmastering fury. He rushed toward Tom through the alleyway the men had automatically opened at Tom's command. But Petersen stepped quickly out, a couple of paces ahead of Tom, to meet him.

" Out o' the way, youse! " he snarled.

But Petersen did not get out of the way, and before Tom could interfere to save the fight for himself, Foley struck out savagely. Petersen gave back a blow, just one, the blow that had gained the fight for him a week ago. Foley went to the floor, and lay there.

This flash of action released the crowd from the spell that held them. They were roused from statues to a mob. " Kill him! Kill him! " someone shouted, and instantly the single cry swelled to a tremendous roar.

Had it not been for Tom, Foley would have come to his end then and there. The fifteen hundred men started forward, crushing through aisles, upsetting the folding chairs and tramping over their collapsed frames, pushing and tearing at each other to get to where Foley lay. Tom saw that in an instant the front of that vindictive mob would be stamping the limp body of the walking delegate into pulp. He sprang to Foley's side, seized him by his collar and dragged him forward into the space between the piano and the end wall, so that the heavy instrument was a breastwork against the union's fury.

"Here Petersen, Pete, the rest of you!" he cried. The little group that had stood round him during the meeting rushed forward. "In there!" He pushed them, as a guard, into the gap before Foley's body.

Then he faced about. The fore of that great tumult of wrath was already pressing upon him and the little guard, and the men behind were fighting forward over chairs, over each other, swearing and crying for Foley's death.

"Stop!" shouted Tom. Connelly, stricken with helplessness, completely lost, pounded weakly with his gavel.

"Kill him!" roared the mob. "Kill the traitor!"

"Disgrace the union by murder?" Tom shouted. "Kill him?—what punishment is that? Nothing at all! Let the law give him justice!"

The cries from the rear of the hall still went up, but the half dozen men who had crowded, and been crowded, upon the little guard now drew back, and Tom thought his words were having their effect. But a quick glance over his shoulder showed him Petersen, in fighting posture—and he knew why the front men had hesitated; and also showed him Foley leaning dizzily against the piano.

The hesitation on the part of the front rank lasted for but an instant. They were swept forward by the hundreds behind them, and Foley's line of defenders was crushed against the wall. It was all up with Foley, Tom thought; this onslaught would be the last of him. And as his own body went against the wall under the mob's terrific pressure, he had a gasping wish that he had not interfered two minutes before. The breath was all out of him, he thought his ribs were going to crack, he was growing faint and dizzy—when the pressure suddenly released and the furious uproar hushed almost to stillness. He regained his balance and his breath and glanced dazedly about.

There, calmly standing on the piano and leaning against the wall, was Foley, his left hand in his trousers pocket, his right uplifted to command attention.

" Boys, I feel it sorter embarrassin' to interrupt your little entertainment like this," he began blandly, but breathing very heavily. " But I suppose I won't have many more chances to make speeches before youse, an' I want to make about a remark an' a half. What's past—well, youse know. But what I got to say about the future is all on the level. Go in an' beat the contractors! Youse can beat 'em. An' beat 'em like hell! "

He paused, and gave an almost imperceptible glance toward an open window a few feet away, and moved a step nearer it. A look of baiting defiance came over his face, and he went on: " As for youse fellows. The whole crowd o' youse just tried to do me up—a thousand or two again' one. I fooled the whole bunch o' youse once. An' I can lick the whole bunch o' youse, too!—one at a time. But not just now! "

With his last word he sprang across to the sill of the open window, five feet away. Tom had noted Foley's glance and his edging toward the window, and guessing that Foley contemplated some new move, he had held himself in readiness for anything. He sprang after Foley, thinking the walking delegate meant to leap to his death on the stone-paved court below, and threw his arms about the other's knees. In the instant of embracing he noticed a fire-escape landing across the narrow court, an easy jump —and he knew that Foley had had no thought of death.

As Tom jerked Foley from the window sill he tripped over a chair and fell backward to the floor, the walking delegate's body upon him.   Foley was on his feet in an instant, but Tom lay where he was with the breath knocked out of him.   He dimly heard the union break again into cries; feet trampled him; he felt a keen shooting pain.   Then he was conscious that some force was turning the edge of the mob from its path; then he was lifted up and placed at the window out of which he had just dragged Foley; and then, Petersen's arm supporting him, he stood weakly on one foot holding to the sill.

For an instant he had a glimpse of Foley, on the platform, his back to the wall.   During the minute Tom had been on the floor a group of Foley's roughs, moved by some strange reawakening of loyalty, had rushed to his aid, but they had gone down; and now Foley stood alone, behind a table, sneering at the crowd.

" Come on ! " he shouted, with something between

a snarl and a laugh, shaking his clenched fist. " Come on, one at a time, an' I'll do up every one o' youse! "

The next instant he went down, and at the spot where he sank the crowd swayed and writhed as the vortex of a whirlpool. Tom, sickened, turned his eyes away.

Turned them to see three policemen and two men in plain clothes with badges on their lapels enter the hall, stand an instant taking in the scene, and then with drawn clubs plunge forward into the crowd. The cry of " Police! " swept from the rear to the front of the hall.

" We're after Foley! " shouted the foremost officer, a huge fellow with a huge voice, by way of explanation. " Get out o' the way! "

The last cry he repeated at every step. The crowd pressed to either side, and the five men shouldered slowly toward the vortex of the whirlpool. At length they gained this fiercely swaying tangle of men.

" If youse kill that man, we'll arrest every one o' youse for murder! " boomed the voice of the big policeman.

The vortex became suddenly less violent. The five officers pulled man after man back, and reached Foley's body. He was lying on his side, almost against the wall, eyes closed, mouth slightly gaping. He did not move.

" Too late! " said the big policeman. " He's dead! "

His words ran back through the crowd which had so lusted for this very event. Stillness fell upon it.

The big policeman stooped and gently turned the

long figure over and placed his hand above the heart. The inner circle of the crowd looked on, waiting. After a moment the policeman's head nodded.

" Beatin'? " asked one of the plain clothes men.

" Yes. But mighty weak."

" I'll be all right in a minute," said a faint voice.

The big policeman started and glanced at Foley's face. The eyes were open, and looking at him.

" I s'pose youse 're from Baxter? " the faint voice continued.

" From the District Attorney."

" Yes." A whimsical lightness appeared in the voice. " I been waitin' for youse. Lucky youse come when youse did. A few minutes later an' youse might not 'a' found me still waitin'."

He placed his hands beside him and weakly tried to rise, but fell back with a little groan. The big policeman and another officer helped him to his feet. The big policeman tried to keep an arm round him for support, but Foley pushed it away and leaned against the wall, where he stood a moment gazing down on the hundreds of faces. His shirt was ripped open at the neck and down to the waist; one sleeve was almost torn off; his vest was open and hung in two halves from the back of his neck; coat he had not had on. His face was beginning to swell, his lips were bloody, and there was a dripping cut on his forehead.

One of the plain clothes men drew out a pair of handcuffs.

" Youse needn't put them on me," Foley said. " I'll go with youse. Anyhow——"

He glanced down at his right hand. It was swollen, and was turning purple.

The plain clothes man hesitated.

" Oh, he can't give us no trouble," said the big policeman.

The handcuffs were pocketed.

" I'm ready," said Foley.

It was arranged that two of the uniformed men were to lead the way out, the big policeman was to come next with Foley, and the two plain clothes men were to be the rearguard.

The big policeman placed an arm round Foley's waist. " I better give youse a lift," he said.

" Oh, I ain't that weak! " returned Foley. " Come on." He started off steadily. Certainly he had regained strength in the last few minutes.

As the six men started a passage opened before them. The little group of roughs who had come to Foley's defense a few minutes before now fell in behind.

Half-way to the door Foley stopped, and addressed the crowd at large:

" Where's Keating? "

" Up by the piano," came the answer.

" Take me to him for a minute, won't youse? " he asked of his guard.

They consulted, then turned back. Again a passage opened and they marched to where Tom sat, very pale, leaning against the piano. The crowd pressed up, eager to get a glimpse of these two enemies, now face to face for the last time.

" Look out, Tom! " a voice warned, as Foley, with

the policeman at his side, stepped forth from his guard.

"Oh, our fight's all over," said Foley.   He paused and gazed steadily down at Tom.   None of those looking on could have said there was any softness in his face, yet few had ever before seen so little harshness there.

"I don't know of a man that, an hour ago, I'd 'a' rather put out o' business than youse, Keating," he at length said quietly.   "I don't love youse now.   But the real article is scarce, an' when I meet it—well, I like to shake hands."

He held out his left hand.   Tom looked hesitantly up into the face of the man who had brought him to fortune's lowest ebb—and who was now yet lower himself.   Then he laid his left hand in Foley's left.

Suddenly Foley leaned over and whispered in Tom's ear.   Then he straightened up.   "Luck with youse!" he said shortly and turned to his guards. "Come on."

Again the crowd made way.   Foley marched through the passage, his head erect, meeting every gaze unshrinkingly.   The greater part of the crowd looked on silently at the passing of their old leader, now torn and bruised and bleeding, but as defiant as in his best days. A few laughed and jeered and flung toward him contemptuous words, but Foley heeded them not, marching steadily on, looking into every face.

At the door he paused, and with a lean, blood-trickled smile of mockery, and of an indefinite something else—perhaps regret?—gazed back for a mo-

ment on the men he had led for seven years. Then
he called out, " So-long, boys! " and waved his left
hand with an air that was both jaunty and sardonic.

He turned about, and wiping the red drops from
his face with his bare left hand, passed out of Potomac Hall. Just behind him and his guard came the
little group of roughs, slipping covert glances among
themselves. And behind them the rest of the union
fell in; and the head of the procession led down the
broad stairway and forth into the street.

Then, without warning, there was a charge of the
roughs. The five officers were in an instant overwhelmed—tripped, or overpowered and hurled to the
pavement—and the roughs swept on. The men behind rushed forward, and without any such purpose
entangled the policemen among their numbers. It
was a minute or more before the five officers were free
and had their bearings, and could begin pursuit and
search.

But Buck Foley was not to be found.

Chapter XXXI

TOM'S LEVEE

IT was seven o'clock the next morning. Tom lay propped up on the couch in his sitting-room, his foot on a pillow, waiting for Maggie to come back with the morning papers. A minute before he had asked Ferdinand to run down and get them for him, but Maggie, who just then had been starting out for a loaf of bread, had said shortly to the boy that she would get them herself.

When Maggie had opened the door the night before, while Petersen was clumsily trying to fit Tom's key into the keyhole, the sight of Tom standing against the wall on one foot, his clothes in disorder, had been to her imagination a full explanation of what had happened. Her face had hardened and she had flung up her clenched hands in fierce helplessness. "Oh, my God! So you've been at Foley again!" she had burst out. "More trouble! My God, my God! I can't stand it any longer!" She would have gone on, but the presence of a third person had suddenly checked her. She had stood unmoving in the doorway, her eyes flashing, her breast rising and falling. For an instant Tom, remembering a former declaration, had expected her to close the door in his

348

face, but with a gesture of infinite, rageful despair she had stepped back from the door without a word, and Petersen had supported him to the couch. Almost immediately a doctor had appeared, for whom Tom and Petersen had left a message on their way home; and by the time the doctor and Petersen had gone, leaving Tom in bed, her fury had solidified into that obdurate, resentful silence which was the characteristic second stage of her wrath. Her injustice had roused Tom's antagonism, and thus far not a word had passed between them.

The nearest newsstand was only a dozen steps from the tenement's door, but minute after minute passed and still Maggie did not return. After a quarter hour's waiting Tom heard the hall door open and close, and then Maggie came into the sitting-room. He was startled at the change fifteen minutes had made in her expression. The look of set hardness was gone; the face was white and drawn, almost staring. She dropped the papers on a chair beside the couch. The top one, crumpled, explained the length of her absence and her altered look.

Tom's heart began to beat wildly; she knew it then! She paused beside him, and with his eyes downturned he waited for her to speak. Seconds passed. He could see her hands straining, and hear her deep breath coming and going. Suddenly she turned about abruptly and went into the kitchen.

Tom looked wonderingly after her a moment; then his eyes were caught by a black line half across the top of the crumpled paper: "Contractors Trap Foley." He seized the paper and his eyes took in the rest of the headline at a glance. "Arrested, But Makes Spectacular Escape"; a dozen words about the contractors' plan; and then at the very end, in smallest display type: "Also Exposed in Union." He quickly glanced through the headlines of the other papers. In substance they were the same.

Utterly astounded, he raced through the several accounts of Foley's exposure. They were practically alike. They told of Mr. Baxter's visit to the District Attorney, and then recited the events of the past three weeks just as Mr. Baxter had given them to the official prosecutor: How Foley had tried to hold the Executive Committee up for fifty thousand dollars; how the committee had seen in his demand a chance to get him into the hands of the law, and so rid labor and capital of a common enemy; how, after much deliberation, they had decided to make the attempt; how the sham negotiations had proceeded; how yesterday, to make the evidence perfect, Foley had been given the fifty thousand dollars he had demanded as the price of settlement—altogether a most complete and plausible story. "A perfect case," the District Attorney had called it. Tom's part in the affair was told in a couple of paragraphs under a subhead.

One of the papers had managed to get in a hurried editorial on Mr. Baxter's story. "Perhaps their way of trapping Foley smacks strongly of gum-shoe detective methods," the editorial concluded; "but their end, the exposure of a notorious labor brigand, will in the mind of the public entirely justify their means. They have earned the right to be called public benefactors." Such in tone was the whole editorial. It was a prophecy of the editorial praise that was to be heaped upon the contractors in the afternoon papers and those of the next morning.

Tom flung the papers from him in sickened, bewildered wrath. He had expected a personal triumph before the public. He felt there was something wrong; he felt Mr. Baxter had robbed him of his glory, just as Foley had robbed him of his strike. But in the first dazedness of his disappointment he could not understand. He hardly touched the breakfast Maggie had quietly put upon the chair while he had been reading, but sank back and, his eyes on the ceiling with its circle of clustered grapes, began to go over the situation.

At the end of a few minutes he was interrupted by Ferdinand, whom Maggie had sent in with a letter that had just been delivered by a messenger. Tom took it mechanically, then eagerly tore open the envelope. The letter was from the detective agency, and its greater part was the report of the observations made the previous evening by the detectives detailed to watch Mr. Baxter. Tom read it through repeatedly. It brought Foley's whispered words flashing back upon him: "I give it to youse for what it's worth; Baxter started this trick." He began slowly to understand.

But before he had fully mastered the situation there was a loud knock at the hall door. Maggie opened it, and Tom heard a hearty voice sound out: "Good-mornin', Mrs. Keating. How's your husband?"

"You'll find him in the front room, Mrs. Barry,"
Maggie answered. "All of you go right in."

There was the sound of several feet, and then Mrs.
Barry came in and after her Barry and Pete. "Say,
Tom, I'm just tickled to death!" she cried, with a
smile of ruddy delight. She held out a stubby, pil-
lowy hand and shook Tom's till her black straw hat,
that the two preceding summers had done their best
to turn brown, was bobbing over one ear. "Every
rib I've got is laughin'. How're you feelin'?"

"First rate, except for my ankle. How're you,
boys?" He shook hands with Barry and Pete.

"Well, you want to lay still as a bed-slat for a
week or two. A sprain ain't nothin' to monkey with,
I tell you what. Mrs. Keating, you see't your
husband keeps still."

"Yes," said Maggie, setting chairs for the three
about the couch, and herself slipping into one at the
couch's foot.

Mrs. Barry sank back, breathing heavily, and
wiped her moist face. "I said to the men this
mornin' that I'd give 'em their breakfast, but I
wouldn't wash a dish till I'd been over to see you.
Tom, you've come out on top, all right! An' nobody's gladder 'n me. Unless, o' course, your wife."

Maggie gave a little nod, and her hands clasped
each other in her lap.

"It's easy to guess how proud you must be o' your
man!" Mrs. Barry's red face beamed with sympathetic exultation.

Maggie gulped; her strained lips parted: "Of
course I'm proud."

" I wish you could 'a' heard the boys last night, Tom," cried Pete. " Are they for you? Well, I should say! You'll be made walkin' delegate at the very next meetin', sure."

" Well, I'd like to know what else they could do? " Mrs. Barry demanded indignantly. " With him havin' fought an' sacrificed as he has for 'em! "

" He can have anything he wants now. Tokens of appreciation? They'll be givin' you a gold watch an' chain for every pocket."

" But what 'll they think after they've read the papers? " asked Tom.

" I saw how the bosses' fairy story goes. But the boys ain't kids, an' they ain't goin' to swallow all that down. They'll think about the same as me, an' I think them bosses ain't such holy guys as they say they are. I think there was somethin' else we don't know nothin' about, or else the bosses 'd 'a' gone right through with the game. An' the boys'll not give credit to a boss when they can give credit to a union man. You can bet your false teeth on that. Anyhow, Tom, you could fall a big bunch o' miles an' still be in heaven."

" Now, the strike, Tom; what d'you think about the strike? " Mrs. Barry asked.

Before Tom could answer there was another knock. Maggie slipped away and ushered in Petersen, who hung back abashed at this gathering.

" Hello, Petersen," Tom called out. " Come in. How are you? "

Petersen advanced into the room, took a chair and sat holding his derby hat on his knees with both hands. "I be purty good,—oh, yah," he answered, smiling happily. "I be movin' to-day."

"Where?" Tom asked. "But you haven't met Mrs. Barry, have you?"

"Glad to know you, Mr. Petersen." Mrs. Barry held out her hand, and Petersen, without getting up, took it in his great embarrassed fist.

She turned quickly about on Tom. "What d'you think about the strike?" she repeated.

"Yes, what about it?" echoed Barry and Pete.

"We're going to win it," Tom answered, with quiet confidence.

"You think so?"

"I do. We're going to win—certain!"

"If you do, we women 'll all take turns kissin' your shoes."

"You'll be, all in a jump, the biggest labor leader in New York City!" cried Pete. "What, to put Buck Foley out o' business, an' to win a strike after the union had give it up!"

Within Tom responded to this by a wild exultation, but he maintained an outward calm. "Don't lay it on so thick, Pete."

He stole a glance at Maggie. She was very pale. Her eyes, coming up from her lap, met his. She rose abruptly.

"I must see to my work," she said, and hurried into the kitchen.

Tom's eyes came back to his friends. "Have you boys heard anything about Foley?"

"He ain't been caught yet," answered Pete.

"He'll never be," Tom declared. Then after a

moment's thought he went on with conviction:
" Boys, if Foley had had a fair start and had been
honest, he'd have been the biggest thing that ever
happened in the labor world."

Their loyalty prompted the others to take strong
exception to this.

" No, I wouldn't have been in his class," Tom
said decidedly, and led the talk to the probabilities of
the next few days. They chatted on for half an hour
longer, then all four departed. Pete, however, turned
at the door and came back.

" I almost forgot, Tom. There was something
else. O' course you didn't hear about Johnson. You
know there's been someone in the union—more'n one,
I bet—that's been keepin' the bosses posted on all
we do. Well, Johnson got himself outside o' more'n
a few last night, an' began to get in some lively jaw-
work. The boys got on from what he said that he'd
been doin' the spy business for a long time—that he'd
seen Baxter just before the meetin'. Well, a few
things happened right then an' there. I won't tell
you what, but I got an idea Johnson sorter thinks
this ain't just the health resort for his kind o' disease."

Tom said nothing. Here was confirmation of, and
addition to, one sentence in the detectives' report.

Pete had been gone hardly more than a minute
when he was back for the third time. " Say, Tom,
guess where Petersen's movin'? " he called out from
the dining-room door.

" I never can."

" On the floor above! A wagon load o' new
furniture just pulled up down in front. I met Peter-

sen an' his wife comin' in. Petersen was carryin' a bran' new baby carriage."

Pete's news had immediate corroboration. As he was going out Tom heard a thin voice ask, " Is Mr. Keating in? " and heard Maggie answer, " Go right through the next door; " and there was Mrs. Petersen, her child in her arms, coming radiantly toward him.

" Bless you, brother! " she said. " I've heard all about your glorious victory. I could hardly wait to come over an' tell you how glad I am. I'd 'a' come with Nels, but I wasn't ready an' he had to hurry here to be ready to look after the furniture when it come. I'm so glad! But things had to come out that way. The Lord never lets sin prevail!—praise His name! "

" Won't you sit down, Mrs. Petersen? " Tom said, in some embarrassment, relinquishing the slight hand she had given him.

" I can't stop a minute, we're so busy. You must come up an' see us. I pray God 'll prosper you in your new work, an' make you a power for right. Good-by."

As she passed through the dining-room Tom heard her thin vibrant voice sound out again: " You ought to be the proudest an' happiest woman in America, Mrs. Keating." There was no answer, and Tom heard the door close.

In a few minutes Maggie came in and stood leaning against the back of one of the chairs. " Tom," she said; and her voice was forced and unnatural.

Tom knew that the scene he had been expecting so

long was now at hand. "Yes," he answered, in a kind of triumphant dread.

She did not speak at once, but stood looking down on him, her throat pulsing, her face puckered in its effort to be immobile. "Well, it was about time something of this sort was happening. You know what I've had to put up with in the last five months. I suppose you think I ought to beg your pardon. But you know what I said, I said because I thought it was to our interest to do that. And you know if we'd done what I said we'd never have seen the hard times we have."

"I suppose not," Tom admitted, with a dull sinking of his heart.

She stood looking down on him for a moment longer, then turned abruptly about and went into the kitchen. These five sentences were her only verbal acknowledgment that she had been wrong, and her only verbal apology. She felt much more than this —grudgingly, she was proud that he had succeeded, she was proud that others praised him, she was pleased at the prospect of better times—but more than this she could not bend to admit.

While Tom lay on the couch reasoning himself into a fuller and fuller understanding of Mr. Baxter's part in last night's events, out in the kitchen Maggie's resentment over having been proved wrong was slowly disappearing under the genial influence of thoughts of the better days ahead. Her mind ran with eagerness over the many things that could be done with the thirty-five dollars a week Tom would get as walking delegate—new dresses, better than she had ever had before; new things for the house; a better table. And she thought of the social elevation Tom's new importance in the union would give her. She forgot her bitterness. She became satisfied; then exultant; then, unconsciously, she began humming.

Presently her new pride had an unexpected gratification. In the midst of her dreams there was a rapping at the hall door. Opening it she found before her a man she had seen only once—Tom had pointed him out to her one Sunday when they had walked on Fifth Avenue—but she recognized him immediately.

" Is Mr. Keating at home? " the man asked.

" Yes." Maggie, awed and embarrassed, led the way into the sitting-room.

" Mr. Keating," said the man, in a quiet, even voice.

" Mr. Baxter! " Tom ejaculated.

" I saw in the papers this morning that you were hurt. Thank you very much, Mrs. Keating." He closed the door after Maggie had withdrawn, as though paying her a courtesy by the act, and sat down in the chair she had pushed beside the couch for him. " Your injury is not serious, I hope."

Tom regarded the contractor with open amazement. " No," he managed to say. " It will keep me in the house for a while, though."

" I thought so, and that's why I came. I saw from the papers that you would doubtless be the next leader of the union. As you know, it is highly important to both sides that we come to an agreement about the strike as early as possible. It seemed to me desirable that you and I have a chat first and arrange

for a meeting of our respective committees. And
since I knew you could not come to see me, I have
come to see you."

Mr. Baxter delivered these prepared sentences
smoothly, showing his white teeth in a slight smile.
This was the most plausible reason his brain had been
able to lay hold of to explain his coming. And come
he must, for he had a terrifying dread that Tom knew
the facts he was trying to keep from the public. It
had taxed his ingenuity frightfully that morning to
make an explanation to his wife that would clear himself. If Tom did know, and were to speak—there
would be public disgrace, and no explaining to his
wife.

Tom's control came back to him, and he was filled
with a sudden exultant sense of mastery over this
keen, powerful man. "It is of course desirable that
we settle the strike as soon as possible," he agreed
calmly, not revealing that he recognized Mr. Baxter's explanation to be a fraud.

"It certainly will be a relief to us to deal with a
man of integrity. I think we have both had not very
agreeable experiences with one whose strong point
was not his honor."

"Yes."

There was that in Mr. Baxter's manner which was
very near frank cordiality. "Has it not occurred to
you as somewhat remarkable, Mr. Keating, that both
of us, acting independently, have been working to
expose Mr. Foley?"

Tom had never had the patience necessary to beat
long about the bush. He was master, and he swept

Mr. Baxter's method aside. "The sad feature of both our efforts," he said calmly, but with fierce joy, "has been that we have failed, so far, to expose the chief villain."

The corners of Mr. Baxter's mouth twitched the least trifle, but when he spoke he showed the proper surprise. "Have we, indeed! Whom do you mean?"

Tom looked him straight in the eyes. "I wonder if you'd care to know what I think of you?"

"That's an unusual question. But—it might be interesting."

"I think you are an infernal hypocrite!—and a villain to boot!"

"What?" Mr. Baxter sprang to his feet, trying to look angry and amazed.

"Sit down, Mr. Baxter," Tom said quietly. "That don't work with me. I'm on to you. We got Foley, but you're the man we've failed to expose—so far."

Mr. Baxter resumed his chair, and for an instant looked with piercing steadiness at Tom's square face.

"What do you know?—think you know?"

"I'll tell you, be glad to, for I want you to know I'm thoroughly on to you. You suggested this scheme to Foley, and it wasn't a scheme to catch Foley, but to cheat the union." And Tom went on to outline the parts of the story Mr. Baxter had withheld from the newspapers.

"That sounds very interesting, Mr. Keating," Mr. Baxter said, his lips trembling back from his teeth.

"But even supposing that were true, it isn't evidence."

"I didn't say it was—though part of it is. But suppose I gave to the papers what I've said to you? Suppose I made this point: if Baxter had really intended to trap Foley, wouldn't he have had him arrested the minute after the money had been turned over, so that he would have stood in no danger of losing the money, and so Foley would have been caught with the goods on? And suppose I presented these facts: Mr. Baxter had tickets bought for ' The Maid of Mexico,' and was on the point of leaving for the theater with his wife when a union man, his spy, who had learned of my plan to expose the scheme, came to his house and told him I was on to the game and was going to expose it. Mr. Baxter suddenly decides not to go to the theater, and rushes off to the District Attorney with his story of having trapped Foley. Suppose I said these things to the papers—they'd be glad to get 'em, for it's as good a story as the one this morning—what'd people be saying about you to-morrow? They'd say this: Up to the time he heard from his spy Baxter had no idea of going to the District Attorney. He was in the game for all it was worth, and only went to the District Attorney when he saw it was his only chance to save himself. They'd size you up for what you are—a briber and a liar! "

A faint tinge of color showed in Mr. Baxter's white cheeks. " I see you're a grafter, too! " he said, yielding to an uncontrollable desire to strike back. " Well—what's *your* price? "

Tom sat bolt upright and glared at the contractor.

"Damn you!" he burst out. "If it wasn't for this ankle, I'd kick you out of the room, and down to the street, a kick to every step! Now you get out of here! —and quick!"

"I'm always glad to leave the presence of a blackmailer, my dear sir." Mr. Baxter turned with a bow and went out.

Tom, in a fury, swung his feet off the couch and started to rise, only to sink back with a groan.

At the door of the flat Mr. Baxter thought of the morrow, of what the public would say, of what his wife would say. He came back, closed the door, and stood looking steadily down on Tom. "Well—what are you going to do about it?"

"Give it to the papers, that's what!"

"Suppose you do, and suppose a few persons believe it. Suppose, even, people say what you think they will. What then? You will have given your—ah—your information away, and how much better off are you for it?"

"Blackmailer, did you call me!"

Mr. Baxter did not heed the exclamation, but continued to look steadily downward, waiting.

A little while before Tom had been thinking vaguely of the possible use he could make of his power over Mr. Baxter. With lowered gaze, he now thought clearly, rapidly. The moral element of the situation did not appeal to him as strongly at that moment as did the practical. If he exposed Mr. Baxter it would bring himself great credit and prominence, but what material benefit would that exposure bring the union? Very little. Would it be right then for him, the actual head of the union, to use an advantage for his self-glorification that could be turned to the profit of the whole union?

After a minute Tom looked up. " No, I shall not give this to the newspapers. I'm going to use it otherwise—as a lever to get from you bosses what belongs to us. I hate to dirty my hands by using such means; but in fighting men of your sort we've got to take every advantage we get. If I had a thief by the throat I'd hardly let go so we could fight fair. I wouldn't be doing the square thing by the union if I refused to use an advantage of this sort."

He paused an instant and looked squarely into Mr. Baxter's eyes. " Yes, I have a price, and here it is. We're going to win this strike. You understand? "

" I think I do."

" Well? "

" You are very modest in your demands,"—sarcastically. Tom did not heed the remark.

Mr. Baxter half closed his eyes and thought a moment. " What guarantee have I of your silence? "

" My word."

" Nothing else? "

" Nothing else."

Mr. Baxter was again silent for a thoughtful moment.

" Well? " Tom demanded.

Mr. Baxter's face gave a faint suggestion that a struggle was going on within. Then his little smile came out, and he said:

" Permit me to be the first to congratulate you, Mr. Keating, on having won the strike."

Chapter XXXII

THE THORN OF THE ROSE

SHORTLY after lunch Mr. Driscoll called Ruth into his office. " Dr. Hall has just sent me word that he wants to meet the building committee on important business this afternoon, so if you'll get ready we'll start right off."

A few minutes later the two were on a north-bound Broadway car. Presently Mr. Driscoll blinked his bulging eyes thoughtfully at his watch. " I want to run in and see Keating a minute sometime this afternoon," he remarked. " He's just been doing some great work, Miss Arnold. If we hurry we've got time to crowd it in now." A pudgy forefinger went up into the air. " Oh, conductor—let us off here!"

Before Ruth had recovered the power to object they were out of the car and walking westward through a narrow cross street. Her first frantic impulse was to make some hurried excuse and turn back. She could not face him again!—and in his own home!—never! But a sudden fear restrained this impulse: to follow it might reveal to Mr. Driscoll the real state of affairs, or at least rouse his suspicions. She had to go; there was nothing else she could do. And so she walked on beside her employer, all her soul pulsing and throbbing.

Soon a change began to work within her—the reassertion of her love. She would have avoided the meeting if she could, but now fate was forcing her into it. She abandoned herself to fate's irresistible arrangement. A wild, excruciating joy began to possess her. She was going to see him again!

But in the last minute there came a choking revulsion of feeling. She could not go up—she could not face him. Her mind, as though it had been working all the time beneath her consciousness, presented her instantly with a natural plan of avoiding the meeting. She paused at the stoop of Tom's tenement. "I'll wait here till you come down, or walk about the block," she said.

"All right; I'll be gone only a few minutes," returned the unobservant Mr. Driscoll. He mounted the stoop, but drew aside at the door to let a woman with a boy come out, then entered. Ruth's glance rested upon the woman and child, and she instinctively guessed who they were, and her conjecture was instantly made certain knowledge by a voice from a window addressing the woman as Mrs. Keating. She gripped the iron hand-rail and, swaying, stared at Maggie as she stood chatting on the top step. Her fixed eyes photographed the cheap beauty of Maggie's face, and her supreme insight, the gift of the moment, took the likeness of Maggie's soul. She gazed at Maggie with tense, white face, lips parted, hardly breathing, all wildness within, till Maggie started to turn from her neighbor. Then she herself turned about and walked dizzily away.

In the meantime Mr. Driscoll had gained Tom's

flat and was knocking on the door. When Maggie had gone out—the silent accusation of Tom's presence irked her so, she was glad to escape it for an hour or two—she had left the door unlocked that Tom might have no trouble in admitting possible callers. Mr. Driscoll entered in response to Tom's "Come in," and crossed heavily into the sitting-room. "Hello there! How are you?" he called out, taking Tom's hand in a hearty grasp.

"Why, Mr. Driscoll!" Tom exclaimed, with a smile of pleasure.

Mr. Driscoll sank with a gasp into a chair beside the couch. "Well, I suppose you think you're about everybody," he said with a genial glare. "Of course you think I ought to congratulate you. Well, I might as well, since that's one thing I came here for. I do congratulate you, and I mean it."

He again grasped Tom's hand. "I've been thinking of the time, about five months ago, when you stood in my office and called me a coward and a few other nice things, and said you were going to put Foley out of business. I didn't think you could do it. But you have! You've done a mighty big thing."

He checked himself, but his discretion was not strong enough to force him to complete silence, nor to keep a faint suggestion of mystery out of his manner. "And you deserve a lot more credit than you're getting. You've done a lot more than people think you have—than you yourself think you have. If you knew what I know——!"

He nodded his head, with one eye closed.

" There's some people I'd back any day to beat the devil. Well, well! And so you're to be walking delegate, hey? That's what I hear."

" I understand the boys are talking about electing me."

"Well, if you come around trying to graft off me, or calling strikes on my jobs, there'll be trouble—I tell you that."

" I'll make you an exception. I'll not graft off you, and I'll let you work scabs and work 'em twenty-four hours a day, if you want to."

" I know how!" Mr. Driscoll mopped his face again. " I came around here, Keating, to say about three things to you. I wanted to congratulate you, and that I've done. And I wanted to tell you the latest in the Avon affair. I heard just before I left the office that those thugs of Foley's, hearing that he'd skipped and left 'em in the lurch, had confessed that you didn't have a thing to do with the Avon explosion—that Foley'd put them up to it, and so on. " It 'll be in the papers this afternoon. Even if your case comes to trial, you'll be discharged in a minute. The other thing——"

"Mr. Driscoll——" Tom began gratefully.

Mr. Driscoll saw what was coming, and rushed on at full speed. " The other thing is this: I'm speaking serious now, and just as your father might, and it's for your own good, and nothing else. What I've got to say is, get out of the union. You're too good for it. A man's got to do the best he can for himself in this world; it's his duty to make a place for himself. And what are you doing for yourself in the union? Nothing. They've turned you down, and turned you down hard, in the last few months. It's all hip-hip-hurrah for you to-day, but they'll turn you down again just as soon as they get a chance. Mark what I say! Now here's the thing for you to do. You can get out of the union now with glory. Get out, and take the job I offered you five months ago. Or a better one, if you want it."

" I can't tell you how much I thank you, Mr. Driscoll," said Tom. " But that's all been settled before. I can't."

" Now you see here! "—and Mr. Driscoll leaned forward and with the help of a gesticulating fist launched into an emphatic presentation of " an old man's advice " on the subject of looking out for number one.

While he had been talking Ruth had walked about the block in dazing pain, and now she had been brought back to the tenement door by the combined strength of love and duty. During the last two weeks she had often wished that she might speak a moment with Tom, to efface the impression she had given him on that tragic evening when they had been last together, that knowing him could mean to her only great pain. That she should tell him otherwise, that she should yield him the forgiveness she had withheld, had assumed to her the seriousness of a great debt she must discharge. The present was her best chance— perhaps she could see him for a moment alone. And so, duty justifying love, she entered the tenement and mounted the stairs.

Tom's " Come in! " answered her knock. Clutching her self-control in both her hands, she entered. At sight of her Tom rose upon his elbow, then sank back, as pale as she, his fingers turned into his palms.

" Mr. Keating," she said, with the slightest of bows, and lowered herself into a chair by the door.

He could merely incline his head.

" You got tired waiting, did you," said Mr. Driscoll, who had turned his short-sighted eyes about at her entrance. " I'll be through in just a minute." He looked back at Tom, and could but notice the latter's white, set face. " Why, what's the matter? "

" I twisted my ankle a bit; it's nothing," Tom answered.

Mr. Driscoll went on with his discourse, to ears that now heard not a word. Ruth glanced about the room. The high-colored sentimental pictures, the cheap showy furniture, the ornaments on the mantel-piece—all that she saw corroborated the revelation she had had of Maggie's character. Inspiration in neither wife nor home. Thus he had to live, who needed inspiration—whom inspiration and sympathy would help develop to a fitness for great ends. Thus he had to live!—dwarfed!

She filled with frantic rebellion in his behalf. Surely it did not have to be so, always. Surely the home could be changed, the wife roused to sympathy —a little—at least a little! . . . There must be a way! Yes, yes; surely. There must be a way! . . . Later, somehow, she would find it. . . .

In this moment of upheaving ideas and emotions she had the first vague stirring of a new purpose—

the very earliest conception of the part she was to play in the future, the part of an unseen and unrecognized influence. She was brought out of her chaotic thoughts by Mr. Driscoll rising from his chair and saying: "There's no turning a fool from his folly, I suppose. Well, we'd better be going, Miss Arnold."

She rose, too. Her eyes and Tom's met. He wondered, choking, if she would speak to him.

"Good-by, Mr. Keating," she said—and that was all.

"Good-by, Miss Arnold."

With a great sinking, as though all were going from beneath him, he watched her go out . . . heard the outer door close . . . and lay exhausted, gazing wide-eyed at the door frame in which he had last seen her.

A minute passed so, and then his eyes, falling, saw a pair of gray silk gloves on the table just before him. They were hers. He had risen upon his elbow with the purpose of getting to the table, by help of a chair back, and securing them, when he heard the hall door open gently and close. He sank back upon the couch.

The next minute he saw her in the doorway again, pale and with a composure that was the balance between paroxysm and supreme repression. She paused there, one hand against the frame, and then walked up to the little table. "I came back for my gloves," she said, picking them up.

"Yes," his lips whispered, his eyes fastened on her white face.

But she did not go. She stood looking down upon him, one hand resting on the table, the other on a chair back. " I left my gloves on purpose; there is something I want to say to you," she said, with her tense calm. " You remember—when I saw you last— I practically said that knowing you could in the future mean nothing to me but pain. I do not feel so now. Knowing you has given me inspiration. There is nothing for me to forgive—but if it means anything to you . . . I forgive you."

Tom could only hold his eyes on her pale face.

" And I want to congratulate you," she went on. " I know how another is getting the praise that belongs to you. I know how much more you deserve than is being given you."

" Chance helped me much—at the end."

" It is the man who is always striving that is ready for the chance when it comes," she returned.

Tom, lying back, gazing fixedly up into her dark eyes, could not gather hold of a word. The gilded clock counted off several seconds.

" Mr. Driscoll is waiting for me," she said, in a voice that was weaker and less forcedly steady. She had not changed her position all the time she had spoken. Her arms now dropped to her side, and she moved back ever so little.

" I hope . . . you'll be happy . . . always," she said.

" Yes . . . and I hope you . . ."

" Good-by."

" Good-by."

Their eyes held steadfastly to each other for a

moment; she seemed to waver, and she caught the back of a chair; then she turned and went out. . . .

For long he watched the door out of which she had gone; then, heedless of the pain, he rolled over and stared at one great poppy in the back of the couch.

THE END